A veiled figure appeared before Quintus. Her face was hidden by the saffron veil of a Roman bride, but the fabric was so thin he could see her eyes clearly. They were long and dark, their almond shape marked with kohl. A crimson gem glinted on her brow, and long gold earrings swung enticingly. She stood circled by fires that burned with fragrance, as if she had scattered incense upon the flames.

"What must I do?" he asked this vision.

"You must follow the eagle to where the water rises in the desert, where the stone gapes open and where serpents grow from stone. Follow me and follow the eagle—or remain here, for as long as 'here' remains." The fires at her feet flared, and smoke rose up quickly, to snatch her from his sight.

"Lady! Draupadi, don't go!" Quintus cried, reaching forward. The earth cracked open, and then Quintus was falling, falling and the speed of his fall snatched thought and breath from him...

"Plenty of authentic, historic detail, good characters, and restrained fantasy elements. *Empire of the Eagle* is a superior piece of work."

—*Kirkus Reviews*

Tor books by Susan Shwartz

The Grail of Hearts
Heritage of Flight
Imperial Lady (with Andre Norton)
Moonsinger's Friends (editor)
Silk Roads and Shadows
White Wing (with S.N. Lewitt, as "Gordon Kendall")

Tor books by Andre Norton

Caroline (with Enid Cushing)
The Crystal Gryphon
Dare to Go A-Hunting
Elvenbane (with Mercedes Lackey)
Flight in Yiktor
Forerunner
Forerunner: The Second Venture
Gryphon's Eyrie (with A.C. Crispin)
Grand Masters' Choice (editor)
Here Abide Monsters
House of Shadows (with Phyllis Miller)
Imperial Lady (with Susan Shwartz)
The Jekyll Legacy (with Robert Bloch)
Moon Called
Moon Mirror
The Prince Commands
Ralestone Luck
Redline the Stars
Sneeze on Sunday (with Grace Allen Hogarth)
Songsmith (with A.C. Crispin)
Stand and Deliver
Wheel of Stars
Wizards' Worlds
Wraiths of Time

TALES OF THE WITCH WORLD (editor)

Tales of the Witch World 1
Tales of the Witch World 2
Four from the Witch World
Tales of the Witch World 3

WITCH WORLD: THE TURNING

Storms of Victory (with P.M. Griffin)
Flight of Vengeance (with P.M. Griffin and Mary H. Schaub)

Magic in Ithkar
(editor, with Robert Adams)

EMPIRE
OF THE
EAGLE

ANDRE NORTON
AND
SUSAN SHWARTZ

TOR
fantasy®

A TOM DOHERTY ASSOCIATES BOOK
NEW YORK

This is a work of fiction. All the characters and events portrayed in this book are fictitious, and any resemblance to real people or events is purely coincidental.

EMPIRE OF THE EAGLE

Cover art by Peter Goodfellow

A Tor Book
Published by Tom Doherty Associates, Inc.
175 Fifth Avenue
New York, NY 10010

Tor® is a registered trademark of Tom Doherty Associates, Inc.

ISBN: 0-812-51393-2
Library of Congress Catalog Card Number: 93-26551

First edition: November 1993
First mass market edition: May 1995

Printed in the United States of America

0 9 8 7 6 5 4 3 2 1

Introduction
by
Andre Norton

IT WAS A soldier of hardly more than peasant birth, but possessing the spark of military genius and practical knowledge, who forged that steel-hard backbone which upheld first the Roman republic, and then the Empire—the Legion. Up to the time of Marius, men had fought hard and well, but the loose formation of an army founded on what had been a militia of citizens called out in times of national danger was not the weapon a leader convinced of his own destiny needed—or wanted.

The concept of the professional soldier, whose home was truly the army itself and whose god was the Eagle of the Legion to which he was oathed, was born. In spite of the bloodbath ordered by Sulla, jealous of his predecessor's power, the idea of the Legion—and the Eagle—remained until it was accepted as the only possible answer to warfare with both barbarians of the borders and the trained armies of any others who dared to resist the expansion of Rome.

To suffer such defeat as to lose an Eagle was a shame so dark that it could only be washed out in blood. Probably the most notable of such losses was the massacre of three of Augustus Caesar's Legions—and the loss of their Eagles—by Quinctilius Varus in the Teutoberger Wald; Augustus is said to have lamented, "Varus, Varus, give me back my Legions!"

But an earlier defeat was suffered by the Proconsul Crassus (of the first Triumvirate). Envious of Julius Caesar and greedy for the fabled treasures of the Middle East, he marched his army to a bloody defeat at Carrhae in 43 B.C.

It is always wise to explore the footnotes in any history. While gathering material for the novel *Imperial Lady*, we found it necessary to read the history of the Han Dynasty—a remnant from nearly two thousand years ago. And in a translation of those very ancient pages, there exists a footnote that proved to be an open door for imagination's sweep.

We are told in a very brief paragraph that a portion of the Han Army, which had poured its might along the Silk Road conquering all that it met, rode into the Middle East and was present as audience to the defeat of the Legions.

Impressed by the way these Westerners stood up to disaster and death, the commander of the Han force who had reached that point so far from his homeland claimed a cohort of these prisoners as a novel gift for his emperor.

So baldly, the paragraph states a fact and mentions nothing more about the Romans' fate in a land so far away that they had no way of measuring the distance.

What did become of the Romans? Because history does not tell us, perhaps we can try to guess. A handful out of a Legion, looking to their Eagle for inspiration and guide—what could chance thereafter?

Andre Norton
December 1992

Introduction
by
Susan Shwartz

I WELL REMEMBER the first time I heard of the Romans who became the protagonists of *Empire of the Eagle*. It was in 1964, and I had been spending my lunch hour reading *The Last Planet*, by Andre Norton. Those of you who know this book know that it opens with a description of Romans in Asia, marching east, always marching east, and, unnoticed to history, forming their last square somewhere in Asia—a perfect prelude to a tale of decaying empire.

Her *Operation Timesearch* brought my attention to the Motherland of Mu, the Atlanteans, and the Uighurs; I was delighted, much later, to discover on the map a *real* Uighur Autonomous Republic in western China, on the border of what was formerly the Soviet Union. Several books later—*Silk Roads and Shadows* and *Imperial Lady* (written with Andre Norton)—I have still not visited this area in any way but research and dreams. Nevertheless, when the subject was proposed, I found myself ready to return in my writing to those places, and more than ready to deal with the enigma of Romans, marching across the Tarim Basin.

How did they get there? With only a few records in Chinese history of people who *might* be Romans, we can only conjecture. On one such conjecture we built this book: the defeat of Crassus and his Legions at Carrhae in 43 B.C. A few things are certain: During the first century B.C., Rome first became aware of the trade routes now known as the Silk Roads and the wealth that travelled west along them.

Especially interested was Crassus, already a spectacularly wealthy man, but one who envied his fellow triumvir Julius Caesar and sought victories of his own by campaigning in the Near East as a proconsul. Unfortunately, in addition to his greed and ambition, Crassus was a poor general.

He was profoundly either unwise or unfortunate in his choice of allies, and was betrayed both by the Nabataean Arabs and the king of Armenia. In addition, he made several strategic and tactical blunders that doomed his campaign. Goaded by the Nabataeans, he allowed himself to be convinced to march his Legions at a cavalry pace. He waited for his son Publius's crack Gallic cavalry. And he fought his Legions under the hot sun near Carrhae, a garrison town near present-day Haran, without rest or water. Worse luck, he fought against The Surena, a charismatic, powerful, and skilled Parthian clan leader, who was later killed by his own king for Caesar's own fault—overmuch ambition.

Those interested in this time and this part of the world know that the Parthians were skilled horse archers. Faced with archers, the Romans formed their *testudo,* or tortoise, shields over their heads to protect themselves against the arrow barrage and wait for the Parthians to exhaust their supply of ammunition. However, they had not counted on the heat, the thirst—or The Surena's bringing up additional supplies. Nor did they count on Crassus's collapse when his son's head was paraded before him.

The defeat was staggering: Rome lost not only tens of thousands of men, but the Eagles of their Legions, the sign of their power and their honor. Abandoning the dead and wounded, Crassus and the remnants of his command holed up in Carrhae and, ultimately, sought terms.

What happened to the remnants of the Legions—and the captured Eagles? Most likely, they finished out their days in captivity, the Romans as slaves, the Eagles as trophies.

That is the story that has intrigued Andre Norton for decades. And that was our jumping-off point. What if, as they marched east into captivity, they marched straight into myths? Asia—especially Central Asia—is an incredible nexus for myths; and we had two extraordinary storehouses of such myths to hand. We had the stories of fabled Mu, often combined with Atlantis and solar mythology in inimitable nineteenth-century-type scholarship that seeks to prove survivals of a lost culture and a lost continent. And we had the ancient Indian epic, *The Mahabharata*, with its gods, demigods, and princes striding among mortals in epic battle. I had become fascinated with it after seeing a performance of Peter Brooks's adaptation at the Brooklyn Academy of Music, and I was intrigued to learn that the stories of Krishna and of his human allies, Arjuna the hero and his brothers, their wife, Draupadi, and their wars are still loved, taught to children, and even form the inspiration of modern comic books.

Certainly, this combination removes *Empire of the Eagle* firmly from the realm of historical fiction and into fantasy such as, I like to think, the elephant-headed Ganesha records in *The Mahabharata*.

Imagine him opening his story. It is dark. Men are crouching in a swamp, betrayed, defeated, unsure of their leaders. And messengers are coming—bringing terms and, for us and for them, the beginning of a journey across cultures and across time.

Susan Shwartz
December 1992

I

CARRHAE'S WALLS HAD let the survivors of Crassus's Legions slip away as ignominiously as it had admitted them: ridding the town of one more set of masters unable to command it. The remnants of the Legion had no pride left—and very little strength. Blank and indifferent, the outpost might have been as far from them as Rome herself. At this moment, the tribune Quintus longed for the protection of those walls and wished the people within heartily to Tartarus. He fully expected to arrive among the damned sooner or later himself.

Up ahead, his superiors and elders gestured while centurions struck flagging men into one last formation with their vinestaffs in order to follow their guide into the marshes.

"You think we can trust him?"

"You want to eat mud, comrade?"

Someone else drew in his cheeks, making a sucking sound. Amazing anyone had strength and spirit left to raise even so feeble a jest.

"Quiet, you!" Rufus, the senior centurion, reinforced

his order with his staff. Quintus would have expected that tough old man to survive. How he had made it himself, though, was more of a surprise. Perhaps because he did not wholly want to. . . .

They had learned they could not trust their fellow Romans, let alone some of their allies: How then could they trust their guide, who cringed when they laid eyes or hand on him, and glared when their backs were turned? His knowledge gave them a scant chance, yet he promised a better, if less honorable, fate than the drums and the arrows they would probably face again at dawn.

The Parthians were horse archers, not ready to battle at night, which risked killing their prized mounts. If they felt that way about mere men, twenty thousand Romans would still be alive.

Besides, what need would now press The Surena and his warriors to fight at all? The legions of Syria were bled out. Roman cavalry was withdrawn, what survived of it. And the auxiliaries—only a few of them lived or remained loyal to follow the Legionaries marshward.

Now Prince Surena—*The* Surena, ruler of one of the noblest of the Parthian clans—had only to wait for sure-to-be-treacherous guides and the veritable sinks of the marshes to assure him of complete victory.

Near Quintus, someone gagged. Sour sickness rose in his own gullet, triggered by the fetid marsh stench, nearly as foul as the oaths sputtering from First Centurion Rufus, like bubbles popping in the muck. The veteran had not stopped swearing since the orders came to retire. First, they had fought their way from the battlefield, men falling under the horse-archers' bows. They were forced to abandon the wounded, and so their rout was complete and shaming. Then, they had slunk out of Carrhae itself like a man sneaking from the stews, defeated, destroyed.

Dead, as soon as their only probable fate caught up with them.

Under the helm that made Quintus sweat, blood pounded in his temples, seeming as heavy as the enemies' wardrums and those bronze bells that had clanged deafeningly during the battle as The Surena had paraded or that had heralded the severed head of the proconsul's son impaled on a lancepoint before the Roman overlord, whose arrogance turned to grief and fear, robbing his Legions of such leadership as even Crassus might give and even of their will to win. Now that dull throb in the young tribunes head, the rasp of the cooling air he drew into his aching lungs, somehow kept him going even as the drums of a galley set the measure for sweating rowers. They had managed not to run. That was all that could be said for them—the shocked remnants of Crassus's seven Legions.

"Down!" The whisper held a snap.

Quintus flung himself to earth—or mud—by a pool, so scummed over it reflected neither stars nor moon. *The gods have turned their faces from us,* he thought. But what more could they expect after such a defeat as this?

Faintly, his memory sharpened. They had been cursed even as they marched from Rome. Had not tribune Aetius, not satisfied with arguing that Parthia was a neutral kingdom and thus not to be attacked, condemned Crassus and his army openly and sternly? Any sane man would have taken that as an omen and thought twice, thrice on what he would do. They said Crassus had prattled in company of the feats of Alexander, and it was rumored that he envied Caesar, his friend and rival. He would have his victory witnessed by all Rome. And so he had ignored Aetius.

What was that word the Greeks used for going against

the gods? Quintus searched memory again. It was all in a fog.

Hubris. That was right. Well, given his own choice, he himself would have been a farmer, not a scholar. And certainly not a soldier. So plain words were good enough. And the blunt commons had a fit word for such arrogance, too. *Nefas.* Unspeakable evil.

Here all about him was *nefas.*

Around him, men were sinking to their knees or to their bellies by the fetid water, shedding their packs. Romans crouched with Romans; the few auxiliaries companioned one another, by nationality. At night it might be hard to tell *auxilia* from enemies; but they must note how the forces were strung out. Some of them had betrayed their oaths. Still, best not kill the ones who held to their faith.

His ribs ached with every breath he drew. In the battle, something had whined by his head. By unbelievable fortune, he had swerved at just the right time, only to be struck with a near-paralyzing but glancing blow.

I'm hit! he had thought. For a moment he was dazed as might be a gladiator waiting for the final stroke. Sluggishly, he tried to put away memory. *Magna Mater, it hadn't been much of a life!*

No home. No sons. No lands.

Time slowed, and he was back in his memories of the battle. He doubled over, bemused about whether an arrow had hit a lung and how long it might take him to drown in his own blood.

Quintus rubbed his side as he half sat, half lay by a scummy pool. No arrow wound had sapped his strength, but he winced from a burn mark. That blow had struck right above where he stowed the tiny bronze statue that had been his lucky-piece since he found it as a boy on the farm since stolen from his family.

"Don't *drink*, fools! Not that muck." The centurion ordered and enforced the command with a whack of his staff across the back of one impatient man. "No water? You there. Share with Titus here. And both of you, go easy. There is no likely spring *here!*"

No man in the Legion was obeyed more quickly than Rufus. Still a mutter, almost a whine, of protest rose.

"You don't drink standing water. Look at that scum. Smell it. You *want* the flux or a fever that would make Tiberside in the summer seem like a garden? Are you stupid enough to think they'll let us carry you when we move out?"

That, Quintus thought, was what hurt the old veteran worst. On a lost battlefield, Rome had abandoned her wounded. Men he had known, had ordered, had punished and praised as if they were his own sons—and they had been left to have their throats cut (or what more savage ways the Parthians killed those in their power), their screams concealed beneath the beat of the Parthian drums.

Without knowing it, the Primus Pilus took off his helmet and rubbed his graying hair. Rufus no longer: The red hair that had given him that name had long since faded. He had grown old in the Legions. Only the needs of men who feared this battle without him to bully them had stopped him from storming into Crassus's tent and choosing the moment of his death rather than waiting for the Parthians. His men. The only sons he would ever have. He had watched these sons of his die for pride and treachery, shot full of Parthian arrows and now he would watch them die in the marshes outside Carrhae, and no sword or shield of his could be raised in bloody answer.

Unless his heart broke first. Dully, Quintus watched the older man, gathering strength himself from the way the centurion went about his rounds, soldiering as usual. The old man's heart was tougher than the Legions had proved themselves to be. He would live as long as anyone needed him to live. Even when dying was easier.

"Good thing you made it," Rufus came to a halt beside Quintus. They had seen each other after the flight to Carrhae, but not spoken. "I saw you miss the spear . . ."

What spear?

". . . then take that arrow hit. Thought it was a waste, after you'd escaped such a close shave. And I wondered if I'd wasted the time I had put in on you."

Quintus shrugged. His ribs twinged, then subsided. "I am ready to move when orders come." He tried to match some of Rufus's matter-of-fact tone.

Exhaustion forced the men into obedience. Rufus moved among them where they lay, inspecting, and ordering the distribution of what food and safe water remained. Quintus got up to follow nearly blindly. Somehow, the younger man could hear his grandfather's voice: *Watch well, boy. This is one of the* real *soldiers.*

Death lay outside the marsh—Parthians and arrows. And the muck about them was full of its own noises—a maddening buzz of insects that worked their way under clothes and armor. Everywhere rose the rot of dying plants, the stink of frightened men and of blood of those wounded lightly enough so they could flee, not like . . . not like the Romans they were. No one had killed himself for the dishonor as they would have in the old tales. None of these leaders here and now would have understood the gesture or deserved it.

At least the night's darkness had brought relief from

the glare of the Syrian sun on bare land or brown water. However, Quintus's headache worsened—lights seemed to shoot red and white behind his eyelids. Even keeping on his helmet was some kind of small victory. Others, he knew, had hurled theirs away as useless weight, discarding all to stampede like beasts. Shame—the proconsul had made sure they already had their fill of that, if nothing else.

"May as well rest, young one . . . I mean, sir." Rufus's voice was slurred with exhaustion.

Obedient, Quintus dropped once more, covering his face with his hands as he shut his smarting eyes.

After a moment, he was ashamed. Even a most junior tribune who owed his sword to placeseeking and fool luck should set the men a better example. Nearby knelt one of the *signifers*. The standard-bearer had grounded the butt of his Eagle in the mud, and the bronze bird high overhead looked as dispirited as the man who had borne it. At least that had not fallen or been or lost. Not yet. Not like so many of the others. Eagles of Rome's Legions had fallen into enemy hands. That was worse, even more than abandoning their wounded. For the Eagles, most who marched behind them believed, were the very spirit of the Legions as the *genius loci* was the spirit of a place.

Quintus raised his head, startled as he might be at a familiar scent or voice. Best not think of *that* part of the past unless he wanted to run mad and gibber like one of the Asiatics afflicted with the religious mania that passed among them for faith. Hard to believe it, but under the influences of their religions, they would cut at themselves or anyone else. He shuddered, and for once, hoped it was fever, not the beginnings of madness. He was a *Roman*. Prophecy and spirit voices were for lesser peoples.

At least the drums, these damned throbbing drums of

The Surena's victorious Parthians were stilled. Quintus was no soldier, not in the way centurions like Rufus were—bred and wed to the Legions—but his few years as a tribune had taught him a little. The drums were a bad omen: All the omens had been bad since Marcus Licinius Crassus had marched his seven Legions, the *auxilia,* and his gods-be-damned haughty cavalry east of the Euphrates.

Wait for the cavalry, proconsul Crassus had said. Thousands of crack riders from Gaul, led by his son. Wait for them. Then, keep pace with the riders until your lungs ached and you nearly choked with the dust of the plains, and some of the older men were limping while you hoped their hearts didn't burst. Well, all those horsemen had been slaughtered, Publius Crassus with them; and the rest fled, avoiding the panic of the common rout.

Gods, he just wanted to lie down and die in his armor, his already-rusting armor. In the breathless days before his final treachery, that Arab dog Ariamnes had jeered at the Romans' pace. Fine for him: He went mounted, he and his six thousand men that he had promised would fight beside the Romans. He had fawned like the vilest client before the very men he betrayed. Traitors, all of them. Gods, Quintus threw back his head a little to try to see the sky. He wished he were back by the Tiber, on the land no longer his.

The panic of their retreat to the marshes was behind them, he could hear from the mincing voice of that prancing Lucilius.

"Seeing his son's head fly-bit on the spear was what did it. The proconsul gave one stare and screamed like a woman in childbirth," Lucilius reported. "Wept. Offered to fall on his sword, though his hand was shaking the way it does after a three-day drunk. I can't imagine how he could have held any sword steady long enough to fall on it."

Naturally, the young aristocrat had been in Crassus's tent—as Quintus had not—for a very select staff meeting the night Crassus had finally been forced to make any decision at all, let alone the one to abandon the wounded and retreat to Carrhae. Quintus should have known that Lucilius would have joined the other patricians, deciding arbitrarily whose lives would be spared and whose sacrificed.

Now, he was laughing as lightly as if he traded gossip in the baths at home. "I swear, he screamed and shook and nigh-on soiled himself."

Quintus had no love for Crassus, who had tossed the farm his own family had held for generations to a client about as casually as Quintus might toss a coin to a beggar. Still, that a general and a proconsul of Rome could abandon his men on a lost battlefield—best that grandfather had died before this day. The old man had died twice already, once with the loss of his lands, a second time when Quintus had held him for his last breath two years ago. This would have given him a third death.

Lucilius's eyes glinted with that gambler's fervor that had forced him out to Syria, one jump ahead of the creditors he had lived off since putting on the *toga virilis*. This flight too was a kind of gamble, one Lucilius was sure he would win even now. Why not? Hadn't his luck always come around before?

"So who leads?"

"Cassius. Pushing from behind."

Crassus had looked enough like a leader to keep heart in the men. Now, this staff officer stepped into his boots. Quintus had never trusted the lean, saturnine elder tribune, but at that moment he would have followed him as his own grandfather followed Marius to destruction. Cassius was a politician. He might be a tribune—the same rank that Quintus held, however inadequately—but the older man had survived the ambushes of Roman politics, and Quintus reckoned he might survive this, too. Another of Lucilius's friends, sleek even now after a rout and hours in a marsh, bared his teeth in a grin.

"*Pro di,*" Lucilius added, "it was almost worth losing the battle to watch that Cassius slap old moneybags back into decency."

Even in the dark now, Quintus saw Legionaries making gestures to avert evil. Their eyes were wide as the eyes of stalled horses who smelled wildfire. Even Romans had to reckon with defeat, but to learn that their leader had lost his courage . . .

"Keep a decent tongue in your head!" Quintus hissed. Lucilius had powerful friends who could snatch the armor off Quintus's back and blight his last hopes of ever regaining his family's land—if the Parthians didn't stick them all full of thrice-damned arrows first.

"Our *senex* there. We'll all turn old and gray," the young aristocrat mocked. "If we live that long."

But the centurion turned his head and glared, and Lucilius's voice softened to a whisper and a too-hectic laugh. Many of the men had not drunk all day. Despite Rufus's oaths, Quintus knew some of them were stealthily lapping up the thick water. There would be fever in the marsh before dawn.

Behind him, some of the younger tribunes diced. Fortunes could rise and fall on the throw of the dice, even in the Legions. That was one of the ways Lucilius had gotten himself into trouble. Quintus had never had any money to play. Callous to play now, he thought—not that it mattered. Still, if one of Crassus's staff happened by, the gamers would regret it in the short time they probably had left.

But they were undoubtedly privileged, as usual. Cassius and his troops were likelier to stay with the proconsul, enjoying whatever comforts he had been able to wrest from the wreck of his armies. Rufus's deep rumble set about disposing the men as comfortably as might be until dawn, when they must break free of the swamp or die. Quintus heard himself repeat orders—to his surprise, he spoke the right ones—as if in a waking dream that differed totally from the memories he had brushed against.

"Why don't they come after us?" a young Legionary whispered in the darkness, then fell silent when someone chuckled.

"Why should they? Got us pinned here, haven't they? They can just wait and pick us off, unless they get bored and want to go hunting. They'll wait till dawn for anything. Or offer us terms. But that's a hope I wouldn't count on, son. However, they just might want some new slaves to push around."

Mumbles about the guards just sneaking off into the swamp rose. Rufus's eye swept round, and the men were silent. Quintus too had heard those voices in the ranks, careless around a green tribune as they dared not be around the wily old veteran. Only hours ago, he had heard them as he stood sweating in the square, too hot to feel as hungry or thirsty as they all had been kept for days. Some men had collapsed from the heat, from the lack of proper food, water, and rest, which had not been enough to keep the Legions marching at their best-known pace, let alone the cavalry pace Crassus had been goaded into ordering. He had heard their mutters of hope when,

looking out, no one saw any of the deadly Parthian cataphracts.

And then The Surena had signaled. At his command,
the drums and bronze bells throbbed, all over the battlefield. The Parthian prince was tall, handsome for a barbarian, much as Quintus hated to admit it. His eyes were
huge, painted against the sun, which could blind you
here, where even in May the sunlight burned. A dancing
boy's trick, but no one said that after seeing the killing
light in those eyes—and feeling the sun's glare themselves.

Sunlight blazed off the gleaming arms of The Surena's
deadly riders and shimmered from thin, brilliant banners
that floated in the still air like tongues of fire. Helmets
and breastplates caught fire as the light glinted off the
armor of the Parthian horse archers. Some of the men
were Parthians. Others, though, were unlike their prince.
They were rather small and yellow and bowed of leg.
Their eyes seemed hidden in slanted folds, and they
smiled at the Romans as a glutton gloats, facing his feast
table.

"The Seres," Quintus had heard. They had made the
steel that the Romans knew they were about to taste. And
the banners?

"What would that stuff cost in Rome?" some fool
with a patrician accent breathed.

"More than you want to pay . . . sir," rasped a centurion before the drums and bells drowned out his words.

To their eternal credit, none of the Legionaries had
broken. They stood firm in the hollow square, twelve
cohorts on each side, Crassus, his pet cavalry, and the
baggage in the center. Quintus got a glimpse of the proconsul. He was sweating—they all were—and the whites

of his eyes were showing. Even as he watched, Cassius flung down his hands in a gesture of disgust.

"That doesn't look good," muttered the man next to Quintus. "Probably told him that the cavalry should be divided up. We should be spread out, not penned up like this."

Hard to tell when the battle started. At first, it had seemed promising. The Surena's cataphracts raced forward, to be stopped by the deep Roman formation. The arrows fell like deadly rain against the Roman *testudo*. It held, of course: Like a strongly shelled tortoise, they would wait for the archers' quivers to empty.

The Legions had settled in to wait for the archers to run out of arrows. When such flights grew sparser, the Romans cheered. Rufus had started swearing then, in between shouting the orders that let the *buccinatores* horns bray before those trumpeters screamed and died, shot by men who aimed at the glinting metal of their horns. When they fell, he had shouted, reforming his men, cursing and begging them to fight and die like Romans. Ultimately, the drums had drowned out his voice and hopes. You couldn't tell the sweat on his face from the tears.

The drums sounded again as the Romans fled, a hateful mercy, as the Parthians slaughtered the wounded Crassus had ordered must be left behind. Quintus wondered if he would ever forget those screams and cries for aid—or for their mothers.

How long since Quintus had been able to cast his helmet down, bury his face in flowing water, and drink his fill? He could not remember. His canteen held the water and vinegar mixture that now stank of leather, and precious little of it. Water trickled in the swamp near Carrhae. Thirsty, he had always seemed thirsty since they left the Euphrates for the desert that was so different from his home near the Tiber.

One or two of the men had already escaped into memories and tumbled forward like men asleep. Rufus had slain another who refused to move, who curled up like a newborn, whimpering deep in his throat.

"Better than just leaving him, sir," he muttered, then spat, cursing how the desert got into his throat.

Memories flowed on, trickling like the water in the swamp. In the desert, Quintus had dreamed of moisture. Now, he had far too much. Sweat trickled under his filthy tunic. If the night got cold, he could expect fever, and that was probably the best death he *could* expect. Maybe he could rest . . .

The underofficers had hoped to camp their men by the little Ballisur stream for a night, but even that mercy had been denied them by Crassus's son Publius and his Gaulish riders. Press on at the wretched cavalry's pace, press on, without food or water to sustain a mule, let alone Rome's mules, the men of the Legions. It was a gift from Mars that more men had not fallen out, never to rise.

Or perhaps the gift from Mars was embodied in Rufus, whose curses, made more foul and more frightening by the unwonted quiet of his voice, flowed as filthy as the water in the marsh by the walled city—the city they must reach if they hoped to save their lives and the old soldier was to get the wooden sword he joked, in his rare good moods, about looking forward to. Everyone had always played along, though a good First Spear was likelier to get a *castra* to command than the reward of a freed gladiator. Best not think of them either. Life as a slave might be the best fate any of them could face.

Quintus shut his eyes. Life as a gladiator was no mercy while Crassus ruled. Young though Quintus was, he could still remember how brutally the proconsul had put down the gladiators' revolt. The roads had been lined with crosses, and the air smelled like death. Crassus could be ruthless when surrounded by an invincible army. Still, Spartacus . . . the gladiator turned renegade had been the bogey of Quintus's childhood, just as The Surena, no doubt, would haunt the rest of his life, however brief it was.

But nothing, he thought, nothing could have been worse than what had befallen his family—his father killed, his family driven from the comfortable farm that had been theirs since the Tarquins were expelled, and with only him, the only grandson who survived life in a Roman *insula* with its fevers and fires, to try to win it back.

"What's that?"

He started. Requests for orders. Plans. He took it on his own initiative to order that those men who had extra food share with those who had none. Rufus caught his eye and nodded, bleak comfort where he had never expected to find it.

Bowing and saluting and waiting on the family's shrewd patron: He remembered that too. The gifts that meant a week of scant food. The snubs that meant setbacks; the rebukes that almost put paid to his hopes of a place following the Eagles. Jupiter Optimus Maximus knew he did not wish to follow the Eagles. He was a farmer, not a fighter. But they had snatched his farm, and there would be nothing at all for his family unless he earned it back.

If he shut his eyes and forced himself not to hear the prayers and imprecations of his centurion, the marsh sounds made him almost happy. He remembered the light upon the Tiber, the way it shone through the leaves of the twisted olive trees and heated the vines before harvest. He remembered how every clod of earth felt as he ran to his favorite places in the gnarled roots of trees by the river, when the heat hummed and the sun burned almost white. There, he would fling himself down and sleep or watch the blue haze fill the river valley as the afternoon drowsed away.

Voices murmured in the marshes outside the accursed walls of Carrhae. Treachery lay in their whispers. Had the city not been there, perhaps Crassus might have summoned the courage to let them die like Romans, but with a way of escape, the old thief had craft, if not honor.

"Buys his Legions like cupbearers . . ." muttered Rufus, too furious to be prudent. "And pours them out like vinegar before that . . . that . . . Persian with his catamite eyes." Persian, Parthian—Rufus would hardly care. The Surena wore kohl beneath his eyes to cut the glare. Who knew, if they had a chance, how many else might do so if it helped them fight in this land? Maybe, they could make do with mud. Enough of that lying around here.

"He's going to get himself killed talking like that," Lucilius whispered to one of his ten dearest friends.

"Small loss. But hush, you'll wake our graybeard."

The other patrician officer meant Quintus, he knew. And he knew enough to control himself. Don't antagonize anyone, least of all a patrician, even ones as worthless as those two. It was not safe.

A hand on his shoulder brought him back to the stinks of marsh and frightened men. Pain in his ribs, right over the earlier burn, jolted him to full alertness.

The centurion, with at least thirty more years on him to weaken back, ears, and eyes, heard the rustle in the marshes about the time that the guards stirred. Quintus nodded that he had heard it too, glad he had not started, much less cried out. The *you'll do* in Rufus's eyes, squinting even now as if unused to the comfort of darkness, was praise enough.

A moment later, both he and Quintus had risen to their knees, hands snatching at the well-worn hilts of the *gladius* that each of them carried. Their swords drawn, the guards that Rufus and Quintus had posted when they entered the marshes were coming in. Without orders and with . . .

With Parthians under escort. But judging from the assurance of their walk, these were not prisoners.

Quintus hunkered down in the wet and the mud. Despite the chill that had long since crept into his bones, he went suddenly hot, ashamed that the Parthians looked upon Romans defeated yet still alive.

They walked like princes. Or executioners. Their harness held a somber glitter that the marshes reflected, a gleam like rotten wood. One of them turned to rake his eyes across the marsh.

Quintus had seen that one last on horseback, with a long banner like a tongue of flame overhead and the sun glinting on the heavy scales of his armor and his horse's trappings. Then, too, his eyes, the pits darkened against the ferocious desert glare, had stared at his enemies, who had fallen and failed.

Once again, The Surena had come to view the vanquished.

All that was missing was the sound of the drums and bronze bells.

No swords were drawn. That might have been discipline. It was likelier to have been exhaustion. Of course, it was called safe-conduct.

None of the Romans were safe. Or were likely to live much longer.

2

Past Quintus and his men the Parthians marched, almost at parade pace, toward the front of the ragged column, where Crassus's staff would no doubt try to prop their commander up into a semblance of decent bearing. Rustles and faint splashes told Quintus that officers were turning their troops over to centurions and slipping forward, to be in on whatever council their commander might hold.

Quintus saw no reason to believe that his equestrian face would be any more welcome in defeat than it had been in prosperity. And the men . . .

Even the auxiliaries had drawn close, seeking the protection of an officer of Rome. Such protection as it was. Persians, this knot of them. Horsemen condemned to walk, like Rome's own mules. Traitors, perhaps, did Rome not war with Parthia. But loyal thus far.

"Forget you outrank a centurion." Quintus had had it drummed into him in training. "When you don't know what to do, forget your fancy armor—" not that Quintus's harness was anything to boast of, ''—and ask him what is to be done.''

Pride and honor had died under The Surena's arrows, but not good counsel. He found Rufus and hunkered down beside him.

''They've brought The Surena in,'' he muttered. It did not seem at all strange to be reporting to the older man, Rufus.

The older man shrugged, then turned thumbs down. *''Morituri te salutamus,''* he remarked, then spat. ''Doesn't look as if I'll get that wooden sword now, let alone my twenty acres and my mule. Damn. Mule would have been easier to train than some of these boys.''

''You think too, then, that this is surrender.'' Quintus didn't even bother making it a question.

''I think our guide was bought cheaper than a Tiburtine whore,'' muttered the centurion. ''And I think that we're about to see a bargain struck.''

''You think they'll offer terms?'' The younger man kept his question low-voiced.

Rufus nodded once, curtly. ''Unless they want us all dead. And they could have had that a time before if they'd had the mind to. We pass under the slaves' yoke probably,'' he spat. ''Better off dead—all of us.''

Voices rose from the direction that the proconsul had taken, angry, threatening. Crassus had called his officers about him. Predictably enough, Quintus had not been included. He could imagine Lucilius, as he had several times before, telling him, ''We couldn't find you,'' as if tending to his soldiers were somehow a dereliction of duty and reason enough for excluding the man who was not of their inner circle.

''What do you think's going on?''

The centurion grimaced as if he wanted to spit again.

"You saw. The Parthians have offered terms. Now we'll have to have the noble talk about honor. Nobles' talk. It'll probably take all night. In the end, Crassus will deal." Not "the proconsul." Not any one of a number of titles that a centurion should use for his commander. "It's his way."

Quintus could not help but look up sharply.

"Pardon, sir. Strange words for the likes of me. But they'd be the first to tell you. I haven't got honor like . . ." He jerked his chin toward the sound of the conflict.

"You want to know about my honor? It's all about you. Sleeping or talking, or it's—you there, I warned you not to drink! And as long as any of *that* looks to me and obeys me, I have my honor. When they're gone, I can think about dying. But not till then. Meanwhile, we wait."

He settled with a sigh that had more of exhaustion than aggravation to it.

You will never see the land now. At least, though, you leave no one desolate.

Quintus's temples throbbed with new punishments. Too many whispers in the night. Too many sounds in the marshes. The water and the weeds and the trees had murmured by Tiberbank, not whispered this way. And there were other voices too. *Hush,* they murmured at him. *Be comforted.* And, most seductive of all and the most mad, *Live.*

He still wore his child's *bulla* when he had found the little bronze statue that might have been new in the days when the Tarquins ruled Latium. Even now he carried it with him, a solemn little thing with a face worn away under its peaked bronze cap, its stubby arms upraised and bearing torches, its feet eternally dancing, but solemn somehow. Even now he remembered how the earth-warmed metal had felt as he clawed it from the earth and cleaned it. In the next moment, he almost dropped it. A voice, praising him, brought him upright. Yet, when he looked around wildly, the only disturbance was the undergrowth he himself had rustled; the sun glinted off the rippling water.

He had not fled . . . not quite. His grandfather's face rose before him—practical, strong, sure of his rights. His grandfather would frown at a boy who did not master his fears. So he kept the little statue with him. And he had forced himself to return to the spot the next day, unwilling to be run off by what might be no more than his own fancies. Strangely enough, it was the memory of that first all-but-flight from the voices he imagined that had sustained him during the long, long hours in the shrinking square, while the Parthians charged and charged, their banners swooping behind them and turning the sunlight into fire.

The fear of madness, of religious madness at that, made death in battle a cleanliness that, if not to be sought, could be welcomed.

He remembered his fear beside the river and his conquest of fear. A voice had spoken to him, true enough, from the rushes and the trees. It was the *genius loci*, the spirit of the place, as much a guardian of him and his land as the *lares* and *penates* to whom his grandfather, attended by Quintus's father, gravely sacrificed. The voice was deep, sleepy, like bees about their hive on a hot summer's day: honey, strength, and a little fear commingled. It was a woman's voice, not mother or sister or nurse, not any voice Quintus had ever heard; and it made him want to be taller and stronger and wiser than he was.

He feared such voices, of course. He was a Roman who trusted very little in gods. But he did not fear *that* voice; it was part of his soul. An odd thought—had you asked him before he heard it, he would have sworn by all the hardheaded Roman gods that he did not care about such things.

Day after day, like the sort of expensive Greek pedagogue his family would never have approved even if they could have afforded one, the *genius loci* taught him of the land, of the waves of men and women who had strode across it, bled for it, and loved it. One day, he took his own dagger—his first, and a gift—and slashed his finger, letting his blood too drip into the soil. That day, he swore he had seen a figure reflected beside him in the pool—dark hair, honey-dark skin, flickering in and out of his line of vision so quickly he never knew for sure what he had seen. A wave of love and acceptance washed over him. It had felt like his family's approval. It had also felt like the dreams that had, this close to his coming to manhood, begun to haunt his sleep. No matter: The land was his, and he was the land's, whether or not he ever saw it again.

And now it looked as if he would not. Never mind. Even if he left his bones in Syria, a part of him lived forever in the grasses outside Rome.

"This one will make a farmer," his grandsire said approvingly at a supper as frugal as that of their tenants. Chickpeas. Some lettuces. Cheese. Very little meat. His father seemed pleased. His mother, like the good woman that she was, sat and tended her wool.

Quintus slipped a hand into his tunic to feel the small bronze statue. It seemed to warm at the praise. He thought then that his life was beginning. But that was the evening he first heard the name "Sulla." He heard it more in the days to come until he came to hate the sound. Often he heard it coupled with the name "Marius," spoken by his father in a tone of reverence that rivalled the way he addressed to his grandsire.

In the days that followed, Quintus's *bulla* lay upon the house altar. Wrapped in an unfamiliar *toga virilis*, he stood beside his grandsire to watch his father march away. The old man kept a hawk's dignity, but he looked as worn as the tombs on the Via Appia they passed on their way into the City of Seven Hills. Even Quintus's bronze figurine, frozen in its ancient dance, had been no more weathered. But six months later, he saw how much older his grandsire could look. A man had come to the door, his tunic poor, his body twisted by ill-healed wounds. Not the sort of man a gentleman wanted visiting him, Quintus thought, until he saw the care with which the stranger limped over the threshhold, careful not to stumble and thus bring bad luck to the house.

He could not have brought more ill-luck to the house had he fallen flat. The news he brought was the death of Quintus's father.

"Did he die well?" asked the old man.

The visitor nodded.

"Then I have a son yet," he said.

Quintus had clasped his hand about his talisman. It paused in its dance, and one of the bronze torches stung his palm as if it were in truth alight. His mother, who had lingered to hear, had grasped her spindle so hard that blood dripped onto the bleached wool. She opened her mouth to cry out, but the old man's hand forestalled her lamentations. It shook once, then closed, clasping the hand of his son's friend, urging him to accept what hospitality the house could muster.

"Leave that wailing to hired mourners," he commanded. He was *paterfamilias*. He was obeyed.

No body was ever returned to the farmhouse near the

Tiber, just as none would come back from Carrhae. His father slept gods only knew where, not in the roadside tomb carved with a mantling Roman eagle rather than mourning figures. Some whispered that his father had died a rebel and it were best to cut the ceremonies short or omit them altogether: His grandsire stood by the tomb in his toga, dark for mourning, refusing to veil his head with a fold of cloth as anyone had a right to at the funeral of his only son. Perforce, Quintus too did not cover his head or face. He fought to keep his mouth from jerking in grief, trying to convince himself that that battle meant as much to him as the wars between Marius and Sulla that had robbed him of a father and his country of its peace.

Like two dogs, he thought, as curs fight on the paving stones, who fought over a stolen haunch until both beasts were bleeding and the meat was spoiled.

Whenever he might, he escaped to the river. The voice he had come to trust crooned comfort for his loss, a comfort that warmed him even as he returned to a cold hearth and a mother whose life turned feverish, flaming high and fitful like a dancer's torch, then guttering out as if it were thrust into sand.

They had few slaves left. Even Quintus's grandsire took his turn at tending her. But she died, and it seemed to Quintus that his dark mourning toga was made of lead, not his mother's wool. Even the coos of the doves by the riverbank seemed to mourn her.

"She was a good, thrifty woman," said his grandsire. "I have my son's son yet. And my land."

Quintus's mother had served him well and loved his son well, but the old man did not weep. One weakness only he showed: that Decia, who loved her husband so well that she could not live without him, should not lie alone in the family tomb, but instead sleep in peace beneath the olive trees of their farm. She would hear the doves and the voices, Quintus thought. He took comfort from that, if nothing else.

The day after that the orders came: They were displaced, evicted from the farm they had held since the Tarquins ruled.

Come with me, Quintus implored the shadowy figure in the water.

I cannot.

I will win back these lands, he vowed.

Whatever comes, you will see me again.

They had sold his mother's jewelry that should have gone to Quintus's wife, if ever he should be able now to marry and if any decent *gens* would welcome him. They had taken space in one of the *insulae* within the City itself, and the old man had declared his intent of pleading his case to some of the greatest men in the Senate.

Life as a client for such as he—as well ask the cliff to melt as the old eagle to bend his neck and smile. Quintus knew that shuttling between the *insula* and his patron's house on the Palatine shortened his grandfather's life as surely as a fever. It had been harder to be a sycophant, Quintus thought, than to lose at Carrhae.

With each attempt at a bow, each delayed petition, the knowledge came upon him. Their family had no skill at this type of battle. They would never see their farm again.

He thought his grandsire knew it too.

Neither ever spoke the thought aloud.

In the end, the old man had been relieved to die. He had secured for Quintus the little that he could—an appointment as a tribune in Crassus's service. Perhaps the grandson's more supple back could secure what he could not—a return to favor and their old home. If not, it was honorable service, or an honorable death.

*   *   *

Shouts boomed out, echoing in the marsh like a Greek
actor's tragic speech, made louder by the mask. The
voices held an edge of rage, made uglier by panic.

Quintus flicked a glance around his pitiful command.
His men sat, heads between knees. Even in the dark, he
could see that their faces wore the glazed, far-away look
of men about to turn children again, retreating from an
intolerable world.

Rufus met his eyes and shrugged. His hand fell to his
gladius. If the men could not or would not march when
the order came, it would be the blade for them, as it had
been earlier.

Quintus could not permit that. And there was something he could do. At the very least, he could gather
information and perhaps use it to keep his men alive a
little longer.

Pulling away from the centurion, he crept forward, his
boots making sucking noises in the marsh, chafing at his
aching feet. He thought to discard them, then changed
his mind.

He could be no more welcome at this staff meeting
than he had been at any of the others. Lucilius would
raise both supercilious brows. Someone else might sniff,
as if at manure brought within the Senate chamber.
Crassus might damn him with a frown.

Surprising, wasn't it, this close to death, how little
any of that mattered?

There was no *Via Principalis,* no orderly encampment
in the marsh. Quintus wondered if Crassus had ever seen
the need for such a thing, even when he was victorious.
Someone had made a half-hearted attempt to set up a tent
for the proconsul. It leaned drunkenly against some

brush and a half-drowned tree, and every time fresh shouts erupted, it appeared to sag. Even the wings of the Eagle on guard outside seemed to droop as if the standard itself was ashamed.

It had been one thing for Quintus to approach the proconsul enthroned in the midst of a proper camp, with all the other patricians around him, their stares casting him back to his days as a client, cringing on the Palatine. This shabbiness no more meant "proconsul" or "Rome" than some nameless fat man in robes, wallowing drunk in an alley, was the Pontifex Maximus.

They were all going to die, anyhow, weren't they? He was damned if he would observe the false niceties of rank even in death. Squaring his shoulders as a tribune ought to do, he pushed into the sorry tent, drew himself into the salute . . .

. . . and stared straight into Hades.

He had thought on the battlefield outside Carrhae that he was a witness to *nefas*, the unspeakable, incomprehensible evil that all Romans fled as they fled impiety. *Nefas* was not just slaughter: Had that been so, Crassus's earlier campaign against Spartacus might have defined it, and the gods would have punished him.

But this . . . this betrayal!

The Surena stood quietly as one of his men—Quintus would have bet the land he no longer owned that the prince could, but would not speak perfectly adequate Latin—finished his translation of his master's words.

"And he offers you truce and friendship on behalf of Orodes the Great King . . ." a howl of outrage rose from the assembled officers, drowning out the Parthian's other titles, ". . . in return for surrender."

Crassus forced himself to his feet. He was sixty years old and always had the best of everything—food, wine, protection. Why shouldn't he have looked well-preserved, the old mummy? Now, grief and—Quintus had to admit—fear made him look years older than Quintus's grandfather at his death. A torch guttered, then flared up, showing Crassus's face in every detail. Almost as red as the torchlight, it was contorted with a coward's rage. Under the thinning hair, tousled out of its usual careful trim, veins throbbed at the commander's temples.

If he died now, we might escape with our lives, Quintus thought, then despised himself for it.

The torchlight picked out Lucilius's sharp features, intent on his master, and the tall Parthian was watching him too as he might have watched an old dog soil the floor. Put him down now or wait? The question seemed to play about The Surena's scornful eyes and lips.

"Surrender?" Crassus demanded.

"Say, rather, you agree to return to your own place after swearing suitable oaths of friendship to my king." The Surena's words were as silken as his banners, and as deadly. His eyes flicked over to Vargontius and paused: brief respect for the way his twenty surviving men—out of four cohorts—had tried to fight their way through the Parthian ranks to their fellows. The Surena had even ordered his troops to withdraw, a vast honor guard, as the twenty limped into Carrhae.

"I will see you all in Hades first!" Crassus shouted. "And go there myself!"

"That might be arranged," remarked Cassius, never raising his voice. "Out there—" he gestured. "The men are angry. They didn't like leaving the wounded for our friend here to kill. They didn't like it at all."

The mutiny of a Legion—*nefas* such as Quintus had never imagined. And yet, he knew how close his men were to turning on their leaders. Desertion was better than mutiny, he thought and half-turned to go back to his men. Perhaps they could escape the swamp—but for what? To flee into the desert? Even properly equipped, his Legion had found the desert to be an ordeal. And thirst, they said, was an excruciating way to die.

As painful as a cross?

He might be out of choices.

The torch sputtered again, casting the features of Lucilius into high relief. He leaned forward with the intentness of a cur watching two larger dogs fight for mastery of the pack. Once he saw a winner begin to emerge, he would dart in and slash the hamstrings of his enemy. Lucilius's eyes shifted from Crassus to his officer, flashed to The Surena, then back to the Romans. He gestured at the man leaning on his shoulder, the companion of a hundred dice games, and the man got up. Quintus backed up against the entrance to the tent, but the man slipped out *beneath* the soiled fabric.

Was he going to tell the men? Rufus had calculated that some ten thousand yet survived. Some might die still of wounds or fever. Even so, there ought to be enough for one last, bloody fight. And such a battle would take out the Parthians who now watched them. Quintus thought he could die content if he could wash out the contempt in The Surena's eyes with blood.

Voices began to rise from around the tent. The Surena barely raised a long eyebrow.

Cassius leaned forward, slamming his fists on the table before the proconsul. Poorly balanced, it went over, spilling the wine—thick and unwatered—into the trodden muck. The winey mud looked like the ground outside Carrhae once 20,000 Romans had fallen.

"I say we accept the terms. The Senate's far away. Caesar's far away. We have no choice."

"And I say, I'll see you all in Hades first!" Crassus screamed. "Traitor and son of a traitor and a whore!"

"By all the gods, I won't take that from a coward!" the staff officer shouted back. "You and your son have destroyed us all."

With surprising strength, Crassus pushed the younger man aside and strode out of the tent. His staff followed, then split up in several directions. Some, Quintus knew, would disappear, not to return.

The others surrounded the proconsul, shouting, waving their fists. One or two made as if to draw swords and rush at the Parthians. But The Surena shook his head, and they fell back.

Up ahead, the proconsul flinched at last from the anger of his staff.

"We have to have a chance!" A wail, in accented Latin, from one of the auxiliaries. Someone threw a punch, and a scuffle ensued as the auxiliaries fought among themselves. The scuffle ended when half their number fled into the marsh.

"God send they sink," muttered Rufus.

Pleas and imprecations. Quintus flinched as a centurion, a quiet man whom he had never known well, simply opened his tunic to show his general his old scars, gotten in a lifetime of service. He would not beg: He simply wanted a chance to live out what was left of his life.

Crassus's eyes looked over at Vargontius, the officer The Surena had approved, appealing for some stroke of magic. Silently, the veteran turned his back.

Quintus heard scuffling, the snicks and hisses of weapons drawn, and over the tumult, Rufus's voice shouting, "I'll gut any of you who lifts a finger. Hold! You, gods rot you, don't let that Eagle fall in the mud."

Such pockets of discipline like that were rare. Thanks to Lucilius and his friends, news of the proposed terms had swept the Legions like blazing naphtha. If Crassus did not accept, he was a dead man.

And if he *did* accept?

Quintus knew what his grandfather would have said. *He should have fallen on his sword before he ever saw this day.*

The proconsul looked about desperately for a distraction.

"You!" he snarled at the guide who had led them from Carrhae's walls by night and into the marsh. "You led us astray. You sold yourself!"

It was as bad as ever Quintus had thought. A trick, entirely a trick: The guide had been as much in the Parthian pay as the yellow-skinned barbarians who had fired arrow after arrow at the Romans as they stood in the sun, unable to rest, unable to drink, and after a time unable to do aught but die. How could anyone ever have suspected otherwise, even for an instant? What Asiatics would ever help the Romans? Romans were for battening off of, then betraying them—even as the easterners might do to one of their own. He knew that well. He might have said as much, but who would have listened to him, a mere equestrian, when patricians, from Crassus's now-dead son down to the merest aristocratic time-server, leaned on his shoulder, ready to tell him what he wanted to hear?

The guide cringed, reeled under a blow from a ringed fist that sent blood spurting from mouth and nose. Then, drawing himself up, he spat.

Abruptly, Rufus appeared between the guide and the mob that had once been members of Rome's proudest Legions. Beside him was the *signifer*, Eagle proudly aloft. It seemed to glint with a light all its own. Even as Quintus watched, that light intensified—and then, as a man drew his dagger with a scream of rage against the traitor guide, the light blazed out.

When the red streaks and black splotches faded from Quintus's field of vision, he saw a man down on the ground, nursing a burnt hand. And the guide lay face down in the water, the smell of burnt flesh and singed, wet plants rank about him.

Odd. You would have thought the guide's body would have made a louder splash as it fell. He floated, face down. Quintus could imagine the staring eyes, the blood, trailing from the treacherous mouth. They were all treacherous here, all the easterners.

"No loss," someone muttered. "The Harpies spit on his liver."

Quintus stumbled forward, dimly aware that earth ought to be sprinkled on the dead man, a coin placed in his mouth.

"Let him rot," came a vengeful whisper.

That was more impiety. He would pay for it: They all would.

Crassus gestured. *Out. That way.* The Surena took his place with his men at the head of a ragged and very dispirited file that prepared to escape the marsh with even less honor than it had used to enter it.

And following the Parthians, the luster of its metal tarnished, was the Eagle of Quintus's Legion.

3

THE SUN WAS rising far over Asia when the remnants of Crassus's great army finally came to The Surena's camp. Save for a small group, the Parthians had ridden away, "to prepare a welcome," someone had said bleakly. *"Morituri te* . . . We who are about to die . . ."

"Quiet there!" a centurion shouted before one of the Parthians could enforce silence. All told, it was a small group of guards. Possibly, the Romans could have broken free. But the Parthians had bows, and the Romans' will to fight was gone with their leader's. The Surena had promised a truce; a truce they would have.

Quintus forced himself not to stagger into the great square outside the prince's tent. From the corner of his eye, he saw the *signifer* raise his battered Eagle proudly, as if its presence alone could turn the camp into a Roman conquest.

Remember, you are a Roman, he told himself as he put foot ahead of foot. It was an effort not to shake or weave, and his kit felt as if he carried all Rome upon his back. Crassus and some of the other, most senior officers had

been given horses and Quintus saw sidelong smiles at
how poorly they sat them, tired as they were and as
unused to the breeds of Parthia and Persia. (Lucilius,
Quintus noticed, had somehow acquired a horse too and
rode with a grace that made the other tribune, worn as he
was, want to pull him out of the saddle.) Their world was
ending, but Lucilius managed to look almost jaunty
ahorse.

Remember you are a Roman.

Tramp, tramp, tramp. The Parthians were watching . . .
long sidelong glances and sly smiles were as much of
their faces as you could see under their helms.

Tramp, tramp, tramp. *Remember you are mortal.* Remembering that was all too easy, even though Crassus
had probably dreamed of returning in triumph to Rome,
throwing down his colleague Caesar (who would never
have permitted such a defeat as this), and becoming a
Sulla who never, never resigned his power. Of the great
army that had marched from Armenia—28,000 Legionaries, 3,000 Asian mounted auxiliaries, and 100 Gaulish
cavalry—perhaps 10,000 Romans survived.

As captives, no matter what sort of gloss was put
on it.

Outside the camp, bland-faced guards requested they
stack their arms. There were more guards than Romans.

"Where's the yoke?" muttered Rufus, marching with
his men. Quintus was willing to wager the pay he'd never
see now that most of the men had hidden daggers or even
a *gladius* somewhere about them. He had sanctioned
enough of a departure from the ranks that hale men bore
along those who were wounded or nigh dropping from
exhaustion or fever.

It was a Roman custom, marching captives beneath
the *iugum,* their necks bent in token of servitude.

"Vae victis," Quintus muttered out of his memories of boyhood Livy. Woe to the conquered. It had happened to Romans before. It was still a disgrace.

The sun's first rays shot down over the great plain, turning the sallow land ruddy as if the rays were arrows. And fine scale armor and weapons blazed as the light rose toward full dawn. It kindled on the fittings of drums and brass bells, which rang as the Romans marched toward inevitable dishonor. Only the Legion's Eagle did not shine.

Outside the prince's great tent, troops were drawn up—proud Parthians, their Persian auxiliaries so like those of Rome (and possibly men who had eaten Roman bread among them), the tall Saka, masters of horse, and, strangest of all, the Yueh-chih with their sallow skins, narrow, slanting eyes, and those bandy legs that only were revealed on the rare occasions when these mercenaries from the steppes and high deserts of Asia dismounted. Their battle standards were strange: But last time that Quintus had seen such men in the field, it had not been their standards that concerned him.

There were even officials of Carrhae, that whore of garrisons, and some wealthy merchants whose long, rich robes bloused over their bellies, making them look slack and weak by contrast with the men who had destroyed Rome's greatest army. Their eyes were eager, though: the clever, ancient eyes of the Levantine, eager for advantage, hoping now that Rome's defeat meant the end of Rome's taxes.

All watched the sorry remnants of what had been the greatest army in Asia. *Romans in defeat. Remarkable: They bleed like other men. Can they also serve as slaves?*

The princes held the arms; the merchants held other power. Quintus fancied that they cast knowledgeable eyes over the conquered Romans, assessing this one's strength and that one's skills, where each might be needed, and how to dispose of the infirm, the useless, and the merely dangerous.

Quintus and the standard-bearer found themselves shunted subtly toward the front of the Roman column, away from the remnants of the cohort that Rufus had managed to keep together. To his horror, he realized he might well have welcomed a command to kneel: At this point, "kneel" meant "rest," not disgrace. He thought that even Rufus would have accepted it if it meant his sons, the Legionaries, could rest. There he waited, disarmed, his body shivering a little in the dawn wind. The scarlet silk banners of Parthia lifted in the wind and the rising sunlight turned the sallow plain to gold.

It was not the blue river valleys of his home, but it was, nevertheless, beautiful country. Would he have chosen it as a place in which to die? Better the square amid his troops, he realized. Better yet the farm, with its river and the mourning voice of the spirit who touched his mind and heart. Better than all, however, would have been to go on living with health and honor. Since that did not seem possible, Quintus tried to tell himself he had no regrets. He thought he could believe that the dancing feet of his amulet would tread out the measures long after he would cease to breathe. It had existed so long that it challenged time itself.

Crassus sat his horse before his army, preserving the illusion, for one last moment, of a general, not a suppliant come to submit to whatever terms The Surena thought good. Then an officer emerged from The Surena's tent and gestured. Crassus began to dismount and wavered. His face twisted.

Cassius slid out of his saddle quickly and was at the

wretched proconsul's side, aiding him to dismount, keeping a supportive hold on his arm as master and officer vanished into the tent. Sunlight struck the doorflap, making the space within look very dark. Other officers followed the proconsul, last of them Lucilius. His eyes, despite the circles beneath them, were bright as if he were about to spend the day dicing.

Perhaps he was. They all were. The difference was that Lucilius had no doubts he would emerge with his hands full of coin.

A cataphract in full heavy armor rode by and shoved Quintus on the shoulder. Pointless to resent the petty insult, and worse than that: He knew how quickly the Parthians could nock and shoot when they wished. He wore an officer's sigils; he must go inside.

He caught Rufus's eyes. They narrowed and the old soldier tightened his lips, wishing him good luck without speech, as was safest.

Then, as best he could, he marched into the dark maw of The Surena's tent.

The air was thick with mansmell: sweat, leather, armor, and the perfumes that these easterners used to scent themselves, even in battle. Too many men crowded into the huge tent; as one of the last and least of the Romans, Quintus would have found himself pressing against the tent wall, had a guard not stood between him and any quick knifeslash up that wall that might have bought a few Romans at least a chance for freedom had he still a ready knife.

Even though it was dawn, torches still flared, and he blinked. It took some time to become accustomed to the changing light and shadow in the prince's tent. The torchlight danced, a flickering, treacherous pattern in which partners changed and betrayed each other in the flickering of an eye. The Surena and his men. Representatives of the six other great Parthian families—and probably even a spy or two from Pacorus, the king's renegade son. Arabs from Edessa, no doubt servants of Ariamnes and Alchaudonius, the chieftains who had snatched their six thousand riders away.

And even though Orodes of Parthia had led half his army into Armenia to punish Artavasdos for sending troops to Crassus, Armenian lords sat as witnesses. No doubt their king prepared to turn his coat, too. Empty chairs, richly draped, stood at the center of the cluster of Rome's enemies. They did not face the chief of them, yet.

Crassus stood before the men who had destroyed him. Despite the weathered armor he wore and the sword he had been allowed to keep, he looked like an old man, a sick man, a man who had lost his son. Like Priam in Achilles's tent, stripped of his pride. Cassius stood away from him, and Crassus raised his chin. That gesture took an effort which impressed Quintus.

Achilles had raised Priam, offered him food and wine, honor and even mercy of a sort. These princes were slow to offer the proconsul even a chair, much less the honor due a patrician of Rome. The one they finally brought him was low; he must look up into the conqueror's eyes. Cassius stood stiffly at his back.

Quintus wondered if Lucilius would still place odds on Crassus.

The Surena chose that moment to take his seat. As if to underline his disdain for his adversaries, he had taken the time to bathe and put on fresh robes. Now he was resplendent in shimmering fabrics brought all the way from the Land of Gold—some of the very wealth Crassus had hoped to gain by taking this land.

No sooner than Crassus sat, he must rise in reluctant homage. He glared at the guard who hissed at him, but submitted. With the Parthian general came officers—men of the Saka and of the Yueh-chih.

The morning passed in a blaze of misery. Quintus, his jaw set against a protest that might have meant the death of all of them, listened to the terms of "truce" and "friendship" promised them the night before as they lay in the marsh. Some part of him might have rejoiced. It was a balancing of the scales for him and his family. It was vengeance, even, for those deaths whose stench polluted the great roads outside Rome.

It was disgrace, not truce.

"You might as well decimate what's left and have done!" sputtered one officer. Cassius hissed at him and, had he been nearer, looked as if he might have struck the speaker.

"That too might be arranged," purred The Surena. "The decision lies in your hands."

The proconsul stiffened. For a moment it looked as if he would hurl himself from his chair, but his staff officers' hands dropped upon his shoulders. Comfort, it looked like, until one remembered that only last night, The Surena had given him a clear choice: Surrender or die.

Now Crassus removed his helm. His thinning hair lay sweat-plastered to his skull. He shook his head. "That decision has already been made. We will have peace."

"That is what you call it when your men, when your son, all lie dead, is it? Peace? We would call it. . . ."

Quintus shivered. From the soles of his feet, he could sense the hot hate of other Romans in the tent. Outside the tent, the Parthians might be relaying this conversation to the survivors of the Legions: Asiatics loved to boast and gloat. He tensed, waiting for the first man to leap forward. The tiny statue in his breast warmed, as if the two torches it had held aloft all these centuries suddenly kindled.

Outside the tent came a clamor that made the Romans start. Better coached, the Parthians, Saka, and Persians did not move from their seats around the table. The Yueh-chih reached for weapons, but subsided at a glare from their master.

Warriors unlike any Quintus had ever seen entered the Prince's tent, led by a man who was too young to be a general, but whose manner clearly proclaimed that he had a right to take a place at least the equal of those who sat at their ease in judgment upon Rome. His armor, like that of his guard, was scaled, his garments quilted, and his boots high, adapted for riding. He was stocky, four-square; and if his eyes were slanted like those of the Yueh-chih, he was not bandy-legged like them. Despite the season, he wore a leopard's skin over his armor, as if the heat that would soon rise from the earth was nothing to him. Oddest of all was his skin, which was the color of gold.

Placing himself well away from the Yueh-chih, who muttered but gave place to him, he seated himself near The Surena with the air of one taking a throne by right.

Now he was actually looking at a warrior of the Land of Gold, from beyond the eastern deserts, Quintus realized. It was said—by those eager for riches—that this land was so wealthy that the dust of gold had sunk into the skins of its inhabitants. And enough Romans had believed that legend to bring them to this place where they might die. Parthia, he had heard rumors, paid tribute to that realm in return for trade. At the time he found it hard to believe. Now, seeing the man's imperial composure even though he was too young to hold rank equal to that of The Surena or Crassus before his downfall, Quintus wondered. It would be a great thing to control access to such a realm—great enough to make the downfall of Rome even more worthwhile than hatred could account for.

He stared at the cause of an army's death, meeting for a sharp second the eastern warrior's gaze. The eyes of that one flicked over the assembled princes as a dog-breeder might regard an unsatisfactory litter, then fastened completely on the Romans.

A small wave brought to his side a man with the quick, mobile features of a Sogdian, who—oddly enough—wore the same livery of scales and quilted fabric. He spoke.

"My lord says your men fought well. But they lost. And your son died. Now my lord asks you—" he jerked his chin at Crassus, "—why you yet live."

"I still have an army to protect. They are all my sons," said the proconsul. He drew himself up as proudly as he might.

If they all survived this day, Lucilius might laugh at Crassus's words. But for the first time, Quintus saw the old man as one who could have been followed had Fortune not turned the scale.

Quintus felt his eyes sting, and another sting besides. Moving very slowly, mindful always of the watchful Saka guard beside him, he raised one hand to where the little bronze statue danced above his heart. A warmth, pervasive but not unpleasant, radiated from it as a promise of comfort. He felt, if not rested, fit to march or fight. Or, likelier than either, to endure what must be.

The Sogdian eyed Crassus, skepticism writ large on his mobile features. He glanced at The Surena as if for permission to smile. But the Parthian lord's face was as impassive as that of the man from the Land of Gold.

The noble from the East nodded gravely, accepting the words as if they came from a victor and general, not a beaten man. "You said, Prince of An'Hsi, that this was the Prince of Ta'Tsien . . . that land to the west . . . who would turn his land to gold and count it? Who would venture to trade with us of the Han? Is he a noble, or is he a merchant?"

Again, the Sogdian spoke. Had the *auxilia* Quintus saw in the marsh survived? He would have been glad of an interpreter of his own. Some of the princes were shifting, impatient, in their seats. It was always dangerous when barbarians became restive. Apparently, the man from the Land of Gold—*the Han*, he called it—thought so too.

The Surena laughed now, a sound echoed by his Persian nobles, whose pride it was to live off their lands and never soil their fingers with trade. These patricians, these patricians, Quintus thought. They would be the death of him as they had been of his family's hopes. The statue over his heart pricked at his flesh. *Pay attention, fool.* He all but heard his grandfather's voice exhort him.

"How can this be?"

Abruptly, one of the deadly steppe riders broke into a tumult of words that sounded much like the speech of the man of the Han—and that young lordly officer listened, then spoke.

"Their gods, you say," the interpreter repeated. "Their gods travel with their armies? Careless of them, should they lose. My most excellent Lord Surena, this insignificant one would see these gods of the West."

The Surena clapped his hands.

And, carried any which way, as slaves would drag bodies out of a prison, Parthians brought the Eagles of Crassus's slain Legions into the tent and hurled them onto the table.

The clash of the metal made everyone start. The Yueh-chih muttered as if they expected the Eagles to leap from their standards, mantle, and strike with beaks and claws. Several men, and those not the least in rank, muttered, gestured, and fumbled at amulets.

The captive Eagles of the Legions lay there on the table: no gods, but tarnished metal, hacked with sword-thrusts, stained with the blood of their Roman bearers.

The blood was fresh on one.

"We found this one just outside. He who carried it . . . fought us."

Crassus half rose from his chair, then sank down at a glance from his staff officers.

Quintus closed his eyes. That Eagle's bearer had been a brave man. Then he forced his eyes open again, condemning himself to watch every last instant of his country's disgrace.

"It seems," said the man of the Han through his interpreter, "that even some gods can be overpowered. What shall you do with these?"

"They go to our temples, especially the one at Merv," said The Surena. "To commemorate my victory."

Behind him, several warriors on embassy from the King Orodes flickered glances at one another. Powerful The Surena was; had he become so powerful that the king would have to risk removing him or losing his own crown? Quintus knew he would never have time to learn.

The Han officer rose. "Metal gods for which men

die," he mused, putting out a well-kept hand to touch the nearest Eagle—Quintus's own.

"My *tu hu* must see this. It will be for my commander to decide, but this foolish one should think that the Son of Heaven in Ch'ang-an must see these Eagles, and that the exalted one's learned men should unravel the mystery of the power that makes men die for them."

He raised the Eagle as if it had been a standard of his own. SPQR, half covered by blood, shone in the firelight. Crassus stared at it as a drowning man stares at the faintest beam of light taunting him at a horizon of air and water that he is fated never to reach, struggle as he may.

"I take this," the officer of Han announced. "As part of An'Hsi's tribute to the Son of Heaven."

He bowed as courteously as if he had done no more than accept a cup of wine among his brothers, then strode from the tent, taking the Eagle with him.

Two men strode forward to gather up the remaining standards.

"No . . ." whispered Crassus, echoing Quintus's longing. "By all the gods of hell, *no!*"

They were Crassus's son, Quintus's friends, Rufus's very lifeblood; and should they be borne in triumph to a barbarian shrine, witness of Rome's failure to protect them? They *were* Rome herself. Surely, great Romulus himself would turn his face away from the army that lost them.

Vargontius and Cassius had their hands on the proconsul's shoulders, but he shook them off with the strength of a much younger man whom despair has made strong.

"Give me back my Eagles!" he howled and hurled himself forward.

He crashed against a warrior and the table, one arm

flung out to capture as many of the precious *signa* as he could, the other snatching a dagger from the nearest Parthian's belt. He could have struck in that moment when everyone stood shocked into stillness, avenged his son and his army and his Eagles with one stroke, deep in The Surena's throat.

Instead, he whirled, the dagger out as if to defend the Eagles he held before him as shield and as standards. The torchlight gleamed off them, splintering the light so that the tent walls seemed patterned by a forest of shadows, oak, and pine, and piercing it, the standards of Rome.

The old proconsul's eyes were alight, but not with battle madness.

"Romans! he screamed. "*Comites*, to me! Finish what we should have ended! *Roma!*"

His staff officers leapt, calculating as great cats: Help the proconsul or take their chances on escape?

"Out!" cried Vargontius. "Someone bring them word!" His hand shoved Cassius from the tent, which seem to shrink inward, holding still the iron reek of blood and metal and sweat. Screams came from outside the tent as merchants fled from riot, and Romans and Parthians sought each other's throats.

Pain thrust Quintus forward, his hand falling past his side to the blade of the nearest guard. How slowly the man moved. Seizing the sword was like taking a pine branch from a girl-child.

"*Roma!*" shouted Crassus as if he had not tried, all his life, to turn Rome into sesterces and hoard them all. Quintus fought forward, struggling to reach the proconsul's side. Crassus had stolen his land, but he had called on Rome. Well, he should have what he could of it. This was a better death than Quintus had expected. It was even honorable. He could meet his grandfather's eyes on the other side of the Styx, assuming someone spared him the coin for passage.

"Someone get the torches!" The heavy braziers toppled, and flames licked up blood and dirt before they, like so many within the tent, died.

Crassus might be sane in his wish to die, but now Pan piped within the tent, and madness struck. Quintus slashed down with his stolen sword. As if in a dream, he saw the man before him spew blood and fall upon another. There must have been screams and groans but the pounding in his temples, harsher than the Parthians' drums, drowned out all other sounds as Romans and Parthians and Yueh-chih contended in what light the tent let in now that the torches had died. It was a mad dance, a fever in the blood, Quintus thought. He might as well be a woman, carrying a cone-tipped wand and screaming paeans to Bacchus and Bromius.

He caught a glimpse of Lucilius, his fair hair smeared with blood, his eyes bright as if Fortuna drank to him and his dice. He had despised them all, but they were Romans.

"Crassus!" Quintus screamed, trying to hack through to the old man. Weakened by age and defeat, the commander would not be able to defend himself and his Eagles for long. One more man—the tribune used the fine steel of the Parthian's sword as if it were a *gladius* to stab him in the throat. And then he reeled before the proconsul, gasping. His heart rose as Crassus's eyes brightened at the sight of him.

"Behind you! Down!" the old man gasped at the same time that fire burned his chest—the bronze statue again? Quintus doubled over, then curved around, almost on his knees. He brought his blade up and around, spitting the man who had thought to slay him from behind.

Quintus turned, and the thanks died on his lips. He lunged but, even as his sword thrust home, the Parthian's blade fell on Crassus's hand as it clutched the Eagles, severing it at the wrist. It fell on Quintus's head in a macabre parody of the blessings his grandfather had once given him.

His shout of horror and Crassus's scream rang out. He hurled himself forward to defend the man who had become—against all reason—*his* proconsul and general. The old man sagged, the Eagles dropping from his arm in a clatter of heavy bronze. He started to fall—too slowly. A Parthian's blade took him at the nape of the neck, and his head fell first.

"No!" screamed Quintus. He fought as he did not know he could, until a space cleared between him and his dead and the Parthians. Sobbing for breath, he paused, his sword as steady as if it did not feel made of lead. The Parthians circled him. It was just a matter of time till they cut him down. Just a matter of time.

But he would sell himself as dearly as he could. How many could he take with him? And where should he start? He eyed the warriors speculatively, and he could see that they knew it. Came a commotion and movement underfoot. He lashed out, but his blade hit the edge of the table and rebounded. He recovered his guard and struck again. . . .

To his horror, one of his enemies parried not with a sword but with the Eagle he had snatched up.

If Quintus died for it, he could not strike that Eagle: as well as strike down his grandfather or Rome herself. They had struck down Crassus. He feinted, then attacked viciously. The Parthian dodged and laughed. Again, he tried; and again.

They were laughing at him, teasing him as wanton

boys tease a chained beast. With a scream, he threw himself forward, determined to take as many of his enemies with him as he could . . .

. . . and what felt like a bar of red-hot iron smashed across his neck. The roaring of the battlefield died away to the murmur of a river on a hazy day, and then into silence.

4

QUINTUS WAS BLIND. He would have been terrified, but fear had been pounded out of him by the Parthian wardrums and bells proclaiming victory. Nearer and nearer they seemed to come. A few paces more, and they would trample him.

And then he would join his comrades in death. He lowered his head like a beast before the altar of sacrifice. It was fated: Let it happen.

Death might be worth it, if only the dryness in his throat went away. They had fought for hours outside Carrhae in the hot sun, with the stinks of blood and dead men and horses, and the flies buzzing as loud as drums and bells.

"Damned if we're leaving him behind. I'm not losing one more." The voice was harsh. Your voice got that way when they kept you out fighting in the sun and wouldn't let you rest or drink.

"What's the worst they can do? Kill me? I'd fall on my own sword if I had one."

"Think it through, centurion! You'll have to get men to

*carry him. He'll slow us down. And he'll have no more wits
than a babe if he lives. . . ."*

The voice was cultured and persuasive. Quintus decided he didn't like it. One more word and he'd silence it,
if he could only get up, but even the effort of raising his
head . . .

*"Do you have to shout? He can hear every word you say,
can't you, sir?"*

The voices subsided to a muttering. Footsteps
pounded, moving blessedly in the direction of *away.*

*"Never fear, he'll live if he wants to. He's a countryman.
His head's as hard as the rock that breaks your plow."*

Long pause while the drums and bells pounded in
Quintus's head as he fought to overhear the argument
that went on somewhere above him. Other voices entered—too many more. He was tired. He let himself drift.

It was the heat and the thirst. They could strike you as
dead as The Surena's arrows or a sword. He was dead,
and they couldn't even let him lie in peace. He thought
death meant stillness, rest—he had seen his grandfather
and his mother laid out before the shrouds covered them
up. Their faces had been strained and twisted during the
ordeals of their last days, but death had smoothed the
lines of care and anguish into the serenity of a country
sculptor's tomb carving.

*"Well, then you bring your imperial whatever-it-calls-itself
over here, and I'll tell him* myself! *I'm not leaving this man
to die. And if you don't like it, you know where you can shove
it. Die fast; die slow—it's no difference. They're not giving the
men they're sending—Mars watch them—to Merv, honorable
retirement, land, and a mule. Or . . ."*

Anger burst out of the voice in a sort of cough. . . .
"Curse this sand to the pit! They're selling *them. Selling free-
born Romans, men of the Legions, as slaves. Do you really think*

*those merchants—Persian merchants, mind you—are going to
waste their time on a man they can't sell fast?"*

More mutters. The sound of a language like horns and
bells. Footsteps. Hoofbeats. A hand on his head. *"Rest
easy, lad, I mean, sir. I think Fortuna's going to let me pull this
off. . . ."*

"I may have found a horse. . . ." A new voice, heavily
accented with the tones of Persia. Quintus tensed.

*"How much . . . never mind . . . If you think it's sound
enough."*

A snort of scorn, a chuckle, broken off.

*"Take my pouch. . . . Lad, the men need you. . . . Come on
back to us."*

So easy to drift away. Just leave.

Footsteps—the crunch of nailed boots on grit and
sand, the quicker, softer stride of a horseman. He could
even hear aging knees creak as someone settled mas-
sively by his side.

*"Tribune, in the name of all the gods, don't leave me to lead
them alone. . . ."*

The appeal was unfair; it drew him back to the world.
He moaned, fighting its claim upon him.

They had left their wounded and their dead outside
Carrhae, unburied, unattended. He had not consented to
that decision, had had no choice in it. But it was *nefas,*
and now he too must suffer for it.

Suffer it and what lay after—to lack the coin for
Charon and to wander bodiless and moaning, on this side
of the river Styx. His grandfather and mother would lack
him forever, unless some pious soul dropped earth on
him and mimed, at least, the rites of proper burial.

Quintus would wander? He was wandering now. Perhaps his father wandered unburied, too. Perhaps they
would meet each other. But would they be able to em-

brace, there on the bank of the Styx, and take comfort in each other's presence? Or would knowing that the other suffered too add only to their pain? Perhaps they would not recognize each other at all. It would be a lonely eternity without kin, without rest.

Something caught him up, and he protested wildly.

"Quiet! Make me out to be a liar, when I said you just got knocked on the head a little? Good thing you had your helmet on. It'll never be good for anything again. Ought to make you pay for it. That was some fight you put up over his body, the poor old bastard. Funny to call him *poor, but what's all his wealth brought him to? Butcher's meat, like the rawest recruit who didn't guard his back. Still, in the end, he fought like a Roman. Guess he had something in him after all."*

The "something" that had caught him shifted and resolved itself into arms, awkward in how they bore him.

"Why am I talking to him? He may never hear me, and all that hard work wasted. Dis take them all, this one would have made a soldier, too."

Quintus's eyes rolled open; he caught a glimpse of the sun, spinning, as it seemed, overhead; and he gagged. Immediately, rough hands clasped his head.

"Have a care! That's a man you're lifting, not a sack of meal. Yes, you too, sir. Easy there."

The manhandling stopped. He felt himself bound to a padded surface. Perhaps now, the voices would leave him alone, and he could retreat into the blackness. It lured him.

Yet now he was rocked back and forward, as if he indeed lay on Charon's boat. Huge flies buzzed, and the drums and bells pounded. And thirst, as if he had drunk naphtha on the field of battle, burned him, so that he fought not to moan.

It was shameful to moan. But his throat burned. A

sudden jolt at his breast made him cry aloud, forgetting shame, forgetting all but the pain. He thought he screamed to be let alone, to be taken down from the wheel, to be buried. . . . He screamed till his throat was even more raw than before. His lips cracked, but the blood brought him no relief.

Bitterness touched his lips. He longed for the moisture that underlay the bitterness, but he spat it away.

"He's not drinking." Again the cultured, hateful voice.

"Sometimes after a head wound, they can't. They just spew it back up. Waste it."

After a long pause, *"I was thinking. We need all the Romans we can get. Now . . ."* A new note crept into the light, patrician tones—self-conscious cleverness. *"I've heard that these people have good physicians. . . ."*

"And have them come and knock the tribune on the head again so he doesn't thrash or throw a fit or slow us up? This time, they'll kill him for sure. He makes it out of the dark on his own, or not at all, I'm afraid."

And then, something blessedly cool, like freshly turned earth, overlay his eyes and throbbing brow.

He sobbed once, unashamedly, and felt a hand press his shoulder, a touch he took with him into a darkness that was now restful. The lurching from side to side that had sickened him before now lulled him as if, in truth, he rode Charon's boat toward peace. Gods . . . water, rippling through shadows, bringing peace.

Animals screamed and fought while men's voices rose in entreaty and command. Quintus flinched, retreating into the blackness before his eyes until red lights erupted there and cautioned him to go carefully. A hot wind rose. Silence again. Someone had thrown the cake to Cerberus. At least, he hoped so. Already, he had made it farther than he dreamed—across the River. Soon, he would walk on asphodels. . . .

. . . but there was the judgment. Dreadful names, clamorous as bronze, Minos and Rhadamanthus, and one more. Which one? He must know the third judge, or his spirit would be hurled to the forges of Tartarus. Briefly he struggled from the blackness and found himself restrained.

Condemned already? He forced himself to think. The name of the third judge! He had to know the name!

Aeacus, came a voice. *He will not harm you.* The voice was gentle, like a hand laid on his brow.

He groaned and to his shamed relief, swooned.

Quintus awoke, if he could call it that, in darkness. He still lay on that warm, rocking surface. He still was bound. But he felt stronger. Carefully, he flexed one arm, then the other. Well enough. He slipped them free of the restraints and slid cautiously onto his feet. Better yet. Something damp slithered from his brow, and he caught it before he could think to flinch from what it might be.

It was a damp cloth. Even in the dusky light, it had the sheen of cloth brought from the farthest east.

So he was not blind, then? Thank all the gods for that. He glanced round as greedily as a man deprived of water plunges his head into a clean pool. What had he expected? The asphodels, certainly, of childhood tales . . . long green meadows with heroes striding over them, or perhaps a bank, mounded with treeroots, overlooking the lazy ripples of the Tiber near his home.

He would have liked that. Instead, he found himself standing in a cave vast as an amphitheatre, with passageways stretching in five directions. He could smell water. Yes, that was right. He had passed over the Styx, had he not? He glanced quickly, a soldier's wary glance, at the other rock-hewn passageways.

He dared to touch his head. No helm. Yes, that was right. The voice of—Rufus, wasn't it?—in the waking dream that had been his life had said his helm would never be of use to anyone. It had saved his life for the moment. Waste of a good helm, perhaps?

His hair was crusted with what he decided must be blood. It was still wet, but the wetness was cool. Moving slowly, like an old man, he walked over to one of the passageways. His caution was well-founded: "Live" he might be, here in this anteroom to eternity, but he had not the strength he always had taken for granted. A few wounds and sprains—nothing compared with the devouring agony of the head-blow he had taken—ached. He ignored them and started down the passage.

Wailing rang out from the passageway, and he recoiled. Not that way. With more haste than he would have thought possible, he found himself back in the main cave. Red light flickered over its rocky ceiling and reflected from the huge gems, set into the living rock, that lit it.

The light came from yet another passageway. He started down it. Heat lashed at him, hungry as fire. Shadows leapt against the walls and were themselves consumed, as the white heat at a flame's core overpowers the reds and yellows that surround it. He looked down: Not sand but grit lay underfoot. He kicked at it, and saw more clearly: bones, calcined almost to powder by the heat that lay before him. He had suffered, when he first came to the East, from exposure to the desert. He had suffered at Carrhae, standing fully armed and afraid in the square, pressed in among the Eagles, as arrows, not rain, fell from the sky. And yet, compared with the heat that roared like a bellows through the passageway, that might have been a vision of Thule. Neither man nor shade could pass much further along that corridor, let alone cross the river, and emerge in any recognizable form. This was not forgetfulness: It was utter annihilation.

The flame shadows—red on gold on white—flickered up like The Surena's deadly banners. They formed into a figure that danced for Quintus, bearing inexhaustible torches. His hand went to his breast and withdrew his bronze talisman. It caught the light and glowed as if its metal had just been cast. Tiny fires sprang up on its palms, upheld forever in the motion of a funeral dance. A fire brushed against his own hand, and he stepped back. Warned again? Carefully, he brushed his boots against the rock, that no trace of burnt bone cling to the sturdy nails. Let the dead keep their own. What lay at the end of the passageway was Phlegethon, river of fire. What emerged from *that* crossing would be unrecognizable as man *or* shade. His head whirled at how closely his thoughts brushed the unthinkable, and he reeled back into the anteroom.

He was a Roman. The great ceremonies and great names of the gods were for the priests and senators, not the likes of him. He had come here to die and to be judged. *Get on with it.* Bad enough to be kept waiting, like a Legionary found drunk and sent in for discipline.

Air and darkness brushed his face like cool hands. Quintus sighed. Before common sense could tell him that there were no hands, there was no touch in this place, he reached to grasp what had soothed his parched brow and cheeks with that flicker of sensation. A ripple of sound in the air taunted his failure, drew him forward to yet another passageway.

"I ought to wait here until . . . whatever . . . comes to summon me," he muttered.

But the air rippled again, a sound so sweet that he followed it. No white powder of ancient bone lay underfoot. Gradually the rock took on a familiar feel. He liked this path. *Why* did he like this path? *Why* did it feel as if he had always known it? It looked no different from any other cave floor. He shut his eyes. *Now* he had it: It was the pattern of stones and roots, the very shape of the path he had taken during his childhood to his favorite riverside lair.

Moving eagerly, a scout returning home after perils, he moved down the corridor and into his memories. The drowsy breeze that had fanned him asleep on the bank of the Tiber soothed him once again. The air was heavy with bees and birdsong. Leaves closed in overhead.

Light rippled on the walls and the roof of the caveway, glinting up from the river Quintus knew lay at the end of the passage. Surely no flowing water had ever smelled so sweet, and no summer sun had shone so kindly. How did sunlight pierce the earth to shine upon a river in the Underworld? He puzzled that question for a moment, then moved on.

He was a farmer and a soldier, not one of his Legion's engineers. It was not for him to say. He sighed again, then yawned, as he emerged from the passageway. Here the cave widened. He had the impression of a vast space through which a river ran. It looked like his river valley. Even the feel of the rock and earth underfoot was familiar—he knew, at this point in the path, to turn his foot *this* way because of a boulder; at that fork between the overhanging bushes, there was a slight depression in the earth so he didn't have to duck.

Merciful gods, was he home? Had he slept, unaware,

and been judged in his sleep? Beyond him lay the river, glistening in the bright . . . it could not be sunlight, could it, striking down through a fissure in the very bones of the earth? This could not be the Underworld, could it? It looked so innocent, so peaceful.

He came out upon the bank from which he had so often fished as a boy and looked down into the summer haze. Here he sat and leaned against his favorite tree. His hand brushed something smooth, and he brought it, dappled with gold powder, up to his face. He rested not only on grass, but on lilies, the very asphodels of Hades such as Achilles had strode upon. For a moment, he wanted to giggle like a boy: to think of him, lolling among flowers. He sniffed at the pollen. It smelled sweeter than the clovers and violets from which he had sucked the syrup on hot afternoons.

Tender amusement stroked his thoughts. His eyes filled. He *was* home. Even the *genius loci* had come out to greet him. "I thought I'd lost you forever," he told the voice. He thought he heard a rippling laugh, but it might have been a fish, leaping back into a blindingly bright circle at the middle of the river.

"*Did you? So foolish, so tired—and dearest of all to me,*" the voice murmured.

Like a child who grasps everything to taste it, he raised his fingers to his lips.

"*You must be hungry and thirsty. Here is food. Here is water. Never leave me.*"

The last time he had heard that voice, he had been a grieving boy, struggling to behave like a man as he went into exile. Now, against all hopes, he had returned. In death, perhaps; but he was home again. Here was the *genius loci*. She would take care of him. Cool hands touched his temples, eased the ache that had never left him since Crassus marched his legions at a cavalry pace and he began to know that he was not only mad but doomed.

The *genius loci* made a wordless sound of pain as those cool, cool hands stroked his face and hair. It was pain for him, for what he had suffered. He could feel even the hurt from the last blow from the *signum*, the one that had cast him into the Underworld, easing. Yes, it was an indignity to have been struck by one of the Eagles he was trying to defend. But it was so long ago; and he was here; and none of it needed to mean anything from now on.

It would be good to be young again. It would be good to forget all that had passed since the day that the stern-faced man had come to his grandfather and announced his father's death. And if he could not forget, well, then, he was man, not boy; and the *genius loci's* voice reminded him of that, too. His eyes filled once again, and he wept for the first time since he and his grandfather had been forced from their home. Wept without shame for sheer relief that the pressure was gone, that he was home again, loved again, protected once again.

After a fierce, brief spate of weeping, Quintus was silent, at peace as he had seldom been. He rubbed his hands across his eyes, breathing in the overpowering scent of the asphodels. Then he chuckled. For the first time since Crassus's Legions had entered the desert, he realized he was truly at rest.

The upper air seemed very far away. He had sunlight and growing things and fresh water here: He had his land. What more could he need? This was all his grandfather had taught him ever to want.

Rest with me, stay with me, crooned the spirit. How sweet her voice was. It was no longer mother, no longer sister or friend, but the wife he knew his poverty would

never have let him take. And more still: "Wife" would
have been a woman of a family equal to his, a practical
woman, a keeper of his hearth. This voice promised him
not just bread, but dreams.

The bout of weeping had made him thirsty.

*There is water, there is even food. It all can be yours. And
afterward* . . .

"Why can I not see you? Why can we not touch hand
to hand?" he asked. He was suddenly afire, athirst, and
for more than water. He reached quickly behind his back,
trying to capture the slender wrists of what seemed more
woman now than spirit.

With a laugh and a fragrant breeze, she eluded him.
The world was vanishing. Names . . . Syria . . . Armenia . . . Crassus . . . were fading from his consciousness.
Another name . . . *Rufus?* He ought to remember that one,
he thought. A voice roughened by breathing grit and
walking too long rang in his head, then faded. No, no
point in remembering Rufus, who would soon find his
own peace.

First, refresh yourself. Such a small thing I ask. . . .

It was no small thing to Quintus. How long had it
been since he could drink his fill in peace? He leaned out
over the water, scooped out a palmful of it, raised it to his
lips . . .

. . . and sneezed at the combined scents of the pollen
of the immortal asphodels and the river water. The *genius
loci* laughed playfully.

He scrubbed his hands and dried them against his
tunic. Then he dipped again into the river, held up his
hands, which dripped with water that smelled more in-
toxicating than unwatered Falernian, and pledged the
woman he could not see.

No! Do not *drink!*

The water trickled out of his cupped hands, casting rainbows onto the asphodels. Their scent grew richer, and he felt his belly rumble with hunger.

That *is real. That is* alive, said this new voice. It too was a woman's voice, but deeper and more strongly accented than the voice of what Quintus thought was his *genius loci.*

And you can only satisfy it under the sun. All else is illusion.

He heard a scream overhead and looked up to see a flash of brazen wings. Eagle's wings. The great bird mantled and cried out a challenge. The cry echoed in the rock. Like the horns that called him to wakefulness or battle, it reminded him: a world. A river. Names and living faces, marred by cuts or sweat or tears. The dead, contorted, bloody, or bled out.

A shapely hand held water to his lips. He could *see* it now, could reach out and grasp it.

Fool! came the second voice. *If you remember names, what is the name of this river?*

"Why, Lethe, of course," he mumbled. The water spilled. Memory returned.

Lethe—river of forgetfulness.

No, you must trust me. Stay with me, love me, forget the rest.

Get away *from him!*

Scented air wafted about him, as if the woman who stood above him was roughly jerked away. Even her hand—which was all Quintus had ever seen—vanished.

A veiled figure appeared before him. Like the vanished spirit, she was scented, but with sandalwood, cinnamon, and cardamom, rather than the flowers he remembered from his childhood. Her perfume was strange, a little daunting, but he found it curiously refreshing. Her face was hidden by the saffron veil of a Roman bride, but the fabric was so thin, so delicate he could see her eyes clearly. They were long and dark, their almond shape marked with kohl. On The Surena, that had been frightening. On this newcomer, it intrigued him. A crimson gem glinted on her brow, and long gold earrings swung enticingly.

He looked up at her. Slowly, she removed the veil. Her hair flowed like a stream at night over shoulders held as straight as any soldier standing in the square, ready to fight. As she had fought for him, Quintus realized, against the creature he had hoped had been his boyhood's dream, restored to him.

"Why did you drive her away?" he demanded. "My lifelong friend, my companion . . ." *And more, had Fortuna favored me.*

"*She* was the companion of your childhood? That one? *She* who would have deluded you, given you drink to rob you of your mind, and kept you prisoner here before your time and with your work yet undone? *She*— your friend? As well go to the serpent mages . . ." the woman glanced around as if even here she feared danger, ". . . and ask for kindness."

Quintus rose. He was much taller than the woman he faced. Taller, but so insignificant compared to her, like a thousand other Romans with his dark hair and eyes, but so less dark than hers; his sturdiness, against her grace, his stubborn mouth against hers—oh Venus, *that* was a thought! At first, he had thought her a creature of Ch'in, like the officer who had laid arrogant claim to the Eagle with the *signifer's* blood still wet upon it. Now, he thought otherwise. He suspected her to be a woman of Hind, far to the south and east of any place Rome's Legions marched.

"Who *are* you?" he asked. He was certain he was

going mad. Here in Erebus, he must face the judges Minos, Aeacus, and Rhadamanthus, not this woman with skin of amber and the carriage of a dark goddess.

Perhaps he had already drunk of Lethe. Perhaps he could find forgetfulness with this woman. He took a step forward, and she held up a hand.

She stood circled by fires that had sprung up amidst the asphodels. They burned with fragrance, as if she had scattered incense upon their tiny flames. Beneath her veil, she wore gauzes of amber and scarlet. Gems glinted at throat, fingers, wrist, and even on bare feet.

"Did *she* give you a gift? Was it *she* who led you to the figure you bear and that saved you when so many good men died?"

Quintus's hands went to his breast, and he drew out the tiny bronze dancer he had found so many years ago. She laughed with delight, her earlier fire vanishing.

"You gave me my luck piece?" he asked.

She reached out long fingers, tipped with some crimson stain, to touch it. Fires sprang up on the torches that the dancer eternally bore.

"I do not call Krishna luck," she whispered. "But necessity. And your fate.

"Krishna," she mused. "Once again, you return to drive us, as you have driven this man across half the world."

She handed him back the dancer. To his astonishment, the fires did not go out, not immediately. The sound of flute music went up, mingled with a thin, high drumming. As much as the bells and drums of the Parthians had repelled and frightened him, this music drew him. Drew him from this trap of Lethe and the asphodels that looked so much like his lost home back into consciousness. Other voices impinged, other sounds—the rustle of sand, the distant rattle and clang of tethered beasts. His sight went dim, as if he peered under water.

"*Are* you she—that spirit whom I once knew?" he asked.

"We are all reflections," she whispered. "Some of us are true, and some illusions."

Tears—shameful, un-Roman tears—threatened. "She said she had come back for me. Come to take me home."

The woman shook her head. Dark hair fell smoothly over shoulders the color of amber and the crimson and gold draperies that she wore.

"There is no going back for you. Krishna told you that on the battlefield. Remember? You told me: For a moment, fighting the sons of the man who reared you, you paused, unable to go forward. And Krishna spoke plainly, as he seldom does, and only to those he loves best. There is only the battle, only faring forward."

"Told me? Who are you?"

The woman's long eyes filled and her jeweled hands went out. "Do you not remember Draupadi? You—Quintus? You who are five in one, and those five the ones I wore this robe to marry? It was prophesied that Draupadi would have five husbands—and every one of them a prince or king.

"Long ago, and far away, I was Arjuna's prize. Your brother the king lost me; your brother the hero protected my name. We wandered, we fought, each side using forbidden weapons. We conquered, but we died. Now, we are reborn. Once again, I think, we must find each other."

Overhead the eagle screamed. Lethe and land wavered. Well enough: They had been deceits. But the woman—Draupadi—also wavered. With a final cry, the eagle flew overhead, effortlessly fleeing Erebus for the freedom of the outer air. Quintus raised his head to follow it. Sunlight broke through the light that had shone upon Lethe before, making it a sham and a counterfeit. He was aware of thirst again, but not for this draught of illusions and forgetfulness.

"What must I do?" he asked Draupadi.

"What you did before, without knowing. You must follow the eagle to where the water rises in the desert, where the rock gapes open, and where serpents grow from the stone. You must seek me and my guide. You will be commanded to bow to gods not your own and wield weapons unlike any you have ever known. Do you think you have suffered? In our last battles, we commanded armies. Now, we have only what we can win.

"My dearest, we need you, but I do not beg. Once, I begged not to be stripped before a court. They did not listen, so I never begged again. The only assurance I can give you is of pain worse than any you have known. Choose carefully. If you persevere, there, beyond the circles of the world, we may find triumph."

She stood challenging him like a statue of Roma Dea herself. "Or you can kneel and drink here, and *she* will have you in charge. It is pleasure," she said with faint disdain, "if not life or duty. But you will think you have your farm and your contentment. You may even enjoy it for as long as anything lasts. Which may not be long at all."

The fires at her feet flared, and smoke rose up from them to cover her. When it reached her head, he knew, she would be gone. The high sweet music of flutes and drumbeats grew shrill, but even more compelling. Draupadi hurled her veil over head and face.

"Or you can face trial and judgment in one," she

murmured. "Follow me and follow the eagle—or remain here, for as long as 'here' remains."

She leaned forward and touched her lips to his. Even through the saffron veil, he sensed their warmth and sweetness.

The smoke wreathed up and snatched her from his sight.

"Lady! Draupadi, don't go!" he cried, reaching forward into the smoke. He brought his hands away scented with sandalwood—but empty. It seemed to him that he had spent his life with his hands empty of all but trouble. And now that seemed a grief intolerable to him.

"Come back," he whispered again. His voice broke, and this time the tears did fall upon the asphodels. They melted at his feet. He was blinded, as if the incense fires that swept Draupadi from his sight now enveloped him.

His whisper echoed, distorted by illusion. Once again, the eagle cried from high overhead.

Come back? That was no wisdom for a man, a Roman.

"I will follow you," he whispered with more fervor than he had sworn when the Legion's brand was set into his flesh.

"Well judged!" Three voices so closely linked that they might have come from one throat rang out. "You have passed sentence on yourself.

"You will be removed from Erebus and restored straightaway to the upper air. So let it be set down."

The eagle shrieked. And he was sinking from his knees onto his face lest he see his judges before his death. Flute music and drums went up again, and he lay in darkness. Beneath him, the land shook. He tried to grasp a rock, a root, then anything at all, but it was all illusion.

He cried out once, wildly, as the earth cracked and gaped open, and metal flamed far, far below in the rock that underlay desert deeper than he had ever seen. Then he was falling, falling through it . . . past a blessed glimpse of clear water running over rock onto a woman whose cascade of night-black hair flowed over her wet body and hid it. Just as well, he thought, with other eyes glowing in the night, watching her, watching him. As he fell past them, too, he realized that others were watching them, and the eyes—the lambent hostile eyes—that spied upon the watchers themselves were even farther from being human than they were from being friends. Even the touch of those eyes was intolerable pain. He shouted once, and then the speed of his fall snatched thought and breath from him.

5

His helmet had fallen across his eyes: He was blind, and he was down. Hands pinned Quintus to the ground. Better to die than be taken prisoner by Parthians! He struggled wildly, but in silence. He was no match for the man he fought.

"Dis take you, man, what do you think I'm doing?" came a harsh voice. "Help me hold him. I don't want to put him out again. He might never wake up. Sir, sir, will you stop it! You're among friends!"

The big hands tightened on Quintus's shoulders, shaking him until his ears rung and he lost the will to struggle. He sank back, panting against the rough comfort of rolled cloaks. Raising one hand to his head, he brought it away damp, and a cloth fell to his lap.

Surrounding him, looking more like cutpurses than Legionaries, was a circle of soldiers. It was Rufus, the senior centurion, who had subdued him. There was a bruise starting near his mouth.

Quintus flung up a hand, as if he had taken a telling blow in training.

"Ah! that's better now."

Grins flashed, as if the Legionaries really cared that their tribune had waked. That surprised him. He had heard mutterings about some of the young officers—Lucilius, for example—being arrogant know-nothings, more trouble than they were worth to honest soldiers. He had heard muttering about him, that he had about as much life as a deathmask and couldn't take a joke if he found it in his pack.

But his men were relieved that he had wakened. Quintus found himself almost teary-eyed at that thought. He couldn't let them see it, so he forced himself to look around, as if inspecting them.

Squatting a little behind them was Arsaces, the Persian, his eyes and teeth flashing in the light of a tiny fire. Quintus squinted at it, then sniffed, remembering the sandalwood and frankincense of Draupadi's incense.

No such luck. Surrounding him were the smells not of a Roman force correctly dug in for the night, but of the confusion that passed among the easterners for camps: dung, smoke, sweat, and beasts. The fire hurt his eyes. Looking away Quintus saw the bulk of camels out beyond the tents and bedrolls of . . . was this a caravan?

Where were they? It felt strange, almost naked, to lie around a fire like a boy, camping out on the hillside, rather than in the orderly security of a proper *castra*.

Everything had changed. He looked up into the sky, searching for some sort of permanence—Orion hunting his Bear, perhaps. Here in the deep desert, the stars too looked different. Orion might still hunt somewhere, for all Quintus knew, but the stars were not the familiar twinkles of Tiber valley, blurred by the mists from the water or even the aloof gleams of the sky above the dry-lands of Syria. Above this land, enormous fires burned in the clear blackness. Daunted, his gaze slipped to the crest of a hill. The night wind blew, and pale swirls rose from the crest, dancing down the ridge like dust from the coils of a huge serpent. Was this the deep desert? He had thought Syria had been barren. He had never imagined such desolation. And he feared worse was to come.

But there was another question he must ask first.

"The men?" he whispered. "Our Eagle?"

Rufus brought a fist down slowly onto the blankets in which Quintus was wrapped.

"You saw the proconsul." The senior centurion didn't ask a question, but stated fact.

They all bent their heads, nodded. No point in asking about the Eagle, then, and making Rufus drag it out of the silences in which he buried dishonor.

"Died like a Roman, at the last. He got his honor back. Protecting the Eagles. That was when you fell. Trying to guard him.

"Aren't many of us left. We started out with—what? Some twenty-eight thousand of us and four thousand cavalry? Maybe ten thousand made it out. Most of them—they're sending them on to Merv along with the standards."

Yes. Quintus remembered. The Eagles would tarnish on the altars of whatever gods the Parthians worshipped.

The young man gestured vaguely. He didn't see ten thousand captive Romans, much less hear them or smell the wounds or sickness that must inevitably accompany so great a throng of prisoners. He thought he remembered. . . . He dropped his hand to his waist. No belt. His fingers groped at his side for the weapons he had been trained to keep ready to hand. Nothing.

He should have expected that.

Seeing him search for weapons, Rufus went expressionless. It was worse than rage.

"They disarmed us, of course. Not that they think they need to worry. Just leave troublemakers and mutineers behind, and the desert will even save you the trouble of a burial party."

"How long have I been out?" Quintus whispered it because he was afraid to ask. He held up a hand and was surprised at how it trembled—and that it did not hold the marks of great age.

"Long enough."

It was not an answer.

"Why didn't they . . . ?"

Rufus looked grim. "We have lost enough Romans. We convinced these . . ."

Quintus stared at the centurion till the older man looked away. "We carried you ourselves. We tended you ourselves."

"And they let you?"

"Drink this—no, slowly if you want to keep it down. Don't spill any."

The watered vinegar stung in his throat on the way down and brought tears to eyes made sore by the desert heat. Yet it tasted sweeter than the Lethe-water he had refused to accept from the treacherous creature who had posed as his own *genius loci.*

He felt strong enough to press the matter.

"They let you?" he repeated. "I want an answer, Centurion."

"We were granted that much grace," said Rufus. "I . . . convinced them." The Roman's powerful hand clasped and unclasped on the skin canteen he held.

Quintus glanced around the circle of Romans. They looked down. *He must have begged.* It would be poor thanks for his life to press the issue. Glancing up at the huge stars, he sought to change the subject.

"*Is* this the deep desert?" He had to ask it.

"This trifle of sand and stone? Hardly. The Ch'in tell me that we'll be climbing into mountains that make the Alps look like meadows," Lucilius's light, cultivated voice came from across the tiny fire, like a surgeon's fingers searching out a wound. "Then, the desert gets really bad. Like the stories of Trachonitis. Didn't you ever learn about that from your tutors?"

Quintus could all but see the young patrician's eyebrow arch up in disdain. However, they were now heading into a land where patrician, equestrian, and plebeian, or even officer and soldier, made less difference than the distinction between Roman and outsider—or between quick and dead. Even so, Lucilius couldn't let go of his ingrained superiority.

Maybe it's all he has. That voice in Quintus's ears again. Was it the woman—Draupadi—he had dreamed of, or had he actually gained some wisdom in that nightmare vision of Hades?

"No? Where *did* you grow . . . well, not to make a short story longer than need be, Trachonitis is serpent and basilisk country. They say it is so bare that if the shadow of a bird falls across it, the bird falls dead.

"We owe you, though, Quintus. If it weren't for those very convincing fits you threw, we'd have stopped in Merv. Forever."

"With . . . the others?" He was glad for the darkness, which hid his blush at how hard it was to ask. "What happened to . . ."

Rufus hung his head. "Slaves, gods help them. Leastways, they've got skills, maybe they can buy themselves out. . . ."

"If these barbarians follow decent laws," Lucilius cut in.

"They've got the Eagles too. All but the one you almost got brained with. *That's* the personal property of this Ssu-ma Chao, who wants to take it back with him to Ch'in to his Emperor. And us with it. He's decided we're auspicious for him, or some such thing. Strange fellows, these yellow barbarians, thinking defeated Romans a good omen. But it's not for me to turn down a chance of not putting my head under the yoke.

"So we're making the trip Alexander didn't live long enough to complete. From Nisibis past Merv, upcountry to Marakanda and into the hills. Then down into the *real* desert that would have fried any Macedonian born. Dis take me, how *do* they pronounce these names?"

"*Takla Makan Shamo,*" Arsaces said. For once the mockery, an unwelcome twin to Lucilius's scorn, was missing from his voice. That shook Quintus worse than a warning.

"It means, 'If you go in here, you don't come out.' I have seen this desert. When I was young, I ventured across some small corner of it as a caravan guard. It is terrible, littered with the bleached bones of man, beast, and town. Truly, they also call it the Realm of Fire, but this fire is far from sacred."

He watched the Romans with a mischief that had just better not turn to malice. "I would not swear this or take haoma to prove its truth, but this I will tell you." He glanced about, as if searching for eavesdroppers. "Some say the desert is full of demons."

Did the eavesdroppers for whom he sought have bodies at all? Arsaces gestured, a warding-off sign Quintus had seen before, though not from the usually skeptical Persian.

"Desert's bad enough without you filling it with demons, man," Rufus growled. His fingers went to his throat though he wore no amulet.

So. Disregarding Arsaces's gabble about demons and bleached bones, Quintus looked out at the desert. If he judged by the number of riding animals alone, this was a smaller, faster caravan with which Quintus and the survivors closest to him rode. Travelling faster than the survivors of Crassus's Legions, but by far on a longer journey.

He would never see his farm again.

He had not expected to. But then, he had not expected to live this long, either. Quintus glanced out beyond the flicker of tiny fires, the kneeling bulks of camels, into the desert. The night wind, cooling now, sent swirls of sand dancing up the dunes. In the firelight, the sand looked saffron, the color of a veil that a lady—or a spirit—might wear.

Far overhead, a star shot down through the heavens toward the eastern horizon. Quintus might have been a boy again, walking in the hills with his father or grandfather. Involuntarily, he smiled. His jaws ached, unfamiliar as the exercise was to them. It had fallen to the right: a favorable omen, thank all the gods.

He stared across the fire at the men who had kept by his side the most closely: Rufus, Arsaces, even Lucilius, and beyond them, other survivors of his Legion. Already, many had wrapped their heads in cloth, a trick borrowed from the caravan routes. Their eyes and teeth—almost all he could see for the swathings of coarse cloth—gleamed red in the firelight as they watched. He could see it now: If they wished to live, they would take on the ways of the desert until they ceased to look like Romans. Gradually, they would cease to be Romans, too. And then what would they be?

Subject people? People without a City or a name? You could not un-name Romans; you could only kill them. His father had died for that truth.

Best not think of it. He was alive. These were his men. They needed each other.

The wind danced down from the dunes he had mistaken for hills. So, he would never see his farm again, never buy it back and purify its altars. But what would he see? A new excitement flashed across his consciousness like the shooting star of a few instants back. It had looked like an eagle, returning in victory to its lofty nest.

Only imagine. He would see Marakanda, he thought. *Who would have dreamed his path would cross Alexander's?* For a moment, joy blazed up in him. He suppressed it. It was unworthy, he told himself, to feel anticipation in the face of disgrace and defeat.

"Make no doubt about it," Lucilius said. "We're slaves too. Not fancy ones, the sort you show off at banquets. Gladiators, maybe." He spoke as though he hated Quintus for smiling even briefly and all of them for continuing to exist.

He got up and wandered from the small fire.

Gladiators. Crassus, who had wreaked such vengeance when the gladiators revolted, had failed miserably against barbarians; Lucilius was never going to forget it. No wonder he didn't seem as burdened by the loss of weapons as the rest of the veterans.

"Who needs a *gladius* when he's got a tongue like that?" Rufus asked. His mouth worked as if he wanted to spit, but he forebore, as if oppressed by the dryness all around him.

In the darkness, a darker bulk rose. They could see a

campfire shine as this new man moved away from it. The silhouette of helmet, padded armor, and spear was unfamiliar. By that, Quintus assumed the man must be a warrior of Ch'in, who had been watching his Roman captives. Lucilius pointed at the fire, then at a larger fire at the center of the camp. The man nodded. "No doubt he's already started bargaining with the Ch'in," Quintus murmured to the centurion. Rufus nodded, not bothering to look shocked as he might have done when they were all still an army and the distinction between patrician/officer and everyone else was still good for some power.

"At least he's won us the partial freedom of the camp, sir. The Ch'in figure, if they guard the water, the desert will guard us."

Quintus chuckled. "I won't give them a fight about that. They know this land."

"And I think they're curious about what we'll do. The tribune says they have all sorts of notions about us. The merchants?" he shrugged. "A couple of them have women along."

Quintus tensed.

"That Lucilius tried. Didn't get anywhere, but you had to expect him to try."

Their eyes met. Every Legion had one—at least. A man who was an accomplished scrounger. Or who could talk his way out of any punishment. Or help his friends get round the centurion or the tribunes. Perhaps that was one reason why Lucilius had approached the female merchants. Odd concept, that. Foolishness, perhaps, to think they might be softer-hearted.

Usually, the Legion scrounger was not a patrician. But then, he usually scrounged for wood or leather straps or food or wine. Not for political favor, like a client.

But all the Romans who survived here had been bred

in a Rome shadowed by the terrors of Marius and Sulla. And Lucilius had sucked up politics with the mists of the Tiber. If Fortune favored them, he would protect their interests as well as his own. If not . . . Quintus shrugged. Long-disused muscles protested. If not, how much worse could things get?

An uproar brought their heads up. Bells clanged from harness as a small camel caravan approached the pass. Camels groaned, a rebellious clamor that sounded echoes as camels already unloaded for the night remembered their own grievances. Voices shouted in at least three languages.

"Others approach from Nisibis," Arsaces said. "It is best to travel with friends."

The auxiliary's head came up. "They drive their beasts hard," he commented. "Too hard. Unwise . . ."

"Friends?" Rufus half rounded on the Persian.

"Compared with the desert, all honest men," he paused, with conscious irony, on the word, "are friends. Of course, there are also the bandits. Thus, honest . . ." again that pause, ". . . caravans join together for the journey east."

Quintus could understand it. The Ch'in, with their well-armed troops, would stand a good chance of surviving anything but an attack by an army—and no huge army (such as the doomed Legions of which he had been such a guileless and reluctant part) could safely cross. Just the supplies of water and food for man and beast would require a caravan of their own. Thus, a small, well-equipped military party, their small entourage of captive Romans, and . . .

"Who comes?" Quintus asked.

"Some merchant or other," Rufus muttered. "Armed. I saw spears, guards."

"Nisibis is one of the staging points for the road east." Arsaces's voice took on a chanting overtone. "From Nisibis to Boukhara, Boukhara to Marakanda, to Ferghana of the blood-sweating steeds . . . into the hills and down from the high pass to Kashgar, before we venture across the Anvil of Fire. . . ."

"If this were a merchant caravan, we would wait . . . oh, a long, long time, excellent sirs, until all who wanted to cross had assembled. And then, we would depart. It can be a long time until the next caravan . . . especially in the high summer."

A roar, of laughter and surprise mixed, came from the central fire. The shouts reminded Quintus of the fight in The Surena's camp. He grabbed again for the sword he no longer owned. No weapons at all, let alone the miracle weapons that Draupadi had promised could be—might be—found in the desert.

Damn! Had she been only a fever dream?

A crunch of the grit that passed for sand in this god-forsaken wilderness brought him around, his head and heart pounding.

"Stop there . . . hold it, it's the tribune!"

Lucilius broke back into the firelit circle. Even in the play of firelight and darkness, his face was red, and his breathing came too rapidly.

All around the fire, the surviving Romans leapt up. Arsaces glanced beyond, out at the beasts where they were staked out—and guarded—then set himself to listen.

"You saw that caravan come in," Lucilius said. "You saw how fast it was moving. Well, I found out why."

Long ago, Quintus had found out that when the patrician "found out" anything, he kept it to himself unless he could trade it for greater benefit.

What does he want this time?

"It came here from Artaxata," he went on. "From the court of Artavasdos in Armenia."

Arsaces whistled. "How many of their beasts did they kill?" he muttered to himself. "What news from the wedding?"

The Romans stared at the slight, dark auxiliary, who laughed softly at them. "Oh, aye, there was sure to be a wedding. As soon as Artavasdos and the . . . most worthy proconsul parted company, those of us born in this land knew there would be a new alliance."

"As long as Rome was strong, Artavasdos, like a dockside . . ."

Quintus raised a hand, cutting off Lucilius as his voice rose in a kind of vicious anger. *Gravitas* was a virtue, one—of many—that Lucilius lost sight of all too frequently. And if he lost control now, how could they expect the men he—or someone—must command to keep it? They would become a rabble of slaves, not veterans who had managed to survive. And they would die in the desert, names and souls as lost as their bodies.

"You heard the tribune," Rufus growled.

Quintus flicked a glance at Lucilius. Like a bowstring stressed near to snapping, he was no good for his proper job until the tension was removed. *Well enough,* he thought. *The men will need time to think of* me *as their leader.*

The idea was presumptuous, impossible, probably even treasonous, but who remained to say so? Crassus, who nailed traitors to crosses, was dead, and Quintus had all but died in trying to defend him. He did not want command, any more than he had wanted to take the Legions' brand or leave his farm or lose his father. What decisions he had made before, he had made to survive. Quite simply, he trusted his judgment before he trusted

Lucilius's—and he trusted Rufus's judgment before he trusted his own. If Rufus had decided to follow him—a case of the strong serving the weak, if ever was—he must assume that the wily old man would get him through this, too.

"Armenia could choose its allies. The King of Kings, for so they style themselves in Armenia, chose Rome." Even muffled by wrappings, Arsaces's voice held all the scorn of the Persian for an upstart king.

"Once the most excellent proconsul decided to travel directly across Syria, rather than the safer upland route, Artavasdos realized that he had chosen wrong."

Again the muttering. Lucilius had concurred with that decision to cross Syria, Quintus recalled. When he himself had expressed doubt, he had gotten the lash of the other man's tongue. He said as much, and was gratified to hear a murmur of approval run round the Romans' fire.

"Will you let me speak?" Arsaces demanded. "The King of Kings Artavasdos has a sister. And the King of Parthia, Orodes, has a son, Pacorus. Not always the most faithful man, Prince Pacorus, but I would swear by the Light that Orodes would prefer him as his heir to, say, The Surena. Would not you?"

Lucilius made a warding-off gesture.

"We should have known that this one would pick up all the scandal, working with the grooms," Rufus said. He lumbered to his feet, holding out a hand to Quintus.

Quintus looked at Arsaces, then at the noble. "Is that the entire story?" he asked.

To his shock, Lucilius hung his head. Shame—on him? "Come," he said. "Hear it. I would tell you, but my tongue would wither in my mouth."

Quintus braced himself and took the centurion's hand

up. Once on his feet, he found himself able to walk, however slowly.

"It is beautiful, Artaxata, with its ramparts overlooking the Araxes, which flows swiftly, even in the summer. And Artavasdos is a man of some culture, even if he is not Persian."

Rufus snorted. "Don't play off your airs, horseman. You're a plain soldier like the rest of . . ."

"Artavasdos knows Greek," Lucilius said. "Knows it well enough to write in it. He wrote an ode, they're saying down at the fire. They sang it at the wedding."

"You can translate it for us, if you will," Quintus said. A neat touch that, turning patrician and officer into mere interpreter. Nothing wrong with *his* head, even if he had been struck on it by the Eagle. (Best not think of that. Best not think of their Eagle, captured and packed away, perhaps along with the arms they had been relieved of.) Instead, salve the wound to Lucilius's pride. "Your Greek has always been much better than mine."

Which was close to nonexistent, but don't let on about that.

They walked toward the center of the camp. Quintus's eyes were still quite sensitive from the blow; he found himself able to see quite well in the darkness. One or two of the men scuffled their feet.

"Do you fear serpents, that you walk so clumsily, you who pride yourselves on always marching?" Arsaces jibed. "Now, if you wore proper . . ."

A hiss silenced him, though it came from man, not serpent.

The shouts of the camp grew louder as the firelight brightened. Quintus found himself struggling to set each foot down without testing his footing: Lucilius's nightmare recollection of Trachonitis reminded him that he had strayed far from the lands most Romans knew into lands such as only men like Xenophon or Alexander had seen. You would probably die in them; but the last thing you might see was a creature out of legend, as it reared up out of the sand or plunged from the sky to kill you.

What rose up to block their way, though, was no monster out of the desert, but two long, very deadly spears held by two very determined Ch'in warriors.

The warrior shouted. The moment it took to understand the guard's disastrously accented Parthian was almost their last.

A Ch'in guard's spear pricked at Quintus's throat.

6

LUCILIUS HAD COME this way with barely a check, Quintus thought. Was this betrayal?

A second fear struck him.

Was this betrayal *again?*

Behind him, though, he could hear how the other Romans' boots scraped still, the rasp of nervous breathing. Carefully, he raised his jaw. The spearpoint pressed fractionally closer. Though the desert wind was cool, a warm trickle ran down his neck.

Arsaces, standing next to him, started to protest and took a blow from the butt of a spear. He went down and stayed down, with more prudence than Quintus would have credited him with.

The noise of the camp seemed to drop away from his consciousness. Even Lucilius's news seemed of far less importance than the tiniest noise that a Ch'in guard might make shifting position, or the faint twitch of muscles or gaze that might herald life or death. The wind scooped up coarse sand and flung it in a sort of serpentine swirl, to land with a hiss. Quintus shuddered. Even *one* serpent, crawling, slithering around their feet—he did not think he could stand unmoved, nor could he expect that from any of the men.

The hissing grew. He shut his eyes. He told himself that serpents were as often sacred as accursed. A serpent hallowed the shrine at Delphi. Farmers needed serpents if their land was to thrive. Snakes killed rats. But cold sweat trickled down his sides, nevertheless. If there *were* serpents, someone was bound to break, and then they would all be dead. He could hear his men's breathing grow harsh, rapid.

It might be crawling among them even now. Who knew if his next step . . . if he would *have* a next step . . . He met the Ch'in guard's eyes. They too held fear, but the hands on his spear never wavered. He was all the more dangerous for being afraid.

Quintus forced his breath to steady and to subside even as fear of the serpents he could only imagine threatened to choke him. Someone must get them past the guards. He must try.

Again, the wind blew. This time it didn't stop. Sand rustled and hissed around them, rising in coils as the wind rose. It was at their knees now; it was wreathing them about. . . . It was getting harder to breathe. A cloud seemed to cover the moon, like a face hidden beneath a cloak.

A shout made the Ch'in guardsman's head snap around. With another shout, he lowered his spear. A heavily armed man, accompanied by guards of his own, marched up. With a kind of furious impatience, the leading newcomer knocked away the spear. The wind subsided. Once again, the moon emerged from clouds, red-tinged now.

Arsaces scrambled to his knees and bowed from

them, almost as if the Ch'in officer were the King of Kings. Quintus looked at the man: He had seen him before at The Surena's right hand. The enemy. The captor. The man who had taken his Eagle and his weapons. Who was taking him and his men deep into the great trap of Asia, from which they would never emerge.

"He says this . . . turtle . . . has made a mistake," Arsaces said. His cynical tone was back in place. The officer's Parthian was better than his man's. Quintus could almost understand it. He promised himself that if he were spared, he would learn more.

"Thank him for correcting that thought, will you?" he asked.

"On my head be it," said the Persian and spoke rapidly.

The officer barked laughter.

His man collapsed to his knees and grovelled in the coarse sand. When he raised his head, he looked up. Tiny as his eyes were, Quintus could see how they bulged with terror.

"He says he truly knows not what happened, that he just saw enemies. . . ."

The officer kicked at him and swore.

"Orders are that the prisoners from Ta-Chin are not to be harmed. He is reminding this fellow . . . Wait, he asks why you do not bow."

Rufus snorted. "Like that cringing fool?"

"We are Romans, tell him," Quintus said. "It is not our custom." He remembered how it had all but killed his grandfather even to bow to a patron he came close to respecting: What the old man would have thought of the scrapings and loutings of the East, he had only too good an idea. He had bowed as a client himself. He swore never to fawn like that again even if it cost him his life.

Compared with his honor, what was his life? From Carr-hae on, it had been like borrowed money—no telling when the loan might be recalled and at what interest rate.

Lucilius might be willing to live that way, had indeed lived that way and thus made his way from Rome to the desert. Quintus hoped he could show rather more courage. The desert wind hissed derisively at him.

"He says he is Ssu-ma Chao. It is," Arsaces added, "a name known to me. A noble name."

So was Lucilius's. Whatever else happened, at least he had seen the young patrician meet a man who was more than his match for arrogance about his rank.

"Tell him, it is not our nature to abase ourselves before mere men," he added.

The officer barked laughter and spoke rapidly.

"He says, 'You have stiff necks, you Romans, as long as your heads still wag on them.' We have not seen this type of courage before. Others, but not this. Thus, he says, and therefore, you fare east with him. You—and the Eagle."

It would have been easy in that moment to rush upon the officer and die. Too easy. Somewhere in this camp were arms and the Eagle. They must try to find them; then, they would show these people what stuff Romans had in them.

His anger and his intention must have shown on his face as Ssu-ma Chao stared into his eyes. Then, in turn, he looked narrowly at each of the Romans, pausing to slap Lucilius on the arm. *What agreement* had *that one made already?* Quintus wondered. No doubt it would come out in the worst possible moment.

Ssu-ma Chao still laughed and waved them past, away from the desert and in toward the fires.

It was beneath Quintus's dignity as a Roman and an

officer to glançe back, but he could listen, and he did. The Ch'in noble's heavy felted boots crunched behind them. And behind him blew the wind. Listen as Quintus might, he no longer heard the hissing and rustling he had heard before. He might have longed for silence. It did not reassure him. He suspected that for the rest of his life, he would listen always for drums and bronze bells—sounds that had meant death since The Surena's horsemen broke the square at Carrhae.

The centurion's presence at Quintus's shoulder, in case he staggered, was welcome. (He vowed he would not stagger.) For once, he was even grateful for Lucilius, who, typically, knew every man of substance in the caravan and had managed, somehow, to identify the newcomers. For once, that subtlety of Lucilius's was helpful as, imperceptibly, he guided the other Romans toward the men who had come in that night from the king of Armenia's court.

It was a mixed troop, as caravans went. By now, even Quintus could distinguish the dark brows and proudly hooked noses of the Armenians from, say, the sleekness of the Persians, or the quicksilver intensity of the pure Hellenes. Others there were whom he could not identify—they were not Ch'in, nor Saka, or even the Hsiung-nu who were accursed as marauders much further east. And yet they looked familiar. . . . How?

"We may as well move on," Lucilius muttered. "Asking this lot for anything is like prying bad oysters out of their shells."

So these were the merchants who included women in their numbers? That fined-down look might appeal to a patrician: It made him think of . . . well, of his grand-father's patrons.

What would he want in a woman? Before his family's lands had been lost, he had dreamed, but of very little beside a country girl, perhaps from one of the nearby families who ranked with his, her thick braids bound in a saffron veil. Saffron . . . he remembered saffron and incense from his dreams.

Dark hair flowing like silk or oil down slender shoulders. Deep pools of eyes, watching him intently. *Draupadi.*

Omens of a woman? Such omens are for women. He could all but hear his grandfather growl that at him. And not for any women associated with *their* family, the old man would probably have added.

There had to be another reason, a rational explanation for why these traders looked so familiar. Somewhere before this, he must have seen faces like those of the woman he had dreamed—*impossible; who would allow a woman that beautiful to travel these roads?*—perhaps in caravans in which journeyed men from Hind, or perhaps those dreams he had known while his wits wandered.

Draupadi . . . he remembered her as he remembered the *genius loci* from his farm. The lithe strength of limb, the sidelong glance of eye, the sleekness of hair and sun-darkened skin all reminded Quintus of her. But Draupadi—at least in his dreams—had eyes that almost melted with warmth. These men kept their eyes hooded, except for quick glances upward. Their eyes were dark, true—but flat, as if not fearing those about them as threat or prey. Draupadi's mouth was generous; these merchants' mouths were tight, betraying nothing except a will to snatch and to keep. The resemblance was as cruel a deception as the shimmering glints on a desert horizon that tricked thirsty men into believing they saw water.

As if alerted by Quintus's thoughts, one of the dusky-skinned merchants turned a little in his direction. His glance flicked out, like a spark shooting from charred wood, from beneath lids darkened with kohl. Threat? No threat? Or perhaps, were they sizing up the Romans as lawful prey?

Quintus held himself in check, though that glance made his fingers crook toward the hilt of the missing sword that a captive could not wear. He had seen more sympathetic looks from vipers.

His nostrils twitched. Over his heart came a familiar jabbing. He would have wagered gold he did not own that, if he pulled out the bronze dancing figure he carried there, the torches that it bore would flicker a warning.

Then, the wind blew, and all he smelled was the fire, redolent of dung.

". . . So much for Roman pride? That's a better thing to celebrate than the bedding of the bride!" Quintus could not hear precisely who said that. He suspected it might be one of the men whose nation he could not identify.

A roar of laughter was quickly choked off as some of the men noticed the Romans.

"It's not good," muttered Rufus. "Look at the way the Greeks are slinking back."

Not just the Greeks. The strangers had backed off, leaving the Armenians to answer.

"What do you know about this?" Quintus asked Lucilius in an undertone.

"Let them tell you." The patrician snapped as if he hated them all, Romans and foreigners alike.

"Ask them," Quintus waved Arsaces forward. "Say,

'You are pleased to mention Roma. Now say what you have to say to my face.' "

"Is it that blow on your head or the desert sun that makes you run mad this time?" Lucilius asked.

"You wanted us to learn what we can. Why quarrel, then, with the results you get?" Quintus snapped.

He strode forward. "Tell us," he demanded of the Armenian, pushing close enough to practically rub noses with the other man.

"Great Lords, forgive!" The merchant bowed as if Quintus were the proconsul himself, standing armed with his Legions to back him.

From behind him, out past the camp in the barren lands, came a cry.

"Forgive *what?*"

The other Romans closed behind Quintus.

"It was the wedding, lords. They were feasting and singing. Some sang poems that our Great King wrote. He is very learned. Then the tables were taken away, and Jason was singing. . . . Do you know the *Bacchae* of Euripides?"

Quintus furrowed his brow. Something about a king of Thebes, who opposed the cult of Dionysus and was driven mad, to wander in the hills and be torn apart by kinswomen.

"Bloody songs for a bridal celebration," he said, since, clearly, he must say something.

The Armenian merchant shook his head. Now that he realized that the Romans were not going to—could not—strike him down, he grew visibly arrogant, as it is a merchant's custom to be with those who cannot buy his wares.

"He is a fine singer and much applauded. He bowed before the King of Kings and received a rich reward. Then

Sillaces entered and prostrated himself. When he was told to rise, he threw what he carried into the company." The merchant paused, aping the skill of the actors he had praised.

"It was the head of your leader, noble lords."

"Gods. *Gods,*" muttered a man behind Quintus.

"Steady there, man," Rufus muttered.

Crassus had been half-crazed, but he had howled defiance as The Surena claimed his Eagles, and Quintus had rushed in to protect him, felt the proconsul's severed hand upon his head a moment before the blow came that all but split his own skull.

If he could bear that memory, he could bear this news like a Roman. His father's son.

"The King of Kings called Sillaces his younger brother and gave him the kiss of kinship. And the men cheered and danced and drank wine. When they fell silent somewhat, Jason came forward. He had found a rod and waved it as a Bacchante in her frenzy would wave a *thyrsus.*"

It was true that the East bred strong haters who would never forget and never forgive. With something close to joy, the merchant leaned forward to deliver his last lines. "He took up the head and sang Agave's lines from the play. 'We've hunted down a mighty chase this day and from the mountain bring the noble prey.' *With your master's head!*"

Behind him, a man cleared his throat. Quintus's eyes stung. He wanted to shout aloud full-voiced, never forgive, swear by all the gods to build a column of heads towering to the sky. Not to mourn Crassus, but to lament the disgrace of Rome.

He could sense the tension straining in Rufus beside him, ready to fight at his officer's command or to strike with his vinestaff any fool who might have few enough brains to anticipate his leader's order.

The old bore Livy was right. *Vae victis*. Woe to the conquered.

"Old moneybags's last, best role," came a whisper he knew he must not trace back to its source. Rufus would do that—and did.

Only the memory of Quintus's grandfather, facing the messenger who had come to tell him of his son's death, sustained the younger man. A gesture against despair brought his fingers to the pouch he still wore. By some miracle, there were coins left in it, small ones.

"For your news," he said, tossing the coins to the merchant as he would to a marketplace storyteller. "I will not trouble you for change." His voice came out more calmly than he would have believed possible. Behind him, a Legionary cleared his throat, and Quintus sensed how his hard-held composure steadied them now.

"You show better than your master!" shouted a man standing half in shadow, who wore his cap well pushed down. One of the Persians, Quintus thought, or—no, the man wore Persian garb in somber hues, but he was one of those newcomers that Quintus could not assign tribe or realm to.

"Tell him the rest! Tell him how Orodes promised Sillaces much gold, then how he paid your leader by pouring molten gold into the mouth of that head because, any other way, he never got enough. You could see the burns, Roman! And you could smell him fry!"

With one outthrust hand, Quintus barred a Legionary who had lunged forward. Start a riot? Certainly they could. And just as certainly, Ssu-ma Chao would order their deaths. They would never have the chance to regain their arms, their Eagle, and their honor, even if, in the next moment, they used them only to die in the desert.

"You fool, he *wants* you to fight. Go ahead, then. If the Ch'in don't kill you, by Dis, *I will*," he growled. "Stand firm. By all the gods, we'll *show* them Romans."

If the square had held that strongly at Carrhae, they would not now stand here, facing a jeering crowd of merchants, cameldrivers, and horsemen. They would not be forced to display their mettle, like slaves upon the block, for that sneering Ch'in noble. To Quintus's relief, his men held steady—staring level-eyed at the rabble before them. Gradually, something in their quiet silenced the barbarians baying about them.

There was silence for a long moment as a blood-tinged moon rose higher in the sky. Despite the hiss and moan of wind and sand, the desert itself was very still, as if waiting, listening. Even the bells of the camels' harness—for not all of them had been unloaded yet—ceased their clanging.

"You are here," Quintus said to the Armenian. "And we are here. We must cross this desert together if any of us are to live. Now you see us deprived of our arms, leashed. But do not mistake me: The dog can still bite. Do you understand me?"

The merchant nodded and edged back from the fire, secreting the Roman coins in some hidden fold in his robes.

"Well played!" came the strongly accented voice of Ssu-ma Chao.

Enough laughter, already! Quintus swung around to face the Ch'in officer. But that laughter did not come from the Ch'in officer. It was hard to see his face in the darkness, lit only by flickering torches, and harder yet to read his narrow, slanting eyes. One hand going to his sword—*I am unarmed!* Quintus regretted once again— Ssu-ma Chao jerked his head about, glaring in a way that betokened ill to any of his men who broke discipline.

Rough-voiced laughter rose again. This time, both Romans and Ch'in faced each other, confused and angry, but not yet ready to attack.

"Keep your hands where they can see them," Quintus heard Rufus pass the order to the remnant of Rome's Legions. "But be ready to grab any weapon you can."

More laughter, from a different direction yet. More wind. A gust blew out half the torches. The remaining ones flickered as men hastened to shield them.

Ssu-ma Chao held out his own hands. It was a gesture of fighting man to fighting man. This servant to an unknown king had had enough respect for the Romans to disarm them, but Quintus believed that for all the other's respect, he was going to take no risks.

You didn't have to be a philosopher to guess the stranger was just as confused as Quintus—and just as worried. For a soldier, the unexpected was as much the enemy as the men he must face.

Gesturing to Arsaces, Quintus started forward. Clearly it was time, and past time, to talk to the commander of this caravan.

Harsh sand stung his cheeks like a contemptuous slap.

The wind rose to a derisive howl. Beneath its jeering laughter, Quintus heard the fatal clamor of bells, drums, and gongs.

7

No SWORD, NO shield! Might as well tie them down and leave them to die in the sand. Quintus wasted but a bitter, fleeting thought on that, then wheeled his men.

"Form up!" he shouted over the clamor. Other orders rang out—the Ch'in officer, for one, and steady as the hills of Rome, Rufus's trained bellow.

And form they did; a diminished, unarmed square. They showed no fear, and Quintus's heart swelled with pride.

Abruptly, the ground shuddered. Quintus fell, floundering onto his knees. His head spun. Around him, horses screamed, and camels, roused from stolid sleep, bellowed outrage. Not far away, two tents swayed—collapsed, one of the torches propped before them falling onto the crumpled stuff of their walls and setting them ablaze.

"Romans!" Rufus again. *"Form up!"*

Some of his men must be still standing, fighting fear before whatever enemy out of the desert struck. Quintus found his feet. He had to get to his men. He had to try, even if the earth opened before him and swallowed him in the next instant—or of what use were all his fine thoughts on honor?

From all across the desert, echoing in the vastness of sand and sky, wild laughter shrieked up. Sand whirled down from the hooded crests of great dunes, hissing like a plague of serpents.

A burning stick rolled clear of the tents. Quintus scooped it up, then grabbed as many other sticks and torches as he could span with two hands. Fire was a weapon, not just against men, but against the dark. Let his men have weapons of fire, and it would not be long before they could win others. Unless there were archers, and he did not think archers could aim true in this wind.

The gongs, drums, and bells made his head ache. Around him, the sky whirled even as the earth rocked under his nailed boots. The never-to-be-forgotten clash of swords on shields, the screams of dying men rose again: The Ch'in were under attack.

His men could do nothing without arms, and it was he who must arm them. Mindful of his footing on this treacherous ground, Quintus could not carry enough, and if he fell, he could well become a torch himself.

"Torches! Get torches!" he shouted.

The hissing rose. "Serpents! Dis take them, snakes!" A man screamed in panic, then fell silent. Quintus hoped he had not died, either by snakebite or as a bad example. Briefly, he envied the Persian horseman his boots. Then, he had staggered within reach of the pitifully small Roman square and pressed torches into the hands of the men in the front ranks.

Hard to fight without the Eagles gleaming overhead, a reflection of a Legion's honor. But Rufus was at his shoulder, the aristocratic tribune nearby.

"Let's make a break for it!" Quintus heard one of them urging. They were prisoners; they were Romans, bred to war, in the midst of clients and barbarians. In the confusion that was battle, how difficult would it be to overpower a merchant train, compelling wagons and beasts to take them where they wanted to go?

And where was that? Without a guide, into a painful death by thirst in the waste. And without their Legion's Eagle, having no honor to return with, they might as well be dead. Assuming they survived the earth tremors, the snakes that even now men were screaming about, and whatever bandits who now attacked Ssu-ma Chao and his men.

"Don't be an ass!" By all the gods, Lucilius, talking of courage for once. "All these damned merchants have guards, anyhow."

Quintus had not forgotten that either. Ssu-ma Chao's curiosity had saved their lives . . . with such honor as might be in these queer lands. He gestured Rufus to order the men forward.

When the order came for a *testudo*, he had to choke back laughter that threatened to unman him. How could men lacking shields form that tortoise that so often let Romans advance under a hail of sword strokes and arrows?

"Use your torches! One man guards, one picks up swords or shields, one passes them on!"

It was some slight hope. If the men used the torch as they might use the *gladius*, then they might even have some slight chance to take an enemy's weapons.

So Rufus too must be counting on the high winds to discourage archers. No archers? Quintus could not see past the blowing sand. The laughter that rode it haunted him. In the instant it cleared, would he see again the sight that robbed them of hope at Carrhae? Thousands upon thousands of riders, and The Surena himself, his face like a mask of Pluto with its too-large dark eyes? With every hiss of the wind, every beat of the drums or peal of bells, he thought of the death of Legions and fought despair.

In front of him, shields were going up—of no design he was familiar with, but shields nonetheless. Bearing almost the first of them, a Legionary stepped before him, guarding him. Now they were marching over twisted bodies.

Blood seeping from the dead men's wounds should have turned the sand into slippery muck. But no blood had flowed. And after their first, initial panic, no Romans screamed of snakes, even though the sounds of hissing and huge, thick bodies cutting through the sand made each waking thought a victory against horror.

Sand and sound enveloped them. This was like fighting in a fog—like the foul mist in the swamp they'd hidden in after the massacre. Quintus's throat was dry from fear and from screaming orders, constant shouting so his men would know he still lived.

Again, the ground shook. A rumbling and a sort of *pouring* sound reminded Quintus of stories he had heard of the mountains beyond Gallia Transalpina, how snow slid in vast waves down their slopes, breaking and burying men and towns unfortunate enough to be engulfed. This would be a dry death, burial by sand—though burial it was.

A crack formed in the earth, and he jerked one of his men back before he stumbled into that dark crevasse. If this kept on, the earth itself might snap them up. On they moved with the purpose that long discipline had fixed in them, ready to fight with what arms they could pick up from those bodies on the ground. Mysteriously dead; or were they? After all, a man could die of fear.

His grandfather would have scoffed at that. But the old man would have scoffed too at the dreams Quintus had had, dreams that had proven to aid him. And he certainly would have made Quintus throw away as a folly the little Etruscan dancer that had already saved his life so many times.

He bit back a cry. The tiny bronze had heated once again.

Once more, the earth shuddered. This time many of the men toppled, shouting their anger and fear against ground that could not keep still. The haze of sand and sweat in which they moved seemed to thicken—to darken, in one part, as if something swept past them. The screams from the Ch'in fighting somewhere ahead of them grew louder, taking on an edge of despair.

There was always that moment when you expected relief or at least nothing worse to happen; then you saw thousands of Parthians coming up, reinforcements for the ones that were already butchering you; and you knew everything was lost. The Ch'in general must feel like that now. What good would his high birth do him if he never returned home to the family and servants and clients who would bow before him?

Quintus could let these easterners die. But then whatever enemy they faced might turn on the Romans. And so they would all go down . . . and the Eagle would be lost. Quintus could not allow that, if there were any way of stopping it. And he needed Ssu-ma Chao to get to the Eagle. Standing straight, he brandished his torch. Overhead, as if in response, a streak of light shone in the night sky flying to the East. It looked like an eagle. The thought heartened him.

Do you see us? Do we do well? We who are about to die . . .
He hoped they had more honor than that.

"Get ready! Hold your square!" he shouted, obedient
to his talisman's warning. He stooped, just as a spear
whined overhead.

Abruptly, a blade met his torch. It was a clumsy blow;
he parried it almost as if he met a staff, rather than a
sword. Then, he thrust forward with the flame, straight
into his enemy's face. The man fell, screaming out of a
charred mouth. Quintus grabbed up what weapons he
could. Around him, his men were doing the same. Even
Lucilius was fighting with a persistent viciousness that
won Quintus's unwilling respect.

They did have *live* adversaries, with swords and
shields and faces that grimaced as the bodies beneath
them took their death wounds. As if to atone for the
humiliation of Carrhae, the Romans fought hard. Those
who fell died with a groan of protest at being balked of
their quarry. The wind and sand cloaked their enemies,
though—those fought in grim silence, not crying out
even when mortally wounded.

Slowly, the wind's force died, then was gone. Above,
abruptly, the night sky was very clear, framing a shimmering mirror of a moon. Now Quintus could see where
Ssu-ma Chao and his men struggled. The men they
fought against were darkly clad; only hands and faces
showed—and the gleam of weapons where blood had not
hidden the bright metal.

Bandits would have arrows, Quintus thought. And
with the wind dying, soon those arrows would fly.

"*Testudo!*" he screamed the order. Shields went up
overhead.

"March!"

Their ranks might be diminished, but their precision

was not. And they were protected as they marched toward the embattled Ch'in, trapping the men they fought against between two armed and desperate forces.

The Romans spread out into their battle lines, allowing the Ch'in to retreat behind them, then return as reinforcements.

Why do I permit this? Quintus wondered. The answer came as quickly as parry and thrust (and *another* man crumpled onto the thirsty sand!): Whatever they faced had not scrupled to use horror as a weapon; all men must band against an enemy who did that. Superstition, perhaps. Well then, reassure yourself, Quintus my lad. These Ch'in have your Eagle, and you cannot go home without it. Assuming you can get home at all.

He cried out, not at a wound that scored his arm red, but at the way his bronze talisman heated. In that instant, he whirled and saw the Ch'in general at bay, one facing two of the strangers, and no place to retreat.

He was a farmer, not a fighter, Quintus thought, but Fortune was proving that wrong. Now it seemed his feet hardly touched ground as he leapt into action. He brandished sword and torch, shouting a raw-throated challenge. At this breathless moment, it seemed familiar and right for him to stand champion to the others.

Quintus struck and strode onward. This was more dream than battle. Four men out of memory marched, drove, or rode at his side—a king, the twins, saintly and silent, and a huge, simple man, famous as a Titan for his strength.

His brothers.

But *I* have no brothers! Quintus thought. He shook his head, aimed a vicious blow at one of the desert shadows who sought to stab the man who had run out ahead of the the battle line.

The tiny talisman he bore kindled once again. *Krishna,* Draupadi had called the dancer: his long-time ally, the strange one who danced while mourning.

Quintus whirled the torch to kindle its flame and send it higher. This should have been a stronger, a greater weapon. Such did exist, the thought flickered in his consciousness. It might be given to such as he to find them as he once had done.

These are not my thoughts! The desert night was cold, but a greater chill wrapped him in an instant. He needed weapons, he and his . . .

No! Whatever it was that sought to speak to him, it seemed as alien to him as the men who died, soundlessly, under his blade. The short sword was the weapon of Rome. It would be enough, or he would die here, he vowed.

"Sir . . . sir! Hold!" Quintus realized that Rufus was shouting, had caught at him in restraint. Quintus plunged another step forward and would have fallen, were it not for the centurion's grip. He looked down. He had tripped over the bodies of three men, all clad in black. Near them, Ssu-ma Chao struggled up from his knees onto unsteady feet, watching the Roman as if he had suddenly begun to breathe fire.

Abruptly, as the strength that had driven Quintus melted from his limbs, he sagged. He leaned on his shield, half bent over, breathing in gasps while his heart felt as if it would wrench itself asunder. Ssu-ma Chao gasped, gagged, then brought himself under control.

But they were all veterans. After Carrhae, even Lucilius was no part-time warrior.

The Ch'in leader gestured and spoke. Quintus shook his head, unable to follow the man's accented Parthian.

"He asks you if you know what manner of men you fought?"

Amazingly, Arsaces had insinuated himself between the tribune and the Ch'in general. Good to see the twisty little Persian horseman still lived.

Quintus squinted groundward. All around were bodies. Some Ch'in; a few—but still too many—Roman. Some were even merchants who had found courage enough to join men whose trade it was to fight. Then the tribune stared at their enemies. Parthians rode in silks and rich metals. These men were robed in black. Not Parthians, then. And not bandits, by and large an undisciplined rabble, dying badly and noisily when overwhelmed.

These men's faces were set, impassive despite wounds that meant death in agony. They were not weathered like the other strangers Quintus had seen, the men whose features and coloring were an evil mirror of his Draupadi's. Fairer, these fighters, pale under the huge moon. Pale and incredibly ancient.

Even as he looked, that flesh turned ashen, tightened over the bones, turning speedily to grotesque skulls with flaking skin still stretched over them.

Against Quintus, his talisman cooled now. Yet a wave of reassurance spread from it and flowed into his body.

He turned from those life-in-death enemies. Ssu-ma Chao stood watching him. Catching Quintus's eyes, the easterner bowed deeply, as if to a man of his own rank.

"He also asks what manner of man you are, that you can look on the work of sorcery and not shudder," the Persian said.

A tired one, Quintus thought, an answer that would hardly satisfy the Ch'in.

"Tell him, 'A Roman.' "

"He says," Arsaces went on, "that this miserable one would willingly reward you for your aid."

Well enough. Give us the Eagle and send us home.

"He adds, however, that he is desolate that he cannot reward you as you would most wish. He is pledged to bring you back to Ch'in, and his head will answer for the deed."

And the Eagle has not been seen here in any case.

The Ch'in general gestured imperatively, and three men raced off, even though each of them dripped blood from some wound or other.

"He suggests that perhaps *this* will serve as an expression of his gratitude even as he lives to obey and serve the Son of Heaven."

The men he despatched returned, heavily laden. Breathing in gasps, they dropped their burdens at Ssu-ma Chao's feet.

Scuta and *gladi;* helms, short swords, daggers, and shields. The weapons of Rome, passed from the Parthians to the Ch'in, and now returned to the Romans—why?

As a bribe, a reward? For good behavior?

"It is this miserable one's hope," Arsaces continued, "that you men of Ta-Chin will assist us as we journey into the deepest desert. And that you will beg whatever spirits that you—sir, I think he probably is calling us barbarians, but doesn't realize that it gives insult—bow to to keep us safe, not only from bandits, but from the demons and their storms that haunt the Takla Makan."

The Ch'in general approached Quintus. Lucilius, the other surviving tribune—who came from a noble family—must stand aside. It was to Quintus that Ssu-ma Chao bowed.

"Tribune!"

Rufus' voice went hollow. Astonishing: Not even the

cracking earth or hissing as of giant serpents frightened him. As one man, Quintus and Ssu-ma Chao pivoted to look where the centurion was staring.

They had a glimpse of yellow-white bone, as the bodies dissolved before their eyes, then those bones themselves became dust, to mingle with the grit.

Even Quintus found his fingers moving in a gesture that the countryfolk along Tiber bank used against demon ills.

The evil laughter had died away along with the clangor of drums, bells, and gongs. No serpents writhed through their minds. Only a slight wind blew, scattering the dust that had been their mysterious enemy.

Quintus rested a hand on the centurion's shoulder. It twitched once, then firmed as Rufus regained his calm.

"Saves us the trouble of burying them. Or burning them." The centurion might never have cried out in alarm. He turned away, as if the entire matter were of little interest to him.

Quintus, following him and Ssu-ma Chao, spared a glance back. Etched into the sand were the shapes of their enemies. Then the wind hissed over them, and even that trace of them disappeared into the desert.

8

"Do you see anything new from that perch of yours?" Lucilius shouted up at Quintus.

He shook his head, then realized that the patrician couldn't see the gesture.

Desert. Always desert. And to think he had found Syria dry. He had never imagined how many shades of gray and dirty yellow a desert might hold. The Takla Makan was so dry that he couldn't even test out if Lucilius had been right in comparing it to Trachonitis, where birds fell dead when a serpent crossed their shadows: There were no birds. Here even carrion eaters could not beat the desert sun and sand to their prey.

From his perch on Ssu-ma Chao's chariot, with its high wheels that made it impressive, if foolish, for desert travel, its built-up body, and its crow's nest of a tower that let a battle commander observe beyond the fog of grit and dust that accompanied battle or the passage of its spoked wheels, all Quintus could see was desert. Dunes coiled like the skeletons of sea-serpents preserved beneath the immense, distant bowl of the cloudless sky.

One day, you saw another one writhing on the horizon. An hour, a day's march, you thought, and you would pass it by. Three days later, camels, carts, horses, and weary men trudged by it, antlike against its immensity. And if it chose, at that moment, to fall . . .

To drown in sand. Best not to think of it; such ideas dried the mouth, and it was not yet time to drink.

By all the gods, even the scummiest puddle left in a Tiberside backwash would taste like wine. And the most priceless of the drivers' hopes was the least likely: that somewhere in the midst of the Takla Makan, in the deepest, most cruel heart of the waste lay an oasis in which a crystal spring bubbled forever. Visions were not for Romans, of course; but Quintus would not need to be a soothsayer to think of men dying in the sand, dragging themselves forward in the hope of reaching such a place or calling for it with their last breath.

It would be easy, in that monotony, to drift away from the caravan, away from the path that must be seared into the eldest drivers' memories. It would be easy, in a wilderness in which all sounds were strange and it was impossible to tell what was near from what was afar, to miss the onset of bandits from behind some dune and to leave one's bones along the line of march beside those other sand-etched skeletons of heedless men and their beasts. They had already passed too many such.

The Ch'in general's chariot might be an old-fashioned, cumbrous thing, but its tower provided a vantage point from which a canny leader might spot raiders and save his men's lives . . . until the next peril.

There were no bandits today. Those were said to be mostly Parthians, whose skill with horse and bow (Quintus winced) fitted them well for a guard's role. And he had seen none of the men native to this area—Hsiung-nu or Yueh-Chih. Ssu-ma Chao seemed to regard those tribesmen as a ferocious cross between barbarians and vermin, and at perpetual war with his Empire.

Quintus wondered if he would ever wish to see bandits, just to break the monotony. Now the world seemed to have fallen away from them. There was only desert. True, the North showed blue shadows that Arsaces swore were mountains. And Ssu-ma Chao had actually consented to speak of them, calling them heavenly, longing in his voice as he described the snow melting and round lakes hidden like treasure in silent valleys. After weeks in the desert, Quintus no longer believed in such possibilities. There was only desert: Where the desert stopped, chaos began—or perhaps those rivers of Hell that he remembered from his dream.

He no longer dreamed of the Tiber, and for that he was dimly glad. This was no land for dreams of home or that gentle spirit he remembered. Instead, sometimes, he woke, breathing hard, almost remembering the shadows he thought had impelled him forward the night they had fought those black-clad . . . creatures he could not name men. Demons, were they? He dared not say, and the merchants who prodded each other and muttered among themselves when he passed were not saying either.

However, if that battle had not won them the Eagle, it had won them Ssu-ma Chao's gratitude for as long as it might last. It had earned them their weapons back. A fine thing, that—for while even Ch'in soldiers valued fire as a weapon, Quintus never wanted again to order an advance armed only with torches.

In that night, they had gone from prisoners and slaves to honored hostages, almost guests and allies. There were camels to ride and carts to bear whatever burdens Rufus would permit them to: "Rome's pace, Rome's race" meant very little here.

And Quintus thanked all the gods for these concessions. It was hard enough to travel the waste as hostages; it would have been intolerable to march as slaves, bound and guarded, in the dust-choked tail of the caravans.

"Descend from Olympus, why don't you, oh lofty one? Lucilius's voice took on an edge. Ssu-ma Chao's favor extended to all the Romans. But he treated Quintus as their leader, and the equestrian tribune knew that rankled in what passed for the aristocrat's heart.

"Right now!"

He wished he didn't have to. Somehow, the chariot felt right—albeit toplofty. It would balance poorly in a fight. But then it was for a king or general, not a warrior. You wanted a lower chariot and a driver as close to you as your own heart to guard you while you drew arrow, your focus so intense that you saw not a man, not a limb, but only the spot to be pierced. He had been a charioteer, and he had been a warrior, driven by . . . Involuntarily, Quintus's hand sought out the bronze talisman.

What *were* these fancies? They were not his memories. The desert bred madness in a man. The drivers swore that a man who strode out at noon with an uncovered head would die, his brains seethed to mush in his skull. Most of the Legionaries carried their helms and wore instead woven hats. (Rufus had broken at least one vinestaff across the back of a fool who thought to lighten his load by discarding his helm. Rome's mules they were and would remain, even here as they marched on World's End.) Alexander, in the waste of Gedrosia, must have worn similar headgear. The thought brought him no comfort. Alexander had all but died in the waste, and his stars—unlike Quintus's own—were fortunate.

Nor did the stories that the camel drivers told in gleeful singsong around the fire, with sidelong looks to make certain that the strangers, the Romans, were sufficiently horrified as Arsaces translated them: storms bad enough to flense skin off bone and suck the water from a man's body, leaving it a husk as if the embalmers of Egypt had been at it; the demons of the waste that gibbered at noon or whenever a man was too tired to turn a deaf ear to them; the treacherous sands that could engulf a town as easily as a man, then spit it up the way the Maelstrom with one contemptuous swirl could hurl the shattered remnants of a ship onto shore.

Best come down to earth now, before the whispers started that he had sold his loyalty to the Ch'in.

Beware.

The gentle voice touched his mind as soothingly as oil on a parched skin. One last look, then.

What was that on the horizon? Not a cloud, surely. You needed moisture for clouds, and there was, all the gods knew, no moisture in this wilderness.

His temples throbbed as if the air itself squeezed at them. Not all clouds held rain, he remembered.

Balancing skillfully, he climbed down the tower, dismounted, and bowed to Ssu-ma Chao, where he rode nearby. Those memories, or fantasies of his were worth something. Of all the Romans, he was the most skilled with the Ch'in chariots. *". . . Easy enough when you remember that he rode in a farmer's wagon* if *his family had any oxen that weren't confiscated for debt. . . ."* He had heard Lucilius whisper spitefully.

Quintus shook the grit out of his clothing and armor. As bad as swamp bugs, the grit was. If you didn't watch, grit might give you bleeding sores that stuck to clothes and never healed.

"Well, did you see anything?" Quickly Lucilius asserted his right to demand information.

"Cloud from the east," the tribune said. "I don't like the looks of it."

He used precious energy to jog forward to where Ssuma Chao rode. Behind him, the predictable murmurs started. Jupiter Optimus Maximus, he knew you could engrave what he knew about deserts on the pommel of his sword and still have room to list what else he didn't know. But he had lived on the land too long not to know when the weather was changing, and he had heard too many fireside terrors not to respect desert storms.

He didn't need to feel the way the air pressured his temples to know that weather threatened any more than a farmer or a sailor did. Interesting . . . the glare winking up from the sand seemed slightly less harsh, as if the sunlight were somehow diminished. He signaled the Ch'in leaders and pushed forward with a burst of wasteful speed. He was sweating, but the sweat dried as rapidly as it formed, forming a white, salty powder on his skin.

Hmmm . . . that was curious. The sand . . . beneath the endless yellowish-gray grit and pebbles, he saw patches of white. Quickly, he bent. Scooping up a pinch of it, he brought it to nose and lips. Salty. He glanced out. Now that he looked, he could see the desert as flatness interrupted by huge dunes, each one of them like an immense tide.

He had heard that in Judaea there did exist a sea so filled with salt that a man could lie in it and never sink. Easy to believe that such a sea had once existed here and had dried totally. Easy to believe? Nothing was easy here.

But imagine it—water, sluicing down from the mountains like the Flood Jupiter had once sent, filling this desert like a basin, sinking all that was in it, letting the earth roil until all was buried as deep as Atlantis. Once he had spoken of this—no more, surely, than a fireside fancy and Lucilius had arched a pale eyebrow in derision that a bumpkin had read Plato.

Shouts broke his musings.

"Buran! Kuraburan!"

Buran, he knew, meant storm. And *kuraburan*—black storm? Demon storm? All of the now-vanished tribunes who had been Lucilius's companions had been pleased to dismiss them as tales told to scare newcomers to this barbarian land.

All along the line of march, camels were moaning, lowering their heads to the sand, dropping ponderously to their ungainly knees. Horsemen galloped the length of the caravans. Carts ground to a stop. From carpets and from gaudy woven bags (now much dimmed with the sand), men pulled swathings of thick flannel the color of the desert itself.

Arsaces tossed a wad of felt at Quintus. It tumbled out of his arms to his feet.

"There's a storm coming up. The camels always know. Wrap up! This sand could carve the flesh from your bones."

Ssu-ma Chao rode toward him. Already he was muffled in the heavy fabric until only his eyes showed. They were bright, alert as if he sensed danger.

"Bandits strike under cover of these storms," he said. "Will your men fight with mine?"

He barely needed Arsaces's translations now. In the weeks of march past Merv, the caravan had evolved its own tongue—part Parthian, part Persian, and, inevitably, even part Latin and Ch'in. And in all of them, everyone knew the words for "bandits" and "storms."

"We will justify your faith in us," he declared. "Rufus!"

The centurion came on the double, gesturing for the maniples to form up.

"This one's officers will show you where to take your stations." Already, some of them were drawing weapons—the huge, cumbersome swords and wicked long spears of the Ch'in soldier. Were they for defense against the bandits—Saka, Yueh-chih, or Parthians—whom the desert might cast up against them, or against the Romans themselves?

A camel groaned, horses screamed, and a soldier who should have had better control yelped in surprise as the gritty sand whipped up to sting at unexposed flesh.

"Keep your heads down. You've seen sandstorms before!" Rufus shouted, then was interrupted by coughing.

The sky turned an evil yellow-gray. Then the air seemed to congeal and whirl about them, and the full fury of the storm struck.

Quintus sank his head on his breast. He had to see— he *had* to, yet some bits of the flying sand could have put out an eye. He felt as if he stood lost in a fog, but a fog that bit shrewdly, burrowing into every fold of the felt that stifled and protected him. A drop of sweat ran down his forehead, blissfully cool in the instant before it dried, leaving an itching salt trail. He was very thirsty.

Dis have mercy, if the grit got into the waterskins, they were all doomed! Someone ought to check. . . .

A hand pulled him down again. "In storms like these, you can wander ten paces from your camp and never be found again!" His companion, no, his rescuer, writhed lips about the words so their shape would convince him, for he could hear nothing but the roaring of the storm.

He would have to wait it out. He had waited out storms before.

Gradually, his ears grew accustomed to the storm—the howl of each new gust, the shriek of a particularly rapid one, the crack as something they would probably need later broke under pressure, and the whine of sand and gravel that sped by like arrows. He had never been as thirsty, not even in the square at Carrhae, and no sun shone here, in the belly of the storm.

Quintus stiffened. Other sounds began to pierce the storm's rage: giggles and whispers and threats. *Come out, come out before the grit buries you. Come, here is sweet water, here are grapes, here is rest. Lie down and take your ease.* He risked raising his head long enough to see one or two of his men shake their heads, then duck them back down against their chests. Hard-headed, Rome's mules: If it didn't present itself before their faces, the Legionaries would dismiss it. He knew his grandfather would have.

You will go mad out here, you know. The sun will bake your brains, and you will babble until they knock you on the head in pity. You never really thought you were fit, did you? All these years, hiding it . . . you're weak, and you're going to lead these men to their deaths in a savage land. . . .

Quiet! he commanded, trying to make his thoughts loud, the way Rufus might bellow at careless recruits.

Shadows that he could make out from the billows of sand only by their darkness capered outside the camp. Surely, that wasn't thunder overhead or the flashes of lightning he remembered from lost humid summer evenings—storms without rain?

You will never see them again.

I know that, he snapped, then regretted it. It was as pointless to argue with whatever rode these winds as to quarrel with a street beggar. And no street beggar sought to draw him out to his death in the waste.

He bent his head and slipped fingers chilled despite the stifling heat within his breast to touch the bronze statue. Its solidity consoled him.

Ah, so wise, he thinks he is. . . . Laughter replaced the whispers, rising and growing shrill until it mingled with the howl of the demon storm's breath.

Sand had blotted out the sky: No sun set, no moon rose, and no stars shone overhead. How much time had passed? Hours? Days? He would have felt hungrier if it had been that long, he thought.

Gradually, the shrieks of the wind grew weaker and less frequent, the gulps of a child making itself sick by a bout of furious crying. From time to time, he could even see beyond the space of a footstep or two. The whispers and giggling seemed to die away entirely. Then, after time he could not measure, came an instant when all was blissfully silent. Men began to rise and shake themselves free of the sand that had turned them into individual tiny hillocks.

"Hold!"

Ssu-ma Chao's shout and the sting of Quintus's bronze talisman came simultaneously.

And in the next minute, he heard the measured boom of drums and the ringing of bells and gongs.

"Yueh-chih!" The cry went up.

Of all the dwellers in this waste, they were the most feared, for they lived as if it held no dread for them. They had no fixed villages, only tents; and they rode where they would. Wise in the ways of storms, they attacked just as a caravan—even one as well-armed as this—began to dig itself out of a dying storm. And they had been at feud with the Ch'in, fighting back and forth across the desert, for more years than anyone but a Ch'in historian could count.

The Yueh-chih rode shrieking as if the *buran* had renewed itself. Nearby, someone screamed, then gurgled as a long lance transfixed him. Two Romans leapt from the sand and hacked at the barbarian with their swords. Hoarse voices shouted in Ch'in. . . . All around the camp, soldiers fought to raise the spears that might give them some defense against a mounted force. The Yueh-chih were counting on speed and confusion, on striking as the caravan struggled out of the sand before its guards, exhausted from simply enduring the *buran*, won back to full strength. It was as good a strategy in its way as the *testudo*, and no doubt as well practiced.

Quintus found himself in a line with the Legionaries, blood drying on his sword from lucky blows at shadows that had turned out to be Yueh-chih. The line was holding. He knew a moment's pride, which faded as he remembered: The Yueh-chih, like all the nomads of the waste, were master archers. Let the wind die, and those of his men whom Parthian arrows had not slain might fall to this new enemy.

As it was, there were too many Yueh-chih. Kill one, or unhorse two, and more hoofbeats pounded out of the swirls of sand and dust. Their screams arched up, savage with hate. They must have known that this caravan was bound for the heartland of Ch'in and was guarded by soldiers in service to its Emperor.

Roman bones as well as Ch'in would litter the salt wastes of the Takla Makan. The drums and the gongs and the wind and the screaming struck like a head blow. Quintus was reeling. . . .

A scream far overhead pierced the fog in which he stumbled. For one precious moment, the warring gusts of

wind allowed a patch of clear sky to be seen. It was the
violent blue that he had seen once or twice in the desert,
broken by a streak of gold, winging to the east. It paused
directly overhead and gave that shrill cry again—the call
of an eagle.

Then battling wind gusts blotted out the sky once
more. But Quintus's head felt clearer than it had for
months.

Will you believe me?

Speak. He greeted the voice erupting in his thoughts
calmly. So many times he had heard it. So many times he
had thought himself mad, unfit. He was about to die.
There was no point in fighting it any longer. He was only
sorry he could not see the spirit who had been first his
genius loci and then the exotic who called herself
Draupadi one last time.

They are too many.

He would have laughed, had his throat not been
parched.

You must flee.

Another reason to laugh.

Where would we go?

Follow me.

He might as well fall on his sword now, saving the
Yueh-chih or his own men the trouble of killing him as
he broke his own battle line to listen to a demon.

I am no demon!

Not a demon? In the *kuraburan*, he had heard demons, giggling, threatening, hinting as this voice did not.
And the bronze figure he bore had not grown hot. He
thought that if he followed a demon's advice, it might
heat so that it would burn out his heart.

Show me, then.

There is a way. Follow. I will guide you.

"We can't stay here!" he shouted.

Rufus's eyes bulged in amazement.

"You want to be ridden down? The storm can't last forever, and the instant it stops . . ."

Ssu-ma Chao, behind his guards and his shields, eyed him. The time Quintus had saved his life, he thought madness had inspired him. Now he was glad. The Ch'in officer might believe that he acted under some sort of inspiration. "Is this another of your omens?"

The gods bless him, even if he *were* their captor!

"Yes! Follow me!"

"Get the wagons!"

By all the gods, how much had the merchants paid Lucilius, that he took care for the wagons?

"No! They'll protect us from arrows, maybe!" Rufus drew on his years of experience as the senior centurion of a Legion. "All right, sloggers, we're moving out. Follow the tribune. . . ."

One of the men swore horribly at the wind. Once again, it shrieked up into a gale. "We're marching into *that?*"

"You want them drinking wine out of *your* skull?"

Carts creaked, beasts brayed or neighed in protest or fear. Someone shouted in outrage as a camel bit him. Incongruously, another driver laughed. And the Yueh-chih kept coming.

"Wait for the next gust!" Quintus screamed before he knew the words were out of his mouth.

He had no weather wisdom here, but he knew storms. The worst wind and rain storms to beat his valley often struck once, tempted people and animals out of shelter into a brief, sunlit calm, then hit again with renewed fury. This storm, after a brief lull, was building up again.

Only this time, it might be their friend.

Now!

The gust he was hoping for struck, and he bowed beneath it, letting it pass by.

"Move!" he shrieked, wild as the Yueh-chih himself.

Beasts and carts struggled forward. He had the sense of struggling forward down a corridor formed of blowing sand. Shadows formed, and he heard roaring, as if the river of lamentation he had once heard in his dreams flowed outside the "walls."

No sand stung his face. He put up a hand. No grit, flying by, cut into it. The only sand, in fact, that he saw formed the walls of the passage that engulfed them. Outside, the triumphant screams of the Yueh-chih died. How long before they realized they had been balked of their prey?

Go while you can.

He gestured and shouted, his order seconded from among the clutter of carts along the battered line of march, and what beasts still survived.

The carts creaked. The beasts moaned resentment at having to move directly into what they must surely fear as wind and pain. Whips cracked; the bells on the harnesses of horses and camels rang; and the remnants of the caravan lurched forward.

"To the cross with it! I can't see a damned thing!"

Lucilius's voice, from high overhead. By all the gods, the shifty bastard had gotten Ssu-ma Chao's chariot moving, had climbed its tower, and was getting a free ride.

If you laugh now, you won't be able to stop. Rufus will punch you out, and they'll load you on the wagons. And what will you do then?

A high giggle broke through, but he suppressed the gales of laughter that would have unmanned him.

*   *   *

They plowed onward through the sand. They had been marching for hours. They had never done anything else but march. Their service in the Legions before Syria, the destruction of their fellows at Carrhae and their proconsul, their betrayal, their enslavement—all that seemed far away. The world had narrowed—from the desert to this corridor of still air in the midst of the worst storm Quintus had ever dreamed of.

Was he dreaming of this? Dreaming men did not thirst or hunger as he did: He was sure of that.

He marched, the ground-eating steady Legions' pace. After awhile, Rufus barked the first words of a marching song. His cracked voice made a horrible hash of the tune, but he sang it through to the end, and some of the men echoed him. Damn, was a hobnail working through Quintus's boot into his foot? It felt that way.

Equally barbarous to the ear was the babble of chants and frantic prayers to what had to be at least three separate barbarian pantheons. At a signal from Ssu-ma Chao, Ch'in soldiers fell back, lest the merchants panic and try to break away, perhaps through the wall, thus betraying all of them to the Yueh-chih.

That was prudent. But Quintus thought it was misplaced precaution. Already they had marched for hours and come—how far? Farther than could be guessed in that time, he imagined . . . and he felt as worn as if he had marched for a full day at a cavalry pace again.

Nearby, Ssu-ma Chao's huge chariot rattled and creaked. Long ago, the senior officer had abandoned it, to walk or ride alongside his men. Lucilius, though, remained in its tower. For what advantage his presence as a lookout might provide, Quintus forebore to protest.

"Do you see anything now?" From time to time, he would call up to Lucilius. The answers grew lurid, then puzzled. Then Lucilius fell silent.

Arsaces joined Quintus as he marched. He led a horse, he who never willingly walked when he could ride. He paused, and Quintus, perforce, had to pause also. "The horses are tiring. If we don't rest them, they'll drop where they are."

"When you know where we are, we can rest," Quintus snapped. He was sorry he had stopped. The brief pause had freed his body from a merciful numbness in which leaden arms and legs performed their duty. Now his back was afire from the weight of his kit, and his limbs prickled as if he had been staked out on an anthill.

Arsaces's bloodshot eyes would have flashed with anger if he had had the strength.

"Some deva has us in his hand," he muttered. "May he set us down soon."

The march dragged out. No one bothered now to question or to speak. They were all too weary. *Bona dea,* Quintus longed for sunlight, for water, even for a chance to drop to the sand and sleep.

Come. This way.

He shouted, wordlessly. All along the line of march, people cried out in surprise and spurred camels and horses to new effort. Their last effort, Quintus felt certain.

This had better be quick, he told . . . whatever. *Who do I think I'm talking to? We are all dreaming, and soon we are all going to be dead, wandering in the desert after a storm and a battle.*

"Ho!"

Lucilius's voice, arching up, and cracking as he called out.

"What . . . you see?" Rufus grunted, not waiting for a tribune to ask.

"Up ahead," he called. "The clouds are breaking up!" His voice cracked once again, this time not from thirst. "By the breasts of Venus, I can see the sun!"

9

"FASTER," SSU-MA CHAO muttered. His chariot rumbled forward, the tower to which Lucilius climbed creaking as the wheels bumped over the rock-strewn sand. "The sun . . ."

The Ch'in soldiers urged men and beasts to greater efforts. A packhorse tried to hurl its head up and scream defiance as if it were a warhorse, but its heart broke, its knees buckled, and it sank dead in its traces. Too desperate to unload it, the merchants pushed on by. After a moment, the driving yellow sand behind them hid it.

And still the Ch'in officer pushed for greater speed.

Bleary-eyed, Quintus looked along the plodding line of Legionaries. Could they even complete this day's march—whatever you called a day in this no-place of driving sand—let alone quicken their pace? Their faces were gray with exhaustion and grit, but their eyes blazed.

"At the cavalry's pace," he ordered. He remembered how they had marched, hours upon hours in the hot Syrian sun, with those Nabataean and Armenian traitors jeering and the proconsul thinking only of his precious son and his horses. His heart would burst, and he would lie beneath the sand, like that packhorse. They all would, except maybe Lucilius. He wanted him to come down from his perch and march like a Roman, but . . .

"Sun. And sky! It's blue. By all the gods, it's a beautiful day!" Lucilius shouted.

A weak cheer rose from the Legionaries.

"All right now, none of that," Rufus ordered. "On the double, now!"

Ahead of them, a ray of sun broke through the opaque walls that had encompassed them for so long. One ray, then another, then seven, brushing across their foreheads with the touch of a mother on a fevered child's brow.

Ssu-ma Chao tripped and measured his length. Instead of struggling to his knees and glaring at anyone who had seen him lose his dignity, he knocked his head against the sand as if the light were his Emperor. That was not sweat that ran down a nearby soldier's drawn face, leaving a clean streak in the mask of sand and dried sweat that coated it. It was not sweat that ran down Quintus's face, either.

With the sunlight came fresh breaths of air. He would have thought he'd had enough winds for a lifetime—the howls, the screams, the battering gusts. This came as a reminder of green hills and hidden valleys, of the blue mists and shadows of his lost home. It soothed his parched skin as if he ducked his head into a mountain stream. And, despite its gentleness, where it brushed against the walls that had been their protection and their trap the rush of sand and gravel thinned and the thin shriek of the wind that kept it blowing about them grew fainter than the highest notes of a flute, rising past a man's hearing to the level of a night flyer's hunting song. Now the sunlight filtered through it, kindling the ugly ochres and gray into rich saffrons and golds. And ahead of them, they could see the glowing blue of a tranquil sky.

Behind the Romans, wailing prayers of thanks rose up, almost as hideous as the wind. Quintus could imagine how the barbarians were kneeling and rubbing their faces on the rock. Not so much as one Roman broke ranks: They stood, waiting for orders. And Lucilius dropped with more speed than Quintus would have thought he had left from the chariot's tower to stand with his fellows.

"You put heart into us for this last dash," Quintus said.

For once, there was no mockery in the patrician's gaze.

"Last dash to where?" he asked.

Perhaps he had earned the right to that much irony.

With a final sigh, the last of the sand fell. And the lost caravan stood forth on land that was not covered with grit and gobi, but honest rock. Ahead of them stretched a narrow course sloping down past tall poplars and gleaming rhododendrons into a valley guardéd by rock cliffs that jutted up like columns carved and melded together in the morning of the world. The pathway—wide enough for six men to walk abreast or a wagon to traverse carefully—wound past a rock spire. Some cut in the rock caught the sunlight, which pooled there, forming a globe of light from which rays issued.

The light brightened past bearing, then faded. Beyond that rock spire, as much as they could see, stretched a green field tippled with gold and red wildflowers. Willows swayed gently by the deep blue curve of a mountain lake. Beyond, more cliffs rose, sheltering the valley.

The quiet all but sang in their ears. No screams, no hoofbeats or drums, and no whine of Yueh-chih arrows, thank all the gods. Without need of orders, Roman and Ch'in soldiers wheeled to guard the rest of the caravan as it coiled about the entrance to the valley. One by one, they stripped themselves of the heavy felts they no longer needed to wear.

Were they dead? Quintus saw no asphodel on the valley floor. Nothing dead could be as thirsty as Quintus, or as tired. "We are far off my reckoning," Ssu-ma Chao murmured. "I have never heard of this place, and no one I know has ever seen it. I see no mountains, or I would swear we had passed over the desert into the Heavenly Mountains of the North."

He clapped his hands. Merchants, horsemen, and camel drivers attended him while restraining their eager beasts, but their eyes constantly wandered to feast on the green and blue that stretched out below them.

For all his cynicism, the horseman Arsaces swore by his many devas, then choked, "In the midst of the desert, a crystal fountain," he whispered. "I would have taken haoma that it was but a tale told round a fire in the desert."

Rufus cleared his throat, looked for a place to spit, then, obviously, thought better of it. "That looks like real water to me," he said. "Are we going to just stand and admire it?"

Already scenting it, the horses had pressed forward. Even the camels moaned and quickened their gait. Saddles and packs hung low on their backs: The humps in which they stored the precious fluid that made them such fine desert travellers were almost flat. A cart overturned as the beasts drawing it swerved too sharply in their eagerness to get to the water.

"All right, wait your turns!"

The wind blew, overpowering the stinks of frightened, sweaty men and animals with the temptations of water and growing things. The same longing that drove the beasts forward shone in the Romans' eyes. Quintus wanted nothing as much as to stretch out full length by that blue pool and slake his thirst. He and his men joined the other soldiers and the caravan drivers in restraining the animals. After surviving a desert storm and the Yueh-chih, they should not fall victim to their own eagerness in sight of rest and water.

The air filled with noises as those beasts too weak to go any further in safety were unharnessed or relieved of packs and led down to the pool, where others would have to restrain them from drinking till they swelled from it. But the choking dust that rose in the desert was absent: Quintus watched the tally of soldiers, merchants, beasts, and carts.

He had seen that horse collapse in the last rush from the blowing sand. Who else had been lost? Some, wounded, clung to carts, were loaded face-down across pack-animals or tied to their mounts.

"That one won't last the night," Arsaces pointed as a driver clung to one of his charges that was too weary to shy away from the blood scent. "At least he'll have enough water while he dies."

No one will die.

"What did you say?" Quintus started.

No one has died here for . . . the voice trailed off.

"Sir, are you all right? Your eyes just rolled up. . . ."

"I'm fine." Quintus waved off the concern with what he hoped could pass for irritation. The Romans owed what freedom they had to Ssu-ma Chao's belief they brought him fortune: no use frightening everyone else. Or, he thought, with a countryman's shrewdness, letting the rest of them know.

You are wise, though you are a warrior, not a priest. I have always thought so.

The tattered caravan staggered past him into safe haven. He started to ask if any others had been lost, but his words were lost in the clatter of warped cartwheels on rock. The men of Hind. The Persians. Even the wagons of that fat man who had been so afraid outside Merv, and the man himself, now not nearly so fat and moving the faster for it.

Then, leading their horses, heads down and shuddering, passed the merchants Quintus had seen the night he had emerged from long, long dreams. Seen and distrusted, with their high-bred faces, their hooded eyes, and their tightly held mouths. There had been—how many of them?

More, it was certain, than now passed under his gaze. And there had been women in their numbers, gone now, too. Had part of their train perished under the blades of the Yueh-chih? Or had they decided to take their own escape?

Last of all came the soldiers, limping down the path. Sunlight blazed out overhead, hiding them, for an instant. As the track wound around the spire of dark rock that blocked a full view of the lake below, they paused. Horses and camels balked, but the crack of whips and oaths in a tongue Quintus had never heard (and liked as little as he liked those who spoke it) forced them back up the slope.

"Our beasts . . . cannot make it downhill," said one of the merchants, his face still muffled in the wrappings that had protected him from the storm. "We camp here . . . outside."

He held up a hand, interrupting the instinctive protests of the soldiers at their charges' foolishness. "We have supplies."

If there had been any one group likelier to husband their own goods while all around them went in need, Quintus had yet to see it. *Let* them thirst in sight of a blue lake. Let their beasts eat stored fodder when fresh green stalks waited to be cropped—though it was a shame to treat honest animals that way.

"And we will pay—in gold—for water to be brought."

"Wouldn't you just know it?" Lucilius hissed. "You might as well let them go their own way. They will, anyhow."

"Merchants!" This time, Rufus did spit as he watched the strangers coil about the lip of the valley.

The eyes of tribune, centurion, and Ch'in officer met in perfect understanding: Tonight and all the nights thereafter, these travellers would be placed under watch.

Now that all the others had descended, they too could head for the water and rest their bodies craved. First, Quintus thought, water. Then, perhaps there would be fish or even waterfowl, feeding near the lake. In that moment, he might even have traded his lost farm for rest—for him and all of the Romans who had lived.

Shadows began to deepen in the valley. The sky turned indigo, as it did in the hills, and a long sunbeam slanted down the track, pointing out the way.

He nodded to Rufus, who raised a battered vinestaff. "Let's show them how *Romans* do it, lads," he rasped.

They formed ranks and marched: Rome's pace, Rome's race, down the path toward safety. If the rock slabs underfoot were not the good roads of the Republic, at least they did not shift underfoot.

Another ray from the sun, heading like they themselves to its well-earned rest, struck the rock spire as they passed. Perhaps it was a trick of the light, but as it died, Quintus thought he saw etched into the rock a serpent, seven heads crowning its sinuous body. Wherever the light touched it, it was slow to fade.

He waited for whatever voice had guided him into safety or madness—whichever—to offer an explanation. None came. But reassurance seemed to radiate from his bronze talisman.

I know, he told it. *Fare forward*.

They passed under the shelter of the rock spire and into a circular valley so pure it made his heart ache.

Fire crackled, casting long shadows on the grimy tents that Rufus had insisted the men pitch even here. Quintus shivered. The heat, the twilight wind, cooked food, fresh clothing, the cold water drying in his hair, even the small, familiar camp sounds of men repairing gear and dicing, luxuries he had forgotten.

The last sunlight winked at the horizon like the eye of a sleepy creature, urging all in the valley to rest. Not all could, or would. Some would stand guard, while others would sit up tonight with wounded or dying men and beasts. When Quintus was certain that the last stake that could be pounded, bandage that could be wrapped, or Legionary to be stationed were all in place, he would be free to rest. The other tribune had retired, and even Rufus, yawning ferociously, had threatened him with feeling like grim Orcus himself on the morrow.

So it stood to reason that he could not sleep. Too far gone, he told himself. Let him be less tired, and sleep would come. But the exhaustion that had numbed his mind and body had vanished. He would have been glad, had it been suitable, to trade tales with Arsaces—he

would have bet the pay he would never collect that the
Persian auxiliary knew more about this place than he
would say. But fed, secured, with a proper camp set up
and officers near his own rank within earshot, he could
not properly do so. Besides, the horseman had gone off
after referring to the valley as a "pardesh." "Garden,"
Quintus knew it meant, but it did seem like some paradise of the Golden Age.

He shifted restlessly, hating the need to remain within
a tent on a night as fine as this one. As a boy, he had
loved to slip out by night and wander in the lands around
his house. Sometimes, sleep would come upon him as he
rested by the river. Drawing his cloak about him, he rose.
Just as he left the tent, he swung back for his sword.

His boots crunched on the trampled long grass and
rocks of their campsite, drawing some anonymous mutters of protest that anyone was stupid enough to be up
and around after all. . . . The complaints trailed off into
snores, which subsided, too.

Nodding to the perimeter guards, he slipped beyond
the camp into the darkness. The water drew him, as it
always had. Swiftly, his feet found a trail that led around
the lake. He heard ripples that told him he neared some
stream or falls. At a boulder that looked as if some enormous hand had sheared it in half, he paused. He did not
know the land. He would be wise to wait for his eyes to
accustom themselves to seeing only by moon- and starlight.

The rushing of the water grew louder. Not just a
stream, then, but a small waterfall, or several, he
thought. He ought to return to the camp for a torch, he
thought. The rocks could be slippery. Asia, he knew,
teemed with serpents of a deadliness unknown in Rome,
except those who walked on two legs. But he pressed

forward, treading carefully. A benediction of mist touched his face and eyelids.

The moon provided enough light for him to see his goal—wide slabs and plinths of rocks, overhung by a huge flat stone from which water cascaded to the right and left. It formed a natural chamber, the "entry" facing him. He peered within, tempted.

Lights sprang up inside the enclosure and even in the still water at the very edge of the pools, reflecting double as if they floated there cased in glass, protected from the spray. Fine scents—cinnamon and fragrant oil—wreathed about him.

Fare forward, traveller, came an ironic voice. He reached down to take out the figure of the dancer. As he had seen once before, lights glimmered upon its tiny, upheld arms, as if, once again, the creature known as Krishna danced to mourn and to rejoice. From overhead came the piping of a flute and the sound of a kind of horn he had never heard before.

Prudence argued that he should return to camp right now. He knew perfectly well what Rufus would object to—and as for his grandfather, he was certain that the old man would say that to go a step further would be to betray Rome *and* the *lares* and *penates* of their old, tarnished line.

I have not survived this far by being prudent, Quintus retorted in his own mind. Besides, perhaps that blow on the head he had taken long ago had spilled his wits; and everything that happened since was a madman's fantasies.

If so, these were the fairest dreams yet.

He pressed forward across the wet rock and into the rocky chamber. It stretched out far beyond what he had expected, turning into a sort of tunnel that led from the falls to a natural enclosure, almost like a theatre. Poplars swayed near high cliffs, surrounding a circular pool that was almost a miniature of the lake as he had first gazed upon it. In the center of the pool, jutting out from the rocky corridor itself, was what might have formed the stage.

Torches flickered at its corners, and tiny lights floated in metal bowls upon the water, dancing in the ripples. The rock was as richly carpeted as any Persian prince or magus could have desired, rug tossed over rug in a wealth of patterns and textures. Sweet smoke trailed up from braziers pierced in intricate patterns: Quintus scented cinnamon and the deeper odors of sandalwood and myrrh. Huge cushions of amber, russet, and deep reds lay upon the carpets. And reclining against a mound of the richest cushions, a figure robed and veiled in saffron . . .

"Hold!"

The command came in Latin. That, as much as the word itself, halted the tribune. His hand flashed to his swordhilt. If he set his back against the rock, at least no enemies could come upon him from behind.

"Who are you to stop me?" Quintus demanded, his back safely against the stone. "And how do you know my tongue?"

Lights seemed to pool about him, and he saw an old man, his skin burned dark from the sun, his thin hair whitened, a red mark gleaming like a dark jewel above the meeting of his brows. At his feet lay a huge shell, a lotus, a discus, an axe, and a tumbled scroll—but no sword. *Arrogant old fool,* Quintus thought. But even old fools dared arrogance if they had warriors to back them.

"I know all tongues. And I know a beggar when I see one. No beggars here. Go away!" In the worst days of waiting in noble patrons' anterooms, Quintus had never imagined that type of contempt. The old man looked down his long nose. The light caught him in profile, distorting it in a shadow cast on the rock wall. For an instant, Quintus thought he saw the image of a beast like those massive terrors Hannibal had brought across the mountains into Latium and nearly marched on Rome; in the old man's command, he heard the arrogant trumpeting of an elephant.

"I am not a beggar, but a Roman." Let the saffron-veiled figure turn its head, let it look upon him, so that he might know whether it was his dream made real . . . or if all of this was an illusion. *A Roman, yes, who owes his life to strangers and must now even depend on them for a sword.*

"Ragtag and sword for hire," scoffed the old man. "A thief, perhaps. I may have been born today, but I know a thief when I see one."

"A Roman," Quintus repeated, low-voiced. "Now, will you let me pass?" Bad enough to be challenged and jeered at; the presence of the woman in her silken veils made it intolerable. He might be her servant: best pay him courtesy.

"Be on your way, whoever, whatever you are. I will be accosted by no more appeals."

"Then I shall not," Quintus snapped.

In the instant, his sword showed bright. *What am I doing?* he demanded of himself and checked that swing. The blow went wild, and the sword rang instead against the rock. Sparks shot from the stone. Much to his humiliation, the blade shattered.

Bad enough: Worse yet was the sudden vision he had of the old man's neck gushing blood and the head, its thinning hair smeared and its eyes wide and glazing, rolling across the rock to splash into the water. For a moment, the light flickered and he even imagined an elephant's head taking the place of the old man's on the plump, rounded shoulders.

Jupiter Optimus Maximus, thought Quintus. *What have I done?* The lights danced in the water like torches in the hands of a dancing bronze figurine.

10

Laughter like a chime of sweet bells rang out from the woman reclining on cushions and carpets. The old man himself joined in her amusement.

"Another mistake?" she called.

To the end of his life, Quintus thought, he would never know if she spoke Latin or not: Her voice was like her skin—dark honey. And what mattered were not the words she spoke, but that she spoke at all.

"Ah no, Draupadi," the old man cried. "I could not be wrong about this one. Not that I have not been wrong before—as I was the first day of my life."

He turned to Quintus, who had retrieved his broken blade, wondering how he would find, among the stores, one that would suit him—or any sword at all. At the worst, he must go to Ssu-ma Chao and beg for arms. The old man must be some sort of soothsayer, then, to call him beggar. Ruefully, he sheathed the metal fragments.

"You do better than a god, young sir. In truth, you outdo my father Shiva, who slew me the day of my birth. I was born full-grown, and my mother Parvati bade me guard the door, that no one disturb her while she was bathing. My father approached and would enter, but in my inexperience I sent him away. Angry, he cut off my head and threw it far beyond the Roof of the World.''

Quintus shook his own head, almost testing its security on his own shoulders at the old man's ravings.

"My mother appeared, weeping. The Lord of All the Worlds, to heal her grief, took up the first head he saw—which happened to be that of an elephant.

"Placing it on my shoulders, he restored me to life. And since then, I have sought only understanding.''

He picked up his scroll. "Welcome to your part in this tale, young lord.''

Again, the woman seated beyond him laughed. Delicate shell bracelets tinkled on her wrists. "You do not explain enough, Ganesha. Is this how our champion must be left—confused? That is not how Arjuna looked the day he won me and brought me home.''

"Let me explain the tale,'' said the creature—man, god, gods-only-knew-what—called Ganesha. "Whoever hears this tale and understands a small bit of it escapes the chains forged by deeds of good or evil. Success he finds, for the tale holds the power of victory! The man who tells it to eager listeners gives them as a gift the Earth with her belt of seas. Stay with me and tell me . . .''

He broke off and shook his head.

"That is not right. It is my turn to tell, not to record, is that so?''

Quintus blinked, not expecting to be addressed. A moment more and he would either laugh or flee.

Ganesha clapped his hands. "Well, follow me.'' He led the way onto that cushioned platform floating upon the glowing lake and gestured to a pile of cushions only slightly less ample than those Draupadi reclined upon.

She bent and, from a golden pitcher richly encrusted with red and green stones, poured a fragrant drink into a matching cup.

The old man threw a wreath of flowers and a white scarf about Quintus's neck.

"We do that for honor," the woman told him.

"Well, why do you tarry?" the scribe demanded. "Sit, sit, sit! And I shall begin."

Quintus laid the cup aside. How was he going to explain the breaking of his short sword?

Draupadi laughed in delight. "We offer him incense, we offer him stories, we offer him even *amrita,* the very nectar of heaven, and, see, he grieves for a weapon. Truly, he is the warrior we seek."

But are you the one I *seek?* Her eyes, elongated by the kohl, challenged him. The fragrance of sandalwood rose from her hair, and a line of red gleamed where she had parted it and dressed it with gems. A wreath of flowers lay beside her, and the odors rising from the cup at his side were very sweet.

If he drank that, what would he be transformed into? Would he, like old Ganesha, bear an elephant's head? *More likely the head of an ass,* he thought. *For leaving my camp; for listening to these lunatics, even for a moment.* In the stories, Circe had transformed Ulysses's men into swine, and the Greek hero had menaced her with his sword. But *his* sword had shattered on the rock.

Once again, he met the woman's eyes. Deep as the Mediterranean, they caught the fires that encircled them. Shapes formed in the fires: his brothers the Pandavas, the eldest, his king with golden eyes, who lost Draupadi in a game of dice and plunged them into war; his enemy, who possessed arms that made him invincible—unless he . . . Arjuna . . . could find weapons to set them at naught.

"This wreath is twin to the one I brought my husband. That was Arjuna, under a vow to share all he won with his brothers. And so, I married five brothers. You are . . ." She paused as if drawing the name from his thoughts, ". . . named Quintus. That is five, is it not? Take the wreath!"

She had it in her slender hands. In an instant, she would have it about his neck, and he would be as bound, he knew, as if he slipped his head beneath a conqueror's yoke. The wreath brushed his hair.

He pushed up onto his feet so fast that his bronze statue of the dancer fell onto the carpets.

"Krishna!" the scribe cried. "You and he have been great friends since . . . tell me you remember. . . ."

"The tree . . ." Quintus shook his head. Again, memories not his own overlay his thoughts. An ironic, enigmatic figure whose gentle humor hid a mind as vast as all heaven. A being who was devoted to . . . to him? Not to him, certainly. To Arjuna, this hero out of some wild collection of Hind stories.

He had been offered a choice—armies or simply Krishna to serve as his charioteer—and he had chosen Krishna. He. Arjuna. He shook his head, trying to separate his thoughts from the spell of these other stories.

He did not want Arjuna's memories. But the tiny dancer was precious to him, and he scooped it up. Mocking flute music rang in his ears.

"This is magic!" he accused them. "All illusion. Even, I would wager, my sword breaking."

He reached to the leather and brass sheath and drew. The blade shone in the firelight, then shimmered . . . the metal length drawing out, blue patterns quivering along it. Even the hilt felt strange. He glanced down: It was decorated with frogs.

"Arjuna's own blade," Ganesha told him. He made a meticulous note in his scroll.

Then the blade shifted form again. Roman issue, the finest in the world. Or so he had always thought.

"Illusions," he whispered. "Is it all illusion?" Abruptly, he was chill with fear. "Is this a dream, too?" Would he wake screaming and find himself bleeding to death from a Yueh-chih arrow? Or would he wake too parched to rave, his tongue swollen in his head as he died of thirst, having led his men to ultimate defeat?

"Illusion?" Draupadi caught up his words.

"You know illusion," she told him. "Do you remember? Maya, god of illusion, made *namaste*, touching your brother's feet. He proclaimed himself a great artist, eager to create. And you asked him for a palace that no one could imitate."

Ganesha unrolled his scroll. "Yes! He found on a mountain slope flat posts shining like a god's face, bordered with gold and set with golden flowers gleaming with jewels. Ages ago, Krishna had set them on the northern slope of the Mother of the World."

"Who lived there?" Quintus found himself asking.

"You—I mean, Arjuna." Ganesha nodded. "We all did, for a long time. It was your home where you found love and grief, happiness and death. And you remember nothing at all. Well, the wheel turns for all of us. You will.

"Maya built his palace. By the front door he put a tree of lights, its leaves cut from thin sheets of emerald, with gold veins. It sang in the wind. He carried full-grown trees and made parks; he brought songbirds and filled the trees; he made ponds and pools and filled them with fish and flowers. And when he was finished . . ."

"Is this Maya's palace?"

"One such, perhaps," Draupadi said. "All is illusion." Her eyes turned sorrowful.

"Then am I dead?"

"Illusion can be as powerful as truth," she told him. "We brought you here. The horsemen who would have slain you were real. The storm you endured was real. The use we made of it, to encompass you as you sped upon the circles of the world, that was illusion. And so is the guise of your sword."

"It was illusion that it broke."

"No; indeed, it shattered on that rock, for it is of Maya's building. You carry Arjuna's sword, disguised now so you can return to your people and bring them to our aid."

Slowly, Quintus folded his arms on his chest. The white scarf and wreath brushed his knee. He started to push them away, then forebore.

"If you are powerful enough to call the desert itself to your aid, you need no help from me or mine. We are prisoners, permitted arms only because the desert holds worse fears than Romans far from their home."

"Then why not turn aside?" Draupadi asked. "Some did."

Ganesha looked down at his scroll as if it were a map.

"They hold our Eagle." It came out sounding flat. How could he explain to these dwellers in illusion what the Eagle meant in terms of loyalty and blood? They looked to be of Hind. Perhaps he could explain it in terms of Alexander, who had journeyed that far. But his mouth went dry. He had never been a scholar, never had much time to study or a good tutor. Even Lucilius would tell the tale better than he.

"Loyal," she pronounced. "Well enough. You are here. And *they* are here. And the talismans. Look you!"

She snapped one of the fragile shells from the bracelet on her slender wrist. "I break this cowrie shell. And I scatter its pieces . . . oh, here . . . and here . . . and here. . . ." She dropped gleaming fragments on the amber and crimson carpet. "But then the need comes for such a shell. A need such as the world has never seen since the stars danced in different patterns in the heavens. So the pieces gather in one place, where the hand that knows them—" her own fingers with their almond-shaped nails were busy collecting the shards, "—and then, they are joined once more. So!"

She raised her hand, and the shell was whole.

"More shadow-play?"

Ganesha shook his head. "That was true transformation. You have grown, Draupadi."

"I *wish* to grow beyond illusions into truth. I can spin shadows into pleasing forms. And I can spin them into shapes that can save a man's life. A little, I can take the fabric of the world and change it in truth. But I cannot do more, not without help."

"I have heard," Quintus said, "that those of Hind are great magicians." His voice was very dry. The cup at his feet beckoned, but he did not dare drink it.

"It would protect you from wounds," Draupadi said, "and make you all but immortal. If you spurn that, drink from the pool."

"We are not from Hind," Ganesha said. "Oh, in latter days, before the stars changed once again and we were driven out once more, we lived there . . . in that palace Maya built at your . . . at Arjuna's . . . command. But this was our home before, and we must hope will be so once again."

Quintus paced about the platform. By rights, he ought to call his men or Ssu-ma Chao to restrain the lunatics.

But, he recalled, perhaps they were oracles. And those sybils who were holiest seemed the maddest. He thought of the woman before him seated by a tripod, a serpent twined round its legs, as fumes rose from a fissure in the earth and dreams erupted from her lips.

"You cast your nets wide, if you draw in such as we."

"Nets! Now you begin to understand," Ganesha nodded approval. "Long ago, this was a plain, rich with water, fertile fields, forests, and lakes. A great city rose not far from here, the home of a race that had journeyed far from the East, from the Motherland known as Mu. From there, they spread out. Here, to the city of the Uighurs. And beyond it to the island in the sea, now sunken. . . ."

Quintus's palms were wet. That much Plato he remembered. "Atlantis, lost when the earth split, sunk beneath the waves."

"We cast our nets wide, as you say. Wide as the waves that overwhelmed our cities." Ganesha's voice was grave. A tear ran down Draupadi's cheek. "On a night of the blackest evil, waves were sent raging down onto the plain that the Uighurs had made into a worthy daughter of the Motherland. Huge rocks shattered the pillars of the temples and palaces and theatres we had built. Those of us who could, those of us with the training of the Naacals, the caste of priests, fled.

"And when we looked back, we saw only desolation. Boulders had scoured the soil, bare to the very bones of the world. The land dried, and sand came, to bury the ruins of Uighur glory.

"Weeping, we made our way overmountain to Hind, those of us who did not despair, or plunge off the great peaks, or die for lack of breath. But we made our way down into rich fields that reminded us of the land we had lost.

"The people greeted us there beside rivers they called holy. When we named ourselves and spoke of our loss, they bowed and touched our feet. They heaped our necks with wreaths and scarves of honor. For 'Naacal,' they heard 'Naga'—a holy people of their own. And indeed, it had been that those 'Nagas' were loyal daughters of the Motherland and Hind had been the jewel on her brow—as much as Mu. Even the symbol was the same. Draupadi?"

The woman gestured. The air around the nearest brazier shimmered, melded with the sparks, and formed the image of the seven-headed serpent that Quintus had convinced himself he had *not* seen on the cliff walls.

"Serpents," she said. "It is the nature of man to fear them, and that is wise. But like fire, there is no need to hate. Do not your own priests venerate the serpent?"

Despite himself, Quintus smiled, remembering as a child how he had laid down a saucer of milk for the garden snake that coiled near the household shrine.

Still it was hard, hard to think of the desert through which he had passed in such pain and peril as a seabed—but his eyes had flinched from the noon glare on slick white patches uncovered by the wind, and when he had touched some of this strange sand to his lips, he had tasted salt.

You could still be in the desert. They could serve your head as they served the proconsul's—hurling it into an entertainment to delight barbarians. Or your head could be curing in some Yueh-chih tent, ready for some unwashed carver to make into a drinking cup.

So he owed these people at least a hearing. And it was

hard to look away from the woman, who spoke with a voice near that of his own *genius loci*.

Her eyes were upon him. "I told you, we cast our nets of illusion wide—and our nets of vision even wider."

He looked down at the statue of Krishna.

"You have pipes—flutes, music, dancing—in your own land," she was continuing. "There can be no pipes without his presence, somehow."

There's Pan or Silenus. It seemed useless to say so, however.

With a stubbornness he thought his grandfather would have approved of, for once, Quintus brought up what seemed to him the most telling argument against this madness. "Lady, you broke that shell. Then you reassembled it—I do not know how. But you knew where all its pieces were and why you did what you did."

"Excellent!" Ganesha said, clapping plump hands together. "Look up!"

Quintus gazed up into the sky. Once again, the stars bloomed, even more brightly than in the deep desert.

"You see the patterns in the stars?"

Ganesha pointed out the ones Quintus had been taught as a boy. "When I was your age, there was no Hunter, no great or lesser Bear. We had the Naga, the Crown . . . ah, they are all passed. But the patterns shift in the sky. And when certain patterns emerge, then it is time for change in the world. *As above, so below.* It is a crucial time, and past time. Does it not seem to you that there is no order, no justice in the world, that all is confusion?"

His father dead afar, his pretty, vigorous mother withering, his grandfather dying, rigid in his bed, their lands lost. Betrayal in the desert, the slithering in the sand of serpents he could not hear, the vanishing of carts from the illusions that should have saved them.

What if you were not mad, but right, to sense that all was amiss?

He sat back down and used the scarf of honor to dab at his brow.

"Have you ever seen," Draupadi asked, "men and women who resemble Ganesha and I? Who look like us, but with whom you would never sit, much less listen to unless you came armed and protected by strong amulets?"

Her hand moved over the water of the pool, and faces formed. "Have you seen any who look like this?"

Dark hair; eyes kept lidded, but dark and with fire in their cores; narrow-lipped mouths; a high-bred look, but one that seemed to raise his hackles the way the rustling of unseen serpents had outside Merv.

Twin to Draupadi, perhaps, but a twin as devoted to darkness as she seemed to the light.

"Those are the Black Naacals," Draupadi told him. "For as the stars moved into their appointed patterns, they stirred. And we have been drawn from our long contemplations, and you from your proper life to stand against them."

He was insane. In the morning, they would miss him. They would seek him out. And they would find him, his face twisted in a madman's grimace, his hair torn out—that is, if they did not count him fled.

"Draupadi!"

Both of the creatures who called themselves Naacals stiffened as if scenting the air. It quivered, seemingly thickening, and from as far off as the cliff walls ringing the valley, Quintus heard the rustle of giant coils. Descending by night, seeking out the warmth of the camp, the lives of his men . . .

"No!"

"*Hold!*"

Ganesha picked up his scroll. Draupadi opened her hands in the gestures that Quintus had seen summon her illusions. For a moment longer, the air thickened and the rustling drew closer. Quintus drew his sword.

"You cannot slay the serpent with a sword," Ganesha told him. "You need a bow—Gandiva, which only Arjuna might draw."

"You do not need me," Quintus told them. "My men do. Let me go to them."

"The serpent has been contained, illusion banished with illusion. But I am no warrior, nor is Ganesha. For the serpent of the Black Naacals to be slain, we must have a man of war. You. And you must have weapons. It seems to me that, just as a bird flies, with the serpent that it has caught dangling from its beak, your Eagle plays a role in what we must do. And it may even be that you, like Arjuna, must seek out weapons that could wreck the earth. But better at your hands, should you err, than at those of the Black Naacals."

From far across the lake, Quintus heard someone call out. The watch? Had the guards found someone slain, or discovered him missing? He glanced up. Banners began to fly at the horizon—crimsons and purples and golds—as the night sky dimmed, hiding the stars that he had heard signalled such war for the world. It was all but dawn, and he had never known.

He had passed the entire night in conversation with these Naacals or spirits—whatever they were, they were beings at least as strange as the *genius loci* of his childhood.

"It is time," Ganesha said. He picked up the huge shell and blew into it, producing a cry that any trumpeter would have praised.

"You've given away your location," Quintus pointed out.

"They do not seek us, but you," Draupadi said. "And they bring news that you must hear."

II

As if he had fallen asleep for a moment, his consciousness shifted. When he returned to awareness, he saw only barren rock: no carpets, no cushions, no old man with an elephant's head and supple hands: only two priests or prophets in clean but threadbare robes, gazing at the sun as they performed morning prayers. Threads of incense spiralled up from sticks driven into the cracks in the stone slab on which they sat. Carpets and cushions were gone, and the lights in the water had winked out as if pulled beneath the ripples.

"Tribune! Where are you?" Quintus knew that familiar rasp, knew the pause that meant that Rufus was hand-signalling for scouts to flank the place on shore and a detachment to rush it.

Three men pounded through the passageway. Their swords were out, and their boots struck sparks from the stone.

"Hold!"

The Romans stood, gazing in amazement at the falls,

the pools, and the priest and priestess seated placidly, their heels turned up in their laps, opposite one of their own officers.

The Legionaries firmed their grips on their swords. Ssu-ma Chao and his guards, spears at the ready, appeared behind them. The morning sun glinted on Lucilius's fair hair.

Rufus glared, not at the priests, but at his officer. For going missing, for leaving him with another tribune whose orders he did not rely on. Quintus could only thank the gods he was an officer and not one of the men under the senior centurion's authority. But there was more to his anger than that.

"These people are unarmed. Friends," Quintus snapped. "What's your report?"

The centurion ushered two men forward.

"Gaius, Decimus, tell the tribune what you told me." *And it better be the same story, if you know what's good for you,* was the accompanying threat.

Draupadi and Ganesha ceased their prayers and sat watching, serenely interested and unafraid, despite the intrusion of so many armed men into their shrine. The sun beat down on their heads. Even if they were surrounded by water falling into a pool, and growing things, it would be a hot day. It was hard to remain on guard in such a place. The very sound of water falling over ancient rocks promised rest and peace.

But they were adepts in illusion, Quintus reminded himself.

"Sir, the centurion set us to guard the wagons that camped outside the causeway."

Very properly done, of course. Quintus had not liked the look of those particular wagons or the way they had struggled halfway down the slope into the valley, then turned around.

Seeing no apparent danger from a priest and priestess in shabby robes, Rufus sheathed his short sword. Despite the sunlight, he wore his metal helm. Lovingly, he tapped his vinestaff against his palm.

"Sleeping on duty . . ."

"Sir, by all the gods, I swear it, we never took our eyes off them. They camped; they built a fire; they drew from their own stores. . . ." Gaius, a man young in the Legions and with the stocky build of the Italian provincial, all but stammered.

Behind him, Arsaces struggled to translate his words into Parthian for Ssu-ma Chao and his soldiers, who shifted from foot to foot, not in impatience but with increasing suspicion. Ganesha gestured with his hand, and the Persian looked up, astonished. Ssu-ma Chao barked laughter once, then fell silent too.

"Didn't you find it strange that they would use their stores when they had a chance at fresh water and grazing?"

Both Legionaries had to fight from shrugging. They had never lived so long and so closely with strangers from so many nations. To them, *anything* any of these people did was strange. "Then, the wind started to blow. A cloud covered the moon. And we heard hissing. . . ."

"We heard that before, the night you woke up, sir."

Outside Merv, when the fear of giant serpents had struck the entire camp. Quintus didn't need to know that Draupadi and Ganesha were leaning forward, as intent on the Legionaries' story as their officers.

"And so they ran, didn't they?" Lucilius drawled. He slipped past the first rank of armed men to run his eyes over Quintus's companions. They lit appreciatively at the sight of Draupadi. She caught his glance and looked aside.

"No, sir!" The denial came too fast, and, despite the differences in rank and status between them and a patrician tribune, too hotly.

"So you heard . . . what? What you thought were serpents? So you went quiet, with your swords ready, in case they got closer?"

Gaius had one hand on his breast, as if he reached for the comfort of some amulet. *Lad*, Quintus thought at the Legionary, who was not all that much younger than he, *I know just how you feel*. The man had begun to sweat, and whites showed all around the pupils of his eyes.

"The rustling . . . I'm from Arpinum, sir, and I've grown up around fields, and I've been in the desert, but this was worse . . . I mean louder than I have ever heard. It came between us and the . . . the merchants. I could see light . . . oh, a *black* light, if you see what I mean. And we could not move."

"I thought we were done for," Decimus interrupted. "Like a bird, staring at a big snake. Couldn't even shout for help, not that we'd have done so."

"It was like everything went away. Then the light went away, too. The rustling died, and the moon came out from behind the clouds. And they were gone, the wagons were. Not even cart tracks to show the path they'd taken."

Draupadi rose to her knees and bent over the water. She stretched out her hands to the right and left; and the water was still.

"Are these the ones whom you have lost?"

Figures moved in the shining depths, so clear that more than one man looked over his shoulder. Even Quintus, who had seen her illusions before, was tempted.

Surely, those carts, those beasts, those lean merchants with the faces of traitors—but so like in feature to the priest and priestess before him—had to be reflections of *something*.

She raised her head commandingly, gazing at the two guards. They nodded and looked away from her.

"We lost more of them," Quintus said. "When you brought us here . . ."

Murmurs rose at his back.

". . . Some of their party were missing. We thought the Yueh-chih had slain them, or they had taken their own way, betraying even their comrades."

"Ahhhhh, tribune, betrayal is ever the way of the Black Naacal."

Ganesha chuckled richly. "Do not fear here, warriors. This place is protected. When we came here, fleeing over-mountain, we expended our last strength in warding it. You saw the Naga, the snake with seven heads, as you approached."

"They could not pass," Ssu-ma Chao muttered. For an instant Quintus heard the nasal tones of Ch'in speech before the cultivated Latin of a noble officer replaced them. "They dared not. You are—what? Wizards, alchemists—or are you witches?"

Ssu-ma Chao drew steel on Ganesha and advanced, holding the tip of his blade at the man's throat.

"I will have the answer from you," he ordered. "Or I will cut it out of your treacherous throat."

"Another mistake," Ganesha said, even as Draupadi cried out. If she asked him to spare the old scribe's life, Quintus did not know if he could withstand her plea.

"You are afraid," the scribe said. "You know what I am, and I am not the first to travel in these lands which your Son of Heaven waters with the lives of his soldiers."

"You look like one of the beggar monks from the south and west. . . ."

"And truly, we have come from over the mountain."

"But . . ." Ssu-ma Chao jerked his head toward the priestess. "She is a great witch."

"She believes us!" One of the Roman guards ran toward Draupadi and hurled himself, forgetful of all discipline, at her feet. "She is a sybil, a prophetess. She knows I have not lied, my soul upon it!"

Rufus strode forward, grabbed the man by his tunic, and jerked him back. "Sir, I'd be inclined to say he believes that. Why else break ranks where I could see him? That's a brave man." He gave the Legionary a last shove. "That's for stepping out of formation, and there'll be more tonight. Remind me."

It was hard to laugh with a Ch'in noble's blade at one's throat: Ganesha managed it. If Ssu-ma Chao swapped off his head, would the scribe return as Quintus had seen him? A shadow, as of an elephant, seemed to shimmer on the stone behind him.

"Show the warrior, Draupadi. Quickly."

"Another brave man." Rufus, speaking out of turn.

Two of the patrician officers raised their brows at Rufus, who saluted offhandedly enough with his vine-staff that it was an insult. Quintus thought he didn't need Ganesha to interpret the centurion's thoughts. *Proconsul's dead, the old fox, and we're a long way from Rome, boys.*

"Let him go." Her words dropped into the crowd of anxious men like oil, calming turbulent waters. Once again, she held out her hands over the pool, where the images of wagons, frightened beasts, and Black Naacals had waited for her notice.

"Until all is made ready, there are limits on my strength. I had not known that others of their number had fled," she mused and knelt, staring into the water as the sun rose in the sky. Its flat surface glared like molten bronze, reflecting the great climbing disk and its rays, like a shrine to the ancient religion she and the scribe had claimed they served.

Only an eagle might look into the sun without being blinded.

"Lady," Quintus asked, "what of our Eagle? I see it flying to the West, even as the one we served heads east."

"The Eagle!" The woman clapped her hands in discovery.

Beneath them, as if a servant had been summoned, the water shifted. The image of the Black Naacals vanished. Replacing it came a picture of rammed-earth walls, a high tower from which soldiers in Ch'in uniform shot arrows while others built high a fire that smoked. Even as they watched, the men interrupted the billowing smoke.

"The fort at Miran!" Ssu-ma Chao cried. "Who would strike the Empire in the heart of the desert?"

"Those for whom the desert holds no fear," Draupadi said.

"These people claim they have enemies who can . . ."

"We do not *claim*, tribune," Ganesha cut in. "Should they gain the power they seek, the Black Naacals could wreak such devastation that the sandstorm you rode through to come here would look like a garden by comparison."

"My general! The Son of Heaven's town. What will become of them?" Ssu-ma Chao demanded.

Smoke swirled in the water that held the images of an embattled garrison. As they watched, a volley of arrows whined out and men, chariots, and carts retreated. Arrows and smoke from the tower persisted some while longer. Then, when the arrows ceased, the smoke billowed, covering the entire scene. It cleared and the tower lay in waste, thin smoke trailing up forlornly into the desert sky.

"And how do we know this is true?" Lucilius demanded, an instant behind Ssu-ma Chao.

"Draupadi," Ganesha asked. "Are you able?"

She held out a hand. For the first time, Quintus noticed the sweat on her brow, the deep circles—wider than made by any kohl—beneath her dark eyes.

The water shifted once again. When it cleared, it revealed an officer garbed similarly, but much more richly, to Ssu-ma Chao. But his cloak was torn. Padding gaped from his quilted tunic, and his scale armor was smeared. The tiny figure looked so real that when he shouted, Ch'in soldiers and Romans alike started, surprised that no sound emerged from his squared mouth.

"Not just anger," muttered Ssu-ma Chao. "If this one did not know better . . ."

"He has seen the face of a new kind of battle," Ganesha mused. "And he fears it. With reason."

Behind the Ch'in general rode his guard, with soldiers marching as fast as they could or driving the lumbering carts.

"Arjuna, I can hold no longer!" Draupadi cried. The illusion in the water vanished as her hands shook. She rose, almost falling.

Before he knew what he was doing, Quintus caught her and steadied her against his own body. For a moment, she relaxed into his hold. Her hair smelled of sandalwood, and the tribune was abruptly dizzy.

"*What* did she call him?" Ssu-ma Chao grimaced. Arsaces shook his head.

"Nice bit of work there," Lucilius observed. "What

will you do when she finds out you're not this whoever-he-is?"

"He is! He was!" Draupadi insisted.

"She has overspent her strength," Ganesha said. "A wise man, Vyasa, told me she was born of the very fire of Shiva, whose third eye will consume heaven and earth."

She was—*what?* Quintus thought. Now, she was shivering, and he drew her closer.

Her hands, with their gleaming nails, went up to clutch his armor. One lay over his heart, and he felt himself breathe as if he had been running.

"Arjuna, I tell you, you must do as you did before when you fought the hundred Kaurovas. Bow you have and sword, but you will need weapons of greater power. Claim them from all your lives—the Eagle in this one, Pasupata in your last!"

"She raves," Lucilius said. "Someone should restrain her—*not* as our good tribune is doing, though. Enjoying yourself, Quintus?"

"She is of Hind," Arsaces dared to contradict. "They say there that all men are reborn until, by doing good deeds, they escape the Wheel of Life."

"She's holy." Rufus pushed between Quintus and the other Romans. The two guards, Gaius and Decimus, nodded. "Like the sybils or pythonesses in the old stories."

Then, surprisingly, he blushed the color of roof tiles back in Italy.

"We must reinforce our general!" Ssu-ma Chao ordered. "Draw water, ready the carts, and let us be on our way!" He eyed Quintus.

"You know what *we* seek," he said.

"That is the prize of the Son of Heaven," the Ch'in officer said. "This one would promise it to you but you would know that for a . . . I do not want to lie to you,

Roman. We have fought well together. This one gives you his word that he will plead your case. When we arrive."

"You'll be safe enough here," Quintus found himself murmuring into Draupadi's ear.

"No! You will not leave me!"

"She won't, you know," Ganesha put in. "They know where we are now. And there are enough of them that we must no longer count on luck and illusions to defend ourselves.

"We go with you."

12

"Surely that's the Alai Valley." The sage who called himself Ganesha pointed at the land that lay far below the rocky point on which they stood, bracing themselves against the wind. He spoke as if he remembered.

"You remember too." Draupadi breathed. "You must remember how you came to the hills, searching for weapons. Searching for Pasupata."

That name struck the tribune's ear like the blast of a horn in battle. The sword—now that was a weapon that Quintus understood. And he had his sword, or he had the blade that, long ago, had been borne by this Arjuna whom Draupadi claimed as one of her five husbands. Arjuna, that very Mars of Hind, had visited the hills as a Greek might go to Delphi, in search of weapons to aid his family in a war that threatened to engulf the world.

Hard to believe that that Draupadi of legend was the same woman who stood here, amber robes concealed beneath heavy sheepskins, sandalwood fragrances obscured by smoke and the womanscent that made him wake at night and station one of the older Legionaries near where she slept. But it was hard to believe that that woman was mad.

If Draupadi spoke truth and not the illusions that were her great skill, Quintus too might face such a war. He had Arjuna's sword. But Arjuna had been a master of the bow; and bows Quintus knew chiefly as a weapon of the Parthians that had already cost him more than he had to give. But, again, if Draupadi and Ganesha spoke truth, the Parthians were no longer his problem, save as the Black Naacals might use them—or any other people—as pawns.

And meanwhile, the rocks themselves could prove enemy enough.

Quintus took a deep breath of the mountain air. Still cold, still sharp; but the knives that had seemed to stab at his chest during the highest part of the climb had long been sheathed. They had made the crossing—up from the stone and water sanctuary to which they had fled in the belly of a sandstorm and into the high hills Arsaces called *bam i dunya*, the Roof of the World. If, as he said, this route took them merely over the foothills, Quintus had no desire to see the true mountains.

He could never quite remember at what point the narrow path levelled out. At one moment, it seemed as if he had always been climbing, edging precariously past bundles and packs that had been torn away from the drying bones of beasts and men who had fallen behind their caravans and lacked the strength or will to go on.

For worse hills there were—mountains whose very names referred to their peril. There were the Killers of Hindus, named for the countless lives of those they had frozen or cast down or starved when men who looked enough like Draupadi to be her close kin tried to cross them from Hind. Those fortunate enough to survive that crossing ventured then across the desert into what even Romans had heard of as Serica, the lands of silk. And then there were the Heavenly Mountains, which people roundabout called the Onion Mountains. Harmless things, onions—a part of any Legionary's or any farmer's diet as long as fresh supplies came—except that the onions in this part of the world were commonly held to poison travellers. How else to explain the giddiness, the shortness of breath, the suddenness with which some men collapsed and died even below the peaks? Hannibal and his beasts, Quintus thought, would never have dared these heights.

None of Ssu-ma Chao's men had died in the hills and very few had faltered; but then they had made this climb before, when they had come west to Parthia—An'Hsi as they called it—from their own lands. The Romans, well, Marius's mules had trudged along. There had been a small revolt when they had sought to lighten their packs by loading the heaviest items on the beasts. For the worst climbs, Quintus had weighed the breach in discipline with the possibility that more lightly burdened men had a better chance of life—and had chosen for life.

But he still mourned the loss of three Romans. One soldier simply failed to wake up in the pallid mountain dawn. Another fell to his knees in a high pass, then cooled before he could even clasp a friend's hand in farewell. *His heart burst*, Ganesha said. And one had been dragged off a cliff when the pack animal he was leading panicked, thrashed until he was caught in its harness, and fell before he could cut himself free. A brave man, he had refused to scream as he fell. Even the Ch'in had mourned him.

Of course, Lucilius had thrived. Quintus hated himself for the unworthiness of that thought. The patrician's lips had cracked from the cold. His hands had turned white, then healed and hardened without the blackening and sloughing off of rotten flesh that could kill as surely as a rockfall in these heights. The ladies of the Palatine Hill would never recognize in this wiry, weary man, wrapped in every warm garment he owned or could dice for, the aristocrat in his white toga with the broad purple stripe. Just as well. They were unlikely to see one another, ever again. In a way that was just, as the lady Draupadi had taught him to look upon the just—hadn't Lucilius wanted to journey to the land of silk? He was making the trip—if not in the manner or the company he expected.

And then there was Draupadi herself. Wrapped in sheepskins and her amber robes, a fold of them pulled up to warm her breath, she made the climb with even less difficulty than the Ch'in or Arsaces, who had survived it before. From time to time, she rested when the rest of the caravan did, but always, her hand was out to support Ganesha (who waved it off with some disdain) or to encourage a man who might falter. Seeing her, a woman and obviously no Amazon, they took renewed heart as they climbed.

Mistress of illusions she might be but she had done nothing to ease the journey. Lucilius had taxed her with that once, and she had glanced away.

"The hardships of the mountains are like pain to the body," she murmured, feeding the small fire with a niggardly cake of dung. "They are given you as warnings so you do not exceed your strength."

Or what a madwoman might think that strength to be.

Her eyes met those of Quintus, who had struggled to conceal his fear for her and his admiration of her hardihood. *Do you recall how, when the king your brother lost all at dice, we lived in the wilderness?*

She had told him that story one night. So vivid was her retelling as the wind whined about them, nosing at the fire they had all but buried in its own pit, that now he didn't know whether he remembered those years of living wild as if they had really happened or from her account of them.

Once again, memory oppressed him. The air was very thin on the Roof of the World. What air there was tasted like wine in the throat. During the long, cold nights, memories, dreams, and illusions danced in his mind like the tiny bronze figure he still carried against his heart. Since they left the sanctuary, it had not alerted him to any dangers beyond the perils of the journey. And he had seen no signs of wagons or beasts or anything else that might reveal a trace of the Black Naacals.

Ssu-ma Chao came up beside the younger tribune.

"Do you see the Tower?" he asked, pointing down and across the valley.

Incredibly, there were birds flying *beneath* them. Quintus tore his eyes from that marvel to follow where the Ch'in officer pointed. On the valley floor, what looked like a rock outcropping jutted up, as if it had been an ashlar left behind while the gods were building the Roof of the World. And toward it, tiny figures trudged, file after file, the humans specks where they marched alongside their beasts.

"The Stone Tower," Ssu-ma Chao explained. "When the Son of Heaven Han Wu-ti—" scarred fingers sketched a gesture that resembled a prostration, "—first sent armies past the Jade Gate and out into the Land of Fire, and they took it on their way to An'Hsi, the men of Han built that."

Quintus studied the Stone Tower. A legion of engineers, much less armed men so far from his home, could not have built that tower had they labored on it from the two generations between Wu-ti's time and this of the current Emperor, Han Yuan-ti. It was half in ruins, assailed repeatedly as it had been by Ch'in and Parthian, Hsiung-nu, Saka, and Yueh-chih. He had seen tombs like that in his own country. His bronze statue—Krishna? however he had come there—had been found in such a place.

"It looks older than that," was all he said.

Ssu-ma Chao nodded. "We built it on a ruin that we found. We think it must always have been used as a trade site, the last before Su-le."

Su-le . . . once again, they were out of Quintus's reckoning. Ganesha had spoken of the trade town of Kacha. He wondered if it were the same as the Kasia, or Kashgar, mentioned so long ago outside the walls of Carrhae by the most adventurous of the Greeks Quintus had huddled with after the defeat.

His eyes grew used to the distances. Viewed from here, the Stone Tower did not seem that far away. But he knew it might take days to reach it and weeks more to reach this Su-le, or Kashgar, or whatever they called it, on the edge of the true desert.

At the very limits of his vision, the horizon shimmered. Down, down, always down into the waste and then down beyond it into the amphitheatre that was the Land of Fire, a desolation of salt flats and gravel and twisting dunes. Some said that a river wound through its depths to a pool at its heart. Hard to believe, but Quintus thought of the sanctuary that he and his men had received, with wonder lying at heart.

It might be possible once again. And then again, the

heart might be rotten, if the Black Naacals reached it first. He reached out, trying to *sense* any danger. Almost, he laughed. He was a Roman, not a magus, and certainly not this hero-god that Draupadi called him. This Arjuna. Had *he* been Arjuna, he would not have shared such a woman with his brothers, he thought suddenly.

Then he shook his head. Folly to even think so of her.

He had other problems. Such as what might befall him and his men at the Stone Tower. Or at Su-le.

As if on command, Ssu-ma Chao spoke. "This one regrets . . ." The formality that had been lost in battle, sandstorm, and mountain pass had returned.

"You regret what?" So it was over, now that they neared the *limes,* the borders of the Ch'in Empire, and Ssu-ma Chao approached the network of forts, officers, and reports that any nation must have. Compared with that, compared with whatever oaths the Ch'in officer had spoken, what was the deepening partnership between Roman and Ch'in?

Still, might as well make him say it straight out.

"When we reach Su-le . . . there is a garrison there. And reports go out, to the four Commands of the West and the Commandery at Wu-liang by the Jade Gate."

Ssu-ma Chao would not wish it known to these personages that he owed his life and the lives of his command to the human tribute they had taken in An'Hsi from the Parthians. Naturally not. Quintus wondered briefly what was contained in the ink scratching upon narrow wood strips that he had seen, once or twice, as the officer prepared them.

"It is different, so many thousands of *li* from Ch'ang-an," said the Ch'in aristocrat. "But as I hope to return to the home of my ancestors . . ."

They would confiscate the Romans' weapons once

again. And the relationship of equals that had begun to grow between the men of Ch'in and the Legions would fade away.

The gods only knew what would become of them. It might be that they would come to envy the men who had been enslaved at Merv. They were in the hands of Fortune. And they had not yet reached Su-le. Much could happen. Once again, he tried to see ahead, tried to *sense* what might happen.

Nothing. No sense of impending danger. No sense, even of power. *Gods send it that the Black Naacals perished on the heights,* he thought, flinching briefly from the deaths he had seen in the mountains.

And knew it for a prayer that would not be granted.

13

"I WILL BE left alone!"

Draupadi had flung aside the sheepskins she had worn in the heights and strode away from the throng of barbarians who troubled her. There were too many people, eyes and voices; they pressed against her awareness after so long in sanctuary, with only Ganesha, the waters, the trees, and the ageless crests of the mountains for companionship.

Ageless, Draupadi? You have seen mountains fall.

A shout—"Don't go alone!"—had followed her, angering her still further. Not Ganesha: After this long, she knew him well enough to know he wandered back and forth, from the men of gold to the men of the West, practicing these new tongues, making notes for one of his endless histories on their ways, their gear, their looks.

Now, she stood on a ledge, surveying the valley. The caravan had drawn nearer the Stone Tower—but it was still quite a journey away.

Don't go alone! As if her illusions would not speedily convince a snow leopard or a serpent to turn aside! He should know that! Draupadi stamped a foot. Or if he thought she was so feeble, why did Arjuna not come with her? Even now, even this far from their shared past, his eyes followed her as they had when he won her in tournament and brought her back to be wife to him and his four brothers, one of them a king. And before that . . . he had been the bravest of them, the most loyal to his duty.

If his duty demanded him to shout "Don't go alone," rather than come with her, she would walk alone. She had lived in the wilderness. She had survived war. But now, Draupadi was not sure she cared to be alone. Arjuna's were not the only eyes that followed her. There was that other officer, the fair-haired one, who bore himself as if he ruled a city. His smiles made her want to wish for a dagger. She was glad that the men she had marked as being the most trustworthy did not trust *him* at their backs, nobleborn though he claimed to be. *His* eyes followed her as if she were a pastime to be enjoyed, then tossed aside like a game of dice.

Dice, in her family, had always cost her too dearly. Her eldest husband had thrown away palaces and kingdom for it—and ultimately herself. She did not trust dice, nor this man who bore himself like a skilled gambler.

All her long life, she had been a mistress of illusion. What if she showed him a few truths? He would flee in loathing.

She held out her hands. Smooth, unstained, unwrinkled, though hardened from the rigors of her recent journey. Draupadi had learned her lessons well, hadn't she? After all these years, she still looked—no, she was no longer the slender girl who had slipped from cell to library of the Temple school in the city by the shore and through the inner passages to share her fears with Ganesha and the other students she had trusted.

Since then, since the city fell and the sea shrank back into the earth, Draupadi had seen herself mirrored in the water of sea or fountain, in silver, in the metal of shields *in all the years of my exile*.

Leaving the valley of her sanctuary, looking down upon a place that bore a name she knew had suddenly made those years sink upon her like a burden. Astonishing that they were not reflected in her face—as she saw it in Arjuna's eyes. She knew he was called Quintus in this place and time. She knew that his name meant "five." The fifth son, perhaps. Or, in his case, the avatar of her five husbands. He was so different. As reserved as the twins, he was: It was hard to see in him the kingliness of one of the brothers, the fighting heart of another. *Arjuna himself had been a quiet man*, she reassured herself. Like Arjuna, this man had suffered, had lost much, had wandered far. Unlike him, though, he had never been acclaimed.

So different—and yet she had known him the instant he strode onto the tiny island of her refuge.

So far they had travelled apart. Please all the gods that they could join together.

A saffron drift of dust cleared away, like a fading spell of illusion, and Draupadi stared down at the Stone Tower. It was closer than it had been after days of necessarily slow downhill travel, but still far away. Years ago, so many years ago—she wished she had Ganesha's memories or, failing them, the scrolls he had left in their retreat, to remind her.

Had the Stone Tower always looked out upon dry lands? She rather thought so: The basin in which she had spent the first part of her life lay far beyond the town called Su-le by the golden-skinned warriors she travelled among. She remembered it as a town near the shore, its breezes rich and wet, refreshing as the grapes that grew on the slopes and near the towns that surrounded a long-gone sea.

How long had it been? Even the dances of the stars had changed!

The wind blew. Again, dust rose. Draupadi smelled dung, some crushed greens, the smoke of a fire, the wildness of true desert, with salt underlying it, the salt of a sea that had lapped its shores when the patterns of the stars overhead were very, very different.

She shut her eyes, casting her thoughts as far back as she could. If she thought of the night sky, she knew what stars she would see, and in what ordered dances. Now, memory was easier: the blue of the sea between snow-capped mountain ranges; towns with tile roofs and thick-walled buildings, temple walls and towers overshadowing them, shining with pure light to guide the slim, graceful ships to harbor, heavy with the treasures they carried. She saw the Naacals in the Temple worshipping the flame as an embodiment of the flame of pure thought, a reflection of the Mind and time beyond all worlds. She saw her own cell in that Temple and felt the hopes and growing power of the young student she had been.

Ganesha would remember better than she. Her skill had been mainly with the spinning of illusions. A humble choice, and there were those in the Temple who had hoped to guide her toward greater skill. But she had never been troubled overmuch by pride in those serene days when sunlight shone on the Inland Sea.

There had been so many worthier students in those days. So many fine men and women. All young, save for Ganesha, who had taught them. Strong or stronger than they had believed.

Some said that the Naacals' teachings in such temples

were themselves illusions as the crafts she wrought at feasts. They believed that beneath the light, the thought, lurked another truth, and that truth dark. Just as great fish leapt upon the surface of the sea to rescue the occasional sailor, such people said other creatures lurked in its depth to swallow the unwary and, ultimately, to swallow all. Such were the Black Naacals, who saw life as a feast of such creatures, writ large and dread upon the pages of the world, and who saw a share of that feast as the best that they might gain.

Even a practitioner of illusion could see how such a belief would turn treason into necessity, if a Black Naacal wished to be feaster and not fast. She had not, she thought, the strength to withstand them: How should she, when what she made faded? The mastery of true change lay lifetimes away—time that she was grateful to be permitted to spend in study. She had had—what was it they said in these days? *All the time in the worlds?* Ganesha, to whom she brought her fears, had told her so, and she had trusted him.

Where could I have gone right? She had not been believed at first. Ganesha had his scrolls, his studies. Seeing patterns in the stars as in the land, he had not seen this new threat. *In all these years,* Draupadi thought, *he has kept his memory unclouded.* Was that his punishment?

She had realized that for the first time—in so many years—when he looked down about the valley and named it. As the very stars had circled into new patterns, they had mercifully forgotten . . . forgotten much. He had forgotten nothing, not even consciousness of the errors he had made.

She too had forgotten in those years of exile. But she had not forgotten her illusions. If she dropped them, she wondered, would they show a woman as far beyond a

crone in age and looks as a bone buried deep in the rock
is beyond a living creature? She laughed angrily. This
creature of an instant, who called himself Lucilius and
bore himself like a prince, would flee from her—

And what of Arjuna? In this body, he barely remembered even his name, like a word spoken in the ear of a
dreaming man.

Ah, they had travelled so long down different roads,
even long after the glory of Mu was swallowed with the
Inmost Sea.

Memory, as unwelcome as Ganesha's, struck, and she
sank to her knees. She gazed out at the Stone Tower, but
saw a gentler, richer—and far older—land instead.

For all of them, life had seemed very sweet in the
palaces, in the sunlit towns by that Inmost Sea—until the
Black Naacals' greed broke all asunder. They no longer
wished to wait for their feast: They wished it now, and
they sought ways of binding man and earth and water to
their will.

Clouds hid the sun, lit only by lightning with never a
drop of rain. The hills shook; they cracked; smoke and
molten rock rolled down their slopes. The very seabeds
trembled, and great waves began to pound the harbor.
Ganesha might have been resigned: He had collected the
wisdom of many lives already, and would be quite content to add his light to the eternal flame. Still, she knew,
he could be enticed by his love of knowledge—and his
love of his students. They were still so young, with the
tales of many lives yet to come. In the end, Ganesha's
compassion conquered his resignation, and he taught his
students one last set of lessons: survival.

The students prepared: boats, food, weapons, and a
clear passage to escape. And Draupadi spun the illusions
that would let them reach the harbor.

After a week of darkness even at noon, the thunder pealed: as above, so below. The earth rumbled and, with a roar, the sea rushed in to devour the cities that had claimed it as their tributary. Their ship had sailed until the wind had stripped the cloth from its masts, and then those aboard had turned the very force of their minds to keep their course. To the mountains of the west, always west, while the waves roiled about them and Draupadi lashed herself to a mast, singing illusions to keep the creatures at the deep from swallowing her ship along with the other fugitives.

"Draupadi?" The smooth voice stumbled over the syllables of her name. It was the one called Lucilius. Perhaps if she pretended not to hear him, he would go away. It was not worth turning from her memories to squander an illusion on him.

She had known that her fellow students, her teacher, and she would pay a dire price for their flight. By what right did they survive their motherland?

The right of a beast, seeking to survive at all costs? If that were the reason, the price would be beyond bearing. But what if they sought to preserve wisdom against future need as they told themselves they did? How they survived their ordeal would tell them whether they spoke the truth or not.

And then it began. As the seabeds cracked and the sea itself drained away into the depths of the earth, the reckoning came due. They floated till there was no more water. Then, abandoning the ship, they set out on foot through the muck of the seabed, then through what dried into the salt and rock of a desolation such as not even Ganesha ever imagined.

"Lady? Draupadi!"

That one dared to make demands when she was meditating! She turned her shoulder on the young Roman, and then her back, sinking deeper into contemplation of her memories.

There was the night that one of the students had disappeared—he who had been their guide and watchman. Ganesha was old. She had no warrior's training. They held the others back, but the others sustained her and Ganesha as they trudged toward the hills.

"Leave us," she had whispered.

"We are bound."

An old man and a weak woman, and five strong men who might have a chance to live, were they not burdened. It was not even a choice; Draupadi stripped herself of her remaining strength to cast what she hoped would be the greatest of her illusions: *We are dead; go on without us; remember us gently.*

And so they had, those five men. But they had been right. They had all been bound. And thus, in the twists and dances of time, they had met over and over again. As they did now. But five in one, rather than five brothers? Surely that betokened some change in the patterns of things.

"You should not be here alone." Lucilius dared to lay a hand upon Draupadi's shoulder. She could feel the heat of his fingers circling the joint, stroking down her arm, and pulled away.

"So your officer said," she told him, watching him sidelong.

"That garlic-scented rustic?" Lucilius barked a laugh lacking pleasure or true mirth. "Some senator's errand boy, rather, allowed into the Legion instead of starving like the son of a traitor that he is!"

Draupadi tossed her head. Let him see that she was displeased. It was not like the time that Dushassana had sought to enslave her and strip her, even though she had cried out that she was in the midst of her courses. Nor like the time she had served in a king's court as a serving woman.

She had come far in time and place. She could ignore what she chose.

Ganesha and she had lain in the drying salt and grit of what had been the seabed, dying, as they thought, without hope of rebirth. Her mind had wandered far; Ganesha's, she thought, had journeyed farther yet.

"They will survive," he told her. *"They will prevail. Do not weep, my daughter, for we shall surely meet them again."*

But her head drooped and illusions stranger than any she had seen danced before her eyes.

Then the Flame appeared. Surely it was right to hide one's eyes from a thing that holy; surely it was right to look away lest she be blinded. Neither she nor Ganesha could do aught but kneel before it. They had feared; they had faltered; and for that, there would be payment. But where they had loved and trusted greatly, that payment would not be beyond them. And they would live.

"And I say you will look at me when I speak to you, seeress or woman or whatever you are!" Lucilius's voice was angry, demanding now.

What did this creature of less than an instant, who dared to touch her, know of such a life?

How long it had taken her and Ganesha to make their way past the mountains and to the homes of living people! How much longer to make themselves places of respect? Illusion wrapped her about: the splendor of fabrics embroidered with gems, the scent of sandalwood and cardamom, the allure of eyes circled with kohl, and fingers tipped with red.

Old she thought she must be, and tried to dispel the

illusion that created beauty of such age. *And they would live.* It was no illusion. The Flame had seen to that.

How Arjuna had smiled the day he had won her! Over all the princes of the earth, he had triumphed. And, as the conch shells blew, he claimed her, and she saw a man whom she remembered in his eyes, though he wore the flesh of a son of these hills. He brought her home to the Pandavas—his mother Kunti and his four brothers. She remembered them too—reborn as many times as they must have been.

In Mu, their minds had joined. Now their bodies joined, too; she had companied with them in palaces and in wilderness until that age ended. They had decided, she recalled, to leave the world, to return to the hills that Arjuna had loved. But the hills had trembled, and they had fallen, one by one.

They had fallen far. She woke in tranquillity, sunlight and water playing about her. Again, she and Ganesha were alone.

"You might listen when a man talks," said Lucilius. "I could make it worth your while."

Finally, she turned and looked at the westerner. Fair hair, pale eyes, skin that was weathered, but that otherwise would have been pale: No, there was nothing there for her. And the look on his face—as if he needed only to put out his hand.

On the mountain heights, he could ignore her presence because of the peril of the journey. Now, once again, she saw the expression she had seen in sanctuary—a hunter sure of his prey. He put out his hand again and touched her, not as if he had a right but as if whether he had such a right or not did not matter.

Eyes and lewd hands had followed her at Virata's court when she had been disguised as a serving girl and her husbands

as a cook, a dancing teacher, a gambler . . . and Kitchaka the
general, most of all, had pursued her. He had even caught her
and held her, a knife to her throat. She had pleaded with him
for a later assignation, which he had granted.

Then she had realized how, stripped of power,
stripped of rank, separated from the others with whom
she had come down the ages, she was powerless. Then,
she had run to seek help.

Now, she cried out wordlessly in anger and slapped him.

And was surprised by the rage that flashed in his
green eyes, like a predator caught in torchlight.

"You dare strike me, a patrician of the Lucilian
gens. . . . I suppose you prefer that ploughboy who's
got the stink of the armies on top of the stink of the
fields. . . ."

Again, he had her by the arm but her own rage, just
as much as his grip, was making her shake. She tried to
breathe deeply, to wish calm on herself, and to look into
this one's eyes seeking understanding.

She saw pride of family without obligation; greed—a
desire to possess, never mind how, and especially if his
own possession meant that his enemies went without;
anger at being checked by anyone, anything—since he
truly considered only those in a position to help him or to
order him to be human—whom he had not considered as
more than a convenience. She saw contrivance for its
own sake, with little guile and less skill; worse yet, she
saw the potential that might have made him a man and
a warrior, but had, for reasons she could not understand,
gone sour. Worse yet, she perceived that he knew he had
failed, somehow, of that considerable promise.

How could he live with the horror he was becoming? If they
were in the sanctuary, she would not lack for water to
form a mirror sufficient to show himself to himself. She

could manage without. She raised a hand to gesture, to begin the first of the illusion spells that might tell him what he was becoming.

"You would claw my eyes, would you?" He shoved her to the ground. "I should mark you."

It was Virata's court all over again. Submit or be marked. Fight, or accept the self-contempt that yielding brought. Die nobly, perhaps, when every nerve in her body cried out to live until better times came.

He was bending over her, had a knee between her legs. She cried out and struggled furiously. Nails scratched and gritted in the rocky ground, the hobnails of the footgear that Quintus/Arjuna wore in this guise.

"Don't we have enough trouble, Lucilius, without you trying to hurt one of our guides? With the Ch'in watching. They already think we're barbarians."

"Native women, ploughboy. They don't know their place."

"Draupadi's no camp follower, *tribune*. It's not your place to teach her anything."

Behind Quintus she could hear other footsteps. She wanted to shout with embarrassment. She should have foreseen this. And Quintus had told her not to go by herself: Had *he* foreseen?

"You don't order me, ploughboy. Why don't you bow? Scrape for me like the client you are. Call me 'Dominus'—as you called my uncle when you licked his feet on the Palatine!"

The dark-haired tribune pushed Lucilius away from Draupadi, gave him one shrewd shove; the lighter man went sprawling. There was satisfaction on Quintus's face as he faced a man who had been his enemy for years.

Lucilius sprang to his feet in a fighting crouch.

Draupadi saw Quintus begin to lurch forward—*she*

*had seen Arjuna throw his brothers in practice thus a thousand
times.* But this was not practice. Their people were strangers here. That they were not prisoners was only by the
grace of the Ch'in, who guarded them. Let them fight, and
they would lose all that they had gained.

And so would she and Ganesha, who required their aid.

"Sir, sirs! Stop it! Break it up!"

It was the older one, the one with hair like burning
coals, angry red frosted with gray. He seized Quintus/
Arjuna and held him.

"You want *them* to see the two of you brawling?" he
warned. "What do you think they'll do if they see you at
each other's throats? Might as well—both of you fools—
turn in your weapons now to the yellow-skins. Go ahead.
Yes, I know. You're tribunes. I'm just a centurion. Spent
my life in the Legions. Call out the men. Tell them to get
ready. Go ahead and punish me."

He looked upslope. The Ch'in commander had come
out, drawn by the shouts and the scuffle. Shaking his
head *no danger,* Quintus reassured the man.

Did he lie, though?

The three men glared at each other. Let them *all* fight,
and they all would lose everything. Draupadi shook her
head, remembering the last time. She had run to Bhima,
burliest and fiercest of the brothers. Working, incongruously, as a cook. He had scented and silked himself and
taken her place in the General's bed. When Kitchaka
attempted to embrace what he thought was a frightened
woman, Bhima had taken him in a wrestler's hold and
squeezed until only a ball of flesh, wrapped in sagging,
gaudy, and ruined silks, was left.

How shocked Virata's court had been. And how she
had laughed!

Once again, Draupadi laughed. She scrambled to her

feet and gestured—and the crushed ball that had been her assailant materialized before Lucilius's eyes.

"Is that what you want?" she demanded. "It was the fate of the last man who touched me."

Lucilius backed up a step, but only one: She would give him credit for that.

But for nothing else.

"You do not want me. You want power to enforce your will. And you take power as you see it—like this!"

Another gesture, and her hands filled with gold . . . ringing metal rounds that she hurled at the Roman aristocrat's feet. He was scrabbling in the dust for them when she clapped her hands; the coins changed from cold hard metal into chips of scarce-dried dung.

The tribune flung the chips from him, his mouth twisting in revulsion. Rufus roared with laughter. Quintus took the opportunity to break loose from his grasp. His mouth worked, and then he too laughed. A moment later, the Ch'in soldiers had neared. Draupadi heard Ganesha speaking to them in their own language—some version of the truth, she assumed. They too laughed, and the echoes spread out across the horizon until it seemed that they would reverberate off the Stone Tower far below.

She herself, however, kept face and voice severe. "I am not some follower of camp and soldiers, to be taken up, used, and cast away. Do you need another lesson?" she demanded.

Quintus smiled at her. "Lady, you need no man's protection."

Then he turned to Lucilius. "Maybe we can't roll you into a ball, but I promise you, if you ever again approach Draupadi or any woman in this caravan, I will *try*. Is that clear?"

Cleaning his hands, his face scarlet at the laughter that welled up around him, echoing, as it seemed, almost as far as the Stone Tower, Lucilius nodded, then left. Though he took care to keep his back straight and his steps measured, almost as if he marched, it had the impact of a rout.

"There will be consequences of this action, daughter," Ganesha told Draupadi. Bending laboriously, he picked up something from the ground. It was a gold coin.

"As always now," Ganesha added, "you wrought better than you knew."

She had meant those coins as illusions, shifting form and aspect for the sake of confusing her enemy. She had wrought better than she knew. The young girl who had been a scholar woke in her once more. She lifted her hand to take the coin . . .

. . . and from down in the valley, as if borne in response to their laughter, came the chanting of a mantra. Each tone in the incantation quivered with menace. And replying to it came a wail of pure fear.

14

Mists rose as if upborne by the force of mantra chanting and screams—mists in a land so seldom touched by moisture that even the white glint of salt mimicked natural rock. The coils of thickened moisture filled the valley, concealing the Stone Tower. Lazily, they wafted upward, licking at the higher rocks. Though they cloaked now what lay below, they did not deaden the clatter of falling stones, first singly, then in a cascade. The ground trembled in a dreadful warning.

"We have to get down!"

Romans and Ch'in soldiers alike grabbed for handholds. Then, they fought to harness frightened, plunging beasts, to snatch up baggage. . . .

"You cannot reach them in time!" Quintus shouted at Ssu-ma Chao in Parthian.

"Those are our people down there! We have to try!"

Quintus surveyed the mists. He had survived demon storms, but this was no such thing. Not sand, but vapor rose to engulf them. In his boyhood, he had seen such mists rise from the Tiber, bearing fevers with them. Almost he thought that he could smell water—not a river, but a sea: wet, cold, alien in this land of deserts.

Again, the earth shuddered underfoot. Now came the wild screams of panicking animals. The Romans, blessed—or cursed—with pride, cloaked their fear with curses as they fought to pack (but a few prayers rose with the oaths). The Ch'in pleas for protection were as shrill as the cries of the beasts.

Like his men, Quintus swore. *Damn* all cumbersome Ch'in armies to the cross or the fires of Acheron! So much easier with Marius's mules, to pack up and—ahhhhh, there went Rufus, taking a much-needed part in making those crying barbarians *move!*

"Load up, you mules! Do Marius proud—who knows, maybe he's watching you! We're getting out of here." Legionaries bore their kit, too much lightened now, but still a burden, on their backs. It let them break camp quickly and move without the complex impediment of baggage trains (unless, gods look kindly on him, you were Crassus) such as these easterners had dragged across mountains and desert. It would not help, Quintus thought, if the mountainside peeled away and they were sent hurtling. He had a sudden, nightmare vision of a Roman lying broken on his back in the shattered frame of his pack, kicking feebly, briefly, like a beetle before sandals crushed the life from it.

No time for that, man. Take Draupadi, be sure of her safety—if he could. He grabbed her by the elbow, pushed her roughly toward Ganesha. "You two! Join the others. Keep up and keep safe!"

A foolish command, and he knew it.

The woman clung to the old sage, her eyes wide, but not with fear. Why should she fear? After all, hadn't she lived through worse . . . many times, if he could believe the tales she told? To his astonishment, he realized what shone in her eyes was courage and reassurance for him. He wanted—gods, he wanted—to promise her she would never again face such an ordeal, to hold her and touch her face.

Once again, the earth shuddered. Not far from where they were working their way down, a chunk fell off the ledge.

"Get back! Now!"

Quintus ran with the others. And as his breath sobbed and stabbed in his chest, memory overtook him.

. . . In Virata's court, he had been useless. Worse than that, he had been a laughingstock, and his brother the king, the hapless player of dice, had been a gambler who couldn't lose. But he, Arjuna, the champion of that Yuga or any other age, had been a dancing master. No, worse: dressed as a woman, cossetted by the royal ladies, and consulted about brocades and paints as well as the placement of hands and feet in the ancient dances. He had not been able to shield Draupadi then either. . . .

He ran toward his own kit, propelling the woman and the old man before him. Shouldering into his gear with the ease of long practice, he jogged toward where the others had formed up. Even Lucilius was ready, his gambler's eyes glistening with appreciation of the danger.

"They're screaming down there," someone remarked. "The wind brings up the sound."

"You think there's enough of us to take them?" Lucilius asked.

Quintus's eyes flickered from the Romans to the Ch'in soldiers. Were they all ready? Could they finally move, please all the gods? Damn all, why not *abandon* that stupid chariot!

Because it is like an Eagle to the Ch'in, the answer came swiftly to his mind.

Those of the Legion were ready. Rufus had barely had to use his vinestaff. The Ch'in, though . . . Ssu-ma Chao, heedless of his dignity, was harnessing his own beasts. His eyes swept over the Romans and his sallow face sagged.

Easy enough for those now to abandon the Ch'in. Lighter armed, lighter equipped, they could flee, leaving the men they had marched with to whatever hazards the mountains threatened as the earth threatened to burst asunder. Maybe they could double back later and, if the Ch'in were not already dead, prepare an ambush. . . .

"Let's move," Lucilius muttered, his fingers tapping against his sword.

"We wait for our comrades."

Rufus swore under his breath, but he had been swearing steadily since the first tremors: Quintus ignored him.

"We are ready," came Draupadi's voice. Ganesha, steadier than the rock that still upheld them, eyed the Romans and the Ch'in.

If he was deciding with whom to cast his lot, Quintus thought, he might die right there from the betrayal.

He caught just such a speculative gleam in Lucilius's face. The Romans were ready; let them claim their Eagle and flee west. Assuming the mountains did not rise and crush them for their betrayal—as well as their cowardice in surviving Carrhae. And the abandonment of their Eagle.

For an instant, Quintus felt the weight of an Eagle against arm and shoulder. Go without winning that, and they were no Legion—but a rabble of defeated men. True, it wasn't as if the Ch'in really were federates, allies. They had bought them, imprisoned them, and Ssu-ma Chao was taking them as captives to his Emperor as if they were strange beasts intended to deck a Triumph—if they lived that long.

But the Easterner had treated them as comrades, had returned some of their battered dignity to them with their weapons. He had let them—let Quintus—redeem some of the honor he felt he had forfeited by their defeat.

"The Eagle ahead—where—we cannot get it!" Lucilius whispered it, intent as he had been moments before on the pursuit of Draupadi. His hands flexed and cupped as if closing on a woman's breast.

"Are we men or runaway slaves?" Quintus spat.

Lucilius spared him a twisted grin.

Surely, he wanted the Eagle, yes, and his freedom. Well, Quintus wanted his freedom, even if he wasted it in a vain bid to return to Rome.

But not at the cost of betrayal. Not after he himself had been betrayed so many times. The Eagle itself would lift from its bronze perch above the SPQR and stoop to rend a man guilty of that disloyalty.

"Help them! We go together or no one moves at all!"

Ssu-ma Chao's weary face lit with a relief that had nothing to do with temporary freedom from the racking earth tremors. Rufus headed toward the plunging beasts. Sweat from their fear lathered them despite the cold and the high altitudes and the swearing men attempting to manhandle the chariot down the side of a shaky hill. But he paused to clap Quintus on the shoulder—a liberty Quintus took as an honor. Ganesha, before gliding down the path with more composure than any of the younger men showed, nodded gravely in tribute.

The horse Ssu-ma Chao had saddled plunged and reared. Quintus moved to reassure it with words and actions he had used a thousand times on his farm. This decision would cut him off once again from his home, his grandfather's bones, and everything he had dreamed of winning back.

Except himself. He felt warm despite the heights, sure despite the fear of the earth tremors and whatever damnable slaughter was going on far below. He had seldom felt such confidence, except of course the rare times his grandsire had praised him.

He and the Ch'in officer slammed a packsaddle onto the last beast, trying simultaneously to soothe and subdue it. Once more, the earth shook. Rocks shivered loose from the peaks and rained down among them as if shot from some Titan's catapult. Two men screamed, but their screams were cut sharply as rock blotted them from sight.

"Forgive, forgive this turtle's pace. . . . They are dying down there and I fail them, I fail my brothers. . . ." Ssu-ma Chao would be weeping in a moment, and then there really would be Charon to pay.

All day they stood in the hot sun with no water. The lucky ones were those who had died early, a Parthian arrow in their eyes or hearts.

But now they were ready. Perhaps they could stop *this* slaughter.

"MARCH!" Rufus shouted, a cracked shout that surely cost him lung pain in these heights. Roman and Ch'in picked their way down the trembling path. The mountain labored, as that old Greek slave had said, and gave birth to a mouse. But not here. Not here. For what prodigy did this rumbling serve as the midwife?

Probably Orcus himself, Quintus thought. They would all be cast down into Hades without coin enough to pay the ferryman. At least, with the rocks tumbling about, they would not have to worry about burial.

Do not speak to me of death, a voice whispered in his

head. It hissed like wind across sand. *They are dead on the road below. You may come there if you can. You may bury their bodies, if you choose, just as you have the choice to waste your lives. . . . These are not your people . . . not your land . . . not your battle. . . . Why do you fear a brutish death when you face life as a slave? In Roma the slaves themselves rebelled against their lives.*

Lick my sandals, Lucilius had added.

Watch that boulder. . . . Quintus sought safer footing, guided a man's hand to a more secure handhold. *His grandsire had bent his back and slashed his pride, scraping like a client, but he had never faltered.*

He nearly stumbled. A stupid fall would be fine, wouldn't it? Tell Minos and Rhadamanthus at the Judgment below, *I fell. I was feeling sorry for myself.* It would be Tartarus for certain; not that Romans truly believed in such places, but after what he had seen in dreams and in exile, best not risk it.

Quiet, he told the voices that battled in his skull. They seemed to echo in his helmet. Gravel rattled against it, and dust rose until his eyes squinted tears. The lucky men were the ones who died.

You would never get the old man to bend. You will not get me to bend either.

Step by step, battling the very rock and earth of their passage, they struggled down the slope. Depending on how you looked at it, the gods were either favoring them or wishing to punish them further, because most of them survived to reach the valley floor.

The wailing they had heard as the earth began to shake had died away. No one could remember at what point the rumbling under the ground had ceased. No one could remember when the screams borne up to them by the winds and mists had been put to silence.

A few last rocks fell and stuttered into quiet as the Romans and Ch'in staggered to a halt on the plains. None of them fell to their knees in relief, and Quintus felt the warmth of pride. Even the wind that swiftly dried the sweat from their heaving bodies had fallen silent. Mist licked them around and brought a thick silence.

Grayish-white, that mist writhed up to billow against them. Moving through it was like scouting through a ruin, not so much festooned with cobwebs but barriered with them. Soft as the mist was, the brush of it on gaunt faces and bleeding hands was something subtly vile. Lucilius grimaced as if touching carrion.

"Ugh!"

"Quiet there!" grumbled Rufus.

Draupadi wrapped a grimy saffron fold of her garments over her face. Quintus found himself breathing thinly as if still on the heights, unwilling to draw any more of this mist-laden, unwholesome air into his lungs. *The mist will breed in you,* came the unwelcome voice in his head. *The webs will ensnare you, and you will gasp and cough until blood spurts from your mouth, staining the webs. Thus shall you leave your bones here, where corpses of mighty cities have vanished without a trace.*

Working through that smell of must, of something old, salty, and spoiled like rotten shellfish were the desert smells. That made it somehow worse.

"Steady, boy, steady," came Rufus's voice as a horse panted and struggled. The mount lacked the strength to put up a convincing fight: It was too tired and too afraid to panic. Up and down the line of march, eyes showed white rimmed in fear. The men sagged, exhausted with more than their mad plunge in the path of the earthquake to the desert floor.

"Mists are getting thicker, sir," someone muttered.

Cocooned in mists the way a spider entraps a fly, would they encounter worse the further they moved into the true desert?

Draupadi was a mistress of illusion, came the thought. Surely, she . . .

"*Domina*?" Gently, Quintus addressed the sorceress as if she were a great lady of his own race.

"In this mist," he told her, "we will wander lost until we die."

Her eyes met his, then fell. "Later would be better," she admitted. "They watch, or something does. Already, I make shields. . . ." She put out a hand that trembled. "I promise."

Abruptly, even an instant longer spent in those mists seemed about an age too long. Thicker and thicker they grew, as if they drew strength from the men trapped to wander in them. The stink of something messily dead grew stronger.

"I would spare you what you will see," she said.

For the first time since Quintus had known her, Draupadi seemed unsure of herself. "You are on the proper trail, I beg you to believe me," she said. Briefly, she shut her eyes. When she opened them again, she flinched as if she gazed upon horrors hidden to the others.

None of them shared her sight—if true sight she had. In the silence, a horse stumbled, and Quintus heard a bone snap. A moment later, the coppery scent of blood filled the air as a Ch'in armsman ended the creature's thrashing pain. Trying to see where the horse had fallen,

Quintus set his foot down awry, and nearly measured his length in the grit. He saved himself, but at the cost of the skin on one palm and knee and a sharp pain in his chest like unto the Legions' brand touching him once more. He did not like to think of the way the mist seemed to lick at the blood that oozed from his scratches.

The image of a slender figure, torches held aloft in its hands, kindled in Quintus's thoughts. "Krishna," he whispered to himself. His bronze talisman, the last link between his home and this gods-forsaken place, the guardian that had always warned him of danger.

As it warned him now against the lure of protection from piercing the mists that wreathed them about.

Quintus strode toward the sybil from Hind. "Can you end this spell?" he demanded in a voice he never had used to her before. "Never mind what we may or may not wish to see. We don't—none of us—wish to be here anyhow, let alone with our legs and necks broken from falls."

Draupadi studied his face through the mists as if finding in it something she had loved and had missed for a long, long time. As her voice rose in a chant, she raised her hands in slow gestures. Her eyes rolled in her head. Drained from the effort of lifting whatever illusion she fought against, she sagged, and he caught her just in time. The fragrance of sandalwood and musk, the salt of her sweat, were the most wholesome things he had smelled for weeks.

The mist dissipated. As the last tendrils vanished, the muffled clangor of harness bells was heard, subdued and strangely echoing, as one of the caravan beasts bearing them appeared in sight.

With a cry that was half oath, half laughter, one of the

Romans dropped his hand from his *pilum*. No sense killing a beast they might need.

The reek of terror and of ancient seabeds evaporated with the mists. Someone caught the wandering pack beast and silenced its bells. In this waste, their release from fear seemed almost obscene.

The beast coughed once and toppled, as if only the sound of its bells had kept it alive that long. With the mists gone, they could indeed see clearly. All along their path, camels and horses were lying as if whatever had shaken the earth had stolen their lives from them.

Near them, all about, were their masters—untidy bundles of travel-worn robes. And all of them were dead too.

15

A FINAL WISP of mist faded, taking with it the incongruous reek of brine. Desert wind tugged Quintus forward. For a moment, he inhaled the scents of this dry place as if they were fine incense: dry stone, salt, and the sweat of fearful men and laboring beasts. Then, as the wind urged him forward, his talisman jolted. No stench of plague or rot, but death was there. *Fare forward*.

Quintus strode into a field of corpses.

Bells tinkled on the harnesses of dead horses and camels as the wind tugged at saddle cloths and the robes of the dead merchants and guards. For the caravan was dead, the little world made up of Parthians, Syrians, Jews, Persians, men of the Ch'in, and guides from the perimeters of the desert blotted out. The journey had leached color and texture from those robes: Display and finery were for towns. But even beyond the drabness of the old robes that men might wear in the waste, these bodies seemed drained of natural color.

Ssu-ma Chao gestured. "Within bow-shot of the Stone Tower," he muttered.

It would have to be a very long bow-shot, nevertheless.

"That would take quite an archer," Lucilius shot out with a barbed tongue. Predictable that he would be the one to point that out.

A soldier laughed at the retort. Other laughter rose in the ranks. Hysteria of a sort, born of relief, could be as deadly a thing as panic, Quintus knew.

"Quiet!" A crack of Rufus's vinestaff reinforced the order, bringing the laughter to a quick stop.

"That will not work, sir," said Ganesha. He had picked his way over to the man who had laughed.

"You show no respect to the dead, younger brother," he spoke softly. "Or to yourself or your comrades."

"Burial detail, sir?" Rufus asked as crisply as if organizing camp for a night.

However, Quintus truly was not commander here—had the centurion forgotten? It was Ssu-ma Chao who ruled, little as the man looked as if he were in any shape to give orders. The line of march had broken. Men were leading beasts to the rear, lest they panic and bolt with what remained of their supplies.

Reason? Quintus knew his men better than that—hard-headed peasant stock. They did have discipline: they had loyalty; they had customs—customs that had been violated at Carrhae, when the Romans had fled, leaving the dead and wounded untended behind them. But they were Romans, not a rabble, and if they had cheated death once again, well and good. If not, they each owed a death, and it were better to die as Romans.

Grandsire, do you see? Be proud of me. The familiar appeal echoed in Quintus's heart. Always before it had brought him only doubt. This time, the doubt was gone. He might walk a grim path, but he walked it as a Roman and a man of whom his grandsire could be proud.

Rufus sketched a tactful salute to Lucilius, then gestured for the men nearest him to unpack their shovels and start digging. "Come on, lads. Respect the dead. We can at least cover their faces, see they've got coins for the Boatman. You'd want someone to do that for you. . . ."

We may yet need it.

Every impulse in Quintus's body urged him to fly. He looked over at Ssu-ma Chao, who stood motionless. Then he compelled himself to step toward the bodies. He stooped to tug the headcloth of the nearest man decently over his face. He had been a merchant of some standing, judging by the excellent quality of his robes, even if they were battered by rough travel. The leather of his weapons harness was finely tooled, while his ornaments and the hilt of his sword . . . no sword? It had been taken.

The merchant did not look as if he had died in pain—but he looked old, far older than any man had a right to be if he chose to take these caravan routes. Old and drained, as if the sun had leached him dry for months, instead of just the time Quintus knew it had taken for the entire caravan to die. At his touch, the corpse seemed to shiver in on itself. Quintus would not have been surprised if it had turned to dust. He shuddered and turned over the next body.

"It does not matter," Arsaces cut in. "Soon enough, the sand will come and bury these men, as it has buried countless caravans and towns." He tried to sound offhand, but one hand fumbled for the blue amulet he wore beneath his robes.

What was this death that left a caravan stark in the sand, stole its weapons, but did not touch its wares—*and what was* that?

"This one's unarmed!" Quintus shouted. "Check to see if the others . . ."

"All the weapons are gone. Even broken arrows," Rufus was first to obey.

Down the line, Arsaces rummaged in the beasts' packs. One toppled, spilling wrappings of cloth. The Persian recoiled. Running from pack animal to pack animal, he tore open the saddlebags reserved for the costliest goods, spilling spices and glass onto the sands as he went. A waste: They dared not burden themselves with such luxuries.

"By the flame, nothing's been touched!" the Persian exclaimed. His voice shook. Not to loot when there was a chance . . .

"This one isn't armed either!" Lucilius shouted, which reassured Quintus not at all. The tribune turned from one prone figure to another, who had died, seemingly, when his horse fell and now lay half-hidden beneath it. A caravan was a small army. Merchants needed men able and willing to fight. *Edepol*, had this been a caravan of old men?

"They might carry gems on their persons," Arsaces's battered boots cracked through the salt crust upon the grit. He seemed as reluctant as Quintus felt to investigate. "An entire caravan struck dead, no signs of plague or bandits or even blood and—Mithras aid us!"

As Arsaces spoke, the tribune knelt by the dead merchant's body. *Be a man*. Battlefield loot—no, this was no true battlefield, and these were not the enemy. He compelled himself to touch the body but not to rob. Under his fingers the corpse seemed to collapse in on itself, like a wineskin that has been drained, but has retained its fullness until a careless hand brushes it.

Oaths and prayers rose as others of the Romans and the Ch'in made the same gruesome discovery almost all at once. This caravan of the dead seemed to be a caravan in which all had died at once—seemingly of old age. Even the bodies dressed as young men dress—apprentices, guards, slim forms that might have been favored sons making their first desert crossing—looked as ancient as some mummy cast up out of a dune.

And when they were touched, they crumpled.

From behind the Romans rose commands screamed out in Ch'in. Ssu-ma Chao's voice cracked up toward hysteria. Arsaces laid a hand on Quintus's arm.

"He wants us to leave *now*. It is a day's march to the Stone Tower and . . ."

Quintus squinted toward the sun. Already it had sunk low in the direction that he dearly wished to go, as if a fire barred the Romans from their home. So, was this the prelude to Carrhae all over again—the brutal forced march to a field of slaughter, followed by other, equally harsh demands?

The Ch'in commander's voice rose to a scream. The best thing for that one, Quintus thought, would be silence. For him; for the Ch'in soldiers; and for the Romans especially. Ssu-ma Chao had eased the terms of the Romans' captivity. He had ordered their arms returned. They owed him—more than somewhat. But they still had the Eagle to regain if they could. What he gave with one hand, he could take back with the other—aye, and their lives with their privileges, should he meet up with others of his race.

It was one thing to die on a battlefield. To die here, among corpses drained by—Quintus shuddered, remembering childhood nightmares haunted by tales of the Lamia.

"By all the gods, there's riches here," Lucilius muttered. "Play for time, would you? We can't leave yet. Not when—"

In a moment, he would start rummaging in each dead man's robes. It was one thing to search the dead for what might sustain the living, another to strip them for gain, here in this wasteland where extra treasure might mean extra burden to all. Quintus would have bet any coin he happened to have about him that Lucilius had already robbed some of the nearest bodies.

Draupadi drew near and spoke to him since the earth had begun to shake. "You need to see what Ganesha has found."

"I also need to obey that man." Quintus pointed at Ssu-ma Chao. "It is only by his grace we are not slaves." Let him crack, and they might be slaves again, Draupadi with them.

"Arjuna—" she began to protest.

"Will you stop that!" All Quintus's fear, all his anger, and even the sense of self-respect he had gained this day went into that demand. "I am *Quintus,* only myself; yet you load me with the baggage of five princes, one of them a hero. Don't you understand? I am not he!"

Her eyes grew enormous, hurt, and he hated himself for that hurt—and the pain he caused himself. Let her know the truth. Let her turn from him now, before it grew any harder to lose her. But the sight of her pain grieved him, and he added in a gentler tone, "If I *am* he, I truly do not know it. I am sorry."

Now the Ch'in soldiers were closing in, encircling their former allies. Some of them were drawing their weapons. If even one Roman drew sword or fingered spear . . . perhaps the Ch'in could wipe out their small force. They would have to. Very likely, Ch'in and Roman would be the death of each other.

And with all that, he had to contend with a weeping princess! "Do you truly not know me?" Her hand touched his chest precisely where the bronze statuette of Krishna lay. It warmed under those delicate-seeming, capable fingers. "I thought you did."

"Perhaps," Quintus said. "But perhaps, too, we must take care that this is not illusion."

She nodded sorrowfully. "I wish for only the truth to lie between us. To give you—"

In that moment, he longed to gather her into his arms; and let the Ch'in skewer him.

"But you do not believe . . ."

"Do *you* believe it?" he demanded.

"Believe it? I *know* it. I remember."

"I remember that I have men to get to safety before he—" a gesture at Ssu-ma Chao and his warriors alerted her to their danger, "—attacks."

"You are all . . . you call it 'Roman' in this life, are you not?" All duty, she meant. All discipline. Damn.

But he nodded as he must. "Aye, *Domina.*"

"That too is like the man who won me." She laughed sadly. "Even at Virata's court, he was intent on the role he played, blind to all else. Perhaps I too have been blind, thinking only of what *I* see, what *I* know, not you as you are in this life. . . ."

"I have it!" Ganesha shouted. For an instant his voice rang with the authority of a battle trumpet, summoning Quintus to the head of the column. Light gathered, shimmered over the old man, who moved with a sureness unlike the careful steps of any man his apparent age over the dead land.

Quintus headed toward the old sage. He stumbled, cursed what he tripped over, then recovered. A length of horn and wood conjoined jutted from the sand, and he snatched it up, using it to break his fall, then as a staff to speed him to Ganesha's side.

The old man held a body in his arms, though already it had withered to flaps of drying skin over bone even as he watched it with somber eyes. This one wore the dress of a guard. Quintus forced himself to look at the face. Already, the lips had peeled back from the jaws, revealing not the expressionless faces of the dead man's comrades, but something different. Younger than the others, this face still possessed a measure of individuality. And it wore a look of hate and terror, as if this guard had seen his death coming and fought frenziedly with what pitiful means he had. Last of all, Quintus saw what else Ganesha bore—a bow, broken as if the guard would yield it in no other way to enemy hands.

Ganesha laid the dead guard down in line with the others. The man's hands thudded to the ground, wasted fingers still clamped shut. "Look you," ordered the sage. He had pried one of the bony fists open to display a dark scrap of fabric.

"What is that?" Quintus asked, leaning forward to examine it even as Ganesha shouted rapid-fire Ch'in orders to Ssu-ma Chao.

"Do not touch it! This poor one did, and thus he died. . . ." Carefully, Ganesha bent forward and breathed on the scrap.

"From a Black Naacal's robe?"

"I feel such a one up ahead," said Ganesha. "Waiting for us in the direction that we must go."

We could circle about, Quintus thought of saying. Arsaces knew the stars; he could guide them.

"But it is in that direction," Ssu-ma Chao stated, "that we must go." Some measure of sanity had returned to him, and he looked just as dangerous as he truly was.

"And so we do, Excellency," said the sage, bowing in Ch'in fashion. "But we do not take that road unwarned.

I say to you: Beware. Trust no one, nothing, even though it wears the semblance of your eldest brother, until we have proved the truth of it.''

''Why?'' demanded Ssu-ma Chao.

''They seek weapons, perhaps that very Pasupata that Arjuna sought in the last age. They must not have found it for, if they had, we should be as dead as their victims here—or praying to all our gods or to those of our enemies for release. But they have found something almost as deadly to us—and deadlier still to these poor fools.''

''And what is that?''

''Life,'' Ganesha said simply. ''Life and health. Possibly spirit. These men are all drained, not just of life, but of what makes them men and not beast. I would pray peace to their souls and better aspects to their lives the next time the wheel turns, but there will be no next time for them. These men's souls have been consumed.''

16

UNDER THE COATING of sweat and grime, even the swarthiest of the men still alive on that plain and within hearing went pale. Quintus saw Rufus battle a shudder and win—just. To have nothing left. No body to be entombed, no soul to travel across the river and face the Judgment that he had approached in dreams, yet evaded as it was not yet his time. Whatever his time was.

He had time enough to fare across a waste seemingly the size of Gaea herself. His time, indeed. When would it be his time not to suffer, not to endure, but to act—either as a Roman or this ghostly hero that Ganesha and Draupadi insisted on believing him to be?

Quintus would have been content only to sit and rest in clean air, away from these strange corpses. He would have been very well content to wrest the Eagles from the temples of those who had slain his comrades—the sign of his own Legion as well as those that had been sent to Merv. But it seemed that none of that was to be.

Why not make your life easier? came a voice. *You want your gods, your freedom? They can be yours, along with*

*sweet water flowing free over the rock in the shade at noon. . . .
Only . . .*

The bronze talisman over his heart twinged unnecessarily. Quintus tightened his hand on the stick he held, seeking relief from his anger.

That is excellent. Feel the anger. All that delectable rage. Let it out. Let it blaze like a fire at midnight when naphtha is tossed into it. Let it. We will reward you for your service.

The tribune's fingers tightened on the wood. In an instant, the frail staff would snap, he feared, and his control along with it. Let it snap like a stick, a broken bone, the spine of his enemy who stymied him and held in his keeping the terms and key to freedom that Quintus desired. *And why should you—of all men—be balked of your desires?*

Quintus's glance fell to what he held. It was not a staff at all, but a bow, the deadly recurved Parthian weapon that had destroyed his old, ordered life at Carrhae, complete even to its string.

"There are arrows in our supply for such bows," said a man from Ch'in. "Unless you expect—" his hand gestured about the endless arena of grit and salt flat as if he expected arrows and quiver to materialize.

With a Legion or two of good lads, Quintus mused. The gods forbid, though, that other Romans be lured out into the desert in which he was now certain he would spend the rest of an exceedingly short and unpleasant life. He nodded thanks to the soldier.

"So," Ganesha said. "You have found your bow. Will you not be convinced even now of who you are? I am an old man and never was a warrior; but it seems to me that when a warrior finds his weapon, then is battle near."

Nearer than you think, old man.

The old one's eyes focussed upon Quintus, compelling belief and more than belief. He had seen what he had seen. He had fought against belief, just as he fought now against what he feared, demanded a surrender of himself more total than even his obedience to the Legion or the way that all of the Romans had surrendered at Carrhae.

Silence him. Do it.

Be quiet, he told the voice inside his skull.

He stared at the sunlight lancing sharply downward, like the swoop of some great raptor flying West. Let it be a good omen, he prayed.

Whatever Ganesha was, he had never lied, never betrayed Quintus.

Would Lucilius laugh? Before a battle, Quintus told himself firmly, a wise leader listened to augury and to the thoughts of his own heart.

"I have heard," he began slowly, "I have heard a voice speaking to me. Promising me . . ."

Ganesha held up his hand as if warning him not to reveal his secret before the entire company. The wise, weary old eyes transfixed his and grew even brighter.

"Be assured, Warrior—" the title sounded more proud than that of "prince," "—that I shall watch and guard, and that Draupadi shall weave us such protection that only our worst enemies can pierce the veil of blindness and illusion she will cast upon the land."

Of course, it was their worst enemies that they had to face: Nevertheless, this was better than nothing.

Ssu-ma Chao beckoned. "This one . . ." Then he dropped the formality. "I heard what you did *not* say to the old alchemist. You hear them too? The voices, promising you your most hidden desires, if only . . ."

Tell him you hear this. He will say you are mad and give your body to the desert so you do not poison the minds of the others. And then, we will have you, and we will eat your soul as we drank the souls from those fools scattered about you. Tell him, and learn the price for going against our will.

Quintus touched the talisman he carried, as if soothing it and his flesh at once. "Is it not said that there are dreams in the wind and the storm? These are not demands to obey that I hear, but the threats of evil men, thieves who steal life and the bandits of the waste who steal treasure."

For the first time, he saw Ssu-ma Chao not just as a captor turned ally, but a man as harried and afraid as he.

"And it does not drive you mad? You can sleep?" Ssu-ma Chao was too fine-drawn, had been too fine-drawn for too long. His face bore the expression Quintus had seen when, after heaving up his guts after his first battle, he had staggered off to wash and stared at his own face mirrored in the blessedly clean water.

Water flowing free over the rocks . . .

"Roman," said the Ch'in officer, for a wonder, getting the name right, "are you and yours for hire?"

"We are not gladiators or guards," said Quintus, even as Lucilius's eyes brightened. *Ask how much.* "And we do not desire gold. You hold in your possession the treasures we would seek—the Eagle and our freedom to leave this place."

"It is my death and my family's if you are not brought to Su-le. But in the garrison at Kashgar I shall myself pray that you be given back your honor and this war god of your worship which has arrived there by now. Would that suffice you?"

"Suffice for what?"

"To have your swords beside ours on the trail to Kashgar."

"You have had our word already," Quintus said. (Behind him, Lucilius hissed in anger.) "Or do you think we march now into greater danger than any we have faced?''

Ganesha had held his gaze, compelling honesty, compelling Quintus to admit that he had been under some sort of attack. Now he borrowed the tactic to use upon the Ch'in commander. *Let him respond with the truth*, he wished. *Please let him.*

''Aye, we have endured storms before. But in the deep desert, surrounded by enemies, we may endure tempests that make what we have faced seem like grains of sand in a light breeze. Get us to the garrison at Kashgar, and I swear to you that you shall have my voice for your Eagle and your friends, even if I must cross the desert on my knees myself and make petition to the Son of Heaven.''

The bronze dancer twinged in its hiding place. *Answer him. The man suffers.*

''I am content,'' said Quintus. He shouted for the men to prepare to march. There would be a moon tonight: no reason to waste the light in sleep when danger was so near. ''Are you?'' he asked in an undertone.

Ssu-ma Chao bowed agreement. Then he gestured at his men. ''If I fall,'' said the Ch'in officer, ''take care of them.''

17

DOWN TO SU-LE and the garrison at Kashgar they headed, finally—as Arsaces said—into the true desert. It was bleaker than even the wastes Quintus had seen, and likely to be bleaker yet. "Enter here and never emerge." That was the desert's name, they said all along the caravan routes and made signs against ill omen. How Arsaces chuckled when he saw the Romans, from half the world away, making similar signs.

"Enter here and never emerge," was not ill omen at all, Quintus thought, but stark truth. From where he stood, the desert, ringed by mountains whose snowy peaks were but inadequate substitutes for clouds, stretched out like an amphitheatre in which all men entering it were gladiators. It was a wasteland of gravel and dunes, broken by the glint of salt flats, whitened occasionally by bones. Pray all the gods they did not add their own.

A few dead tamarisks jutted from the grit. There were almost no living plants and no living creatures that they could see by daylight. As for the unliving—Draupadi and

Ganesha stood watch with the Legionaries; for still the most highly strung of the men screamed in the night, declaring that they felt eyes upon them.

From time to time, Quintus saw Ganesha look about him. Not as if he marvelled at him or stood aghast, as any man might, but as if he remembered it in other days.

"A terrible stage," he said finally, "on which the fate of the world and all our lives, past and future, must play themselves out." Those were not words that Quintus, particularly, wanted to hear.

At least, there were no raiders. Wise in the tales of Modun and others of the Hsiung-nu and Yueh-chih from the Ch'in stories (told, Quintus was certain, more to affright than to inform), the Romans were somewhat relieved until their days' marches and their nights' marches made them realize that the waste held no other life at all. After that, they would have welcomed bandits to drive off as evidence that the curse upon this place was not the one that took the caravan by Stone Tower.

Draupadi, mistress of illusions though she was, had no such hopes. She grew pale despite that amber skin of hers. At her request, ultimately, they tied her to the camel with the gentlest gait. *She has depopulated your world, you know*, whispered the sinister voice that was Quintus's constant tempter. *What if she dies? Clearly, she has already run mad—a kindness, perhaps, to kill her swiftly. The people you see now—cherish them, boy, for theirs will be the last faces you see in the world.*

Unless, of course, he succumbed. He took a twisted satisfaction in the fact that the voice had given up trying to offer him rewards.

He tried not to listen and failed. Then he tried not to debate and did little better. He would run mad if he allowed himself to listen freely. Or, if he did not run mad, he could wither from inside, a blight of the spirit destroying him just as surely as the Black Naacals had sucked the life from those merchants whose husks he had watched shrivel under his touch. Then they would all die, yes, and their bones would bleach here in the waste, if the demon storms did not splinter them first. And the last man left alive would curse the fate that allowed him to watch his brothers escape.

His brothers.

Something in Quintus stopped at that thought. Used to the discipline of the Legions, though, he did not break stride—for they were walking now, to spare their exhausted beasts. They were all his brothers—the surviving men of Rome, the Ch'in soldiers, who, if not as far from their homes as his Legionaries, shared their exile and fear. Even Lucilius: for they sprang from the same earth.

But Ganesha, for all his wisdom, and Draupadi? How could he claim "brotherhood" with beings that far removed from him and his nation? As he glanced at Ganesha, did the ancient scholar momentarily shift form so that an elephant's head topped his bowed shoulders? A trick of the light, or the heat, or Quintus's own weary mind, no doubt: his eyes dazzled from the sunlight on the salt flats.

And Draupadi—for an instant, Quintus thought of the legend of Tithonus. Beloved of the dawn, Aurora had promised him whatever gift he might ask of her. He had chosen immortality, and it was granted. But granted without a gift of eternal youth. And after a time, Tithonus gummed his bread and his voice rose shrilly into the air; ultimately, when he was transformed from grandsire to grasshopper, his voice rose higher yet, like a string too tightly plucked. *She is mistress of illusions. But if illusions fail, you might find yourself kissing a skull.*

Birth and rebirth, she had told him. He could either believe that was true—or else the illusions had been spun for so long that they had become real.

So down to Su-le they plodded. Rome's pace. Rome's race. The beasts were rested—at least as rested as they were ever going to be—but they were Romans and they preferred to march.

"As stubborn as one of Marius's mules!" Lucilius called, riding just as Quintus might have expected. He might sound lighthearted, but his lips were as chapped, his body as worn as the rest, and the jeer was softened by the use of the old name. They were all Marius's mules, soldiers of a Rome they would not see again, following a captive Eagle.

One foot before the other, the nails of his sadly worn boots rasping in the grit. *March.* Sunlight flashed and glared off the grit and gypsum that formed the desert here: gravel and salt flat. Ganesha had seen all this when it was seabed. Seabed. Hard to believe this had all been an inland sea like the Middle Sea itself. So much water, Quintus thought. His mind reeled at the thought of such luxury; already, he found it hard enough to imagine the hidden pool by which he had found Draupadi so long ago, seated in the luxury of silken cushions, sandalwood, and amber lights. There was, she had told him, another such place, deep in the desert's heart. If such a desert could be said to have a heart. If they could survive, heart and sinew and soul, long enough to reach it . . . and if their allies did not kill them first.

One foot before the other, steady, firmly planted. *March, Roman.* He heard his grandsire's voice now, strong as it had been in Quintus's boyhood, urging him forward. At first he had protested, but had been shamed into carrying on. Later, he had learned to persevere, even if the old man's demands outstripped his body's strength. Now, as he marched, he remembered the tough, fierce old face, and he blessed it.

Now the bronze talisman he bore near his heart neither heated nor jabbed his flesh. It was as if, somehow, it had achieved a truce with the *genius loci* of this place.

That thought staggered him for a moment. Keep marching. For a heartbeat longer, the marching stride, men coughing at the parched dust cast up by feet and hooves, and the cloudless sky stretching from overhead to an unreachable horizon made him reel. They were not a company, he thought of his men and his allies, but a coffle of slaves. He reeled again and flung out a hand.

"Careful, sir," came a mutter. There was a grin and a good-natured attempt to steady him on his feet. His hand touched the hide of a pack animal. It was dry, scaly: The sun had leached all the sweat from it as soon as it formed.

"Arjuna?" The sibyl's voice was soft and concerned. Sibylla. Now there was a good Latin concept for you. And he wanted badly to be Roman, to be only Quintus, his father's son and his grandsire's heir: not, please gods, this spiritual shuffling, as it seemed, among lives and deaths, all of them violent.

He swerved to tell Draupadi precisely that, but the remnants of her beauty, the dark eyes shadowed not by kohl but by exhaustion, the amber skin parched and dirty, the glorious long hair dried out and straggling, silenced him.

Meeting his eyes, Draupadi's eyes filled, first with anxiety and then with tears. "You always were more than one being," she told him. "When we met, you even swore to share me with your brothers. Yet, Arjuna, I have no complaints . . . but you have always been many men in one. Just as you are now. You are the heart of all of these men . . . and the luck of the men from the Realm of Gold."

He shook his head like a man who has staggered up after a beating.

"Too many," he said, thickly. "It is more than I can bear."

"So, you would be only the loyal heir who follows the head of his family, the loyal soldier who follows his commander? My dearest, I wish you had that luxury. Or that I could cease to be Draupadi and sink her, dreams, illusions, and all, in the cares of a soldier's wife."

Their eyes met. *Do you understand what I am telling you?* each seemed to ask the other.

"*Domina,* had the fates deemed otherwise . . ."

"It is not you, not ever," she murmured. "But . . ." Abruptly, she raised her hand again and smiled ironically, honey with a sting beneath. "You are weary with the cares of duty as well as with the desert. Could you not keep your honor if you consented to ride for a brief time?"

"I must set an example."

"Example—to the cross with it!"

Quintus blinked at her. He had not thought she would have learned that oath, and he was certain he did not approve of her saying it. Between surprise and disapproval, he laughed; he had thought never to laugh again.

He checked the line of march, drawing back to the rear of the column, where the riding animals—horses and camels—and the pack beasts plodded along. The camels' humps were flattening, a sign, he had learned, that even these beasts whose capacity for endurance was legendary in the desert, would soon need water. One of the Ch'in guard, having, as was clear, ideas about the lowliness of any Roman's position in the general order of things, scowled at him; but Arsaces had a grin and a thumbs-up—wherever he had learned that—for him and he gestured him toward the beast likeliest to bear him without either of them suffering more than they must.

Mounted (however reluctantly), he rode past the pack animals. He rode past the column of Romans, inexpressibly proud that they neither faltered nor complained—though the heat and dryness kept them from their usual songs. Rufus saluted him without reproach. Past Draupadi on her camel he rode, and past Lucilius who, as usual, hovered near the Ch'in officers as if seeking to make their power his.

Ssu-ma Chao nodded to Quintus as he pulled into line only slightly behind his captor. He turned the head of his horse—a fine beast from Ferghana, though Quintus could not, for the life of him, make out what was meant by the term "blood-sweating." The beast's stocky neck barely seemed to sweat, much less sweat blood.

"There we are." The Ch'in general rose in his saddle and pointed.

The Roman squinted. Though they were riding away from the light into the east, the glare and the shadows of late afternoon made sight painful. Clouds of dust rose, making matters that much the worse, too.

"Do you see it?" Ssu-ma Chao asked. "The towers of Su-le."

"May I tell my lads?" Quintus asked. They would be glad of a rest. And a meal or so and even a wash, though he knew they could not expect proper Roman baths. He would tell Draupadi, too, and watch her eyes light with pleasure and relief.

A cloud of dust rose between the towers and themselves. Quintus tensed, victim as he had been of battles and double dealings. His hand dropped to the hilt of his sword.

Quietly, imperceptibly, he signaled Rufus; and Rufus took up a posture of defense.

The dust subsided, and he could see Su-le. The town looked preposterously new—a garrison town that paid and treated its soldiers well as a necessity for its survival.

"A strong garrison," Ssu-ma Chao commented, hand on sword. "We know there is mischief afoot in the land. Otherwise, why send the garrison out at all?"

The Ch'in officer stared at Quintus, his eyes narrowing so that he appeared to be regarding the Roman through dark slits. "It is possible, I suppose, that a message might have been sent before the caravan died. . . . There was light enough for the signalling device to work. But from what we saw, I think the men died too suddenly." The Ch'in's face twisted in revulsion. "Still, I hope they succeeded. But, Roman, you stare at Su-le as if it were one huge trap. What makes you so suspicious?"

"I have been abandoned before," Quintus replied. "And betrayed by garrisons." *As you well know.* The words were blurted out before he could guard his tongue. In it, all men were brothers and equals—or else mortal enemies; you could readily tell the difference.

Ssu-ma Chao laughed. After a too-nervous moment, so did one or two members of his staff. "This is why I want their cooperation," the officer stated with the air of one repeating a point on which he had been proud to be right.

I like this man, Quintus thought. *But the gods only know why.*

Behind them, Lucilius edged closer. Hearing laughter, he dared to approach. For Quintus, his ironic presence blunted the mood of only a few moments ago.

"Is that traders," he asked, pointing, "or a welcoming party?"

The sword Quintus again wore by grace of Ssu-ma Chao hung reassuringly against his leg. He signalled the marching column of Romans to alert. Not to attack, please all the gods, no. He did not want to fight the men who had been his allies in the journey overmountain. But if the men from the garrison at Su-le had a mind to attack, they would get more than they wished.

And there was always the chance that he could retrieve the Eagle from wherever they had sent it.

But it took all the discipline he had to sit complacently in the saddle as the shadows lengthened and the dust cloud rising from the garrison's advance party rose in the vast sky. It spewed out before them, then solidified into individual horsemen. And each one of them was not only heavily armed, but bore weapons bared. Bowmen formed a second rank.

Seeing that, Ssu-ma Chao dismounted and walked forward, a posture of submission he maintained as the garrison rode slowly into voice range.

He sank into a deep bow. "This one wishes to ask . . . ."

"You must explain instead why you travel with this excrement of turtles as if they were brothers in arms. And, worse yet, why you have allowed them their weapons!"

Now, how had they discovered that?

The garrison party advanced. It was much larger than either the column of Romans or Ssu-ma Chao's exhausted little force. Quintus let his hand fall away from his sword.

You caused this, you know. It was you who thought of the Roman line as a slave gang. But you could alter that. . . .

Be still! he ordered sharply, the better to concentrate on the outer fear he must now confront.

A hand touched his arm. Draupadi had ridden up beside him. It was not a time to talk with her, not a time to distract himself with thoughts of her. But she could not be denied.

"Already," said Draupadi, "they are different from what they have been. I remember how the earth shivered and swallowed up the water. . . ."

"Is that what you offer me?" Quintus asked. "Memories I do not want?"

Draupadi shook her head. Despite the gesture of negation, her face brightened, youth and life returning. "You know what I offer."

The breeze between them seemed to warm his heart— and the rest of his body. It was not the heat of the sun, reflected from the desert floor, but longing, a longing that possessed him every time he looked at her.

"Not your Eagle or your home," Draupadi surprised him with her words. "Not even the power that would restore you to your birthright. But Quintus, just as you are—you are worthy to go on. That is what we offer. The journey. The life. For as long as we live."

A new ache gripped him in that moment—the urge to lift her down from her mount and hold her for as long as he might. He had always hoped that when a marriage was arranged for him (as in the course of time it would have been, had the Fates been kinder), he would feel a kindness for his bride and she would . . . she would not fear him too badly at first. But this woman, with her powers and her endurance and her memory—this woman claimed to have been his wife in a vanished world. He could not remember. She deserved better than for him simply to trade on that and take her—when the time came, as it surely must—without an oath on his part to match the ritual that, clearly, lived on in her memories.

And if he died in the next hour, at least the words would have been said. She even wore the saffron veil of a Roman bride.

"Where thou art Caia," he began, drawing on the words of the *confarreatio*, the most solemn and binding rite of marriage, "there am I Caius." His voice thickened, and not from the dust.

He had the ring of his service to Rome. He gave it to her.

18

THE GARRISON FORCES fanned out. Quintus sized them up with the sharpened senses of pure despair. They were fresher than the men he and Ssu-ma Chao led. They had archers—and after Carrhae, archers were a thing he had learned to fear. Would there be time enough for his men to seize their shields and form a *testudo?* Even if there were, it would leave unprotected the men they had marched beside all these months.

And he suspected Draupadi and Ganesha would not accept its protection, such as it was. The finger that had been encircled so long by his ring felt lighter, strange. No time to think of that.

Then Quintus looked into the face of the garrison commander. His eyes were flat and cold. And dangerous. No, he did not look like a man to whom anyone could explain why he had allowed prisoners to travel armed. Not, at least, if you were one of the erstwhile prisoners.

The commander barked something angry and explosive in the language of Ch'in, and gestured at the Romans. Even before Ssu-ma Chao tried to translate, Quintus knew what the command was.

"You must disarm," the officer said, almost in a tone of apology.

Quintus handed him his sword.

"This one protests, with submission, that it is folly to disarm capable warriors," the Ch'in aristocrat bowed again, as if pleading forgiveness for rebellion. "We just came from the Stone Tower. We passed a caravan that was well-armed, but even so, it had no chance, snuffed out like flies—"

"Report," said the garrison commander (who had not seen fit to supply a name), "was brought of the Stone Tower. A madman was taken up in his last moments of life. He was a man ancient beyond belief who swore that just the morn before, he had been a young apprentice of the *Hu*-barbarians. Demons wearing black, he said, stole his youth, stole his life, stole his mind! The sun had baked his brains.

"He said he had seen some four demons, but one fell. The other three . . ." The commander broke off, glaring at Ssu-ma Chao.

"You knew of this?"

The loosening of swords in sheaths was the coldest sound Quintus had ever heard. *If no prisoners came to the garrison at Su-le, there would be no prisoners to account for in a report to superiors.* The salt flats might swallow their blood, too.

He hoped his men had taken their time in following his move to surrender his weapon.

Behind him, he could hear Rufus swearing, then subsiding to, "So it's slaves again, not allies? If they want our swords, let's make them *take* them. And why not—"

Mutiny? From the tongue-lashing that the garrison

commander clearly was administering to Ssu-ma Chao and the submission with which he listened, mutiny wasn't a possibility. Say, rather, summary execution.

The garrison commander gestured peremptorily. At his command, Ganesha and Draupadi, on their tired, dusty mounts, rode toward the head of the column. Just in time, Quintus stopped himself from flinging out a hand. It was her old nightmare, the one that she remembered and he didn't—that she had been a prisoner among their enemies, and he could not help her.

Let them touch her, something said inside him. His mind and hands itched for the bow with which Draupadi had told him Arjuna had such matchless, deadly familiarity. Had he his skills and his memories, this wasteland would see a second devastation. They would not even need Pasupata.

"What kind of demons are *these* vagabonds?" Quintus had picked up enough of the language of Ch'in to supply words to that question and to understand Ganesha's reply.

"We are scholars," said the old man. "And alchemists."

The garrison commander actually fell back a pace. "You? Alchemists? You can make the Elixir of Immortality?"

"We grow no older," Ganesha declared. "I myself remember your First Emperor. . . ."

The garrison commander looked almost as if he would prostrate himself before the sage. His men, too, relaxed their threatening stance, but only slightly. Rufus pointed with his chin at where the troops looked weakest. "We could maybe take them. . . ."

Lucilius approached. "Tell him—offer to strike a bargain," he said. Reddened by grit and strain as they were, his eyes brightened. "Our lives, our weapons, even our Eagle . . ." The wastrel might mention the Eagle only as an afterthought, but he mentioned it all the same.

"This one is Li Liang-li," said the garrison commander. Ssu-ma Chao drew breath in at the magnitude of that concession, then, hastily, began again to translate as the language grew complex and potentially treacherous. "And this one declares that the Son of Heaven must see you, must speak to you."

Maybe we could take them, Quintus thought. Now that they were shocked, a smaller, tougher force might have a chance at, if not escape, a soldier's death.

Ssu-ma Chao jerked his head, knowing well the mettle of the men at his back. "No. No. If this one has done aught to deserve well of you—" *he made you allies, not slaves,* "—do not disgrace me before my officers, or I shall have to die, and my men too. In great pain, after witnessing your deaths. And then they would send men to slay my family in the Land of Gold, too, down to the meanest servant. And our memory would be disgraced."

His eyes swept over Lucilius and he spat. "You will win more gold by doing as the commander wishes."

"And we, will we get our freedom?" Lucilius retorted.

The garrison commander Li Liang-li barked a few words. No doubt he suspected this interchange. Ssu-ma Chao sagged in on himself.

"These slaves—" a murmur went up in the ranks as Arsaces, damn his eyes, translated, "—are men of Rhum who have served well and helped us win through many hardships to obey you," Ssu-ma Chao told the commander. His abasement wasn't going to be enough, and he knew it—but it was a try. Ssu-ma Chao offered his pride to save them and perhaps even win them some of the gold pieces for which Lucilius hungered.

"Obedience," said the garrison commander in a heavily accented version of the Parthian current along the caravan roads. "You have a problem with that, have you not?"

He turned to a younger man—his second in command?—who bore the same marks of an aristocratic heir sent out to exotic lands that Lucilius had borne so sleekly long, long before Carrhae.

Patrician, Quintus recognized the breed. *Just as prejudiced and arrogant as our own can be.*

"Younger brother, mark this man and those like him well. And remember when you return to Ch'ang-an and make your bows before the Son of Heaven seated in brightness before the Dragon Throne. This man in the dust is an officer of the border. Men who serve in these distant regions are not necessarily pious sons and obedient grandsons. They have been deported for some offense; this is why you find them serving there on the frontier. As for the barbarians who company with him, look well at them too and regard them as you would wild beasts."

Ssu-ma Chao flushed, with anger or shame at being thus insulted, and before his men.

Rufus threw Quintus a look that would be imploring in anyone else and was only bloodthirsty in the centurion. *Still want us to hold back?*

Clearly, he would have to do something or *he* might have a mutiny on his hands.

He edged up carefully toward Ganesha, showing the garrison troops that he, at least, was unarmed. "Will you translate for me?" he asked. His Parthian was at least as good as this arrogant officer's. But he had seen men like this one—too many times—who drove their soldiers too hard, denying them rest or drink or shade, and whose arrogance and colossal bad judgment could have gotten them killed had his own word—and the words through him, of his men not been pledged to stay their hands.

Ganesha nodded.

"Say then . . . to the . . . use whatever courtesies you think are the best . . ." he had no better idea of it, ". . . for him if he needs to have his pride satisfied that, changeable as we of Rome may be, when we pledge our word, *that* is as fixed as the North Star. And our word is pledged to the officer who treated us with the honor he accords to his own—and expects to have accorded to himself."

Ganesha's sly, warm eyes lit. "Wit, I see, is another bow you can draw. You have hit in the gold this time— right upon the thoughts of one of the Realm of Gold's most honored sages. I shall tell this Li Liang-li that your people do as they would hope to be done by."

Ganesha's voice rose in the rapid tonal babble of the Realm of Gold. So long it took, Quintus thought, to say in his tongue what would be only a few brief words in good, plain Latin. The aristocratic younger officer reacted with an indignant rush of breath and a lift of elegantly slanted brows. "Kung Fu Tse," he exclaimed. His superior officer seemed barely to listen, yet the stiffness of his posture relaxed somewhat.

"Do you want their swords?" Quintus strode forward. Spears levelled at his breast, and he ignored them. It was *right*, what he did: challenge this arrogant man by his own codes to deal with them justly. He could even defend the word of Ssu-ma Chao, who had treated them almost as if he were himself a Roman, and who had been disgraced for it before his soldiers.

Lucilius shot him a look that clearly indicated he had been out in the desert too long with his head uncovered:

Yet, still, he held out his sword, defying the garrison commander to take it and thus confess fear not only of the Romans but of the Ch'in soldiers who had campaigned with them.

A gesture of rejection would have been useful. A word of respect *should* have been his—and would have been, were Quintus dealing with honorable Romans; but he was used enough to less. Li Liang-li simply turned his shoulder. He spoke to Ssu-ma Chao. "The Son of Heaven can be merciful. He has commanded his generals to be lenient to most faults, as long as general discipline is maintained." A dismissive hand gesture showed what he thought of that mercy.

Ssu-ma Chao handed Quintus's sword to a soldier, who took it to the tribune. He received it with as close to a Ch'in bow as he could muster. Again, under a patron's yoke? Quintus had sworn never to bend his back like a client again—but he had his men to think of. He must be hostage to them. He might regret this, but he sheathed it in the instant before the officer turned back toward him.

"The Emperor, my master, has ordered all the people of the south to show their obedience. The heads of the disobedient are exposed at Ch'ang-an, in the sight of all the world. You—you must acknowledge him as sovereign."

"He's pressing his luck," Lucilius muttered. To Quintus's astonishment, he saw the young patrician and the Ch'in aristocrat exchange what could almost have been a wink. Quintus supposed, though, that he should be glad that he had Lucilius's support for at least this much—but he could have done without that wink.

So, it was further exile and what might yet prove to be slavery? He thought of his days as a client as having been hard. He realized now that he had not even begun to test the meaning of the word "hardship" or of his own endurance. He had thought himself bereft to have lost father and grandsire and estates: Now, he had seen Legions raised for the majesty of Rome thrown away by noble fools. And he had survived that much. He had found farmwork and a warrior's training arduous: Now, he had endured heights and deserts that could freeze the blood or make it boil, if demons did not drain it first.

Now, he foresaw his task would be to march even further east into the realms of a gold he would never partake of. *We will show these strangers* Romans! he wanted to shout to his men, to hear them cheer, to see them salute. Here, in Kashgar, or at the throne of the tyrant that ruled all Asia. Armed, or in chains. He would show these people *Romans*. He gestured for Rufus to dress the column. The Legionaries' bodies cast long shadows. A fine drift of grit lined his face; dust, like a saffron veil, skimmed before his eyes, scouring the moisture from them even as it made him want to rub them clean.

The garrison commander shouted more commands. His riders formed up, some riding as exceedingly watchful guards behind the column of Romans. Down the last of the great rocks into the grit the combined forces marched, up the steep ridges of immense, winding dunes, not stopping even long enough for food. It was a deliberate test of their heart and their strength. *Watch, you arrogant barbarian. These are* Romans. Wherever the Eagle was stowed, they would march as proudly as if under its shadow.

The reddening sunlight glinted off the salt flats until they resembled the plain of Carrhae the sunset after the battle had been lost.

As they marched behind the garrison forces, torches sparked up, either to alert guards posted along the line of march or to signify from guardpost to guardpost that troops were approaching Kashgar.

19

SIGNALS AND THE blaze of torches warned the guards posted on the walls of the city of the travellers' approach. Even the fields were guarded by farmers who bore themselves like fighting men, Quintus saw the next day. Only sparse green showed in the dusty soil, somewhat darker near the channels that carried the thin streams of water that made any growth at all possible this close to desolation.

Kashgar, or Su-le as the Ch'in called it, was twice walled: by tall, thin poplars that cast columns of meager shadow on the marching, weary men, and by its actual fortifications—walls as high as forty feet. The walls were whitewashed, and glistened in the sun and they ended in guard platforms and square towers. Quintus could see the poles to which torches or signals could be attached. Knowing how such towers could be stocked, he began to count them. The sum was a city's strength.

A flurry of lights winked from the walls. Scrapings and stampings of feet warned those outside that weapons had been trained on the approaching men. Notwithstanding that soldiers and officers of Su-le—including Li Liang-li—rode with them, the garrison had turned out. Quintus peered past the high, neat walls. He could see piles of wood—a rare treasure in these parts unless you counted brushwood. No doubt it was kept for night signals.

"Fully stocked, I'd wager," Rufus muttered approvingly as they rode toward the gates. The place indeed looked as self-contained as any garrison city in which they had ever been stationed.

"Lucilius is the gambler, not me," the tribune replied. "I wouldn't throw my silver away on a sure thing— assuming we ever see a paymaster again."

That subject touched too close to home. Ch'in was supposed to be the Land of Gold, but they had seen precious little gold, silver, copper, or even brass. Even a Roman slave usually had some coin about him. But prisoners . . . like slaves, prisoners were property: Their status may have shifted, but not by all that much.

"Rough land to farm," the centurion commented, moving away from the sore subject. They had ridden past fields reclaimed from the waste with painstaking care and backbreaking labor, cultivated by strong men and women whose every move seemed as deliberate as it had been taught on the drill field. Wrest the food from the land, green from the ochre and ashen. Husband the water. Make the land—if it couldn't be made to bloom— feed its people. Preserve it against raiders and enemies and whatever demons now stalked it. Even the eldest of the farmers bore himself like a soldier.

"Not where I'd choose to claim my land and mule," Rufus said. "What about you, sir?"

The haze of the river valley Quintus had called home for too short a time rose in his imagination. Even when his family's fortune was at its lowest, that land had held a wealth of water and soil that the sere fields of Kashgar could never hope to reach. This was poor land, but it was home to the soldierly men and sturdy women who worked it. They had land of their own and a future they could count on—a fortune far beyond the reach of the Romans.

Unless, of course, the Black Naacals conquered.

Hot wind fanned Quintus's face. He started. That had felt as if he stood too close to a fire. He had been expecting the damp, Tuscan breezes. They might bear flux and fever, but at that moment, he would have welcomed the dampness against his parched skin and run the risk of illness. The hot winds here ruffled the trappings of his horse and flicked a glint or two from the matted gold of Lucilius's hair, darkened almost to the color of less noble Romans. It was all the gold Lucilius could count on, he often said. Just as well he couldn't gamble it away with older men, or he'd have been bald by now.

Once again, the patrician tribune rode as close as he could to the Ch'in officers. His eyes followed the young underofficer from the capital. *Lucilius is a man for women,* Quintus reminded himself. *That one's another like himself—another noble with his fortune to make by impressing bigger nobles.*

He noted that Lucilius's Parthian was improving. He wondered, however, if the young Ch'in aristocrat would risk a chance of impressing Li Liang-li long enough to speak to any of the Romans. Aha! Now Lucilius managed to meet his eye, nodded; but the other man turned his head away. Quintus suppressed a crack-lipped smile: That was as fine a snub as he had seen in all his days of clienthood. Lucilius flushed, that is, he flushed as much as you could tell from the clean patches in the pale mask of dust and grit that was his face.

Let him try again. Let him know what it feels like. And then, please all the gods, let him succeed. The equivalent of a patrician tribune would be a formidable ally, especially if they were sent on eastward to the capital of Ch'ang-an. Some of them, he was sure, would indeed be sent in just the same way as Crassus and the other proconsuls pillaged the eastern provinces for exotic goods and noble hostages. But who would be among them? Lucilius, if he had his way. Arsaces, perhaps: He was useful with beasts and could be serviceable during the march as well as as a translator. Himself? He was only commander by default. Perhaps it was time to turn command over to Lucilius, if he could accomplish anything with it. And then, perhaps, Quintus could stay here with those of the Romans who were not sent on ahead. He might even get to work this stubborn land.

In a way, it would be little different from the fates of his brother Legionaries at Merv—save that here, perhaps, they would have at least a chance at a kind of freedom. And land. Certainly, it was dry, but there *was* water here. Otherwise, there would be no fields and no poplars. What a cohort or so of Romans, working together, might build . . . aqueducts soaring in the Italian hills flickered in his mind's eye. His head felt as if his brains were boiling under his turban. And beneath his tunic gathered the familiar power of his talisman.

Danger here? Or was it forgetfulness? Folly to dream of land and a future, even as bleak and isolated a one as Su-le, for himself and his followers. Draupadi rode past, and the talisman heated again. Oh gods, she would be sent on, and he could not let her go alone. Not after what he had vowed.

The Ch'in guards closed in around here. A look from Ssu-ma Chao was all the apology he was going to get: the Ch'in officer was a man with two masters to obey now.

The gates of Kashgar opened to engulf them. For an instant, the walls' shadow swallowed them—an instant of blessed coolness and darkness. Then they passed through the stockade into the town itself. Above them on the walls, guards stood prepared.

"Alert," Rufus commented. "Maybe too much so?"

The Ch'in soldiers did have the too-tense look of men who constantly await attack: from what direction or enemy they do not know. You could see that in Li Liang-li: arrogant, high-handed, still ready to jump at shadows with deadly force. Men did that—from the merest recruit to proconsuls in their glory—when they were afraid. And judging from what Quintus had seen, this was a town, a region, a land that had right to be afraid.

Harness jingled amid the cries of sullen, weary beasts that scented water and an end to toil not far ahead. For the first time in months, the clamor of a town enveloped them. Food that was not dried or seared over a dung fire—Quintus's mouth watered. Best not think of it; after all, prisoners' rations might not bear thinking on. And he had no money. Certainly he had none for extra food. And—a more painful thought—he had no coin for even the type of gift that a client, back in Rome, was able to buy for a woman.

A camel snaked out her neck. The foul-breathed jaws snapped. Quintus recognized that beast, as he would have known what it bore if he had seen it in Hades. The Eagle. *Relax,* he told himself. *You are worn out. The gates are shut, and even if that camel breaks loose, it's not going anywhere.*

Clearly, the soldiers on the wall agreed that for now,

the threat was past. They relaxed minutely, no longer considering themselves to be under immediate danger of attack. One or two men who seemed to be off-duty pointed and laughed at the angry beast, which was plunging and snapping in a very determined attempt to live down to camels' reputation for terrible dispositions.

Except that in all the time the beast had been part of the caravan, it had never once spit on or lunged at any of its drivers. That was one reason it had been selected to bear the Eagle sent on before. It had even been the subject of some jokes, though its driver had been much envied. Now it moaned, snapped, and tried to break free, lashing out at the men who dodged and attempted to restrain it. One man went sprawling. He rolled fast, seeking to dodge the beast.

"If that were a dog, I'd swear it was mad," Rufus commented. "About time they brought it under control."

Some of the others thought that way, too. Arsaces was a horseman, but even as he approached the maddened camel, hands out, a man in a mottled robe brought a staff down on the Persian's back. A moment later, he rolled beneath the camel's feet. Even in the noise of the square, Quintus heard the snap of bone. Arsaces's face was bloody and scraped. His neck hung twisted at an impossible angle.

My sword! Damn, I knew this was folly!

Where had Arsaces's damned mount gotten itself to? Ah, there! When Quintus swerved to try to seek out the man who had struck the guide down, he had vanished into the crowd. *Get the sword, in case he comes back.* But a soldier with a drawn sword barred his way.

How did you avenge a comrade on a camel? A Persian, Arsaces was, but he had served the Legions well, with a loyalty exceeding anything they might have expected from a man of the East. Hard to believe that energy was stilled. What folly had prompted Quintus to go unarmed?

Again, the beast plunged and twisted. Its pack started to slip to one side as the girths of its packsaddle weakened. There was that murderer once more! His staff cracked down, this time on the camel's back. Again, the beast lunged. Its saddle jolted farther to the side. Straps snapped, and it fell. So carefully wrapped was the Eagle that Quintus could not hear the clang of metal striking earth. The staff lashed out again, a final blow. With a grunt, as if all the air in its body had been forced from its lungs at once, the beast collapsed on top of Arsaces.

Now the thief and killer in a mottled robe boldly snatched for the roll of fabric that was the Eagle of Rome.

"Get him!"

"Shoot!"

"Kill that thief!"

The man in desert robes had snatched up the pack and hauled it across his back. He swung about, desperately seeking a road of escape. Perhaps he might have made it, had the Romans not been there, had the thing he sought to steal been anything but a Legion's Eagle. But if the Romans' way was blocked, so was his.

The thief's eyes were black, yet they shone strangely in sockets blackened against the sun. His face—Quintus had seen that elegance of feature before, and that supple length of limb—on Draupadi. This ragged, murderous thief looked enough like her to be close kin.

Ssu-ma Chao beckoned his men aside. After all, it wasn't as if the Romans were going anywhere out of town, either. Might as well let them take out the thief. He held his staff out before him.

This murderer had the Eagle, and their way to him was clear!

Quintus hurled himself forward, even as Draupadi cried his name—his or Arjuna's—he no longer cared. All he knew was that no one, no one at all, must be allowed to kill a comrade and steal a pack, least of all when it held the Eagle of the Legion.

He shouted in sheer rage. The man in the shabby robes could escape! Now he was heading toward the gates, but they were shut, blocked by the Ch'in as well as the Romans. Quintus moved into the thief's path. He raised his staff.

"For all the gods' sake! Give me a sword!" he cried. The idea that he might be perceived as begging the Ch'in for the order they should keep in one of their frontier cities enraged him. "Get him!"

"Men of Ta'Chin!" Ssu-ma Chao shouted. Drawing his own sword, he tossed it at Quintus. It glinted as it flew, catching the flash of the hot sun; the Roman caught it in time to bring it up against the thief's staff.

The staff hit the borrowed blade with a ring of two blades clashing. The force of that clash rocked Quintus. Heat flowed up the sword he held into its hilt, from its hilt up his arm, into his body. Flames shot from the sword, wreathing about his enemy. The man swung his staff so that it whistled with the force that sent it passing through the air. Once more came the ring of metal against metal.

Though that weapon had looked to be wood, surely it was fashioned from something harder by far. From the slight hollowness in the ring as his blade clashed against the staff, Quintus sensed that it was past its breaking point. Sweat glued the hilt to his hand.

Another blow. Quintus felt the shock throughout arm and shoulder. His blade rang and then snapped, leaving him holding the hilt and about a foot of less-than-deadly metal. The next blow of that staff . . .

But no blow ever came. From the talisman he wore, warmth flooded out across his chest. Warmth as heady as wine filled him. Quintus saw his enemy's eyes go wide, as those black eyes stared at him. The rising warmth leached away pain and weariness for the Roman, while the broken blade in his hand glowed.

Then the light flooded out from the hilt he still clutched. For an instant, Quintus could see the bones of his hand and arm through his skin. He felt heat, but no burning.

His eyes met those of the thief, dark eyes, almost ophidian with their look of alien hate. Light flashed from the fragment of the blade still clinging to the hilt to engulf his enemy. The man screamed as that point of radiance touched him. Where it touched, his flesh crisped. Still, he held Quintus with that hate-filled, *other* stare, though his face contorted in mortal agony and even fear. Then the eyes blanked, and held nothing at all.

Behind him, Quintus heard men shouting. The flames spread, to engulf the man's robes and dart over to the Eagle he bore on his back. Its wrappings caught fire, and the bundle fell. As the standard rolled free of the charring cloth, every bronze feather on the Eagle glowed.

The fire had all but consumed the thief. However, for a moment, he stood. He was only bones, but still he stood holding that staff. Then that strange weapon dropped with a clang. Defenseless, the skeleton disintegrated and flaked into ash as if the bones had been of tremendous age.

Quintus dropped the broken blade that had, suddenly, cooled. He staggered over to kneel by the Eagle. It was important, just as it had been at Carrhae, that the Legion's standard not lie on the ground. Struggling to his feet with it held close, he planted it upright and leaned against the staff. He was as tired as if he had suffered through a full battle.

The hot sun of Kashgar beat down upon his head. Where had the turban he had worn since the beginning of this fatal trek gone to? He would need it: the gods knew that he would never find another proper Roman helmet.

Draupadi came to him, the dusty roll in her slender hands. She brushed the dust from it and held it out to him. She showed no fear, no revulsion at having seen one man crushed and another man—or perhaps a Black Naacal or one of their agents—burned. But then, she had been the wife of the greatest warrior of one age. And before that—it was too hard to think of what she had been before that. More than anything, Quintus wished to be clean. A plunge in the Tiber, cold from the spring melts—ahhh, that would be better than Elysium.

Draupadi stepped closer, and Quintus rested his arm across her shoulders, appreciating the strength he had found in her supple frame. For a moment, he stood balanced between his Eagle and the lady, as strength from both seemed to flood into him, restoring his soul, if not his worn body.

Gradually, he became aware, as he stood thus holding a lady he had treasured from the first, that the other Romans and Ch'in were staring. Quintus colored. His father had never shown such caring for his mother in public. Even her epitaph, like her mother's before her: "She stayed at home and tended her wool," reflected her worth as a wife and worker, not woman. *But this is my beloved,* Quintus said deep within himself as he tightened his arm about her. It was an un-Roman thought: It was far older than Rome. Draupadi knew his mind, and smiled.

A veil of windborne dust, rattled the thirsty poplars and obscured the faces—appalled, afraid, or calculating—that surrounded him. Mouths worked. Gradually, Quintus heard the shouted concerns and questions that might just as well be commands. The thin dust—mixed over with the powdery ash of his dead enemy—briefly filmed their hands. He brushed it from Draupadi's hair, the black of a mountain stream running free at night. But even before he touched that, the long locks gleamed. He glanced down at his hand. It shone too.

Only moments before, he had been smeared with dust, his entire body coated with the white powder of salt and sweat dried on his skin by the desert heat. Now, he was as clean and shining as if he marched in triumph behind a victorious proconsul. Overhead, the Eagle glowed, drawing all eyes.

Draupadi leaned a hand on the staff that upheld the Eagle and the proud motto of Rome's Republic: *The Senate and the People of Rome.* "It is truly a mighty weapon that you have here," she whispered.

So it was: As much as anything else, it was a sign of Rome and its power. Where the Eagle flew, respect followed, even in this most recent captivity. Draupadi knew his mind, just as she had days before; but she shook her head. "Are you not to seek Pasupata, more powerful than Arjuna's bow? Long and long Arjuna searched in the mountains. He sought out strange teachers. And then he returned. Still, unless a man be fit to wield what weapons he has found, they will turn upon him."

The sun beat down upon the Eagle to cast a sort of glory about them.

Then Li Liang-li approached. Several paces away, he

stopped and snapped a few words at his second in command. The young man frowned. Quintus could guess the order he was so reluctant to obey. The garrison commander meant to claim the Eagle. Quintus's Eagle. His Legion's talisman, and the symbol of Rome—just after he had won it back.

Ch'in soldiers circled him, their faces set. Many of those men had journeyed with him. Would they hesitate to kill a man they had fought beside? If they did, Quintus was certain that other men from the garrison would move in. Lucilius too pushed forward, to be brought up short— if respectfully—by Rufus. He gestured furiously at the centurion to let him through.

"You have to give it up again," he hissed at Quintus. "That commander would think nothing of killing us all."

"And are our lives worth so much without our honor?" Quintus asked. The patrician's face was drawn. With fear? Was he asking a favor, actually begging one from a former client of his *gens?*

Come and take it. He did not dare speak the words, but they must have been revealed on his face. Gently, he began to push Draupadi from him. She moved her hand from the Eagle. Some of the warmth filtering through the two of them abated. She nodded, and edged back into the press of onlookers and soldiers. With one fragment of his awareness, Quintus saw her talking to Ganesha as he stood near the men who had come to bear off Arsaces's body. *Farewell, old friend.* It did not feel strange any more to call the Persian "friend." But calling him "brother" would have hurt, so he did not even try.

If Quintus surrendered the Eagle, it was Carrhae all over again. It was watching The Surena receive the submission of Legionaries and proconsul. Then, Quintus had fought for the Eagles and nearly died of a blow as he tried to save one. Giving back this Eagle he had won would kill him, he thought. He could feel its power working within him. *Let them try to take it.* They could not do so unless he chose.

Or, unless he died. Death before dishonor, perhaps; but his grandsire had bowed as a client for Quintus's sake and suffered no loss of dishonor in Quintus's eyes. And he—he had men who looked to him, and he had Draupadi. He had given up his dreams of home. Did he have to give up this last token of it?

Fool, and look you what Draupadi and Ganesha have given up!

"Quintus . . . comrade . . ." Lucilius, trying again. *Don't try too hard, tribune. Your heart may burst with the effort. Why shouldn't it? Mine is breaking right about now.*

He snarled at the patrician, who went white under his weathering. *Still think you have things to lose? You don't know the half of it.*

"Wait."

Ssu-ma Chao stepped forward. "If this humble one may be permitted . . ." First, he spoke in Ch'in to his commander, then translated it into Parthian. The self-abasement sounded strange in a language suited far better for brittle court intrigues—or caravan oaths.

The garrison commander barked something, and the young city man stepped back, hands at his side, relief writ large on his brow. He returned to his superior and stood waiting. Only the look in his eye boded very ill for Quintus. He would not forget how he had lost face before the rabble and his own commander.

"Comrade," Ssu-ma Chao's use of the word, unlike Lucilius's, did not make Quintus wish his dry mouth would allow him to spit. "I gave you and your men your weapons back. We have fought together. I gave you my word—my ancestors take witness—that I will strive to have you treated well. And I repeat my word to you: You will be treated with all respect. Surely this does not require more blood?''

Oh, but it does, it does. But not this way, Quintus thought. Dying in a fine frenzy, dying with honor—he could understand that. But here was an enemy turned ally, offering him essentially the lives of his men.

Quintus glanced up at the Eagle. Light winked off the wrought bronze of its deadly beak. Then the light faded. The dust-laden wind swept through the square, stinging his eyes.

"Comrade," Quintus said warmly. "You are no servant of the dark. Guard this with all honor. Fortune grant that we may claim again our own."

Gently, he handed over the Eagle to the Ch'in officer, who took it and held it aloft in salute.

20

PITCH FIRES BURNED on Kashgar's walls, casting bloody shadows over their bulk and out into the desert where, under heavy guard, the Romans were camped. All Quintus's submission had been for nothing: He was not trusted as ally and scarcely trusted even as a prisoner—and with him, the rest of the Romans. The fires of the guardposts flickered and the stink of the pitch drifted thickly down to the camp like the fires kindled to burn slums racked by fever.

The garrison commander would not even allow them space inside the walls. Save for the fear that his caution might bring about their deaths, ejection from Kashgar was no great curse. The city seemed fevered, restive, a child crying weakly within a house wherein all others have died; two dogs snapping at a dirty chunk of meat; the acrid spoor of hunting cats; the thick-voiced shouts of men drunk past reason. No, the cleanliness of the desert seemed far preferable. They even had fresh food.

Quintus had seen Li Liang-li's face, though. Even in the brief time he had had to study it, it had aged and grayed, as if the man suffered from a canker not of the body, but of the spirit. He had been sent to push back the Hsiung-nu and keep them in subjection. Yet here he was, facing prisoners unlike any he had seen, and perils he refused to imagine.

Quintus looked at the watchfires as if, at any moment, he might expect to see a pillar of flame rising from one of the braziers placed in the towers, signalling danger. Danger lay in the deserts and the hills alike: Another danger, he was certain, lay within the city, where lurked those newcomers who might become such a formidable enemy. Kashgar was just the farthest outpost of an Empire, but in one way it reminded Quintus of Rome: The stink of factionalism underlay the smoke of three signal beacons.

Two parties of Ch'in soldiers shared the desert with the Romans . . . the now-unarmed Romans. Guards from the garrison, loyal to its commander, and, almost as carefully watched as the Romans, Ssu-ma Chao and his soldiers. He had returned from Parthia, furnished, as he thought, with the means of triumph, only to find himself under suspicion for his survival.

What was the Eastern officer's promise—and the word of his ancestors—worth, given the decline of his future? Quintus sighed. Choose as he would, he must choose wrong. With the Romans' arms gone again, how could they escape? He himself might turn toward the Ch'in and fling himself upon, say, that sleek young officer from the capital. Death would be sure, if not swift. Or he could wait for whatever stalked desert and city— and which regarded Draupadi, Ganesha, and he himself as its mortal enemies.

Footsteps came up beside him; the heavy, weary tread of Ganesha—and how weary he must be after these many, many years—and the delicate pace of Draupadi. He almost thought he could hear the tinkle of tiny bells, copper and gold and silver, accompanying her. As she had done that day, she came to his side and he laid his arm over her shoulders without hesitation.

Ganesha smiled. "That is the one thing," he said, "that is going right. The two of you . . ."

He looked at the woman, wrapped in the saffron that was the color of a Roman bride's veil. *Where I am Caius, be thou Caia,* he repeated the words he had said to her in his mind, savoring them.

She glanced up at him. Here was fire; if there were no doorposts to anoint with fat, no nuts to scatter before a cheering, singing crowd, there was indeed a priest present. And here, on her finger, was the ring of his service, resting above the *vena amoris* that ran all the way up to her heart.

He reached over and touched it. She smiled.

But Ganesha held up a peremptory hand.

The three of them froze where they stood. Ganesha jerked his head, and Draupadi nodded. A moment later, she began to chant softly, up and down on notes that should have lulled Quintus to sleep, but they did not. If she did not wish them to be seen, they would not be.

Lucilius and Wang Tou-fan, the young officer from Ch'ang-an, paced beyond them as if they were not there—never mind the fact that the hilt of the young officer's sword almost brushed Draupadi's robes.

How did Lucilius, who had always been quick to jeer at any evidence of rusticity, enjoy being talked down to as an untutored barbarian?

"You saw it," said the Imperial soldier. "Saw how it blazed. Like the Phoenix, which builds its own pyre, then rises from the ashes, reborn."

"That's *Latin!*" Had Draupadi's spell not held, his incredulous cry would have betrayed them right away. Where had Wang Tou-fan learned their language? The familiar, beloved syllables sounded odd in the aristocrat's mouth. Odd and distasteful: Quintus would have liked to smash them from his lips.

"Strange," murmured Quintus, "I should not have thought they had anything at all in common except pride in their bloodlines. Least of all, a common language."

"*They,*" said Ganesha, "do not. But others might, others for whom the learning of a strange tongue is as easy as the shifting of one robe for another."

"It is not only robes that can be shifted," he added darkly.

"We have no Phoenix, as you call it, but an Eagle," said Lucilius. "Our Legions follow them. If you listened to Ssu-ma Chao . . ."

"A provincial of no particular family—what has such as he to tell me? He brought you here; he brought the Eagle, as you call it. You saw how it blazed, even for him. What could it not do for . . . for us?"

"What of it? A trick of the sunlight, nothing more," Lucilius drawled.

The Ch'in hissed. Quintus pondered Ganesha's words. *As easy to shift from one robe to another* . . . as the Naacals had done. The man whom fire had consumed had died without a scream. But a deathscream had come from behind Quintus.

It was mad. It was pure lunacy beyond any wild fantasy that any man had ever had. What if *two* men in addition to poor Arsaces had died in Kashgar—the one man's body burnt by the power of the Eagle, and the spirit of the other destroyed when the first man's ego conquered and occupied his body. Madness, true. But how else to explain that scream or how an arrogant young officer now spoke polished Latin?

"It is no matter," Lucilius said, sullen. "This Eagle—oh, very well—the Phoenix lies in your power. Or in your commander's. And you and he are, as I observed, on the best of terms."

"It is no matter," said Wang Tou-fan or that which wore his flesh. "He will not permit you to remain here. He said as much while he was . . . tired men drink too deeply, let us say. And, when they are tired and their guard is down . . . I have had my piece of good fortune out of this: I am to return to Ch'ang-an with you. Bearing with us the Eagle."

Lucilius shrugged. Quintus did not even need to see his face to know that the patrician was wearing his "and what do *I* gain from this?" look. Dice, defeat, forced marches: They were all the same. Even this far from home. Lucilius might spy a future and the power he thought he had lost.

"How did he make the Eagle light?" demanded the Ch'in.

Quintus could have laughed at the baffled arrogance in Lucilius's voice. "I don't know. I never saw that happen before. I tell you, there is a strangeness . . . I will be glad when we go to a place where family is respected and a man can be civilized."

"Mud huts and upstarts!" spat the Ch'in noble. Jupiter Optimus Maximus, he was speaking of his own capital! Or of the capital of the young man whose body had been usurped. Then he recovered self-control.

"The man who could teach me the secret of the Eagle's fire—the secret of the Phoenix itself—might find himself honored as if he were a prince, almost as the Son of Heaven himself."

Lucilius almost purred. "You begin to interest me."

"You, not—"

"That peasant? He would not listen to you. But it was he for whom the Eagle lit. I must think. . . ."

"I must see it," said Wang Tou-fan.

"And if you touch it? It may consume you as it consumed . . . how shall we call your former . . . yes, yes, I know. I am all discretion, not that I believe you. Will you risk the chance that the thing has bonded so to him that it will turn on all others?"

"It allowed Ssu-ma Chao to touch it."

"The risk, as I said, is yours."

"He has the place," said Wang Tou-fan, "that should be yours. That can be yours, with far more added to it. That choice, as I said, is yours. Remove him, and perhaps the Eagle will turn to you. And then you and I can talk again."

Quintus stiffened. They had never agreed, he and Lucilius, not from the moment that the patrician had eyed him and marked him as a bumpkin and his family's client; and Quintus had, in return, seen the other as responsible for his family's degradation. All this long round of service and exile, they had been like enemies manacled on a short chain and tossed into deep water, to drown together or, together, struggle onto dry land.

"Here is a blade," said Wang Tou-fan. "And here is a phial. They have fine poisons in the farthest East. But a scratch . . ."

Lucilius made a sound of revulsion.

"Do you want to be a fighting man all your life, one step up from a slave, when Ch'ang-an holds so much promise for a talented man who understands where his advantage lies. Take the knife!"

"He is not *worthy* of my attention," the Roman muttered. "To die at the hands of one of my *gens* is more honor than that rustic deserves."

"Can you be so sure? Or is it that you fear him—or that hulking oaf who marches behind him and serves him? As he should have obeyed you. Tell me, Lucilius, are you afraid?"

Afraid of Rufus? If Lucilius was not, he ought to be— if only for listening to this talk of betrayal. Quintus's belly chilled. He would not have thought . . .

"What's there?" Lucilius whispered and whirled about.

The Ch'in laughed softly. "Afraid? As I thought. Review your enemies; and what is there to fear? The oaf, the young fool, the old man from Hind, perhaps, and she who travels with him."

"She is of interest to me. . . ." Lucilius purred.

"Take her if you wish," said Wang Tou-fan, as if throwing a coin to a whining beggar. "They are not . . . unskilled, adepts like herself. As you may have observed. As your enemy the rustic doubtless has discovered."

The other laughed softly. "She is of interest to many."

"I'll kill him myself!" Quintus got the words out between gritted teeth.

"Quiet!" Draupadi hissed. She flung her arms about him as he started toward Lucilius and Wang Tou-fan and out of the range of the protective illusion she had cast. Her breath against his neck was warm and comforting.

"No, Quintus," Draupadi crooned it almost as if she cast another spell. *Lady, you do bespell me with every move.* "No. Caius. Dear one. Be still, please!" She seemed to rock him back and forth, as if seeking to relax his too-taut body. "I am here. Stay with me."

So it was treachery by Lucilius, was it? Knives in the

back. And not just in his back, but Rufus's. Quintus had known Lucilius to be venal, known him to be ambitious, spoiled, too ready to assume that all good things were his for the asking. But not evil. Now—with a strangled moan, he let his head fall onto Draupadi's shoulder. Her body felt better in his arms than he could have dreamed. And this, he knew, was no illusion.

Nevertheless, he let her go. He needed to get closer, to see the two men, born half a world from each other yet united in treachery. Romans had shamed Rome before, but this . . . this was somehow different. And there were so very few of them left this far from home.

"Who's that?" Lucilius's voice rang out sharply.

"How long have you been in the desert?" asked Wang Tou-fan. "Are you truly fool enough to believe the stories of demons and goblins?"

A hissing began to rise in the outermost range of Quintus's hearing, a hissing of great snakes, their jaws wide, draining the life through shining, hollow fangs until their prey were ancient-seeming, bled-out husks such as he had seen at Stone Tower.

"Yes," Draupadi whispered. "Yes. Surely, he has been touched by their power, promised . . ."

Surely, Lucilius had been promised—what? Draupadi herself? The gold he had always wanted? He would be lucky if he did not find himself, like his master the dead proconsul, with more gold than he could safely swallow—the mock of his enemies.

Still, Lucilius stood. "Why not do it yourself?" he demanded. "You could say he tried to escape. You could say he ran mad and tried to kill someone."

"Perhaps I require proofs of those in my hands. For example, you know, as does every man here, that as long as one of you Romans remains alive, he will not abandon him. He would not even, I imagine, abandon you."

Quintus could guess Lucilius's answering, high-nosed glare. But would he take the knife and the poison?

The Ch'in noble's hands dropped. He stood motionless. Quintus heard other footsteps, passing so close beside him that surely the conspirators must have heard their breath in the stillness of the night.

Ssu-ma Chao! Why had he ventured outside the safety of the camp, unless—and the thought made Quintus's belly chill—he too . . .

"Who goes there?" the frontier officer snapped. Quintus might well have laughed at the way the two conspirators attempted to look casual, guilt-free.

Wang Tou-fan recovered himself first, staring at Ssu-ma Chao—a contest of wills as each sought to make the other cast down his eyes. The younger man was from Ch'ang-an, was in favor with the Court; but Ssu-ma Chao had a will of iron. He might have been called a provincial, accused of filial impiety, and all but accused of treachery to the Son of Heaven, but he knew his own mind. The man from Ch'ang-an had, by his own code, toyed with treachery, conspired with a prisoner; he could not meet the older man's eyes.

"These lands are not safe," Ssu-ma Chao said. "Not just the demons, but our own soldiers have died. When you have ranged the deserts as long as I—which the spirits of your ancestors forbid!—you will know that this land holds traps, even for the wary." Then he bowed ironically and deeply. "This one humbly suggests that one trip across the Takla Makan does not make the esteemed officer from the capital an expert guide. And you—" he turned to Lucilius, "—are under guard, or

should be. So, back to your camp. I will not report this to
your officer, and you will not be punished.''

Lucilius stiffened. *Hoc habet!* Quintus thought, as he
might have applauded a deadly blow. Even in the darkness, Quintus could see how the patrician's light eyes
flamed. A slave and a subordinate—that was what Ssu-
ma Chao had treated him as. Now, he gestured at Wang-
Tou-fan as if requesting him to take charge of a somewhat recalcitrant prisoner so that the ranking Roman
officer—Quintus himself—might not need to be told. And
that, no doubt, would rankle Lucilius worse.

"This is my command now," snapped Wang Tou-fan.

Ssu-ma Chao bowed even more deeply. Then, deliberately, he turned and began to walk back toward the camp,
toward the fire. The hissing Quintus had heard subsided.
There would be no attempt tonight, he thought.

Wang Tou-fan glanced down at a small, poisoned
blade slipped from his sleeve. It would be easy, so easy
for him to run up behind the other officer and stab, not
even stab, but scratch him. At this moment, he hated
Ssu-ma Chao more than he wanted Quintus himself
dead. If he stabbed him, it might even be blamed on the
Romans.

Draupadi raised her hand and made a tiny motion. An
instant later, Wang Tou-fan stopped, as if struck by
something . . . something about the size of a small rock
that clicked off his arm and onto the desert floor.

Draupadi sagged, and Quintus caught her. With her
spell-casting and her sudden move to protect the border
officer, she had come to the limits of her strength, as he
had seen her do before.

"You spin powerful illusions, lady," he whispered
against that silky hair that, even in the desert, never lost
its scent of sandalwood.

"You do not understand," she said. "I had no pebble in my hand when I began. This was not illusion, but true creation."

He embraced her very gently. In the midst of treachery, she had achieved the victory she had sought for so many years.

Lucilius joined Wang Tou-fan. The Ch'in aristocrat was muttering to himself.

"Old men. Always old men. Send me out here where I am slighted. Make your future, they say. Make us proud. How, in the names of my ancestors? Here is just a prison of swords. So I seek power and, should I succeed, not even the Dragon Throne itself would be barred to me. It means power to those who stand with me, and all the gold in the Realm of Gold. Are you with me?"

Lucilius's hand shot out. Had Wang Tou-fan been a Roman, the gesture would have been finished in a clasp of arms or shoulders. "Make a future? So they would keep you short of silver and gold; sit on power till they die."

Wang Tou-fan laughed, softly, almost a hiss of amusement. "Old men. All old men and the younger fools—like those two—who serve them. But men die. Oh yes, they can die. And their power . . . it shall be mine. It will be mine."

Decide, Lucilius, Quintus thought. *Make your soul whole, or sell it. Be a Roman or a traitor, but choose.* It required only for him to take the poisoned blade or not.

The patrician held out his hand for the blade. It glinted in the night, and the poison on its tip seemed the color of rotted wood or of Charon's wharf in Hades.

"Lost," Quintus whispered. The man was his enemy, but his eyes filled with tears. "He is lost. I ought to kill *him,* but—oh gods, he was a man and a Roman and now—"

"In my old life," Draupadi whispered, "I swore not to wash my hair until I could wash it in my enemy's blood. I understand. There, my heart." She laid her hands on Quintus's arms. "There."

The two conspirators wandered off, too casually, in different directions. The wind blew sand about them until it veiled the vast, uncaring sky.

21

THEY HAD BEEN marching forever in a waste that made the Dead Sea, where it rippled sullenly in the depths of Judaea, seem as hospitable as the Tiber Valley in spring.

No merchants now rode with them because Wang Tou-fan, eager to return to the bright center of the Middle Kingdom, had selected a route so risky that no sane merchant would dare it. Ordinarily, caravans turned north at Kashgar to Aksu, Kucha, and Turpan, nestled in the shadows of the distant Heavenly Hills, or south to Khotan, into Hind past the lower lip of the devouring Takla Makan Shamo. By contrast, Wang Tou-fan planned to cut across the desert—across the tongue, as it were, of its mouth—to Miran, ordinarily a stop along the southern route. And then? Quintus had seen a map, and he was troubled. What need of treachery in a wasteland such as that?

Madness, the merchants had shouted in return. Arsaces's shade, Quintus thought, must be shaking with rage for the stupidity and the waste of the beasts he had tended.

They were all correct. After months of marching and of surviving the deserts, Quintus had thought himself inured to it. But all of the wastelands he had traversed had possessed *some* life: Here, there was none. The broken-backed ridges of dunes looked like the bones of some immense kraken, cast up on an intolerable shore. Pale, splintering wood projected from the settlements buried as deep in the sand as the tombs of Egypt to impale the careless or those who travelled by night. And when the wind blew, sometimes, they saw leathery and dried-out huddles that had been man or beast once, before the wind blew and their luck changed.

Long ago "Rome's race, Rome's pace" had given way. Rufus, gasping and almost fatally red in the face, now swayed—under Quintus's orders—upon a camel's back. Others took it in turn to ride or march, while the Ch'in officers had horses and chariots. The only pride was in endurance.

Swaying with the rhythm of his own beast, Quintus edged forward past the other Romans. Lucilius rode his horse with his back as straight as if he were on parade, disdaining what he called a show of weakness and what seemed like common sense to Quintus. Well enough, he had thought as they left Kashgar. Keep him tired and off-guard; sap his strength; whittle away his defenses. If it preserved his life or Rufus's, Lucilius might be as arrogant as he wished. When Rufus had collapsed gasping in the heat, he and Draupadi had examined him minutely for wounds: The clammy skin and stertorous breathing were much like the onset of some poisons.

Now Rufus rode past a maniple or so of Legionaries whose turn it was to march, and none dared to comment that he had a soft ride. They had all lightened their packs as much as they dared—and were permitted. Now they carried only food and water—and their arms. Draupadi rode, of course, swaying in the padded saddle, wrapped in the veils that reduced her face to a mere shadow of beauty, the only fair thing in this desolation. Ganesha rode close beside her, seemingly almost asleep.

Quintus passed several of the Ch'in guard. He called out a hoarse greeting. Turning in his saddle, Ssu-ma Chao nodded permission to Quintus to approach. He lowered the cloth with which he protected his face against the sun and stinging grit, and croaked a question at the officer. They would all drink later, when the desert cooled that night and they dared a few slightly less fearsome hours of travel by starlight.

Moisture was too precious to waste on speech. Still, it had to be said.

"Madness," Ssu-ma Chao husked. "I could almost pray for more deaths—of men or beasts. It would stretch out our water supplies."

It was quite possible for a caravan to founder of its own weight, with more men and beasts along the line of march than the pack animals could provide for. The men and weaker horses would die first, though many of these horses were bred to the heat and grit. Then the camels would start to die. If those perished, all would die, and the great drifts would cover them—until the wind cast them up again, husks to frighten the next travellers rash enough to venture here.

"Miran," Quintus faltered on the unfamiliar name that had become the object of his desire. "Will we really reach Miran?"

"If the ancestors wish," Ssu-ma Chao said. "And they send no storms . . ."

Which, of course, was no answer at all. Desert storms could force them to lie up, sweltering in the heavy felt wrappings that would shield them from the storm-borne sharp pebbles and grit that could scour flesh from bone. Such storms could delay them until their water ran out, and they could only bleed their beasts for fluid for so long.

"Say we reach Miran. And then?"

"The caves . . ." mouthed the Ch'in officer. He was the one who had dared show Quintus the map. The Roman valued him for this, for being unwilling to allow a man he still considered ally, rather than prisoner, to venture into the unknown devastation without some knowledge.

For devastation it was. Once well outside of Kashgar, Draupadi had taken one look and recoiled in horror. Ganesha's wise, sleepy eyes had widened. "So many years for the seabed to dry out and change so," he had mused before talk grew too painful to be much indulged in. "Waves. Capped with white spray, birds soaring on great strong wings like unto the sails of our ships, stroking us forward, as above, so below. . . ."

It was punishment even to think of a galley, cutting through the waters of the Middle Sea—all that blue water. The thoughts of coolness, of wetness, the ability to drink, not to satiation, but to drink at all, could drive a man mad.

For now, at least, there had been no storms. For which mercy they must thank the gods or the ancestors. But there were no birds this deep in the desert. Quintus saw that as a loss.

"An oasis?" he whispered. Shadow, he thought. Shade. Coolness. And, please the gods, a bubbling spring. Draupadi unveiling and freeing that dark wave of hair, her eyes gleaming in fire and starlight—if the sun did not burn out his eyes before he beheld her thus.

"What dangers here?" he husked.

"Storms," Ssu-ma Chao muttered. "Or straying off the path."

Wang Tou-fan had, Quintus knew, an instrument that showed true north. He himself had sought—and failed to find—Polaris, though whether that was his weakness or some shift in the very zodiac itself, he could not tell. He was a simple man and no philosopher. Always before, he had been glad for that to be so.

But now? Quintus wished he had Ganesha's wisdom, his understanding of what they faced, his experience of endurance. Or Draupadi's vision. She had passed this way before; it held no unfamiliar terrors for her. Now, as they travelled toward eternal exile, she still hunted for her enemies in her own way.

Ssu-ma Chao covered his face, veiling his features as had some of the Nabataeans who had betrayed Rome so long ago on the march toward Carrhae. His beast plodded on, complaining as Quintus would have liked to do.

With talk as closely rationed as the water, Quintus fell back on the discomfort of his own thoughts. The desert, it seemed, provoked reflection.

You are a Roman. True. *You must endure.* Unfortunately true. *You are of the Legions.* That was true, too. *Your trade is war.* Ah, that it never had been, fight though he had had to. *He* had asked no more than his family's lands, so richly watered—oh Dis, don't think of the Tiber now, with your mouth as parched as the land around you.

His trade had never *been* war. But was that still true? Here in the desert, a lie could mean your life. When he shut his eyes, sometimes, images of the deep desert replaced the lands he once knew as well as his own heart. He had become a man whose trade was hardship. Whose trade was war, too, if it came to that. And if Quintus, worn out, rode or plodded through an unspeakable present to an incomprehensible future and dreamed only of lying down and dying along the road, it was the warrior spirit—the elements in him Draupadi identified and cherished as Arjuna—that kept him going and even exulted in the chase that brought him closer and closer to his enemy.

For traces of the Black Naacals were all about them. It was only fools and madmen who spoke of the hissing that he heard. They called the sand *ming sha*, or singing sand. But Quintus heard it as the sound of great serpents, surviving even in this desolation. Never again, he knew, would he see a serpent—from the wise snakes at Delphi to the most humble farm or house snake—without an inward shiver or without reaching for a weapon.

He felt such a shiver as Wang Tou-fan turned to stare at him—flat, ophidian hostility. The man swung away and, from his breast, took out the instrument with which he studied the sky. He held it up, pondered, observed again, and paused. The sun was not yet at zenith—the deadly noontide when neither man nor beast dared stir, but, rather, lay flat, trying to sleep and, in sleep, evade fearsome dreams. Now Wang Tou-fan signalled a halt. That was folly, but Quintus was too tired to feel anything but relief. It meant a chance to lie in whatever shadow might be contrived, to rest, and—best of all—to sip some few mouthfuls of water, tasting of the leathern bottles in which it had been carried. It would be the last water he would drink before sunset.

He brushed the pale dust of dried sweat from his brow and turned about. He wanted to be near Draupadi, to aid her from her camel, and for that moment when he lifted her, to be a man rather than a captive wandering through a land of torment.

As he anticipated, she slid willingly down into his hands. Hot as the sun was, closeness to her made Quintus feel as if they lingered beneath green trees by a pool of sweet water.

Lucilius rode by, and the moment shattered as if they had looked into a pool, seen their faces reflected, then recoiled as a rock splashed nearby, destroying their image.

"I should kill him," Quintus muttered.

"And would that be worse than what he has done to himself? Drink, and tell me now if that is what you desire," she rebuked him gently.

He took a sip of the warm, strong-smelling water. Grit wormed its way into water and mouth alike. The water tasted like the ashen fruit that Legionaries too long in Judaea swore grew by the Dead Sea. He started after Lucilius's back, stubbornly upright even after he dismounted and could safely rest.

Gods keep him; he is dead already. Or worse, as if a lamia had him in thrall.

Draupadi inclined her head. "It is not only blood and strength they take, as they did at Stone Tower."

Too soon, the order came to remount. Quintus saw Draupadi settled in her veils on her saddle, her camel complaining as it swayed to his feet, before he himself mounted. Then he went to check on his men.

His beast rose, moaning like an old slave who wasn't sure he could survive another beating. Quintus had heard that song before; the beast would bear him down the line of march. He must review his men. He must check on their mounts and pack animals—especially the stubborn old camel bearing the Eagle.

* * *

Day after day, they rode, and Quintus found one prayer answered. He did not want to see his men divide into those who faltered and suffered in the sun but pressed on until they fell, always facing east, and those who fined down, whose skin blackened and whose eyes grew hidden in the wrinkles caused by squinting against the sun, but who adapted to the desert as if they had been bred there. They must all adapt. Or die.

Their sleep was shallow, dream-filled. It was not a Golden Age that haunted Quintus's rest; it was a Green Age. His home now struck him as unreal as Elysium, more a paradise than the gardens Arsaces had spoken of—and the gods send that the Persian's crafty spirit wandered in such places now. One day, Draupadi mentioned the deodars of the high hills in Hind, and he dreamed of them, too—places he had never seen with his own eyes, but that now seemed as familiar to him as his soul.

Ganesha, learned, enduring, dreamt, he said, of water when he dreamt at all. Inconceivable, what he had said: that all this waste had once lain at the bottom of a great sea.

"Miran?" It was all Quintus had strength to hope for now, as he lifted a packsaddle and fastened it on the protesting beast. The Bactrian's two humps showed still, like the dugs of a woman nursing in a famine—full, for now. They would wither. The water would be consumed; the camels would falter; and they all would begin to die—soon, if they did not reach Miran.

The desert turned cold at night, a deadly blessing against which they built fires of dung and the wood uncovered by the winds. Alternately, they froze and they baked. . . .

. . . To wake when dawn rose like a fireball from some hellish catapult in the east, the direction in which they must go. The camels groaned when shifted to their feet. The men had no strength to waste complaining. Each day, they settled in their saddles or marched, if it were their turn to struggle on foot. Perhaps water might be found today. That was hope enough.

Wang Tou-fan rode by, Lucilius at his horse's heels, ignoring the grit kicked up. The sunrise cast a molten glory over both of them. They were like brothers these days, intent on whatever enterprise they planned in Ch'ang-an. Quintus remembered The Surena. He had seen a similar gloss of hatred and violence and treachery upon him.

Do not resist. Endure.

Quintus started, saving himself from a slide forward that might have unseated him and hurled him into the path of those riding behind him. Where had that voice come from? A long-absent, familiar prickle over his heart: Yes, his talisman, the bronze dancer, had waked from the long sleep that it seemed to have entered when they reached the deep desert. *Or perhaps there was no sufficient danger up till now.* And *that* idea was frightening.

He took the dancer out and regarded it: delicate, ancient, surprisingly strong. Its upraised hands caught and held the last explosions of the sunrise, diminishing now to what was almost bearable splendor. A faint wind stirred the grit, setting swirls arise in an updraft, above the ungainly knees of the camel ahead of his own, veiling him in a world by himself.

Rays of light seemed to erupt from the dancing figure, spooking Wang Tou-fan's horse. It reared, screaming through a throat parched even for a desert beast. It danced on its hind legs, hurling the Ch'in aristocrat forward. He clung to its neck for a moment, then flew off, dust, grit, and small stones scattering about him. The Roman swerved his camel to avoid trampling the officer. A shining arc pierced the veils of dust as the bronze direction finder flew from Wang Tou-fan's hands.

Light overhead . . . was it a trick of the dawn that made its shadow resemble a great winged creature? It swooped, it neared them, and it dropped like a raptor, snatching up the chain of the direction finder as if an eagle spied a serpent and caught it, to fly off, prey in its mouth, to its eyrie.

No, Quintus told himself. It was another trick of this soul-destroying desert. He could *not,* most assuredly not have heard a shriek of triumph. No bird of prey would shriek so close to its prey and, thereafter, it must keep its beak firmly clasped around it.

He would have sworn, though, by all the *lares* and *penates* of his vanished home that he had seen an eagle swoop down to steal Wang Tou-fan's bronze device. But why would an eagle—the Romans' symbol—have chosen precisely the instrument on which all their lives depended?

They would never see Miran; they would die in the desert! Quintus hurled himself off his mount toward the Ch'in officer and Lucilius, who had begun frantically to burrow in the dust and grit. Blood welled from cuts in their hands, drying quickly on their sleeves and in the thirsty desert floor.

''That won't help.'' Rufus's hoarse voice held them all—officers, nobles, horsemen, soldiers—in their place. ''All of you pile into one spot and start kicking up sand . . . rock . . . whatever . . . and what you're looking for will never turn up. You want to do this orderly-like.''

He was in there then, bringing order out of panic with

his raspy-voice commands and occasional blows from a very battered vinestaff. Roman-fashion, the ground was cleared and quartered; the officers helped up, patched up, and brushed to some semblance of order—but no direction finder turned up. Quintus had not expected that it would.

Remounted, Quintus met Draupadi's and Ganesha's eyes as if the three of them studied the wreckage of their futures with the assurance of complete despair.

However, sun, sky, and desert had turned themselves into the usual noontime smelter before the others were able to concede that the bronze direction finder was gone for good. Some hurled themselves, gasping and red-faced despite their weathering, upon the grit in rage. A Ch'in soldier reached for a waterskin.

"Hold!" Rufus was there, his staff striking the man's hand away from the precious water. One of the Ch'in's fellows began to draw on him, and he raised his vinestaff again.

You have stumbled into deep water, old friend, Quintus thought and moved in to back him. The Ch'in soldiers' mood was ugly and could turn uglier. They could not mutiny, but they *must* blame something for their loss of hope. There could easily be more blood on the sand before long.

"Listen to me, man," Rufus spoke Latin, and there was no way the man-at-arms would understand him. Still, the force of his years of command, the assurance his knowledge of soldiers gave him kept the Ch'in soldiers' swords in their sheaths. *"Listen.* We knew this trip was going to be terrible even when His Excellency or whatever *had* that little . . . what-do-you-call-it . . . You know it. Now, with the way finder gone, we are going to have to go forward and find water. But it is going to take us much longer, don't you think?''

The wind had gone dead. Ganesha did not bother to raise his voice, but it rang out anyhow, translating Rufus's words. To Quintus's surprise, Lucilius flung up his hands on which the blood had dried.

''Do you think we will ever last till Miran?'' Quintus asked Ganesha in an undertone.

''There is sun. There are stars. We can travel as sailors do.'' The old priest recited precisely the words they needed to hearten them. Though sailors preferred not to journey out of sight of land, Ganesha had sailed upon some very strange seas. What he said could be relied on—at least to enable them to survive through today.

All might yet be well. Quintus had a sudden vision of Draupadi in her place by the pool, water slicking her hair back, molding her saffron robe to her amber skin. He was hot with more than the sun—useless dream for a man who never would see Miran. All would *not* be well, and they would die in the desert. Wind and sand would cover them, hiding them in a necropolis as vast as Egypt.

He remembered striking men away from the brackish water in the marsh outside Carrhae. That water would be nectar now. Yet it had not been time then to lie down and die. It was not time now. Quintus entered the quarrel between Ch'in and Rome, urging quiet, urging rest, urging travel at night. The setting sun showed them the direction west (and how he wished he were heading that way): They must head opposite to it.

He expected a sneer from Lucilius, but the man was sitting propped against a packsaddle. The sun glinted off his hair, bright as the coins he had never ceased to covet. Draupadi had veiled against the sun. She stood beside him, a hand on his brow. This was no time for even a traitor to be struck down by the sun.

"No birds," he muttered. His lips were pale. "No birds in this Orcus-be-damned waste. But I saw one. I saw an eagle. It came down and snatched our lives away. . . ."

Treason was punishable by death. In Rome, traitors were hurled from the Tarpeian rock, or slain in other, slower ways. When Spartacus and the rebel slaves had been put down, the roads had been lined with crosses. A long death if the man was strong and a painful one.

Was it as painful as dying of thirst?

But why condemn the whole Legion—and those of the Ch'in force who were guiltless? And why condemn . . . fragments from the poetry Quintus had had to learn edged into his mind, all wrapped about the image of Draupadi in that bridal saffron of hers.

"I do not believe that," Quintus said. He was glad he had thought of the fields, of the world of green things, and water half a world away. There was still hope.

Rufus, he saw, was gesturing and shouting at a Ch'in soldier who looked as tough as he. Ssu-ma Chao was translating, a wry smile of perfect hopelessness on his face.

The voices floated in the still air. "Who can we trust? We trust *them!*" Rufus jerked a thumb at Draupadi and Ganesha. "Let the water be under their care. And, for all the gods' sake, let us *do* something before we drink it all!"

They rode or marched because the idea of lying down and dying, ultimately, parched skin chafed raw against the grit, seemed even more loathsome. Better to move until one's tongue blackened and a merciful madness blurred consciousness, until one's heart burst.

That had happened to at least five people since the direction finder had been lost. It was impossible to tell from the husks covered over with blankets whether they had been Ch'in or Roman. And that meant there were five fewer men—the weakest at that—to share the water and food that Draupadi guarded.

They had been wandering for days. By now, surely, they might have found at least the ruins of an outpost. There had been no storms to cover the bodies of a patrol with the ever-present dust and grit; and there should have been patrols out. As for scouts of their own—to send a man alone and on a weak mount was a waste of man, mount, and water supply. And the idea of sending a man out without water was hateful: more merciful to cut his throat on the spot.

Quintus remembered when he knew they were lost. One moment they had struggled to the crest of an enormous dune. For that instant of achievement, the desert had been somewhat less hateful. There had even been a night wind, blessedly cool. A delicate spray of dust had spun near their hands.

And then, even when they looked up again, the stars' patterns had appeared to change, to shift. Oh, somewhere, Orion must surely hunt the Bears, lesser and greater; and Cassiopeia still fled her amorous god, or whatever fables the Ch'in made up about the heavens as they saw them. It was only that now, the patterns did not make sense.

"We are at sea here," he had mouthed to Ganesha.

"Once I saw a ship sail down a wave and plunge into the next. I never saw that ship again," the old man said.

It hurt to talk. Quintus just nodded. It didn't do to

think of that much water, either. The younger man cast a look at Draupadi. He was not the only man to send longing glances in her direction, but the others had eyes only for the waterskins she kept close at hand.

She shook her head. "Even power of illusion is gone," she whispered. Her lovely voice was gone too. "I cannot even provide the dream of water in your throat."

He reached over and took her hand. When it came his turn to die, he wanted to die clasping it, looking up into her eyes. *And then,* he thought, *when we are all dead, she and Ganesha will go on. As they did before.*

She moved her fingers across the callus on his palm. "No. No. For us this is real—too real this time. If you die, we die. Maybe we have had many years, but I am not ready yet to give up!"

Her voice gained strength, then subsided. Could she and the old priest have taken life somehow and gone on—as the Black Naacals had done at Stone Tower? He would have shaken his head, but he found that his brains were already addled enough from the sun without shaking them up further.

Not in all these years. The dancing figure was warming over his heart. Even when they had tossed away everything that might conceivably have held them back, he had refused to part with the tiny bronze. Not the dancer, and not the Eagle, which was borne each day by a different packbeast.

Draupadi pressed his hand. "I wanted reality, not dreams," she said. "This is real. You are real."

Quintus raised her hand with his ring on it to his cracked lips. "And so is this."

They rode on, very calm. Time was when "drifting" was a serious crime. Now, they sought to drift, to go on as painlessly as possible. They drifted between night and day, under unfamiliar star patterns and a sun whose rising and setting brought them no real understanding of where they were. They might as well have been children, turned and spun until they could barely stand, much less find their fellows.

"We are so weak," Quintus rasped to Draupadi when one precious sip of water let him speak. "Why do they not come for us?"

She glanced at the hot chimeras that rose from the desert floor to a cloudless sky. Even the white-fanged mountains so far away were a torment since the whiteness of those peaks meant snow. Precious moisture: for others. Never for them.

"The Black Naacals?" Her lips formed the words as if sound might summon them. "It suits them to torment us and to watch. And even now, I think, they find us." Dismay sharpened her too-thin features beneath the grimy veils.

"You and Ganesha?"

"You knew how long ago we were here," she whispered. "It was you who wandered in the waste, seeking Pasupata. You. Quintus—Arjuna—can you truly not remember?"

Then Ssu-ma Chao croaked out the command to mount, to march, to press on—in whatever direction seemed less useless. It was his turn to march, and they were separated, less by distance on the road than by memories.

Think, he told himself. *Think.* He was marching. It was his turn to march, which was true. But also, he preferred now to march, to feel again the undeviating rhythm of a Legion's pace behind its Eagle and, in that rhythm of so many thousand paces a day under constant discipline, to lose himself.

His arms swung just as they might have done if he formed part of a column marching down a paved road somewhere in Italy. It was, he thought, much like a galley, its oars beating in unison at the commands of the *hortator*. But what beat the rhythm here in his mind was not a great drum but the pounding of the blood in temples and heart. Rome had discovered what rhythms would spare mind and heart as long as possible: Pound too long, too fast, or too hard, and the man died.

But not, please all the gods, before he achieved forgetfulness. I am a *Roman*, his pace said. Left, right; left, right; boots pounding the grit into fine dust. It was all salt here, and he could almost believe in Ganesha's sea stories. Never mind his tales of a sea. You will never see the Middle Sea again. Believe in what lets you march on, he told himself. Left, right.

He was seeking to achieve forgetfulness—but to forget Rome? He had given up family, land, hope of return, even his honor. Now, when he had offered sword to his enemies, must he give up even his *patria?*

His solution, as Draupadi told him, lay in himself.

But not in Quintus: rather, in the man she named Arjuna, this ancient warrior-prince whose soul, as the wizard priests of Egypt taught, had transmigrated into stubborn Roman flesh. Mule-stubborn. Mule-strong. Left, right; left, right. The sun's hammer clanged down upon his skull—far more drum than he needed.

Forget.

Remember.

The air shimmered. His mind spun. He was Quintus—no, he bore a bow; he had a chariot to drive, and a dancing god to drive him; he was . . . a man fell out along the line of march and was packed onto a camel by men too weak to waste their strength on swearing.

The air hurt his chest, and he put his hand up to ease it. His fingers caught as the talisman beneath his garments grew warm again.

Out he drew the tiny image of dancing Krishna, a god old before some artisan who had lived in Italy before his own people made this to be laid in some tomb. How the coins of light had flashed out from it before they flew upward, dazzling man and horse so that the direction finder was lost?

Krishna himself—he had danced with light, mourning and rejoicing with the same movements. Quintus—no, Arjuna—now he remembered that. The god had danced with torches. The one he had been had bent and touched Krishna's feet and asked for the god himself, not his armies. And Krishna had made a pact to drive him.

The one he had been possessed a great weapon. He had sat in a ring of fire to trap power. Now, trapped in another life, he remembered the ultimate weapon he had thus won. But what had it been? That he could not remember, not if he marched until the bones of his feet rubbed away into powder as white as the salt flats on which he stood.

It was not power that he had to seek. It was life. He had sought life before, at the ruin by the pool.

Ah yes. His feet moved now without direct control of his body. He was on the right track. Think of a pool. Think of a river. Draupadi's retreat; his river valley. So far away now—but there had been a tale once, a tale he had heard once under an outcropping of the Roof of the World, where men had huddled together: that in the heart of the desert, found only by men at the extremity of need, there bubbled a spring of clear, pure water. But where it was, no man could say for certain.

An oasis, such as they had in Egypt or Judaea or Syria, perhaps? Or was it something more.

They were lost. They could not be more lost or more desperate. All was failing. Perhaps . . . ?

He had heard of such places, so sacred that animals who were each other's mortal enemies might crouch beside each other and fill their throats with pure water, rather than one another's life blood.

Did that water truce apply to Black Naacals as well? Somehow Quintus doubted that. No, that was not his thought; that had to have been the thought of Arjuna . . . he was far from the discipline he had learned at home. Left, right; left, right.

He was not aware that he had quickened his pace, that gradually he outstripped the other Romans, and was drawing even with the Ch'in. Some still rode, masking mouths and noses against the dust. Some were slung across their saddles. Some marched poorly.

Does the Eagle know? Will it see us? It must. Arjuna's thinking again, perhaps? But one didn't have to be a warrior prince, but just a farm lad to know that birds always knew where there was water. A pity there were no birds in the Takla Makan.

Now he pulled level with the Ch'in soldiers. Ssu-ma Chao, judging the temper of some of his allies, had guards posted to prevent someone from killing Wang Tou-fan.

A pack camel stumbled, then stood swaying. Then, it collapsed; the men and beasts behind it swerved just in time to keep from walking into it.

Quintus too halted. It took an act of genuine will to keep himself out of the line of march.

Up ahead, Ssu-ma Chao signaled orders to unload the dead beast's packs. Odd. Why not leave them where they lay? It hardly seemed as if they could use its burden themselves. Then Quintus's bleary eyes flamed.

The beast had borne the Eagle. Even as he watched, Wang Tou-fan and Ssu-ma Chao came forward. Both men jockeyed for position, worn as they were. Finally, with two or three imperious words and gestures, Wang Tou-fan won the skirmish. *He* was in command of this. He was. No one else. And he reinforced that by a hand on his sword, waving away even Lucilius, who eyed the Eagle with some of the same longing that the other Romans—those who had stayed faithful—displayed.

There was no point, good common sense told Quintus, in edging forward. He would not get even so much of a glimpse of the Eagle, and his presence might just make a bad situation worse. Still, he found himself heading toward the standard, his feet kicking up clouds of fine grit. It rose, coating him. When he licked his lips, he tasted salt; and he had not had so much water that his body could sweat *that* much.

As Quintus reached the dead camel, Wang Tou-fan had laid a hand upon the Eagle. He himself, he declared in words Quintus could not understand—and gestures that he could—would strap the prize to his own pack-saddle.

Quintus gestured to Ganesha. *Interpret. Please.*

"Well enough," Quintus said, Ganesha repeating his words in the language of Ch'in. "Why not take it out and set it up? Let it shine over the place where we lie down to die."

The man glared at Quintus. "You are leading us to death," the Roman spoke, finding words somewhere. "To die is nothing to us. We all owe Rome a death: time we were paying it. But you—have you not a life and a future?"

Lucilius's head came up, sensing a bargain.

"You do not order this one," Wang Tou-fan said through the interpreter.

"No," said Quintus. "But what about *them?*" Suddenly, he remembered how, in another life, his brother the king had wagered all and lost all. Having nothing, though, he had nothing to lose. Except his life; and he had reckoned that as a dead loss for years.

"Perhaps you can lead," he conceded. "But can you endure? We can teach you that. And they—perhaps they can guide you."

"And what would you demand for this service?" Too wise, despite Ganesha's earlier attempt to soften the sting of Wang Tou-fan's lies.

"The Eagle," Quintus said bluntly. "Then, if we die, we die in possession of our standard." He shrugged. "You may yet outlast us, and then it would be your possession once more." Much against his better judgment, he glared at Lucilius. "As it is now."

The patrician glared in return but said nothing.

"Well?" Bluff. Pretend you are in a position of strength. It hardly seemed, he realized, like the Roman Quintus, sober, dull, who was about to gamble with life and honor both. He warned himself not to look weak. For the strong do as they will, while the weak suffer what they must. He had been weak for too long.

"And," he added craftily, "a garrison may come and put paid to our agreement after all. What have you to lose?"

Ssu-ma Chao turned away, as if expressing—what? Laughter? Gods, he had spirit. He should have been a Roman.

There was one problem, Quintus thought. If Ssu-ma Chao assented, he would be on the cross before he clasped arms with him like a brother.

"Have you any idea of where we are?"

Help me, Quintus wished of Ganesha and Draupadi with all his might.

"Before the stars changed," Ganesha said promptly, "all this basin was a great Inland Sea. I have seen the charts. In it were islands at which ships might land and . . ." he allowed himself to look wistful. "They had springs of sweet water, trees bearing fruit. They cannot all have perished wholly; for they were at the very heart of the sea. We might well find water at such a place. But we would need to go into the very bowels of the desert. Have you the courage for it?"

"Say we reach this water. What then?"

"We will have the strength," Quintus said, "to try again for Miran. Or send out a fast scouting party—as we should have done." *Had you been a true officer instead of a wastrel and a traitor.* He fixed his eyes on Lucilius, willing the patrician tribune to shift his loyalties.

"We have no better choice." Lucilius forced the words out as if under torture. As perhaps he was: He suffered more from the heat than some of the others.

Wang Tou-fan stood irresolute. Clearly, he was afraid; clearly he was thinking rapidly as threat, fear, and exhaustion worked in him. Cunning flashed across his features. *Try again. Betray the men who helped you. All of them, especially that stiff-necked oaf who rules an outpost and gives himself the airs of the Son of Heaven. It might not even be necessary to share with the traitor—after all, are they not all barbarians, and the men of the western deserts only slightly better?*

"Done!" he said, forgetting nobility and sounding

like one of the merchants who had predicted nothing but destruction for this caravan.

Trying not to let his hands shake with eagerness, Quintus nodded gravely, and held out his arms to receive the Eagle.

And, although the sky looked as if not enough water to form even the tiniest of clouds had ever touched it, thunder rumbled and lightning danced across the horizon.

22

THE STANDARD EASED into Quintus's hand, and the sun swooped down upon it, picking out each detail of the bird's bronze plumage. It felt right in his hand, fitting like the hilt of a veteran's sword. He shut his eyes against the dazzle of the sun on the Eagle's wings and his own tears.

The first time he had held it, only for a moment, in The Surena's camp, it had been before a blow to his head had nearly driven wits and life from him. He remembered, how he remembered, the reek of blood, sweat, and metal that had been one of the last things he had sensed. But with the fear and the pain had come the realization that he had come, at last, to the right place and done the right thing.

Perhaps he had defended a leader not worthy of his service, but Crassus had been a proconsul of Rome; and that was worth, he thought, any price he might pay. And here, far from Rome, was its very sign. Whether or not any word of his life and service ever reached the *patres conscripti* who were as much an object of his grandsire's veneration as the family altar, or that turbulent, brawling people who had transformed the lands around the Tiber, once again, he had that sense of purpose.

Grounding the standard, as he had in that enemy city not so far in the past, Quintus surveyed the shrunken force. His own renewal of spirit had inspired the others—and it had been a long, long time since he had thought of them as "his men." In the presence of their Eagle, they stood ready, falling perhaps by instinct into the familiar pattern.

Quintus felt himself aglow with a light that did not fade. It fed upon him, yet it returned a new strength in exchange. Using him as a focus, that inner strength reached out to his men, uniting them into not just a fighting force but one spirit.

That dazzle was gone, leaving Quintus with the sense that something profound had been accomplished—but just what, he couldn't find a name for.

Draupadi approached, eyeing the Eagle warily. "That is no less your weapon," she said, "than the sword you bear."

The sword he bore had been Arjuna's. Quintus stared upward—would that proud bronze bird now take wing?

In his grasp, the standard quivered as if the Eagle surmounting it indeed mantled its wings, ready for flight. But that was only the way of eagles in the heights. Aloft in their own place, they swooped down, arcing, and circling, borne by the winds from the peaks. Here were no mountains.

A glow from the Eagle reached to gild the sky. There, the color was deepening and turning sullen. Quintus tore his eyes from the Eagle to look to Ssu-ma Chao. Before any of the *buran*, the great desert storms, the sky turned brazen. Then, as the storm struck, it darkened with wind, thickened and made visible with grit and sand.

A prudent traveller—and Ssu-ma Chao was the best they had—would be alert to such changes and would order out the protective felts in time. Thus, Ssu-ma Chao opened his mouth to shout, scrabbling for his own protective coverings. And then the Easterner paused, as if at a loss. All along the line of march, the camels stood motionless, not complaining the way they did when sensing a storm.

Yet that sky, like a brass bowl overturned above them, was now the color that heralded the worst of storms. Only there was no wind, no stir of sand. The very air itself might now be as dead as the land.

The camels began to crowd together, as if in rebellion against a too-weighty burden. There was a heaviness pressing down upon all until Quintus was certain that even the long dunes would be flattened—even without a wind.

Draupadi whirled about, scanned the horizon, then turned to Ganesha.

"All about us—we are ringed in."

The old man turned to face outward as if confronting a still-invisible enemy.

It was Lucilius who launched into action, breaking the spell. His green eyes wide with fear, he edged closer to the standard, step by heavy step. He might have been struggling against a swollen river current.

"The Eagle," he mouthed. "Give . . ."

Quintus swung the standard out of reach.

"Give it to him," ordered Wang Tou-fan.

"Let him *take* it," Quintus retorted. He spoke without any regard for rank. Surely it must be clear to all that the Eagle chose—men obeyed.

"Let him *try*, that is," the tribune added.

About Quintus, the decimated Roman force came

slowly alive. Some moved forward to stand between Quintus and the Ch'in soldiers. One or two moved in as if to guard Draupadi and Ganesha. The rest, without being commanded, fell into their familiar ranks.

Again, Lucilius grabbed for the Eagle.

"No." Quintus jerked it out of his reach.

Then the sand began to hum. Singing sand, some wayfarers called it. However, this was no howl, but like the flaps of some appalling insect's wings, enticing lesser creatures to come and be devoured.

Beneath their blistered feet, the ground trembled. Thunder drummed, then rumbled again, as if summoning full force. A faint blue spark flew from man to man in the ranks. The sky darkened toward twilight. Now the air seemed to cool. The bedraggled crests on the Romans' helms rose. Quintus sensed energies building up the way the tension builds in a catapult.

"Iron," muttered Ganesha. "There is iron here, and they know it. . . ."

"Quick!" Draupadi cried. "The metal you wear—off with it for your lives' sake!"

Long ago, most of the Romans had stowed their armor on packbeasts. The Ch'in mainly wore harnesses of leather. But still, there were iron nails in the Legions' boots. . . . The matted hair on the back of Quintus's neck stirred. Shed belts, weapons, tools, yes, but to go barefoot in this realm of sharp rocks was a sentence of slow death, and he had a sudden nightmare image of Black Naacals tracking them by sniffing along bloody footprints.

However, it was Draupadi who had warned them. And she knew what might follow. "Off with boots—all iron!" he commanded.

What of his own footcoverings? He could stoop to shed them, but he would have to drop the Eagle to do so.

Better to stand, to feel this immensity of power as it built up. Was *this* what Arjuna had found when he discovered Pasupata and learned to wield it? Was this the ultimate warrior's test? He wished he could remember.

Tension continued to build. Quintus's hands quivered as the metal of the Eagle vibrated, and that movement fed down the staff. He could almost hear the bronze hum.

A savage crack split heaven and earth, blinding Quintus. The bolt of white, tinged with purple, was the last thing he saw. Caught in the darkness, he felt the rumble of the thunder even through his feet, oversetting his balance. He toppled to his knees.

Exhausted as they were, the pack animals plunged and screamed. Someone shrieked, a terrible sound, annihilated by the thunder and the stink of burning. Now the wind did blow, and Quintus scented garlic and approaching rain, incongruous in this waste. His eyes watered, as tears forced themselves out beneath his eyelids.

Voices nearby:

"Jupiter Optimus Maximus, did you see Sextus?"

"Burnt like a pig . . . gods!"

Had he been so frightened, then, that he must weep as he had not done even at his mother's funeral? No: Tears were warm, and the moisture now running down his face was cool. A wind continued—not the Vulcan's forge of the deep desert, but a true breeze, heavy with water and salt.

Rain came in that basin of salt and grit, dried before the stars altered the pattern of their going. In Quintus's hand the standard tingled. A tremendous wave of well-being rushed through him, worn as he was.

Rain was falling with increasing strength, cool on parched skin. The darkness of the sky was now water, released from the clouds that had suddenly gathered.

Quintus's talisman pulsed, and the power he had sensed before built up again, seeking discharge.

"Get down and hold!" he shouted. No need for any man to be the tallest thing on this plain. Please all the gods that his men had shed their metal gear. There might be another lightning strike among them.

I must order burial detail for Sextus, he thought.

The energies vibrating in the Eagle built up nearly past endurance, and he tensed, waiting for the strike.

This time the crack of lightning drew a response from the earth itself, which rumbled accompaniment to the thunder. Far and near, the crash echoed and re-echoed all over the desert basin. Men and horses toppled and fell, rolling upon the wet grit. Even the camels panicked and tried to plunge away. Some of the men rose and staggered after them, unsure of their footing on ground that was suddenly more slick, or higher or lower than it had been moments ago.

The smell of a salt sea intensified as the rain fell. Quintus opened his mouth and gulped a mouthful of water. Such bounty made him drunk. Proconsuls were fools to drink Falernian, he thought giddily, if they could have water like this. Someone cheered, and Rufus silenced him fast.

Another lightning bolt, searing purple-white even despite the barrier of Quintus's eyelids. When the explosion dissipated, he dared to test his sight, to seek sight of the company. . . .

He found himself gazing in dumb amazement over a vast split in the earth, or in the seabed dead so many years, but stirring in its long death with deadly strength.

Draupadi gasped, while Ganesha chanted in a tongue unknown to the Romans and the Ch'in.

"Stay back!" Quintus ordered, but he himself edged

forward over the unsteady ground, holding the standard high as if he headed a proud marching Legion.

Behind him, Rufus shouted to men to catch the rain-water in any container they could find.

Did Quintus indeed carry a weapon stronger than any he had dreamed might exist? Had the Eagle not drawn down the lightnings, aye, and shielded him from that raw force? *May Charon ferry Sextus swiftly; he took a bolt I fear was meant for me,* he thought. And was the standard not the source of the new strength flowing into his body?

He had sought and found weapons—Arjuna's sword, for one, and that length of wood and horn that passed for a bow. Now, he thought, he had sought and found *the* weapon of supreme destruction for this time and place. He could have laughed at the irony of the gods, who decreed that the very weapon he had sought for so long was the Eagle, the loss of which had meant his disgrace.

In what guise did Pasupata come to you, Arjuna? he asked the voice inside his mind. He was not surprised when the Delphic, aggravating voice did not answer.

Whatever form its power took, for this age, Pasupata had now manifested itself in the Eagle. And Quintus was both its master and its servant. His eyes met Draupadi's, and she smiled at him. How beautiful she was with the rain draping the curves of her form. No illusions there. Even during the lightning, she had not removed the ring he had given her.

"Hold firm!" Ganesha cried out in a voice stronger than any Quintus had ever heard him use.

The land quivered with aftershocks. Now even the horizon appeared to their dazed eyes as if it were dancing. Another crack came, again followed by thunder above and below them. Quintus sprawled this time, but fought his way back to his feet, using the standard as lever. Pasupata might for the moment be a lame man's staff. Leaning on that support, Quintus wavered forward.

He came to a halt on the very lip of the chasm that the lightning and earthquakes had opened in the desert. The Ch'in were wailing to their gods, their ancestors, or any other powers that might award them a moment's thought at all. From the Romans came muttered oaths and prayers, all equally useful.

Quintus paused at the edge of the pit, two aftershocks made him reel, back and forth. Only the standard, stabbed deeply into the ground, kept him from falling into the dark depths of the pit that had opened.

All this land *had* been under water once—an inland lake of such a size, perhaps, to rival the Middle Sea. Nor had that forgotten sea been any more unknown in its time than the one serving Roman ships. Ships had also sailed it—and creatures had dwelt in its depths.

Quintus's talisman heated—a warning but not with a real alarm, as he dropped, to creep forward on his belly. Beneath him, as if the seabed had swallowed it at the critical moment, lay a ship of a design unknown to him. *Ganesha might have sailed on such a craft,* he thought.

The seabed had opened and trapped this ship—and apparently, in addition, the sea creature, longer than any kraken, in the very act of opening its jaws to engulf the vessel. It was only bones now, but the length of back and the width of jaws made it by no means certain that it would have failed in the attempt.

Draupadi and Ganesha knelt beside him, staring down at the remains of that Titanic battle.

"The Flame shine upon them," Ganesha murmured.

Water must have been thrashed up over that slanted deck, as the sea creature struck the ship, driven from the depths as the earth shuddered, maddened enough to attack. The thing must have seen the ship as its enemy. Perhaps it was as afraid as the men who watched the water boil as it arrowed up from the deepest water and screamed as its immense jaws opened, distended, and tried to swallow them.

There might have been White Naacals on board like Ganesha himself. But at that moment, none of their prayers and powers had availed them.

The last few moments of the crew—Quintus jerked his gaze away. Too well, he could imagine the water thrashing, the gibbering terror, even the desperate composure of the Naacals as they sought to fight off an impossible enemy.

Time and place flickered for Quintus, as if he could remember it all in truth. *Some had fled below, had turned inward. One or two flung themselves overboard. Others prayed, even as those among them who were warriors struck at the great monster with their weapons, hoping to buy time for the Naacals to bring greater weapons to bear.* But they had failed. Why had they failed? Overpowered by the Black Naacals? Was their power weakened by what they surely fled? Or perhaps it had been the earth itself, not the Black Naacals, which had ultimately killed them, allowing their souls freedom. The monster would grasp their ship by the stern, was pulling it down, and then the earth opened to swallow creature and ship alike in blackness and pressure and, once the heaving ceased, silence.

How had Quintus remembered? *Look again.* He looked down into the pit and into his memories simultaneously, and the effort almost robbed him of his senses.

"Aiyeeeeee! The dragon! The great *lung*, King of Dragons!"

The Ch'in had been slower than he to approach the pit. Now many of them panicked. Some cast themselves face down on the wet salt. Others ran as if attempting to escape what the crew of that long-dead ship had not been able to flee. They ran and fell, and when they could not get up, they crawled, mindless with fear.

Wang Tou-fan's path led him near the pit. Surely he would miss it.

"Come back, man!" Lucilius cried. He even started after the Ch'in—*to stop him or push him in?* Then another tremor sent the Roman sprawling. He turned his sprawl into a desperate grab at the man's knees, caught him, attempting to pull him back.

Wang Tou-fan screamed like a woman in the last stages of giving birth. With astonishing force, he fought to pull free of Lucilius—a ferocious and maddened dance that brought him to the very lip of the chasm.

"You can't save him!" Rufus shouted. "Let him go, lad!"

Whether or not Lucilius would have abandoned his fellow conspirator was never to be known. Once again an aftershock rumbled through the earth, spawning more tremors. Lucilius fell, and Wang Tou-fan, screaming about the great dragon, hurled himself into the pit.

Quintus's talisman heated and he clutched onto whatever flimsy support he might find. What was coming now was no mere tremor. Rocks shook and fell; the lightning exploded in sheets across the sky; and the earth snapped shut like the lid of an enormous chest, reclaiming its secrets and adding yet another victim to its toll.

Once more, the thunder spoke, a prolonged rumble as if the earth now digested what it had engulfed. Then, all was still. The dunes had tumbled and toppled into new shapes smelling of salt and ancient seas. Puddles glistened on the salt flats, rippling as the storm winds brushed them. Already, the heat began to rise.

The talisman fell from Quintus's shaking fingers. At his feet, the tiny bronze dancer, sparks quivering in the torches that it held, danced its dance of grief and exaltation.

He scooped it up one-handed and thrust it back into his tunic.

Then, leaning on the Eagle's staff, he turned and edged painstakingly back to where he had left his men. How many of them had survived?

One of the Ch'in camel drivers had crumpled to his knees, and lay with his head in his arms, whimpering. He could not believe this place, could not accept it. Wails rose from his fellows. They were a superstitious lot who saw demons in every aspect of the desert. A prodigy like this—if something weren't done to quell the panic, they might never recover.

"Get the animals' heads!" someone ordered. The command was repeated in Parthian, then in Ch'in.

The Romans hastened to retrain the animals. The Ch'in soldiers, dazed by the loss of Wang Tou-fan, moved more slowly. At this rate, they might never form back into a party capable of travelling.

"Hold!" Quintus shouted. His voice came out as a croak. Despite the downpour, his mouth was dry with fear of what he had seen. . . .

. . . water in the desert . . . the heave and torrent of the sea as it sank into the earth. . . . Draupadi's and Ganesha's refuge came to his mind as some last glimmer of a Golden Age. He didn't think he would ever cease to thirst. And the rain was stopping.

"Stay where you are." His voice came out a little more strongly, but still, no one heard it. *You must!* he told himself. No lives must be lost because his body failed him.

Grasping the staff of the Eagle, he tried a third time. "Stop there!"

The standard quivered in his hand. Deep clouds in the sky appeared to shift, and sunlight struck the bronze Eagle. Beams of light glittered along its wings, arcing out over the scatter of troops. A steadier light engulfed Quintus: He shivered as strength flowed into him. Gradually, his troops turned. The Ch'in who had collapsed raised themselves from bellies and knees. Those Ch'in, led by Ssu-ma Chao, who had kept their composure by care of animals, reassembled.

Now the clouds dissipated, blown away by a wind tasting of salt. The wind seemed to spread the light from the Eagle Quintus held until it formed a dome beneath the arch of heaven, a dome of protection. The Eagle's wings were over them, he thought.

They gathered close, staring up at it. The light rippled into all the colors of the rainbow. Incredulous smiles appeared on lips that had never thought to do aught again but scream. Then the light vanished. Romans and Ch'in stood on the barren, churned-up ground, staring at each other.

Two men turned to Sextus's body. One scooped up a handful of salt and grit and mud and scattered it about the charred remains.

"He was our comrade," Rufus chided. "We'll make the time to bury him properly."

Then, Quintus knew, they must move on. Perhaps the Eagle could guide them.

23

Light shone overhead as more and more of the layers of clouds were stripped from the sky. Already the wind was dryer and warmer.

Ssu-ma Chao left the camel he had staked down to walk over to Quintus.

"We are far out of our reckoning," he admitted, the first time any of the Ch'in had done so.

Quintus grasped the Eagle's staff more firmly and nodded. He gestured and Rufus came toward him at a trot as brisk as if the world had not suddenly gaped beneath his feet a short time ago. Draupadi too came to his side. He longed to lay his free arm over her slender shoulders, gaining support from her as he had gained it from the Eagle itself.

Ssu-ma Chao looked out over the desert. "*Any* storm at all would have destroyed the tracks of other caravans. Let alone this one. . . . Do you agree? We wait for the sun?"

Sunset would show them the west. Then they could strike due east again, Quintus supposed. The storm had even given them some larger supply of water than they had had. Perhaps they might find a way station that would guide them toward Miran.

Follow the sun? Where was the sun? Light, indeed, shone overhead, but the huge angry disk too bright for anything but an eagle to gaze upon seemed to have been replaced by a glow that spread uniformly over the entire vault of sky.

"Illusion," Draupadi murmured. "They seek to confuse us."

"Lady, they succeed," Ssu-ma Chao said. His eyes held a question.

"Concerted illusion. Several adepts must maintain it. I am only one. I wish it were otherwise," she told him.

"Should we make camp?" It was a bad time to take grim pleasure in the fact that Lucilius's voice still quivered.

"And lie here waiting for whatever-it-is to come eat us?" Forgetting the tribune's higher rank, Rufus cut in. "We had the right of it back in Carrhae. March or die. Keep marching *until* we die—or we prevail."

Ssu-ma Chao regarded the older Roman with what looked like awe. "We have no such spirit left," he said. "Is it because you have . . ." he gestured, ". . . your god back?"

"It is because we are Romans," Quintus replied. "Those two most of all." He nodded respect at the senior centurion and the Eagle itself.

"You said they seek to confuse us," he added to Draupadi. "How can you be sure?"

"Illusion is my art," she reminded him. "And illusion, just as much as truth, comes at a price—a great cost in strength and spirit. And *I*, thank the Flame, have not the means at my disposal of renewing either as the Black

Naacals do. Long ago I took such oaths that I would die first.

"There is great power arrayed against us." She gestured at the light that colored the entire sky and the torn-up horizon. "Now, if they can use that power so that we lose ourselves on the desert, they would count that deed done and well done. Especially now, since they must surely have sensed the use of—" she gestured discreetly at the Eagle, which shone in the false light, "—our weapon here."

"The Eagle? Our standard?" Rufus asked, then looked as apologetic as he ever got.

"You yourself have seen it work. It is the standard of your army, and yet it is also a form of the ultimate weapon that Arjuna, warrior and prince, sought long ago when he fought for his family. It is a mighty weapon for defense or for attack. And they would use it—"

"How, lady?"

Ganesha replied. "They would use it to return things to the way they were. To fill the desolation once more with sea, and to sail over it, uncontested masters of land and water. But I saw the Motherland *sink*. Those days are gone now, and a new age holds sway. It is for other realms to take up the rule of the world."

He met Rufus's glare firmly. "Yes, I say it, even though I remember those days too. The Black Naacals must be stopped. Found and stopped. Destroyed, if needs be. This is no longer their world."

He paused, as if studying the wreckage of the camp. "Now, if we have the strength."

Quintus met Ssu-ma Chao's eyes. The Ch'in soldier bowed profoundly to Ganesha, even more deeply than he had abased himself before the governor in Kashgar.

"When will you be ready to move out?" the Roman asked him.

"At your command." Ssu-ma Chao bowed again, then shouted the orders that they all knew by now meant break camp, pack, and mount.

None of the Ch'in soldiers moved—not even after a shout from Rufus, followed by a swing from his vinestaff at the nearest laggard, sent the Romans scrambling for their packs. Five of the Ch'in soldiers lay on the ground, oblivious to their discomfort, their knees drawn up against their chins, their eyes squeezed shut. Several more knelt by them. All breathed as if they had run for far too long, and they seemed shrunken in upon themselves by more than hunger.

One of the camels protested being loaded, and a soldier jumped away. Then he collapsed, weeping helplessly, first to his knees, then into a ball of utmost rejection.

Ssu-ma Chao walked over to the man, shouted at him, shook him, and slapped him. His face darkened with anger that was mainly fear, and he drew his sword.

"No!" Draupadi ran forward across ground that Quintus still feared might liquefy or gape open at any moment. Her dirty robe, almost dry now, flared out behind her with a fleeting ghost of her old grace. Men drew aside to let her pass.

With a motion like a wave breaking into a gentle foam as it touches shore, she knelt by the afflicted man, took his face in one hand, and, with the other, peeled up his eyelid. His eyes rolled back in his head.

"His spirit has retreated," she told Ssu-ma Chao. "If we can bear him and his comrades to a place where the light is familiar and the earth does not gape open and ancient dangers do not emerge, he may wake and obey you once more. But you do wrong to kill him for what is not his fault.''

The officer glared at her.

''No, you do *not* lose face,'' she insisted. All the care she had taken, as long as Quintus had known her, to speak demurely before the Ch'in, to defer, to work through Ganesha, was gone; her voice bore the authority of a sybil.

''He sees visions from his past, and he cannot bear them. Have you not discovered yet that which will break even *you?* Fortunate man. Let me know when you do, and I shall keep the others from executing you.''

Another soldier began to laugh, a high note ending up in a cry of near madness.

''We have to get out of here, or we'll be awash in lunatics,'' Lucilius muttered.

Well, that much was true.

''No sad words for your comrade?'' Quintus gibed, and then was sorry. Bent as he was, the patrician tribune was wary; and they would need his wits too since so many others' wits seemed to have gone wandering.

Quintus studied the Legionaries. Restored to what order they might manage, they assembled in formation. Their eyes were shadowed; they were tired, bruised, and afraid. But they were all, thank the gods, sane.

Their formation looked blessedly normal. He went over to stand before the line in his proper place. The men straightened as he neared them bearing the Eagle; they saluted, fists to chests, as proudly and precisely as if they prepared to enter the newly surrendered capital of a great empire.

Quintus smiled. ''Brothers,'' he spoke very gently, ''we have our Eagle and our Legion's honor back.'' No one moved, but the sun-blackened faces glowed. He struggled for words to express his pride and his desire to reassure these men, then, as his throat closed, for any words at all. He knew his grandsire would have told him not to babble. The memory gave him the words he needed. "Once again, we may call ourselves Romans."

They had always been Romans, but captives, only half themselves, stripped of their Eagle and their pride, marching at other soldiers' commands. Now, once again, even in a strange place, they led. The formation, small as it was, seemed to draw strength from the bronze Eagle.

Quintus made the decision he had been pondering.

"Break ranks," he told them. "I want each of you to aid them—" he gestured to the Ch'in, who had begun to fight their own way back into some semblance of order. "They are our comrades. Help them now as if they bore the Legion's brand."

"They will slow us," Lucilius hissed.

"Ssu-ma Chao held our lives and honor in the palm of his hand," Quintus snapped. "And returned them to us. Shall we betray him too?"

To abandon the men who had marched with them so long—Quintus's outrage mounted until he realized that it was not just his anger, but the memory of that other life in which he had sought a weapon, wooed a princess, and fought a battle against illusions and evil images. Just as he fought now.

For an instant, the ground trembled underfoot again, as if he balanced on the floor of a great chariot, a chariot such as Arjuna had owned and Krishna had driven. He had no such chariot now, but he remembered that battle, feeling lost, feeling fear and indecision that paralyzed him just as it did the Ch'in soldiers whom he now watched being tied to the groaning packbeasts. As Arjuna, he had known fear and indecision. As Quintus, he would not permit other men to suffer for what he had known.

He had crouched in the center of the battlefield, all eyes upon him. Krishna seemed to have stopped time somehow; and he—Arjuna—knelt at its crux, the hub of the Yuga, or cycle, of this world. Go forward? Go back? Conquer or flee—he had the sense of being transfixed by a hundred fates, all of which clamored, Choose me, choose me! *Self-disgust hit him hard. He was Arjuna, and he had less spirit than a dancing master—less spirit than the eunuch he had been. He dared not look. Everyone he loved had assembled. His brothers were at his back. The men he must kill—his enemy, a man who had cherished him like a father, and even the ancient who had taught him the art of war—they were all arrayed against him.*

The dancing figure heated against his tunic. All his life, it had been Quintus's talisman; now—with his free hand he reached for it and drew it out. It shimmered under his bleary gaze: trove from a tomb in Latium, image of enigmatic Krishna, dancing in grief and joy, urging him to fare forward.

He rose from his knees, staring at the bronze talisman as it lay reassuringly on his hand. Draupadi was waiting for him. Once again, she waited for him to win the battle she was part cause for.

Unwilling to resign the Eagle to a standard-bearer hand, Quintus mounted, still holding it. *Well,* he thought, *here we are. Wherever* here *is. Where shall we go? In what direction?* "Fare forward," thank you very much, was little aid when the sun lay hidden. For all he knew—and he suspected that the Black Naacals intended this—they could wander in circles until the camels collapsed and they all died.

The bronze standard warmed in his hand. He looked up at the Eagle. The diffused light that was all he could see struck it, picking out the fine details that some crafts-man had put into shaping its feathers or the sleek, deadly line of its beak. It was a sign, a weapon—and a guardian of their honor. Would it guide them now?

Light struck the Eagle's head, enveloping the entire standard in a glow that blinded, then moderated. A beam shot from it before him. Taking that as an omen—please all the gods it serve him as a beacon and not a snare—he gestured the soldiers forward.

A horse whinnied in fear. Quintus slowed. Gods only knew what it thought it saw. One man, marching, cried out and looked down at his foot. Rufus gestured the tri-bune forward. He would see to the soldier; let Quintus lead.

The camel seemed to pad through puddles of water. Its huge feet made sucking sounds as it lifted each one free.

"Illusion," Draupadi repeated. "We are fortunate. Thus far, they have not mustered even more strength."

The desert floor shuddered even as she spoke, and a dune began slowly to collapse. Why that particular dune? If the Black Naacals' plan succeeded, they would distrust their very shadows and, at the end, turn on one another.

What might lie buried in that dune, dead as the sea monster whose bones they had seen—or perhaps horror that was *not* dead?

Behind him, someone muttered, and Quintus heard the *thwack* of a vinestaff. Ssu-ma Chao began to protest, then fell silent, as if ashamed of his own reluctance to proceed. If any of them might know this land, it was the Ch'in frontier officer.

"Forward!" Quintus shouted and gestured with the Eagle. The flawed sunlight ran down the shaft and into his eyes. Once again, he felt strong, perhaps even somewhat rested. He could ride for ever, if he must, to achieve his goals.

The light glanced down over his camel. It bawled a protest but lurched forward into the swaying movement that it could keep up for hours upon hours.

They would follow the path of the Eagle. Not even the gods themselves could demand more than that. The caravan gathered what speed it might. The Eagle's presence kept it from feeling as if it fled.

24

THE SUN NEVER rose in the desert sky—only that faint, diffused glow that continued to pool into glory when it rested on the Eagle showed the difference between night and day, if not between morning and noon. For that, they had only the heat as their guide. When the sun made even the strongest of their camels droop as if they inched along the fiery banks of Acheron, Quintus guessed that it was noon and called a halt. Not even the evident desire of some of the Ch'in to flee across the desert until, please their ancestors, they encountered another caravan kept the Romans from obeying orders and enforcing an obedience of their own on would-be stragglers.

Quintus's eyes ached as if hot gold had been poured into them. Still, when they made camp, he forced himself to make a circuit of the paltry space with the Eagle.

Think of green. Think of water. Think of home. But his memories of his Tiber valley were long faded now.

Halfway about the camp, he greeted Ssu-ma Chao. "Your men?" he asked.

"Two still must be tended like babies," the officer

reported. "This one implores that they not be abandoned. . . ."

Quintus felt rage at the suggestion leap from his eyes.

"We leave no one alive in this place," the Roman answered. "If it were possible I would bear even our dead along, lest the Black Naacals work mischief with their corpses."

Ssu-ma Chao nodded. His face was sallow, not the burnished gold it had been in Parthia, which now seemed like a world of safety and comfort away. "This one should not dare to seek to live, for he has fled a battle-field. . . ." He looked as if he might drop to his knees or, worse yet, his belly.

"It is no shame to retreat," Quintus attempted to rally the other officer's courage. "Or even to be vanquished." That sounded hollow, and he knew it.

"You say that *now*," Ssu-ma Chao gestured at the standard. "When I saw you at . . ."

"It would have been enough to die. As you see, we live. *I* live, and I had taken such injuries that I might well have slipped away." He had had the choice, he remembered; and he had chosen to return to life and defeat rather than leave his men without a leader, even into exile.

"You live, and now you . . ." Abruptly, Ssu-ma Chao let out a gust of laughter that brought men's heads up all over the camp. "You prosper? How can you say that anything prospers in this waste?"

Bless Ssu-ma Chao for that laugh. The entire camp was the better for it. He could hear Rufus remarking to someone, "Laughs at misfortune, does he? I'm not saying that that is a Roman thing to do, but it takes a Roman will to look at the Fates and laugh."

Ssu-ma Chao nodded at the centurion. "He knows no fear."

"No," Quintus said. "None. He fears only for his honor; and he is perfect in that."

"Honor—this one's honor is fled. This one would redeem his wretched self." He struggled with the idea, then replaced it with another. "Without the direction finder, we have only your Eagle to guide us. Is that not so?"

Sunlight on bronze—if you called that guidance.

"We do not know that it will bring us out along the caravan routes again. We are in the hands of Fortune," Quintus answered with the truth as he saw it.

"But surely your god . . ."

"It is not a god."

"Can you deny, Roman, that it is a thing of power? Could it not discern other power?"

"You begin to interest me extremely," Quintus said. "Come to my camp, brother, and sit down."

The Ch'in officer's head went up at a word he might once have rejected, and he followed Quintus to the flaps of felt set in the shadow of a reclining camel that Quintus called his camp. They had come down a great way in the world from the meticulous *castra* of his training—but he was grateful for the rest and the shade, and even more grateful for the presence of Draupadi, who greeted him with water and a gentle touch to his shoulder.

She would have withdrawn, but Quintus forestalled her. This was no time for her to mimic a Ch'in lady's manners. She and Ganesha had been scholars alongside the Black Naacals before the world changed: They would best know how their enemies used their power.

Gradually, others joined them: Rufus, Lucilius (there was no keeping him away), Ganesha—the men Quintus most trusted and the man against whom he had most reason to guard himself.

"Speak for this humble one," Ssu-ma Chao appealed to Ganesha. That much the Roman could follow. Then his voice broke, and the spate of rapid-fire Ch'in that followed made even Ganesha blink.

"Slowly, slowly," he said, holding up a hand that even now retained some of its former plumpness. "I am a tired old man."

Ancient, he might be. Even now, Quintus hated to consider how old because, if he calculated Ganesha's years, he must also think of Draupadi's. She looked thin and strained; Ganesha was showing his age. His dark eyes in their pouches of flesh were as reddened and strained by their journey as though he belonged to one of the younger races with whom he companied. But they still gleamed with an alertness a scout might have envied and a relentless intelligence honed by the years, however many.

"I feared," Ganesha translated for Ssu-ma Chao. His own voice quavered. So, did even he fear? "And then I resigned power and sought only to flee from a place of the unquiet dead. But I still digress. So now, it seems to me that I must never return to Ch'ang-an and pollute its precincts with my cowardice. Indeed, I must blot it out. In my blood, if need be; in the blood of my kin, if my sins are discovered. But I would prefer to avenge myself in the blood of those who brought me to this pass. I shall go forward."

Ganesha broke off, one hand upraised in the storyteller's graceful demand for attention. But his hand trembled slightly. "He asks me to ask you whether your Eagle can guide us to our enemies."

Draupadi clasped her hands in her lap so tightly that

the delicate bones showed white beneath the skin. She looked down at them, and Quintus spied what an effort it took for her not to look at Ganesha. The old man also looked down now, as if unwilling to influence any of the others.

"They're the ones who want to steal it—"

"How do you know—"

Rufus and Lucilius broke into the silence at the same moment. At Lucilius's glare, the centurion broke off, muttering to himself. "The day I agree with . . . maybe the sun *hasn't* ridden or it's made me crazy. . . . Oh, to the crows with it."

"*Ask* them!" Lucilius snapped. "How do you know they haven't maneuvered us into just this decision?"

Ssu-ma Chao looked inquiringly at him. Then he retreated into impassivity.

"They want to know," Draupadi spoke slowly in Parthian, "whether you in truth suggest going up against the Black Naacals or whether these are words that Ganesha put into your mouth."

"*He* wants to know," said the Ch'in officer. "Who would have betrayed us all. *Yes,* those were my words, not the man who translates for me. Who is to say that other caravans may not fall prey—may not be engulfed by these evil men?" His eyes were frenzied with memory of the Stone Tower.

"Do you truly believe," Draupadi's voice was consciously sweet, "that I would lead you to your deaths, your tribune with you?" She unclasped her hands and held out the one that bore Quintus's ring.

They were desperate, but Rufus took a moment to grin and thump Quintus on the shoulder.

"I believe in my orders," the tribune said. He would have liked to savor that moment, but every moment was

precious now. "I believe—or believed!—" he shot that at
Lucilius, "—in my elders. And betters, as they insisted
they were to me. But now I believe in the Eagle."

Rufus turned again to the young officer. "You are
Roma for now, son. You decide what is right to do; I'll do
it. Aye, and drive the men to fight past the gods of Hades.
Say the word, sir."

Lucilius rose to his feet. His eyes were wild. He all but
quivered with anger, not unmixed with a tinge of fear.

And why should he not fear? We are all afraid.

All the Romans feared death, feared the worse-than-
death they had seen. And he feared losing what had
become precious to him. But Lucilius—he feared making
the decision to which he had been pushed and which he
could no longer put off.

"Why?" Quintus asked Draupadi and Ganesha.

They fought against the Black Naacals, who had been
of their own blood and faith. But why did they require
allies, when, surely, they had powers of their own?

Draupadi reached over to touch the Eagle. She *could,*
Quintus thought, and the sight reassured him even before
her words.

"We are guests in this age, this Yuga of the world,
Quintus," she told him. "It is no longer ours. It falls to
you now, to the younger races and nations that sprang up
after the Motherland sank beneath the waves. I believe—
Ganesha and I believe—that we survive only to finish
what we began: the overwhelming of this darkness, so
your peoples may attain what fates are destined for
them."

And why me? My return home is lost. . . . He remembered
those saddest of Achilles's words. *Lost in any case,* came
a thought—his or his enemy's. He did not know: In either
case, it was true.

And so, there remained only one question: What the proper course was for a Roman to take. The Eagle gleamed overhead, the only bright thing in a desert of grays and ochres. Decide. Decide, fool, it seemed to say.

The ground trembled, and a salt smell rose from the desert. Rufus thrust out a large hand as he overbalanced, and Ganesha shook his head. "The island we passed that night, Draupadi. . . . Do you recollect it?"

"You do not think it was overwhelmed?" she asked as calmly as if discussing a journey made a day ago, a month ago, and not the great expanse of time that, surely, was the truth. "It was so small, but it possessed that peak with a tabernacle. . . ." She broke off and stared at Ssu-ma Chao.

"There is a story," the Ch'in officer said, "of a fountain of pure water, a shrine in the depths of the waste, found only by people in the most desperate need—and sometimes not even then. I heard the story from a dying man, the last survivor of a caravan. A patrol had turned him up. We took him up and tried to save him, but he died at noon, raving as we thought. Raving," the Ch'in officer added thoughtfully. "We are already off our reckoning."

"Fare forward," Quintus found himself muttering. Arjuna's thought had become his.

"Forward?" Lucilius snapped. "Which way is forward? Can you even tell?" Rufus glared. If Lucilius hadn't been patrician, he would have had a blow for the interruption. It was death to strike an officer. Considering the case they were in, that could hardly make a difference; but it did, for Rufus.

"You'd dare, would you?" Lucilius snarled at the centurion, whose control did *not* extend to his eyes.

"We must move in any case," Draupadi said. "Better

for us to find them than for them to find us at a time of their choosing."

A scream rose from behind them, and they jumped from the shock. One of the soldiers who had collapsed and had lain head down on a camel for the journey yammered in terror, then screamed again, this time in mortal agony. His back arched, and his entire body convulsed until the ropes binding him to the pack animal broke asunder. Before he fell face down, they could see that his face had swollen and turned dark as if he had been strangled.

"Snakes!" screamed a Roman, looking down as if a veritable legion of serpents had attacked. The hiss and scrape of grit in the desert intensified until even Rufus looked uneasy. If you were exhausted or half-mad—and if someone suggested it to you—perhaps you would mistake it for the sound of immense coils, dragging along the desert floor, waiting, preparing to—

Draupadi flung out a hand and chanted. The hissing subsided.

"I distrust things when they're that easy," Rufus observed.

"Your man was mad already. Being mad, he could be worked on to believe, and his belief killed him. I have removed the illusion for now, but I warn you: When you are weariest and weakest, they will strike again."

"So we have to move," Rufus said. "Sir?" He turned to Quintus for orders.

Lucky Rufus, who could unload the burden of leadership on officers who didn't want it either. Ganesha met Quintus's eyes. Either resign authority or be worthy of it and, perhaps, save all of their lives.

But Ganesha was more fit by far to lead!

It is not our world, not our time, he recalled Ganesha's

words. After seeing the means the Black Naacals would use to achieve dominion, Quintus knew that Ganesha feared what he might do if he himself seized great power: Perhaps he would be a benevolent tyrant, but, ultimately, a tyrant nonetheless. It would be hard to go against a beloved tyrant, but Quintus would have to, being Roman. Or, if not he, other Romans.

"Draupadi!" Ganesha snapped, a guard alerting other warriors.

She chanted once more, as the bronze talisman Quintus bore heated. Another of the men who had collapsed during the flight after the earthquake screamed and began to writhe. This one gasped, his face purpling, and Quintus heard the crack and snap as his bones broke.

Draupadi ran to him, as he writhed and twisted, moaning weakly. She stretched out her hands, laid them on the air above the man's chest, and began to tug. Her voice rose strongly. The soldier slumped back, blood dripping from his mouth. It might be that his death was a mercy.

Draupadi's arms stiffened as if she fought to hold off fangs and the coils of an immense, unseen body that sought now to crush her.

"Do you see anything?" Ganesha demanded of Quintus.

He tightened his hand upon the Eagle. Was that a ghost of scales, of green and bronze that he saw? He had heard travellers' tales of serpents so vast that they could swallow cattle—and Draupadi was so much smaller.

Quintus drew his sword and hacked at the shadow. The blade snapped. Draupadi reeled and fell, as if she had been tossed aside. Then it was the Roman's turn to gasp and fight off encircling coils of an astonishing strength, rising up his legs so he couldn't move the few steps necessary to grasp the Eagle, and rising, always rising. He heard Draupadi's voice rise, chanting again, rising almost to a shriek.

I must help her, Quintus thought, but he lacked the breath to tell her he was coming. If he could get to the Eagle, he would have a weapon better than any sword, but he had laid it aside.

His ribs felt as if lead weights were laid about them. He could see Draupadi's face, but it was growing smaller and fainter as if he saw it through a mist of blood. . . . He started to fall but was upheld by the very thing that was attacking him.

Draupadi stepped forward, a tiny knife in her hand. A stab at the serpent's "middle" and the pain in his chest eased. The creature seemed to fall as if poisoned, and Quintus had hard work not to collapse, too.

Dust swirled up from the desert floor, as if some immense creature lashed it up with its tail in its death throes.

Fire seemed to burn in Quintus's chest. The talisman's heat subsided; now the fire was his fight to draw in enough air so he could breathe without gasping.

They would send more serpents, Quintus knew. Sooner or later, everyone would see them, and Draupadi could not fight them all off.

He forced himself to move, then doubled over, almost retching from the pain as if he had run a race and must now collapse. *Chairete, nikomen,* he remembered after Marathon. *Rejoice, we have conquered,* said the runner. And collapsed and died. *You can't die yet. You haven't conquered,* he admonished himself. *No Lethe for you.*

Ganesha's eyes begged him. *Choose. Choose now.* He could see the old man fighting his own battle—to urge rather than to coerce. Perhaps that was a battle he knew.

Perhaps he had seen the Black Naacals fight it and lose it too.

Perhaps that was even how it started, a desire to do good, to protect, to lead—and then the desire grew to overpower all opposition, even to the wrecking of the world.

Ganesha was an ally. Quintus must aid him, just as he had aided Draupadi.

They were out of their reckoning? Well, Ssu-ma Chao's fountain of pure water was as good a goal in this world of illusion as any.

"We ride!" he ordered. He didn't see who came up to lead—or carry—him to his horse because his eyes were fixed on Lucilius. Once again, the patrician had started toward the Eagle.

"No need to trouble yourself with that," Quintus rasped at Lucilius. "Get me over there," he ordered his bearer. He picked up the Eagle before the other man could try.

Quintus's horse screamed and plunged. Desert-bred as they were, even they had a horror of serpents. Did this one sense the illusion serpents? It must be so. A wind began to rise, stirring the sand and grit into swirls that looked like more coils—best not think like that, lest exhaustion and fear and memory of the serpent's coils cause them to manifest once more. Venomous or not, those coils were deadly.

Rufus had bent over, was sprinkling dust over the faces of the two men who had died. Draupadi mounted, chanting as she moved.

"Mount up and take her reins!" Quintus shouted at Rufus. She would need both hands for her work.

"Forward!" he shouted. He had not meant to gesture with the standard as if it were a sword—it had been

Arjuna's blade, but that had snapped. However, the Eagle felt right in his hands, like a sweetly balanced weapon. Once again, light flared from the proudly held bird's head into a crown of glory, lighting sky and ground alike.

Once more he heard hissing, this time in front of them. If they turned to flee, he would wager all that the serpents' hiss would sound again.

Gods help us, he thought. The image of dancing Krishna seemed to stir against his chest.

Again, Quintus raised the Eagle. As the light struck the ground ahead of him and the wind blew, a figure gleaming like the Eagle seemed to gather itself up from the desert floor and leap to its feet. It moved forward, dancing as it went; light gleamed off its raised hands, as if it held torches.

Light from Eagle and dancer intensified until they filled Quintus's consciousness. Tears ran down his face, and he had to look aside. Tears were a waste; he would need that moisture as they rode deeper into the desert.

When the brightness subsided enough to allow him and the others to open their eyes, sand and sky were as they always had been. They stood in a basin in the greater depression. It was only a waste now, not the abode of monsters. It was a marvel to stand thus and look about the cloudless sky, realizing that what looked like clouds were actually far-off mountains to the north and east: a marvel indeed to have north and east again.

Confidence touched Quintus, as it had every time the Eagle manifested its power. No doubt they might cut across a caravan route and reach a town before they consumed the last of their supplies.

They might well, indeed. But instead of counting on that, he turned his mount's head and guided his people deeper into the waste, following a dancing figure that flickered and gleamed ahead of him like sparks from a fire at harvest time.

The sparks brightened and spread out, solidifying into a track of light upon the eternal drabness of the desert. On and on it stretched, inviting them to travel along it.

Some of the men turned away. One screamed, then fell, lying with his face against the grit.

"We have a path," Quintus said. *Try not to hurt at this most recent death,* he told himself. He held aloft the Eagle as he would hold a torch up as he entered a cave. The *signum's* brightness gleamed as if it were molten metal, a beacon not just of power, of the might, of the Senate and the Roman people, but a sign or a promise that here at least, in the wild where madness stalked behind the noonday sun, the Eagle's wings spread out over all who cared to shelter beneath them.

It might not protect them: Romans and Ch'in alike, they were soldiers who must go where they were ordered and, perhaps, die there.

But this was a chance; and more than that, it was uniquely theirs, a memory of governance, land, and homes that existed, even if they never saw them again. Judging by the light in Ssu-ma Chao's eyes, Quintus thought that the Eagle—or as he called it, the Phoenix, meant much the same for him: authority, guidance, loyalty—his ancestors themselves, looking down on him and nodding approval.

Quintus led the Romans and the Ch'in out onto the blazing track.

25

UP AHEAD, THE dancing figure flung up its torches. They blazed brightly as they rose, then exploded into even greater radiance.

"But if that light goes out . . ." came a whisper, followed by the crack of the vinestaff. You followed where you were led. If you were led well, you lived, you received land and a mule, and you retired to enjoy them. If not, you died. But always, you obeyed.

None of them, Quintus knew, had reason to understand this enemy. What had they thought of? Death in battle or even by thirst were things they understood: not this. But they followed him.

Why do you tarry? the tiny figure seemed to ask as it danced. After so long lost, with such a path ahead of them, they might have been riding or marching down a Roman road toward a fate that, for the first time since he was a boy, he was convinced held glory.

He grinned at Ganesha. "Fare forward, just as he told me last time."

"I remember," said the magician. "But fare faster."

Ganesha knew. He remembered and had chronicled how Arjuna had ridden out in his chariot, riding behind Krishna to a battle that would shake the foundations of the world. He had his usual weapons—and he had Pasupata, the ultimate weapon for which he had searched the waste. He, too.

There was no question of it now, Quintus thought, exulting. Faster and faster they travelled, and the *ming sha*, the singing sand, rose up to obscure their passage as if they marched into a place of turned up sand and light where their enemies might not harm them.

The sun sank and set, yet the light persisted. It was too good to lose: Tired though they were, they plodded on. Those who were mounted, marched; those who had marched, rode, resting as they might. There would be time to cease, to camp when the light faded. The hot wind blew. Quintus was very happy.

As the hours passed, the moon rose, climbing high overhead.

Beneath the beacon of the moon, the Eagle glowed not like bronze but the electrum of Egypt. Under that dome cast by its light, Quintus saw the desert transformed—softened by the light and by the *ming sha* itself, as if a veil rested gently over its worst aspects, hinting at the beauty that had once been in this place.

It had all been sea, Ganesha said: easy now to look at the slopes of the dunes and see the waves that had not glittered under the stars since their patterns had changed.

He turned, craning his head to see those he led. Ganesha rode as if in a happy dream. He might have been hastening not toward a battle but a reunion with what he loved best. Draupadi rode veiled once more, more wary than Ganesha, perhaps. But even as he looked, she cast off the veil from head and shoulders. The light touched her, erasing fears and weariness; and the sight of her took Quintus's breath away.

The figure who rode there—that was not *his* Draupadi, as he thought of her: a warmth of saffron and sandalwood, her dark hair flowing down her upright back like hot oil. This woman's face was silver, cooling the beauty of feature into a type of antique mask of the sort he had seen lining the Via Appia, smiling through closed lips like his talisman.

Not Draupadi, he thought, but Diana of the Three Ways, the huntress keen on a trail that would bring her to her quarry, or Selene, overlooking the night land. Or even—and this thought made him shiver—the dark goddess at the crossroads, now manifesting herself in a priestess fully capable of mediating between heaven and Hades.

She was, Quintus recalled, a mistress of illusion; but he saw her as a face of the power she revealed. And as the others rode at her heels, he saw them too, not illusion but truth as the light distilled it from the flesh: the stubborn loyalty of the eldest of them; the strength of Ssu-ma Chao, loyalty unlooked for; even the shiftiness, the fox-like cunning of Lucilius was transformed into a kind of beauty.

Would they be eager to go up against whatever fastness the Black Naacals had taken for their own? In this light, and with the Eagle gleaming beneath the moon, he thought they could do anything. Judging from the rate at which they travelled, the way they held up their heads, so did they. It was so simple, he thought. One simply . . .

. . . The light flickered . . . a veiling of sand or cloud—after months it was odd to think of clouds that were not a desert tempest or the eternal snows of far-off mountains. What was that? An instant ago, he had known with an assurance greater than any he had ever enjoyed before, precisely what to do. The Eagle's staff warmed in his hand. Had he forgotten? It had not, the warning seemed to convey.

Fare forward.

He did. Then another wind blew, casting a pall of sand between the Eagle and the moon. The standard's brightness faded, then blazed up again. The moon was lower in the sky now, slipping toward its rest. Its light diminished, then was extinguished.

Ahead of them, the dancing figure seemed to pause, drawing light about it as a lamp flares up with the last drops of oil. Then that light too was quenched.

They were left standing in the bare desert. The keen, chill night wind wreathed them and cooled their faces. Then that, too, subsided.

After silver, lead. A weariness seized Quintus's limbs. He had time enough to signal a halt and sink the standard of the Eagle deep into the ever-present grit, securing it so whatever protection it might afford would lie over the camp they would now, in the dark of the moon, permit themselves to build. After such a passage, it was time for them to sleep.

Rufus's voice came to the tribune's ears. Not the usual assured bellow—but hoarse, hollow with exhaustion and even a sort of awe.

How far had they come—and what had they reached? They were beyond all reckoning. And they were tired beyond all measure. He yawned hugely. A little longer, and he would be able to sink down and sleep where he fell. Improper: They were Romans. But beneath the Eagle . . .

"To the crows with it," he muttered, and let his legs collapse beneath him.

Draupadi passed by, drifting in her tattered robes. Past him. Past the Eagle. None of the drunken staggering of deep exhaustion for her, but her usual grace.

"Do you know where we are?" he whispered.

Had he lost her to the illusions he had seen? Doubt chilled him more than the wind: He was tired; he must sleep. Sleep brought dreams; dreams were fancies, wafted into his thoughts through the gates of ivory. The gates of illusion.

Draupadi gazed out over the sand.

"Closer to where we need to be," she murmured. "Give me your hand."

That surprised him. She had always been profoundly reserved before the others. Pleased, though, he held out his hand for hers. She touched it and made a small, happy sound in her throat. And he saw what she did: the dome of light cast by the Eagle, even with sun and moon gone from the sky.

"It will not hide us forever," she murmured. "But it will serve for now."

Behind them came the noise of a camp, of soldiers settling, some to sleep, some to guard. He should return, should allow them to see that he was still alert.

"Let them all rest," Draupadi said. "Your minds and gods can do very little against what we face. We have come far and fast, and we need rest."

At that moment, the desert floor looked as comfortable as a silken rug—to sink down upon it, to sink into it as into a bath of deep water. . . . He jolted himself back to full awareness. Then he knelt and thrust his hand down into the grit. Rock, dust, powder, sand—not water at all.

He let the powder pour from his hand.

"They wish to return this world to what it was,"

Draupadi mused. "Even now, because you are weary, they make these little tests." She sighed. "Guard yourself. The tests will worsen before we face them in truth."

Her gaze went to the Eagle, its bronze eyes staring out fiercely over their heads. "It is time now for our weapon to be our shield."

Quintus felt himself falling sideways. Draupadi sank down beside him, and let him pillow his head upon her knees. Sleep covered him like a saffron veil.

26

THERE WERE SHIPS on glinting blue water, small boats floating like swans or larger ones with oars stroking with the rhythm of the great wings of birds of passage, dipping and turning as the ships glided away from coastlines and spears of rock in which birds nested and from which they too sailed. The flags of the Motherland, brave with their disks of the sun, flew from masts. Below, on deck, sailors ran back and forth, steps as ordered as those of a dance but more urgent.

He stood watching as his ship came about between two rocky peaks of some dark stone that glinted in the sunlight and the light reflected from the changeable sea. But those were not just rocks jutting out from the expanse of the sea or markers indicating that the waters roundabout might be treacherous for the uninitiated. Art, science, and craft had labored over them for many years, building piers at their bases and climbing steps up their hard surfaces to platforms that held beacons and gongs to guide ships home and warn off the unwelcome. And, at the rocks' highest crags, engineers had wrought long and skillfully: A triumphal arch joined two of the peaks, with scenes of the Motherland's history sculpted in high relief.

A shadow fell on his face, but his heart lifted and sang as his ship passed beneath the Arch of Memory. For beyond it lay the harbor, and on the hill above the harbor stood the temple where the Naacals studied and where they served the sun. This was home. His home and that of—

Who screamed?

Even before his eyes were open, Quintus's hand flew to his sword—broken now, he must be wary—and he leapt to his feet. Leapt too fast. *Careful, man, or you'll fall overboard*—no! Where was he? *When* was he? The sea of blues and green, with the gold of sunlight gilding a sail or the edge of a seabird's wing or striking fire from the crystal glinting in the living rock of the Arch of Memory—they were all gone, long gone. A sullen dawn glared down from the east like a soldier hoping to flee a battle he has no stomach for.

Again, Quintus heard a bubbling scream. He set out for the edge of the camp. One thing was certain. A man couldn't scream over and over like that if his throat were cut. The voice arched up into pure madness, then ended suddenly.

Ssu-ma Chao rose from his knees beside a limp body. "Dead," he said. "Did you catch that last word?"

"The shadow, the shadow," Draupadi repeated it.

Lucilius ran up, short sword in hand, present when trouble turned up as he always was. "Look you!" He gestured.

On the ground beyond the circle of light still cut by the Eagle, even in this harsh dawn, long shadows fell like bats shrilling to each other at the uttermost edge of a man's hearing, more felt than heard. Shadows like unto the flow and sweep of long, black cloaks, darkening still further as the sun rose.

Draupadi clapped her hands. The shadows remained. She raised her voice in a chant. The words faltered and came out hoarsely. The shadows flickered. She drew breath and sang the more strongly, clapped her hands once again, and they finally withdrew. She almost sagged with weariness, but caught herself.

Ganesha came up behind her. She spoke to him quickly in a language Quintus did not know, dismay in her voice.

"Yes," Ganesha answered her in Parthian. "They get stronger. And will continue to do so the closer we come to them."

"Do they think we are children or fools?" Ssu-ma Chao asked.

"Very likely," said the old magician. He laid his hands on Draupadi's shoulders. "They know we are with you. If it were I, I would seek to drain the two of us, leaving this, our army, without protection."

"Army?" Ssu-ma Chao's bark of laughter sounded almost like a sob. "At every dawn, we become fewer and fewer. Come and see."

It was one of the Ch'in soldiers who had collapsed during the time when the earth shook and time past and time present blurred, seeking to blot out mind and body alike. The man's face was set in what would have been a mask for the theatre signifying panic. For if ever that god had laid his grip upon a man to steal sanity and breath, it was now.

Lucilius muttered something along the lines of "loading up," and "the line of march." Ganesha smoothly interposed his bulk between him and the Ch'in officer, lest Lucilius hear.

"We could send men out to scout, see if those Black Cloaks are anywhere in sight. Or smell," Rufus offered, oddly indecisive.

"No!" Quintus and Lucilius shouted it together. They could not afford to lose more men, soul as well as the mind.

"He was only a common soldier," said the Ch'in officer. "But he served faithfully."

"He served you well even in the manner of his dying," Draupadi told the officer. "For whatever reason, he was—how shall we say it—aware? sensitive? *vulnerable*," she brought out the word with the air of one struggling to express sophisticated concepts in a language more akin to a child's speech, "to the influence sent among us by the Black Naacals. Who knows what they might have done had he not screamed and waked us? Until the end, he was faithful; in the end, he gave up his life for his fellows. His ancestors can look down upon him and be proud."

Even the Ch'in officer's narrow eyes widened in respect. He heaved himself off his knees and saluted the dead armsman as men wrapped him in his cloak and covered him in a shallow, hastily dug grave.

"And now?" he asked. His eyes went to Quintus. Lucilius glared as he always did when Quintus was deferred to as leader.

But it was Ganesha who answered. "We go forward. Always forward."

He gestured at the Eagle, which glinted in the coppery rays of the risen sun. Light welled out from it. "We will be guided—but the path will not be easy."

* * *

Day melted into day, and the dunes through which they passed loomed higher and higher. For some time, as many as possible who could ride, did. Then, as their beasts tired, they walked, leading them.

Rufus muttered, "It's like looking up from the bottom of a well. What sort of pit are we dropping into?"

Of course, no one had any answer for that. Day by day, they *were* descending, perhaps into what would have been the deepest part of the seabed. Day by day, the shadows ranged alongside them. At first, they paused if you looked at them dead-on. And the higher the sun rose in the sky, the smaller they were, vanishing at noon.

Later on, though, later on, it took Draupadi's or Ganesha's knowledge to disperse them. Closer and closer they ranged, not fading even at noon. Even for these men, the strongest who had set out so many months ago, it was hard to rest at noon when no shadows should mark the trail, and see these shadows, as it seemed, in a midday camp of their own, just watching—or ranging out in the late afternoon when all shadows lengthened. Quintus had a private nightmare that, one day, they would curve around one of the larger dunes and find an army of faceless shadow-soldiers between them and their goal.

On the fifth day after the first madman died, a Roman recovered from the stupor into which he had fallen. He recognized his thankful comrades, vowed himself strong enough to march—and disappeared late in the afternoon. The man nearest him had heard his companion shout and run out into the waste, arms outspread in welcome. He had started after the straggler, but two of his fellows had toppled him and sat on him.

"We grow fewer," Ganesha observed again.

As the water grew scarce, they dreamed shallowly, and always of water. When it seemed as if they could descend no further without losing sight of the night sky, Lucilius woke screaming about a well of water. Thirst had made him slow on his feet, or he too might have fled. He would have to ride, even when others walked, until he recovered from the shock. *If* he recovered.

"No loss," Rufus muttered, despite Quintus's glare. Every man incapacitated and needing to be carried weakened them even more than a death. Impossible to abandon a brother-in-arms—even if to do so would not put them on the moral level of the ones they fought.

As their throats grew more parched, Quintus had no more dreams of the sea. Odd: He would have thought he would have dreamed more of water, rather than less. His sleep was shallow. Too often, he woke in a cold sweat that wasted water he could ill afford to replace. He dreamt of sliding down the face of immense dunes. He woke shaking. And *then* he thought of water.

So far they had come, so far: If this had been a futile chase, they must now begin to resign themselves to having lost their way. It was too late now to retrace their steps. Perhaps they had all been befooled, betrayed. Perhaps the *real* Black Naacals marched beside them, a fat man and a slender woman, lithe and careworn, wrapped in tattered veils.

And that thought was worse than any possible dreams that Quintus might have.

The fifth horse died at noon. It had simply collapsed and refused to rise. Lucilius despatched it by cutting its throat, surprising tears drying on his cheeks. The copper stench of blood seemed even hotter than the sun.

One of the Legionaries began to unstrap what the horse bore.

"Leave it," Quintus ordered. The man obeyed.

Do you really think, lad, we are going to need what the poor brute carried? The man might have been Quintus's own age, maybe even a bit older: At this point, they were all "lad" to him. Lucky men, who had someone to shoulder the burden of regret for all the lost lives.

Even if it had been gold or jewels, he would have ordered the pack left. Only food, water, and weapons were of value enough to be borne along—and blankets against the chill of the night.

The blowing grit stung their faces until they bled. They wrapped in the felts designed for storms until, from a distance, they might well have seemed to be a straggling column of mummies, bandages peeling, staggering and lurching from their inquiet sleep. "Look at us," Rufus muttered. "Maybe we'll *scare* those shadows."

That raised a laugh from the men that would have brought tears of pride to Quintus's eyes if they weren't so dry—and if the men didn't waste breath by laughing.

Then, late one afternoon, he looked up. An immense slide was beginning along the slope of a dune not all that far ahead. His heart sank: He had dreamed of an attack, but usually it took the form of the Black Naacals' shades arrayed in a *triplex acies* against them.

Nevertheless, he told himself. *Nevertheless, we fight.*

He grasped the Eagle firmly. "Let me go first." He had heard sweeter tones from a crow. There were no crows here: too dry.

The shadow marched ahead of him. The Eagle showed no soldiers waiting for him, and the tiny bronze dancing Krishna he bore still rested quiescent against his heart.

Something marched alongside his shadow. He chuckled hoarsely, and it all but turned into a sob. The shadow he watched and feared so had been his own—his and the Eagle's. They had reached the depths and were climbing once more.

The grit that crunched underfoot gradually yielded to spurs of rock, then a rocky floor covered with drifts, and worn in patterns that even now showed the smoothing of water upon rock very long ago. They seemed to be marching through the foothills of some mountain range below the surface of the world.

"Move along," Rufus said for what had to be the fiftieth time that day to Ganesha. Once again, the adept had sunk to his knees, staring raptly at the outline of a fish's skeleton embedded in a rock. That is, Quintus thought it was a fish, though he had never seen one that looked that way. "Wouldn't you rather eat a real one?" he asked.

"I would rather be at peace," Ganesha replied. "I am very old, and I would be glad to rest. But the tale is not over yet; and as long as it goes on, I must be part of it—to undo what I did. And what my brothers and sisters, the Flame forgive them, still do."

Rufus shook his head. They looked at each other, *senex* and *senex*. Two old men, old from the desert as well as in years; too old for much more than tending land and handing on their wisdom. Quintus's throat ached. Ganesha should be basking in a temple courtyard someplace— Juno grant—talking to a child who looked like Draupadi or like himself. And Rufus—he should have little more on his mind than showing a child that might have been his grandson how best to tie up vines or, for the hundredth time, allowing him to see his sword, or even hold it, as a very special reward.

Long wrinkles angled down from the corner of Rufus's eyes, squinting shut as always in the desert glare.

He looked older than Ganesha and, in the harness he stubbornly refused to lay aside, far more frightening.

Yet, Ganesha was the elder by far and possessed of powers far more fearsome—those of the White Naacals. Despite the heat, Quintus shuddered. The Naacals' power harnessed the virtue of the sun: Misused by the Black, such power had cracked the land through which they now struggled and a great sea had vanished into the depths.

Better not think of all that water. A drop of sweat ran down Quintus's back. Momentary relief: Now that was a delicious thought, like the time after harvest when he was a boy, his chores over, and free to slip off his tunic and plunge into fresh water. He could dive as deep as he could and emerge, spluttering and laughing on the other side of the arch.

Arch? What arch?

The ebb and flow, the lapping and splashing of water seemed very real in that moment. The arch? Any fool knew the Arch of Memory. And so did he. He had dreamed it long ago: the gateway that welcomed those who served the sun to the island that was one of their schools and fastnesses. Statues had ornamented that arch, statues of ancient heroes and wise men and women, depicted with beasts out of legends that Quintus did not know, all surrounding the great, many-headed serpent that meant wisdom and power—the illumination of the sun.

He did not even need to close his eyes to see that arch. A moment of vertigo came. Place and time flickered in and out of focus. Once again, he could hear seabirds and the splash of oars, the shout of pilot to the guardians of the shore, hailing them from the gateway. And he knew the price of that gate to the unwary. Those who were not expert in the passage were swept onto a rock shore.

Quintus fought not to think of the image of the arch that thrust itself so insistently into his consciousness. Draupadi would tell him that this was illusion, the sort that thrust a man from his wits and off the nearest cliff—or that left him prey to the Black Naacals. The Eagle's staff warmed in his hands, a warmth that ran up from his hand to his shoulder and down into his spine. For a madman, he felt surprisingly well.

Again came one of those flickers between then and now. One of the madmen tied to a camel whimpered and giggled, then fell silent. Now Quintus saw the arch as it was in this time and place. No longer a matter of pride for artisans and engineers in its construction or its ornament, it looked like a skull, most of the teeth rotted out and one temple battered in. The span of the arch was weakened from the many rocks levered out of it by tremors, perhaps, or eroded by countless desert storms.

Most of the gleaming stone was gone, and many of the carvings. The heroes' faces had been blotted out, hammered into nothingness like the tomb of a disgraced ruler. A few statues still raised weapons in defense against ancient enemies. And the great serpent still occupied the space below the keystone. But how changed it was. It was no longer a symbol of light, but of illumination wasted, power turned in on itself, fueled by a hunger that grew from age to age because there was not enough, not ever enough in all the world to feed it. It would devour the world in a rage that it had not even more to eat.

Draupadi caught her breath in a faint sob. "And to think how fair this all was once."

The usual trick of the light in the desert made the

despoiled arch seem much closer to them than it really was. The approach actually took them many hours of hard climbing up an immense hill toward what had once been an island. That rock ahead—was it a cliff or a fortress? Or, all the gods help them, was it the temple that had once graced the height?

They would do well, Quintus thought, to rest and to let their beasts rest and to attempt the gate by full light.

He ached. And he knew that if he suffered, the men behind him had suffered worse and the beasts worse yet. And Draupadi—he ought not to think of her as gentler than he, weaker than he, but he did—until he saw her face, which hardships had refined, instilling dignity and power into already-great beauty.

A flicker of memory lit his consciousness: In the wilderness, when his brother had lost kingdom, crown, freedom, and wife by his gambling, Draupadi had only screamed once—when they had tried to take her. And then she had vowed to wash her hair in the blood of the man who had dared—and kept that vow, as he recalled.

No, it was folly to fear she was too frail for this.

Behind him a horse screamed, and rocks clattered down the slope. Oaths rose, followed by Rufus's rasping shout for quiet. The coppery tang of blood touched the air. One of the dazed men laughed, then sobbed, muffling his face in his hands. *Hurry, fool,* he told himself, *or you'll have no one left at your back but corpses and madmen.* The two magicians. Rufus, until that great heart of his burst. And probably Lucilius, yoked together as they seemed forever to be.

But it was only another pack animal fallen. It might be best to leave all of the beasts here and go on, though what the beasts would do if no one returned. . . . Gods, he *was* his troop, man and beast: Every loss hurt as if it had been carved out of his own flesh and bone, even after so many deaths. The Eagle's standard felt comforting in his hand. And it made a fine staff as they climbed up toward the crumbling arch.

Ssu-ma Chao caught his eye, and Quintus was all attention. He would never forget that he had lived and kept his weapons only by the Ch'in officer's goodwill. He gestured for Quintus to go on ahead. Rufus leaned against the rocks, waiting for the weakest men and beasts to pass. (He would straighten up when they came in sight, of course, lest they see him doing anything that looked like easing up.) The column was, in fact, as carefully guarded as he could make it. The gods only send that it survive to reach what lay beyond the arch. One rockfall, for example . . . gods avert.

And then what? This journey was all "if's." *If* they survived. *If* this place in the center of a desert more fearsome than Tartarus proved to hold the spring of sweet water that travellers' tales had spoken of. *If* they met the Black Naacals and were not blasted into the kind of glossy black stone that littered the sides of a mountain that spat up rock and fire. And finally *if* they were able to retrace their path and be granted safe return out of this desolation.

Keep your head down, he reminded himself. Watch your footing. Watch the rocks up above for what might crawl out from beneath one of them, or come hurtling down. He dug the butt of the standard into the grit and gravel. It bit strongly, and he started up the slope.

And as he climbed, even as he struggled to keep his mind on the immediate problems, Quintus's thoughts wandered. They had been wrong, his father, his grandsire, even the Vestals and the entire college of priests, all the way up to the Pontifex Maximus. It was not the Fates that guided a man's life and wove the thread of it. That was just a pretty story. It was the "if's" that determined within any age of the world whether a man would or would not go on living or whether he would achieve what had been set down—by whomever—for him.

So why try? The question struck with the force of lightning, blinding force followed by darkness. He blinked and looked up. No storms anywhere around. No thunder. No lightning. He shook his head to clear it. He had been warned to expect attacks.

No, he said.

One of the madmen whimpered. The camel bearing him twitched, then plodded onward. Limping. They would have to check all the camels' feet for cuts—a real pleasure to anticipate. When this was over, the kindest thing they could probably do for the wretched creatures— camels and madmen—would be to slit their throats. Then they could fall on their own swords.

No, he said again in his mind, more firmly than before. *If I die, and I do mean if, let me do it in the open, fighting. Or marching east under the Eagle.*

That sense of oppressive blackness pressing down on his mind. The sky was clear, but the smell of salt filled his nostrils. Salt, not sweat. Abruptly—not again! he moaned inwardly—sky and land flickered. A shadow loomed up before him. Entering it created an instant of blessed coolness. The gate shone in that moment, its statues intact and magnificent.

Did Chronos blink again? Are we adrift? A madman's sobbing confirmed his suspicions. After a while, even wonders grew tedious, and this one was a nuisance.

"Ought to knock him on the head," Rufus muttered. "No! You don't have to hit him that hard. Did you kill him? No thanks to you, if you didn't."

In and out of focus the arch wavered. He blinked hard, not wanting to be blinded when he emerged from its shadow. He rested his hand on his sword, painstakingly sharpened once more. Gods save them if they had to fight even as time and place wavered about them.

"Quintus . . ." Draupadi moved to his side. He flinched as a particularly strong tremor made the entire arch waver and even vanish for a dizzying instant.

"Please tell me," he began, despising himself for what was almost a plea in his voice, "that it gets worse this close to the gate."

She laid a hand on his shoulder. Some of the vertigo and fear drained from him. "I hoped you would not feel it so strongly."

Quintus moved his shoulder out from under her hand. He loved her touch, but to be reassured by it, while his men struggled with their fear? That was not right.

She nodded, knowing his mind. "Quintus, do not concern yourself to stay hidden. They know we have come. Otherwise, you would not feel under attack once more." She raised her hand like a sailor, sniffing the air. "They will surely have greater magics prepared. Let Ganesha and I face them first."

An old man and a woman—to lead Romans into battle? Impossible! he started to say.

"We are weapons in your hands," she cut into his objections. "Who knows better than we what they might do, and how to fight them? They destroyed our home! They destroyed our world! We have a right, Quintus!"

Draupadi's eyes grew huge and dark. A man could fall into them. *And how many fools has she beguiled? A man could be bespelled, besotted. . . . She will pass beyond the gate with that old man of hers, and then be gone. And you will die here.*

She has never tricked me and never will! he retorted to the treacherous voice that insinuated itself into his thoughts.

She and Ganesha served the Flame. They were Naacals, White against Black. They had as much right to oppose the Black Naacals as he had had to seek the Eagle.

"Even now, they seek to reach you," Draupadi said, looking into his face. "Even now, don't they?"

His thoughts were more traitorous than any trick of Lucilius. He loved her. He must trust her. He shook his head. Hard enough to fight. Worse, if he had to re-assure her.

She held up her hand on which the ring he had given her shone. "This has power in it, the power of your pledge. I could not wear it if I were false."

Those eyes of hers . . . he could see a tiny version of himself, watching her, watching a slender, tired woman as if she were about to launch an attack he could not withstand. Was he always so solemn? The idea forced a chuckle from him, then a real laugh. "A throw of the dice," he said. "Trust you or lose all."

Gods send it wasn't "trust you *and* lose all."

Draupadi nodded. "Let this sign of yours, this weapon, blast me if I lie." She reached out and laid a hand on the staff that upheld the Eagle.

Thunder rumbled overhead. For a moment, Quintus forgot to breathe. If she were struck down, he would not survive to mourn long, he vowed. But a wave of good feeling flowed up his arm.

"You see?" Draupadi whispered in triumph. "You see I am not false?"

A beam of sunlight seemed to shoot beneath the arch and strike the Eagle. How it glowed! He almost believed that it would wake, mantle, and call out.

"Thank you," he said. "As you have asked, you and Ganesha shall lead."

Mercifully, the madmen were silent, sinking back into unquiet sleep. The Naacals moved to the front of the column and led it out from beneath the Arch of Memory into what had, in years beyond memory, been their refuge.

27

THE TREMORS THAT had cracked the ancient sea basin through which they had marched for so long had dealt more gently with the land here—or perhaps some lingering virtue of the White Naacals had spared it from the worst of the devastation. Perhaps he had picked the memory from Draupadi's thoughts. The water here had been shallow, tricky for mariners. He could all but smell the salt, hear the snap of commands and the song of ropes as a ship neared port, coming about sharply before the arch. Water . . . desire possessed him.

Draupadi and Ganesha marched on ahead. From one of the packs, they had withdrawn robes long stored away, shaken them free of dust, and now led, robed in the white of their old offices.

At a cry from Rufus, the Romans hailed them as they emerged from the great arch and the sunlight touched their robes to flame. The light blazed up, restoring priests and archway briefly to their ancient splendor. For that moment, even the desecrated statues high overhead seemed haloed in light. Even the Eagle glowed as if in homage as Quintus held it aloft.

As the sun sank lower, a trick of the light made Draupadi and Ganesha's forms seem to be a size larger than life. As the soldiers watched, their white robes kindled into pure light. Two white figures glided over the darkening land beyond the arch, leading them.

"They will leave us," Lucilius's hiss echoed the fears of which Quintus was now ashamed. "You had to trust them. . . ."

The very stillness of the waste and the soldiers' awe in the presence of those gleaming white robes silenced him for the moment.

Thunder pealed in a clear sky, a desolate place, a dry month. The Naacals paused, halting the column, raising their arms in homage to the setting sun as it dropped, like fire into a sea of oil, setting the horizon ablaze.

Some portion of that light shone even beneath the great arch. It seemed to tremble. Chunks of rock and masonry—later additions, perhaps by the Black Naacals—toppled from the ancient stone. Again the thunder pealed.

The Eagle warmed in Quintus's hands. *Use it, use the weapon*, whispered the tempter inside his skull. *It is Pasupata, which you have sought. Do you thirst? Strike the rock and draw water. What did you win power for, but to wield it?*

To use it wisely! he retorted. *Now quiet! I promised, and I shall keep my faith.*

The ground trembled underfoot, as if they stood on some great bubble that grew larger and larger and that would inevitably burst. Ssu-ma Chao cleared his throat. *Was* this going on too long? And what was "this"?

You are a Roman, a fighter, a soldier, not a client to mages, hissed the voice. *Shall you bow and scrape to them as you did to the senators? They will take you and you will be worse than a client, worse than a slave—and it will be for all times.*

"Steady there, men," Rufus growled. "For the Eagle."

As the sun sank, the light beneath the arch flashed and went out. And then it rekindled, brighter than before, as if struck from the two flames that were the figures of the White Naacals. Their robes grew so brilliant that it hurt to look on them. Then the pain passed, and vision returned. *And are we ourselves turned to eagles,* Quintus asked himself, *that we can stare at the sun and not go blind?*

The Eagle he bore was a glory overhead. Now he could make out Draupadi's and Ganesha's faces. Under the radiance, they were worn, the eyes deeply circled. Ganesha's jowls drooped as if he were melting, and Draupadi's proud straightness seemed to waver.

"Come now." Only the stillness of the night let him hear her words.

He brought up the Eagle. Rufus gave the command to march. Rome's pace, Rome's race. Left, right; left, right. You have marched beneath an arch. This is your triumph. Now, get on with you.

Remember thou art mortal. Thou fool and slave!

Quintus moved to stand beside Draupadi.

"Tell them to hurry," she gasped. "We cannot hold this forever. . . ."

And then the sun set. They had entered the arch in daylight and emerged in night. The wind blew around the peaks, striking eerie sounds from the rocks it had hollowed over the centuries, like invisible owls.

The ground trembled. Oh gods, this time, it would swallow them all up, and then it would snap shut, and they would be buried alive. Draupadi's fire would go out, but he would see her gasp for air before they died. Quintus stiffened. He heard a splitting sound. That bubble they stood on—it had expanded to breaking, and now it would burst, spraying them with molten rock, fire all over them. They would see each other burn. Reality whirled, fragments of forgotten nightmares and new horrors.

The Eagle's light dropped, a flame swallowed by what fed it.

And Quintus remembered. They had stood on the field of battle, and he had unleashed Pasupata. The price had been paid, and he had earned the right to wield it. And they had stood, very quietly, as its deadly danger passed over them to strike their enemies. He had the right. But there was one who could wield it, he thought, even more fully. However, there was another weapon to be used.

"Take the Eagle," he ordered Draupadi now.

She grasped it, and the standard flared up with the same fierce joy that shone in her eyes. Quintus's hand went to his breast as if in salute, but instead he found the tiny bronze figure that had been his guard.

"Now," he told it, "dance for us. Lead us."

And Krishna danced. Light blossomed on Quintus's palm, and the tiny figure danced its mourning and its joy. Leaping from his hand, it grew in size, leaping and spinning as it danced away from the arch and toward the ruins on the hill.

"Come, lads," Quintus said, his voice gentle. "Hand in hand, like we were back on the farm."

Rufus grasped the tribune's hand. *That grip could crush,* had been Quintus's thought when he had first met the centurion. He had been a boy then, even though permitted to call himself a tribune. Now he met that grasp with a matching strength.

"Don't look," he whispered. "Don't feel. All about

you—it's all lies. Look to the light. Look only to the light.''

"The light," Rufus whispered hoarsely. And then, with a shout of strength, "I see flame!"

He grabbed the next man's hand and pulled him along. "See that light, look at it! What are you afraid of? *I'll* give you something to be afraid of," he shouted.

Someone laughed, which should have gotten him at least one blow—but for the present, Quintus and the big centurion were only too happy to hear it. Laughter, like light, pushed back fear and darkness.

Draupadi laughed and joined hands to link a Ch'in armsman to a Legionary. Hand in hand, the Romans and the Ch'in scrambled past the arch and upslope. If the ragged line lacked the dignity of a parade, it was at least on its feet and refusing to despair. It followed the figure of Krishna, no longer trapped in immobile bronze.

"You too, lad!" Rufus reached for Lucilius's hand. The tribune jerked it away. He had always been distrustful of closeness, but this looked like real revulsion.

They couldn't let him be lost, though. Quintus grimaced.

Having struck off Rufus's hand, Lucilius reeled, his eyes rolling up in his head as if driven nigh-mindless by what his mind—or voices within it—told him he saw. Sweat poured down his face, as he started after his fellows. Each footstep—what did he think he was setting feet to? The very idea made Quintus shudder—was a battle won against deadly illusion, but he made it past the barrage.

"Drive the beasts along!" Ssu-ma Chao shouted. Camels and horses, eyes rolling, came along, many blindfolded.

One man suddenly cried out and pulled free of the

handholds. Not having Lucilius's strength—or stubbornness—he screamed. They heard his body hit the ground.

"His fear devoured him," Draupadi said. "Let us go. Hurry!"

"Go on ahead," Ganesha wheezed. He leaned against the rock. "I'll follow you. No, go on. I *promised*."

"You heard him!" Quintus told Draupadi. She stared at him with a kind of frantic grief. "Go on!"

He turned to Ganesha. The old adept's face was gray. "Come on, old man. Take my arm. You may not be able to dance, but you can stagger. And you will!"

The magician sagged, but Quintus bore him up and forced him upslope. The hallucinations weakened and failed, and they found themselves standing in the clean night air with all the other men—except the one who had fallen—and their beasts waiting.

Draupadi knelt to one side, her hand reaching for something that lay on the ground.

"Look," she said sadly, holding up what had served them so faithfully. The figure of Krishna was a bronze statuette again. But now its arms drooped as if weary after too-long dancing. First one, then the other broke off. It seemed to shrink in upon itself and turn to dust in her palm. "Your talisman has danced its last dance," she said. She laid down the tiny handful of dust and covered it with a flat stone.

Quintus brought his hand up in a very private salute over his heart, to the spot where the talisman had rested practically since he laid his childhood *bulla* on the household altar. It was gone, and so was the boy who had found it. But the man that boy had grown into could almost feel the bruises it had given him in warning him the many times it saved his life.

True, he had the Eagle, but the tiny bronze had been his private guard and treasure. He would miss it.

Draupadi at his side was warm and real to his touch. He thought, perhaps, he might not miss the talisman quite so much if they both lived. Her hand clasped his. The touch made him feel the way he did when the Eagle seemed to stir. In the darkness, the standard's reassuring light glowed, like a fire in the desert glimpsed from far away by a traveller unsure of his path. Roman and Ch'in alike ringed closely around it, basking in the light.

Draupadi shivered. Quintus offered her the Eagle to carry, but she shook her head.

"They are out there. Do you feel them?" she whispered.

"Who?" he asked. Black Naacals? By now they would have attacked, seeking to destroy the remnants of the Romans' and Ch'ins' failing strength.

"Not them. Hush. Wait."

Quintus obeyed. And after awhile, up in the rocks, pinpoints of light winked into tremulous light, strengthened, and resolved themselves into flames that bobbed as if their bearers walked slowly and reluctantly down to the waiting soldiers.

Then the lights stopped. And waited.

28

METAL RASPED BEHIND Quintus, and the line of men drew up, curved, and moved out to flank and protect him.

"Archers," Ssu-ma Chao ordered. Even shooting into the dark, a volley of arrows might take out a number of . . . of whatever laired in that forbidding tumble of rock up ahead. To that extent, the Ch'in officer's command made sense.

Arrows whined and buzzed like some ferocious beehive, struck with a spear in midsummer. A man screamed and died, blood running from his mouth. Drona, teacher to warriors and princes, had died thus, Quintus thought—or was it Arjuna, speaking into his memories?

The trouble was, a volley of arrows would kill some but anger and disperse the others. The wisest policy would be to follow them up into the rocks—but not by night.

Quintus shook his head. *"Testudo,"* he ordered. "Make ready. And make sure that you bring the men of Ch'in into it." They were not trained for such close combat order, but they were allies: and he could hope that this new enemy had not seen such a defense before.

Overhead, the Eagle's light gleamed, a brighter, tinier moon: as above, so below. Quintus thought he could see figures moving down from the heights, their eyes wide, their mouths open, their backs stiff almost as if they forced themselves along. Like the Romans, had they learned to fear newcomers?

"Draupadi, you go to the rear," Quintus gave the shoulder he held a gentle pressure.

"You will need . . ." she began.

Ganesha pushed forward past the Legionaries. "Do not fight," he commanded. "Do not so much as move." So absolute was the authority in his voice, so impressive was he in his wrinkled Naacal's robe, that Quintus's hand fell from his sword. He raised a hand, holding the men in their places before they could raise their shields to form the tortoise defense that would protect them from a flight of arrows.

The old man smoothed out his robe, otherwise untouched by the ever-present hardships and dust of the desert. It bore gold embroidery that shone in the light of moon and Eagle. "Come with me, Draupadi," he said. "We must welcome them."

"Are you mad?" Quintus rounded on the old man with a snarl. One moment, Ganesha had leaned gasping against the rocks; at the next, he was likely to throw lives away.

"Are you? We have tracked the Black Naacals to their lair. *These*—" he gestured at the rocks with their pinpoint torches, steady now, "—have not attacked us as the Black Naacals surely would have done. Therefore, it is not they, perhaps, who are our enemies—"

"They could be spies—" Ssu-ma Chao suggested.

"Or they could be souls in torment!" Draupadi flared. "At the Stone Tower, you know what you saw. You saw what the Dark Ones do. Terror and suffering are their servants, but they have human slaves as well."

"And what is to stop these men slaying us to please their masters?" Lucilius sneered.

Ganesha shook his head. "What stops any slave from turning on his master? Fear. And what gives a man the strength to turn against the master who abuses him? A greater fear, perhaps; aye, or a vision of courage beyond anything such a man has dared to dream."

There had been a road and lining the road crosses, each bearing the tortured body of a man, his chest heaving or too still, his legs broken, and his face blackened from lack of air. Gladiators. Had they seen Spartacus as a greater fear or the image of a type of courage that they, fighters though they were, had never aspired to?

Fellow feeling with gladiators and revolted slaves? And you call yourself a Roman? It was un-Roman. It was subversive. It was also, probably, completely accurate. Imagine a man from Thrace or some other barbarous spot, taken as a slave, sold to a *lanista* to win his life back again and again, or to die, dragged by the heels from the arena. It was a vision of Tartarus to match what he had seen at the Stone Tower.

Narrow of eye, Quintus watched the torches moving so slowly toward the Romans. Slaves, perhaps. Fearful slaves. Jupiter Optimus Maximus, let even some of them have the courage of the gladiators who had followed Spartacus and who had all but marched on Rome. What allies they would make!

He must have looked eager because Ganesha spoke quickly, for his ears alone. "You are a man of war," he said. "And if I am wrong, you are leader here and must not be tossed away. I shall go and speak to them."

"And I." It did not surprise him that Draupadi volunteered.

"If what you say is true, priests enslaved these folk. Would they not fear and hate any priests then?" Quintus asked. "You had far better let me go."

"Not alone," growled Rufus. "Not alone." A gesture from Quintus silenced him.

Draupadi shook her head. Her long black hair whipped about the lustrous cloth of her white robe. "What priests have done that was ill, others must remedy." She stepped close to him and looked into his face. "But, if you will, follow us at several paces' distance and light our way."

Side by side, the way Draupadi and Ganesha had maintained the passage beneath the arch, they walked toward the rocks and the men on them. Quintus followed, holding aloft the Eagle as a standard-bearer might follow his commander. In truth, this was but a paltry thing, this parade of just two priests and one soldier—not all that good at his trade, if it came to that, even after all this time.

The Eagle's light blazed and expanded around them as if, in truth, it spread out mighty, gleaming wings. The Naacals' white robes shone in its light, giving Draupadi and Ganesha additional majesty, like gods appearing before mortals: pristine, austere, white-robed. Impossible to imagine them afraid or weeping or even moving through a land that had been as badly violated as this.

True, there were only two White Naacals here. But as they marched imperturbably forward, Quintus saw what a force they must have been in the fullness of their power—thousands of them in procession, chanting, determined to serve what was not only what was just the law, but what was right. Draupadi and Ganesha might be alone in body, but in spirit, they were part of a host. Now they raised their hands and were singing in a language that Quintus had heard them use once or twice before.

Once again, time and place shifted focus. Incense and the brine of the sea on a fine day wreathed him about as he paced behind priests toward an altar adorned with the Flame itself.

Light welled from the standard he bore, spilling out over the ravaged land, up the rocky slope like a benediction. It was not, he saw now, just a jumble of rocks. Some of that hill—perhaps the greatest part—was a ruin, as if some enormous Temple complex had once stood there, but had fallen in on itself when the land had shifted and drunk the sea dry.

The Naacals' chant took on the aspects of a summons. Tears came to Quintus's eyes. How he remembered— evenings by the Tiber, when the mists rose and turned the air a gentle blue, when the echoes softened, and it was time for boys like him to go home, to wash rapidly, and stand behind father and grandsire as they sacrificed to the family gods before whatever dinner might be prepared from their own fields and very little coin. Such a simple, such a safe life: No wonder it seemed almost sacred to him now. No wonder the Naacals thought it might entice the men upslope, brutalized and terrorized as they doubtless were, to come forward.

He blessed Ganesha and Draupadi for reminding him, even on the brink of the greatest danger he had ever faced, of all he had been given. He had regained all, now, that he had ever lost and more besides, for now he understood the full value of everything he had ever had. And he was not alone. Rocks clattered and spun down from the hill. The torches upslope wavered, then moved forward more confidently. . . .

. . . As Quintus watched, the man in the lead threw down the torch he carried. In the next moment, he had cast himself down at Ganesha's and Draupadi's feet. His shoulders heaved with the force of his sobs. Their song broke off, and the priests diminished into themselves: an aged man and a lovely woman trying to coax up from his humiliation a man who had already suffered much, who had feared and who still feared, but who had seen in them what might be an end to all fear.

Now, from behind him, crept many more men, wary, but making what must surely be the bravest decision of their whole lives: to risk trusting the white-robed priests who called to them.

Having approached, they saw the armed men behind Ganesha and Draupadi, and they froze where they stood or knelt.

Draupadi murmured sorrowfully. She stepped forward, Ganesha following her. Quintus moved as if to accompany them, but she gestured him to remain in place the way he would command one of his Legionaries.

The men—for all here were men—looked like the hungriest dregs of the Subura, who skulked in abandoned buildings, preying on the old, the sick, and the unwary. Only . . . only there were old men among them too, and they stared at the Naacals with a desperate hope.

The white robes seemed to shine more brightly. Another of the newcomers hobbled forward. He was an old man, his cheeks sunken, his back bent, and he hobbled, leaning heavily upon a crutch.

"How may we help you, my son?" Ganesha asked.

Quintus blinked. What language *was* he speaking? It was not Ch'in; his Ch'in was not good enough for him to understand. Nor was it Parthian, not exactly. And it surely was not one of the tongues of Hind. Yet, he understood it as if it were the Latin he had learned as a child.

"Are you hungry? Afraid? These our friends will protect you," Ganesha promised.

Ask if they have water!

The old man, his back bent by rotten living and ever-present fear, began to tremble violently. His crutch fell from his now-strengthless arm, and he began to topple. Draupadi was there before he could abase himself. She raised him to his feet and supported him until a much younger but equally ragged man retrieved the crutch and handed it to him.

Draupadi, ignoring his protests, helped him adjust it. A strand of her black hair fell across his face, its dusty length suddenly sparkling as if a tear fell on it. When the old man could stand on his own, she pulled away. The Eagle's light picked out the joy and those tears on the old man's face, which filled the seams that age and fear had graven in his flesh. Worn he looked, and long abused. But beneath the ragged cloth that bound up his sparse shock of white hair, the man's eyes glowed.

"Two Children of the Sun," he whispered. He broke into a sob of incredulous joy. "At long last, and against all hope, they have come. To shield us from the dark!"

29

SOLDIERS AND SLAVES alike huddled in a hollow that had surely been part of a palace or temple complex. Their feet scrabbled not just on grit but on stone and jagged tile, cracked from years of small, carefully nourished fires. Two fragments of what had been a high wall remained. Part of a once-splendid frieze adorned one of them—the serpent that was the Naacals' god sign—and marching along the other, robed forms of priests approaching an altar.

Now that the slaves had realized that the newcomers were not Black Naacals, to demand immediate victims, the women among them had ventured forth too. A trick of the light made the priests' faces seem very real—the tall fair sons and daughters of the Motherland itself, the shorter Uighurs with their thin eyes, concealed in merry folds, and the Southerners, so like Ganesha and Draupadi as to be closest kin. Below them were those unfortunate folk of the successor races who had been swept up in the Black Naacals' nets—those of Ch'in, those of Hind, even one or two of the Hsiung-nu or their distant cousins, wrapped in felts or pelts. The Ch'in soldiers stared askance at them, but clearly, they felt themselves to be in their own place—if you could call this ruin anyone's home.

With the air of one daring greatly, Ganesha leaned forward and placed a lock of hair upon the fire. It burned the more brightly, though without scent, and its smoke rose into the night sky.

"Will they not know we are here?" Quintus asked.

"They? How shall they not know anything?" asked a man with coloring like Ganesha. "How not? Some of us they actually begot—or our grandsires. Others . . . I thought I would die, my eyes staring straight up at the sun when our last camel died of thirst. But they took me up, me and all of those who otherwise would have perished. At first we thought we had found kindly rescuers and employers. And then . . ."

"How long have you been here?" asked Ganesha. "Valmiki, you have years on you. Do you recall? Look up at the stars and tell me truthfully."

The eldest of the men dwelling in this ruin levered himself up painfully to his feet. Ganesha offered him his arm. "Master, I must not dare."

"Valmiki." The older-seeming man submitted. Adjusting his pace to Valmiki's, Ganesha led him outside to study the patterns of the stars.

"Do you remember the waste?" Draupadi asked a woman with the pure features of the Motherland.

"I remember," she whispered. She was weeping. Her eyes reflected the firelight, but then went opaque with dread. "Oh, do not ask me to say it. The earth trembled. The sun itself seemed to wink out, and we could not see beyond the hill. Kinte's son was born in that hour, and she died of it, without even a sight of the sky. And when we looked out again, the water had drained away, and the ground—which had been seabed—was cracked and already drying.''

"Kinte's son?'' Draupadi asked. "Is he here?''

"I beg you, do not make me remember!'' the woman cried. *"They* took him!''

Lucilius pushed himself away from the fire. Even now, he was fastidious and hated the reek of burning dung—though he had been glad enough to warm himself. Quintus heard him greet Ganesha outside. For Valmiki he had no word.

"Is he not hungry? . . . There will be food. . . ,'' another of the women said.

Draupadi shrugged, too intent on calming the weeping woman.

"You have been generous past praise already,'' she said. "Sharing with us. Giving us water.''

"Watch him?'' suggested one of the Romans. Rufus growled *silence.* Treacherous or not, he was still one of their tribunes. But that was not all that troubled Rufus. A *paterfamilias* could decide which of his children might live and which were unfit and must be abandoned. Could. How many did? Clearly, Rufus thought, too many. And the Black Naacals usurped those rights. . . . Pretty soon, Quintus thought, Rufus was going to want to fight them.

"Like those whoremasters in Carthage,'' he muttered at the soldiers. One of them made a small, shocked sound: There was nothing worse, nothing more scandalous than a mystery cult turned sour; and the Tophet of Carthage combined the hatred of an enemy with the grisly fascination of such a place, its priests turned savage.

The woman who had begged not to be questioned

clung to Draupadi's shoulder. They murmured together, words clearly meant to be kept away from the men.

"She is of the North," Draupadi said. "And she has been here very long, like Valmiki, since the world changed. She is almost my agemate," the priestess added bleakly.

"And the others . . ." Quintus began. He glanced around. All the peoples of Asia seemed to be represented here, some drawn from a dying caravan, one or two lost in the waste, even a few bought in a bazaar—a cast-off concubine, perhaps, or a wounded horseman or just a traveller too old or weak to withstand a day's journey in the deepest desert. Collected and left here.

In the darkness, eyes glowed. There were always different listeners, as men and women came and went on whatever errands they must do. Did the Black Naacals keep watch or revelry tonight? The Romans feared to ask. How many of these castaways survived? And how many served out of fear, not loyal awe? Quintus would have traded a year of his life to ask those questions, even though he realized that a year of his life here might be no valuable commodity.

"We would have fled. But where would we have gone?" the woman cried. "We had the holy writings. Some of us had the golden vestments—not all. Those few who survived and knew where everything was had purposefully clouded minds, lest they torture us and, in crying out, give away all our secrets." She raised her head with bleak pride.

Quintus tightened his hands. Secrets of the Naacals—scrolls, tablets, the gods only knew what else—it was a trove that the Black Naacals would kill to possess. Even if it were useless, they would kill to prevent anyone else from possessing it.

Secrets. He could well imagine that these folk would have them. But was this all they could imagine to do with powers more awesome than any he could conceive of—to serve and to fear and to hate? They had consented to pass under the yoke, after all.

In the next moment, his mouth twisted. How much better had *he* prevailed? And found himself in just the same plight, forced to serve those he hated. But compared with the Black Naacals' mastery, that service seemed like the most loving care.

"I know your thoughts, young lord." The woman's voice was bitter. Draupadi crooned something comforting, but the woman shook her head. "You look at us. You are a warrior and you look at us, and you think, 'Why did they submit? Why did they not all flee?'

"Some of us tried. Hulagu actually made it out of here. He said he was a child of the deep desert: A star had led him to us, and another would whisk him away. He even returned with men of his clan. They had hoped for a fight against the dark. But even they, who made drinking cups out of enemies' skulls, became as we are, the creatures of the Black Naacals."

"After they took Kinte's son—and her poor body for their altars—Rehu and Cho tried. They had all the water we could spare—" The woman held her fingers to her lips. At some point they had been badly broken and poorly set.

"But they came . . . they came by night . . . and they took them and staked them out beyond the arch. And when the sky and sun steadied once more, we saw them again. Or rather their bones. Then the times shifted once again and, when we could look again, nothing was left."

"And you believe what they tell you about the outer world," Rufus mused.

"They broke our world," the woman cried. "I myself saw people fall from the oars to which they tried to cling when the last ships pulled out of harbor. How should we not believe what they say—or dare not to serve them?"

"Lady," Rufus said, "you might have died."

"True, we might. But then, there were the children, and always, always, there was some paltry hope. Hope such as you have," the woman retorted, "or you would have lain down to die too."

Her eyes lit on Draupadi with a terrible surmise. "You, though, you are young. Fair. Perhaps you . . ."

"Do you see them so often?" Quintus broke in. He had seen very few of the Dark Ones, but their traces left him little desire to see more. Could so few terrify a tribe for generations so that they would live here in submission, content to wait each time till their masters returned?

Hard to believe that there existed greater masters of terror than the Legions of Rome. That double line of rotting bodies on their crosses—such a warning would serve as long as any slaves remained alive to see it. Yet, that was physical fear, not this blight of the spirit that oppressed these castaways, with their numberless years.

A glance went around the circle of castaways, judging, summing up, questioning.

Flickers of time and place had bound them together here for all those years. So well they knew each other that it seemed that they could speak without words—or was that a trick they had learned from the priests they served? And if so, could he truly trust them?

How many of these folk, he wondered, had the power that Draupadi and Ganesha did, untrained within them? He might have wagered on the woman Draupadi questioned, she whose hands were so cruelly twisted—from torture, he was certain. She had served, but not submitted.

But why had she not used any power she had? There were, as she said, the children. And there was something else that might have prevented them. They had hidden their little jewels of learning, their devices of power. They claimed they could not remember what they were. And such secrets . . . it would not be hard to forget . . . a man dead here, a woman in her dotage there: and where are the secrets that they themselves harbored? Just meaningless words and clues. After a few generations of such losses, perhaps, that was all they had left.

And even if they preserved every one of the White Naacals' teachings and had the skill to use them, had they still the will?

For that matter, had Draupadi and Ganesha the fighting will after all these years of hiding and studying the Dark Ones?

They had best be done with waiting now, Quintus thought. What had they been waiting for?

The answer, when it came, made him want to shout out a denial. Surely, they had not waited just for him? Why had they not acted when he was Arjuna, who had been a prince, practically a demigod?

Arjuna might be a prince, but he was no Roman. A Pandava, perhaps. A master of his arts. But Rome—Rome spanned the known world and reached out for more, as had Alexander in his pride. And as had the Motherland.

Best to test them. "So you sit here," Quintus asked. "Like rabbits to be fattened for the table?"

The man called Manetho, who had first approached the Naacals, glared at Quintus. "We have some small protection," he said. "Doubtless you would think our resistance paltry. Let us show you our defenses, our walls, our traps. . . ."

Manetho had sense as well as pride. He would not, Quintus suspected, show the Romans all of them.

"If they want us, they must come and claim us," said the lady. "We hide, and we endure. When they are away, we even contrive to live, a little. So it makes it harder when they return, because we dared in that little space of time to hope. As we did this time. And then," she sighed, "they returned and their coming was worse than before."

"But you are here," blurted one of the younger men. "You have withstood the Black Naacals' anger, and you are masters of arms. You can lead us!"

I was a farmer! Quintus thought, *who wanted no more than to settle down with my acres and a mule and as many children with amber skin as Juno Lucina might have granted Draupadi and me*—even though the idea of all that elegance and wisdom in a robust farmer's wife was enough, even now, to make him smile.

"Let us show you what we have."

"Lead us."

"Let them show you," said Draupadi. "It will ease their hearts, if nothing else. And who knows . . . ?"

With him out of her way, perhaps she could learn even more.

Quintus rose, hand-signalled several of the Legionaries to accompany him, and gestured to Rufus. "Take command until I return."

Rufus looked up. "Trouble again?"

Quintus shrugged. Lucilius probably had slipped away long enough to fill his lungs with clean air. Since they were, strictly speaking, equals, Quintus had forborne to set a watch on him: It was better, besides, if he felt himself unguarded to work such treacheries as he had. "If the tribune returns soon, let him think he commands, but . . ."

Rufus nodded. Quintus reached for the standard.

"Lord," said Manetho. "That is a thing of power. Here, the walls of the old shrine shield it. In the stillness of the night, though, its presence will shine up like a pillar of fire."

Leave behind the standard that had cost so much in blood and lives and spirit? That was the weapon that he and the White Naacals had sought? Eyes watched him, and murmurs rose from the circle around the fire. The murmurs deepened to a buzzing in all of the tongues spoken here—but so rapid that he could not understand it.

If they were trapped here, he would have to eat these people's food, drink their water, and trust them, if they were to trust him in return. If he wished to learn the secrets of any power they had, he must share his own.

He placed the staff in Rufus's hands, certain it would accept him. He was right. "On the *manes* of your forefathers," he told him. "And on your oath."

Rufus saluted. "On my soul," swore the centurion.

Quintus followed Manetho outside, slipping past Valmiki and Ganesha, still gazing up at the stars and shaking their heads. They had passed beyond patterns, he realized, to specific stars—talk for adepts or priests, not warriors.

He and Manetho dodged around a rock outcropping that might once have been outer walls. Within that jumble of rocks lay a path that looked very precarious, a tower that looked dangerously ready to collapse. Yet it was along this way that Quintus was guided.

"Follow in my steps," said Manetho.

Quintus followed along a passageway cunningly concealed in the very wreckage of the walls and bearing evidence of some use.

"From here," whispered Manetho, "our youngest men and even girls watch for traces of caravans . . . or . . ." he had not finished the sentence. "And when we see such, we wonder if we can dare contact them. To warn them away from what our life has become."

Quintus bent his head. "You did not warn us."

The man scuffled at a broken tile. It glittered for an instant, then dropped beneath a larger stone. "We saw what you bore and sensed the power in it. And you marched right up to the arch, as if you knew what to expect and how to fight it. The Light defend us—we saw the Naacals and we dared to hope. And now, if things go ill and we do not win and some of us do not die, you will have ages in which to hate us."

"*These* Naacals do not hate," Quintus said.

The path down which Manetho led him wound outward, to the very ramparts of what had once been an immense wall, suitable for processions or defense. What had this palace or temple looked like in its prime, when it rose proudly from the hill that crowned the island on which it had then stood? If he shut his eyes, he thought it might be imprinted there, someplace on his inner eyelid as well as in his deepest memories, memories so old that even the years he had spent living Arjuna's life seemed recent in comparison. The fortress shone in his mind: massive sloping walls between pylons, encircling a core of towers facing the harbor and the great arch that adorned it, reflecting up from the blue water.

The night wind blew. For an instant the smells of salt sweat and salt water mingled—ancient memories of a lost sea.

The night was black here, and the blackness had as

much to do with the feel of this place as the hour. Once light, life, and power had radiated from the crest of the hill—gone now, replaced by the menace and a hunger responsible for that darkness of spirit.

He stiffened. So often, when he had felt that oppression, it had come companied by the hissing of great serpents. He stiffened, and Manetho guessed his thoughts.

"There are no serpents," his guide assured him. "The Black Naacals will not let us suffer from the creatures of the desert: They reserve their cattle for themselves."

He looked shrewdly at Quintus in the starlight. "This is not, the Light knows, a fate you would have chosen or a site for a battle. But we have taken these ruins and made them into our fortress, our redoubt . . ."

And now, yours too. The thought came very clearly, but Manetho did not put it into words. "You have the look," he said instead, "of a man who has lost his home. I am sorry."

"The walls are sound." Quintus made himself reply to at least some of the other man's words. And indeed, he thought a Legion's engineers could work prodigies with them. But his thoughts were on more than fortifications.

Had Quintus pitied himself for his loss? For having to bow and scrape before fools like Lucilius? This man and the people he led had suffered far, far worse. They had endured a slavery more long-lasting and harder than the rulers who had lined the roads of Rome with crucified rebels.

Tears came to his eyes. He squeezed his eyelids shut on them and thinned his lips. So much Manetho and his people had endured, and now Manetho apologized to him? Had he, in truth, pitied himself? He must stand a little straighter now.

He had, he knew, lamented the deaths of the Legions

at Carrhae, and he had mourned each one of his men who had fallen every day since then. At least, however, he had been free to work out his own fate, seek to retrieve the fortunes of his house or the honor of his Legion. The gladiators who had rebelled had no such choices. They were trained as beasts to kill other beasts in the sand of the arena and if they knew a month's respite from the armor or net and trident it was a great deal. They had remembered, though, that they were men, had rebelled, and had died.

These castaways in time and place, shut away from the world in the heart of a desert so harsh that it made Trachonitis seem like Elysium, endured a slavery that jeopardized not just their bodies in the sands of an arena, but their souls on profaned altars.

Surely, the thought must have touched their minds many times during the hideous years. How easy it would be: agree, bow to the altars; grow stronger; escape. Canny slaves had agreed and had won comfort, perhaps even freedom, thus since the dawn of time. Yet Spartacus who might well have been one of the gladiators to survive to be freed had not done so.

"Why?" he asked.

"Why have we not surrendered? Sir, you have seen the handiwork of the Black Naacals, but we have lived with it. When they come to claim one of us for their . . . their rites, their expressions were—how shall I say it? Hungry. As if they cannot be content to snatch us away alive, but they must also drain dry all our fear, all our horror. Not just at that moment, but all that night.

"The air . . . the air grows thick, and we hear terrible thunder. We long for a storm's fury to fill this basin; we even long for another great wave such as that which swamped our Motherland, to fill this basin, wash up and sweep over this place until the rock is clean once more; but it never happens. The air turns thicker and more foul; breathing it, you feel as if your lungs are coated with blood. I have seen an old man die of that alone. I think I must first have sensed that fear, that foulness, while still in my mother's womb, on the night the Naacals snatched up my father."

Quintus glanced away. "I too have lost a father. In battle, too."

"Your father's death was clean," Manetho said. "Mine . . . I tell myself that death puts you beyond pain, beyond a world where you cannot go to sleep and be certain of waking up able to call your spirit your own. But do not think of us as stainless servants of the Light, not all of us. We have had our spies and traitors squatting among us, and we dared not even kill them. Always, they are someone's son, someone's mother, someone we have lived with, wept with, perhaps even loved. And besides, if we killed the spies we knew of, who knows whether we would lose more? So we turn our backs and, after a time, they die, too." Manetho sighed. "It used to be our custom for closest kin to catch a dying man's last breath in their own mouths: These spies' breath is foul, and we no longer have that custom."

Quintus shook his head. It would no longer be enough to escape, he and his people. Somehow, he must think of a way to save these castaways.

"You, at least," said Manetho, "might have died. Fallen on that blade, or turned your face to the wall and starved. We . . . we could not. Not as long as we had a chance."

Think, man, came Arjuna's memories into his mind. *If you believe you are reborn according to how you have lived, think of what these people fear they would be reborn as?*

It was like the Eagle, Quintus thought. Even when it had been only the standard of his Legion, it could not be abandoned as a prisoner among barbarians, not as long as there was a Roman able to risk his life to retrieve it. And, once he realized that the Eagle was far more than just a standard, just as he had learned that his talisman was not just a funeral bronze found in an old tomb, some things became more important than death with honor. Like keeping such things safe. Or, at the worst, making sure that they did not fall into the possession of enemies who would use them to destroy soul and body, both.

"If we had died," said Manetho, "the Dark Ones would only have found another fortress and other folk to be their slaves. We could not allow another people to endure our lives." He looked out over the deep desert. "When this life is over, I shall pray to be reborn as the fattest and richest of merchants in a city by the sea. I shall have earned it."

Quintus wanted to salute the other man as if he were a consul. The honor would have gone unseen: Manetho was staring far out into the desert. The moon had risen and, in its pale light, a whirl of sand danced about, then subsided. At the horizon, faint lights played: heat lightning. He listened for the thunder.

Thunder! What was it that Manetho had warned him about the thunder? Now it rumbled out sullenly, hollowly. The night wind blew, then ceased. And again, the thunder growled, closer this time. The air thickened. Quintus felt the urge to rip at his tunic, to hurl his heavy harness from him, to gasp for breath. He shuddered until he could get enough air to fill his chest.

A third time, the thunder grumbled out.

"Does it rain?" he asked, to forestall words that might have been fearful or hot with the anger born of fear.

"Blood, maybe," said Manetho. "Never pure rain. We must get back, *fast*. I have felt this weight at heart before. It means that the Black Naacals have come among us."

30

Down they swung from the tower, Quintus ready to curse every time his feet, unfamiliar with the footholds, kicked loose a tile or chunk of masonry. Manetho moved fast and far more silently, a scout expert in his own terrain, aware of every hiding place.

How many Naacals, Quintus wondered, ventured out into the ruins and never returned to the black sanctums?

The air thickened still further. The night sky took on the color of onyx appearing to settle, inexorably, upon his shoulders as if he were being tortured, pressed beneath its weight. Heavier and heavier it grew, together with the sense that something was amiss, someone watched him as he might watch a snake before he struck its head off.

Confess and your punishment is less than if your crime is discovered, he had always been told. They lied, oh they lied. But the temptation to run from the path into bright lights and bargain for some shreds of a miserable life added to the oppression of his spirit.

"Quickly!" hissed Manetho.

You are not at risk, at least with me, Quintus thought,

but dismissed that as ignoble. It might be that Manetho's people needed him to put heart in them, the way a good leader must. Or it might be that he did not want to decrease their numbers by staying away, protecting himself if the Black Naacals claimed a victim by lot.

And it might—oh gods, there were *strangers* in their midst. His Legionaries. Rufus. Lucilius. Ganesha, or even Draupadi—priests taken as sacrifices after their many years of struggle and survival. That was *nefas*, blasphemy so vile that Quintus could not imagine it.

"My comrades . . ." he muttered.

"You brought Naacals of the light among us," snapped Manetho as he hastened back toward the ruin. "Children of the Sun, in the fullness of their power. If the Dark Ones take them, they take that power, too. Do you understand? It is not just wiped out; it is absorbed."

A tremor shook the earth. Manetho gasped out something that might have been oath and prayer combined.

"I have to get to them!" Quintus gasped. The Eagle was there, safe—if anything here could be safe—in Rufus's care. But Draupadi—she was young-seeming, fair, almost unmarked by hardship. The Black Naacals would see her and, having seen, how could they do aught but choose her?

"It is *sacrifice*, not lust. Or just lust alone," hissed Manetho. "Will you for the love of the undying sun come *on*? You sacrifice not just to give honor, but to *get*, to compel the spirits to give you of their power to use as you see fit."

And you believe that? Quintus scrambled for a grip on the rocks.

Of course Manetho did. This was not a matter of feeding a horse snake or the python at Delphi—or of bowing before the *lares* and *penates* of his home. It was a sacrifice more evil than any he had heard of, and it brought such power that, years ago, the Black Naacals had cracked the very face of the earth and allowed the sea to drain away.

What would they choose if they found such power available to them once more in the persons of the two White Naacals?

What would they *not* do? *That* was the question.

Twist; turn; tramp back. They had reached the precincts of the Temple itself. Now Quintus could somehow recall the topped columns he had seen before on the half-broken archways through which he had come. Past that toppled wall lay the entrance to the hall where he had sat before. He headed toward it, his hand on the hilt of his sword.

After all, how many Black Naacals could there be? He had fought them; they could die—and once he could lay his hand upon the Eagle . . . he could feel the jolt of energy it sent through him the times when it had worked through him to protect their people. Surely, it would serve him—or he would serve it—now.

Manetho seized his arm. "Not there. Not now. I will take you to a place where we can watch. From which we must watch, the Light shine upon us all."

The castaway steered Quintus to a sort of gallery overlooking the meager fire and the hall where his people had assembled. Several had encircled Draupadi.

"You ask many questions, Lady. You and the old man. You wear the robes; you speak the words that we long to hear, but . . ."

In a glance, Quintus saw what must have happened. They had spies in their midst before, Manetho had told him. How could they think that Draupadi and Ganesha were among them?

They are terrified; they can think anything when the thunder peals and the ground rumbles.

The priestess shook her head. "Ganesha and I . . . we do not steal power, but have learned it . . . year after year, life after life . . ."

That had been the wrong thing to say, obviously.

The others drew back. Draupadi held out her palms. "Look at me," she cried.

They hissed at her to keep her voice down.

"Look!" she continued in an urgent whisper. "Test me by any ordeal you choose. But I tell you, I have seen what the Dark Ones do, and I swear to you by the flame that the only way I would go to their altars is as a sacrifice!"

The ground trembled. A fine dust filtered from the rock overhead and dropped before Quintus's face, momentarily obscuring the people on whom he spied.

Then, from outside the broken hall came measured, sardonic applause. "Excellent, my lady priestess. A noble speech. Shall we go now?"

"This girl, a priestess?" Ganesha rose to his feet more quickly than even a man of his apparent age should. "She is but a—" his voice seemed to change as he spoke what must surely be a title in the long-gone language of the Motherland.

"He just gave himself away," Manetho whispered. "Why?"

Quintus looked at him briefly, bleakly, then turned his eyes back to the hall.

"All the better," said the Black Naacal. His eyes glinted beneath his hood. Quintus shuddered at the pressure of the thickened air and the hunger he saw in the man's face as he looked at Draupadi. He moved forward a step, extending his hand as if to claim her. Ganesha brought his own hand down, barked out a word or two, and the Dark One stopped, and laughed.

"You would protect your—student, is that all she is? Just a student still, after all these endless years? And what of the others? *All* of the others, *Father*. I believe your oath. . . ." He too switched into the ancient mellifluous tongue Ganesha had used.

Three others of the Black Naacals entered the room, their staffs ready in their hands. Slowly, as if enjoying the terror they created, they pointed their staffs spear-fashion at the slaves. One man jerked away. A black-robe chuckled wetly and let the staff tilt upward to tap him on the shoulder. At that touch, the man screamed and fell back.

The others sank down.

Beside Quintus, Manetho drew a deep, sobbing breath.

"Cease!" commanded Ganesha. "That man has not harmed you. Leave him be."

"He is meat," said the Black Naacal, "like all of these, for our altars."

To Quintus's shock, Ganesha laughed. "What do you need such—forgive me, my friends—cattle for?" he asked. Then he drew a deep breath and steadied himself. "Not when you have the Wise themselves. And what need of a very young illusionist—when you have *me*."

Manetho's knees buckled. Quintus bore him up, though he longed to drop the man and race down to stand between the Black Naacals and the White.

"Better yet," said the Black Naacal, all but purring. "A willing sacrifice? It is long since we have had one of such power. And perhaps . . . perhaps you need not be a sacrifice but a celebrant. We have other meat, as I told you.''

Ganesha jerked up his chin. *''No.''*

''Fool, for all your learning. Take him,'' he gestured to his fellows. ''Take the woman, too!''

''I would not stain my lips with even the lie that I would work with you,'' Ganesha said. ''I know what you are. I know what you seek. And I pledge not to hinder you from taking what you will from me. Just let the others go.''

The Black Naacals moved together. Their eyes beneath their hoods were alight, and their whispers were eager. Two approached Ganesha and pointed at him with their staffs.

''Up with you, old man!'' commanded the eldest. ''The slaves can live. Your girl, too.''

For now. Everyone in the room heard that unspoken threat.

They would take Ganesha's power and Ganesha's life, and then they would be back for more. His sacrifice would be meaningless.

''No!'' Draupadi was at the old man's side, her hand on his arm. ''You shall not go.''

Carefully and with surprising strength, Ganesha pried loose her hands. ''Child,'' he said, ''for you have been daughter as well as student to me all the years of our exile, obey me in this last thing as you have in all else. By our oath . . .'' he bent and whispered.

She nodded.

Ganesha squeezed her hands together. He jerked his chin once at Rufus, who rose. Probably the centurion was the only man who could have moved at that moment. Ganesha placed her hands in the Roman's.

''Guard them well,'' he whispered.

Then the old priest straightened himself. His white robe blazing, he allowed the two black-robed priests to take charge of him. Serenely, as if going to officiate in some rite, he left the room, the last of the Black Naacals sullen at his back.

The room boiled. Men darted from it, while women gathered up children, and girls and youths pressed back from the Romans who stood bewildered.

Quintus turned away from his vantage point. He had seen the Naacals stare about the room. It had not only been Draupadi and Ganesha the Black Naacals had sought: It was himself.

"Where are you going?" Manetho hissed.

"We have to stop them!"

"Wait!"

Draupadi sank against Rufus's shoulder, the image of a woman distraught at the loss of one who had been like a father to her. The sight tore at Quintus's heart, even though he suspected her weakness was an illusion born of acting, not of her powers. As the last dark robe swept out, she pushed herself free of the centurion.

"The Eagle," she demanded. "Let me take it."

Rufus froze.

"He is an old man," Draupadi pleaded. "And I can use it well."

"Lady, I have my orders."

"For him, too!" Draupadi cried. "We must fight *now*. Don't you think they'll be back? Don't you think they'll take the strongest, the fittest? They took Ganesha away quickly enough!"

She tried to dart to one side and grasp the standard. *Wrong move, Draupadi.*

"I have my orders."

"With power like that," Manetho said, "they'll have

it all. We cannot wait. I must rouse the people, and we must fight. What if they come back for her? What if they seize your Eagle? It may not be . . .''

"Rufus," Draupadi pleaded, "listen to me. You have no idea how strong Ganesha's power is. It may be enough. How would you feel if you gave your enemies a weapon that could crack this world like an earthen plate?''

Rufus shook his head, stubbornly.

"And what about *him*? He is not back yet," Draupadi told Rufus. "What if they have him already?''

Him? She was speaking of Quintus!

"Come *on!*" said Manetho. "Now, while we have the chance. . . .''

Rufus shook his head back and forth. *No.*

"What do you mean, 'no'? You are the flesh of Rome itself," she told Rufus. Now, I am going to find my friend and my kinsman. Can you do less for your officer?''

Manetho turned to go.

Quintus gestured. *A moment more.* Rufus walked over to the Eagle, gleaming even in the shadow. He saluted it, put out his hand to take it—and Draupadi darted forward and caught it up. The bronze Eagle poised atop its standard did not blaze up, as if it too sensed how great their peril was and that it must stay hidden. But its brightness seemed to subtly intensify, to take on a richness akin to the saffron that Draupadi wore.

She looked upon the Eagle and her lips moved as if she spoke to it in a whisper, or a prayer. Then she nodded. Was it a trick of the light that made Quintus think that the Eagle had dipped its head in assent to whatever she had told it?

"Man, move it! Do you want your people facing the Dark Ones without you!?" Manetho's voice cracked.

He pulled at Quintus's arm. This time, the tribune allowed himself to be drawn through the ruins at a speed he would not have dared by himself. It was too fast, through unfamiliar terrain: He had fears of falling, terrible images of writhing, the yellow bone piercing the flesh of his thigh, crippling him for the rest of his life—assuming he had a "rest of his life."

"Faster," Manetho gasped. He passed a gap in the wall and gestured, once and then again. "In here."

"Where are you taking me?"

Quintus planted his feet, good old Roman stubbornness warming him for the first time, as he thought, for days. Even a dozen Legionaries, with Roman discipline and their swords outthrust, should be able to wreak terror on the Black Naacals—and he, standing with his men, would finally pay Rome the death he owed.

Hot pain lanced into his arm, and he spun around in shock.

Manetho had his dagger out. *Fool, to let yourself be gulled by fear and a sad story!*

"Your men's lives lost? Your lady stolen? And you think that is *all* we have faced?"

Quintus clapped hand to the wound Manetho had made. Not serious. "Tell me why I shouldn't kill you."

"You will never find your way back," Manetho's teeth shone in the darkness. "And your blood will leave a spoor for the Dark Ones to follow."

Quintus's arm had begun to sting as if Manetho had smeared the little blade with poison. *Perhaps he has. Perhaps those gestures were signals for his followers to strike you down, you and all the others. Who knows? Perhaps he has sold you to the Black Naacals himself?*

Temptation threatened to overwhelm him. *Kill this traitor. Find your men. Take the Eagle and fight your way in*

*to reclaim Ganesha and Draupadi. And then get out of this
trap, leaving these fools and slaves behind.*

Manetho folded his arms over his chest. "They're in
your mind," he said. "Pain helps. You can kill me now,
you know. You might be able to find your way back: Who
knows? You found your way here, didn't you? Or you can
come with me and give us all a chance to fight."

The desert wind blew, but Quintus was drenched in
sweat. . . . *After Carrhae, they crouched, betrayed in the dark
swamp. Some of his men drank the foul standing water and
shuddered with fever and flux—to the cross with this madman
and dying in this place.*

"Come on," Manetho almost taunted him. "Decide.
Kill me or help us. But do it quickly. We have run out of
time. They are moving to attack, and it will be as it was
the last time—and they will overwhelm the whole world.
Well, which is it?"

From the rags of his tunic, Manetho pulled out a
dagger with a bone hilt, curiously bright. Light welled
from the blade's point. *If he's fool enough to arm you,
quench us that knife in the slave's blood. We would welcome
news. We would welcome you. Come to us. . . .*

"It will get worse, you know," Manetho told him. His
voice was almost kind. "I will forgive you, too, if you kill
me, strange as it sounds. Life like this has been no great
blessing. I have seen so many of my brothers dead in
ways—do it. Do it quick. I may even thank you. This
way, I would die as a warrior at a warrior's hands—
you're even giving me a chance at a decent rebirth!"

Quintus looked wonderingly at the dagger.

"And leave your people?"

"What have you left for them? You came in as you did
with White Naacals and a weapon that cast trails of
power like a comet from halfway across the waste. You

think the Dark Ones don't want that? That they wouldn't spend all of us to get it? The best any of us can hope for is a quick death before they make the entire world their slave."

Manetho raised his chin to allow Quintus the easy, fast blow to the blood vessels in his throat.

He was so thin! Quintus thought he had never seen such a poor specimen passing for a fighting man. But he stood, trembling only slightly, waiting at a time when waiting was perhaps the riskiest thing in the world to do. What gave him the courage?

Only hope. In hope, Quintus had marched across the desert and reclaimed his Eagle. And now? Taking on the Black Naacals would be like a single cohort toppling The Surena's forces when the Legions of Rome had failed . . .

. . . but he had the Eagle, and with it, a weapon that would alter the balance of power.

Kill the wretch now and come to us!

The intensity of that attack made him sway as if he had taken a blow to the jaw. The carvings on the ruined rock walls seemed to drift in and out of focus. In his mind, processions of White Priests moved toward an altar surmounted by the many-headed serpent that meant—*coils, crushing and constricting, squeezing the life from their victim, draining him, before the great jaws gaped wide for the flesh that remained. . . .*

The serpent seemed to writhe in his consciousness, its eyes stark with ancient malice. Its tongue flickered back and forth.

Use the blade, fool!

Lightning went off inside Quintus's skull. *A nail-sticker like that to take out a giant serpent?* He laughed, the

coarsely cheerful mirth that Rufus reserved for the most
awkward Legionary-in-training.

Not a serpent. Another illusion. The friezes and the
broken walls turned firm again. Once more, the White
Naacals marched over the roughened stone toward their
altar, and power sluiced out like warm water pouring
down an aching back, healing, comforting. . . .

It was all a lie, wasn't it?

He let the dagger drop from his hand. Manetho wavered and sagged, and Quintus reached out to steady
him—almost in the embrace of brothers.

"I've wasted time we can't spare," Quintus said.
"Lead on."

He followed Manetho at a near run through what
quickly seemed so like a maze that he expected a Mino-
taur to bellow and charge them at every crossing of the
ways they passed. He had no thread, though, to mark his
passage, and *his* Ariadne—to whom he would be faithful,
unlike Theseus—lay in the grasp of their enemies.

Draupadi was, he reassured himself, a mistress of
illusion, able to dispel hallucinations that might have
finished off him and the Legionaries. Just as he must trust
Manetho, he must have faith in them and their inborn
strength to hold firm until he could retrieve the Eagle and
lead them.

Now, he and Manetho raced through a narrow passageway. On either side, he heard a rushing sound.
Water, perhaps, coursing through hidden channels as if
through an aqueduct? Or air singing through tunnels set
into the thick walls? Romans were engineers. These
walls, though, made anything built by Rome seem like a
shed flung up out of flat stones.

As they hastened on, it became easier and easier for
Quintus to see the path up ahead. Some trick of the light,

perhaps? He thought he saw a glow welling from the floor wherever Manetho stepped.

"They are coming," he said.

Was this to be a full rising of the slaves, then? Quintus's belly clenched. Was this how the gladiators had felt, turning on their masters, who were vastly more numerous and powerful than they? And yet, they had put Rome in such fear that it would never forget them. Given the Eagle, given its power, how much more could he—

"This used to be a place where the underpriests robed. . . ." Manetho told him.

How long ago? Don't ask, Quintus. Don't even think of asking.

His foot brushed something, and he stumbled. What was *that?*

Something bulky sprawled against the rock. Quintus swerved, but could not avoid it. He went sprawling and fell hard against the wall, the carvings bruising his flesh. And his arm, dropping over what had tripped him, landed hard enough to bring a moan out of the man he had stumbled across.

It was Rufus's voice.

Jupiter Optimus Maximus and all the lesser gods, Quintus thought, as he knelt beside the centurion, feeling for wounds on the man's hard skull. Rufus groaned repeatedly. The light rising from the floor showed his eyes, glazed now, with the pupil of one eye larger than that of the other.

"Lad . . . I mean, sir . . . by all the gods, didn't know you had a twin. You'll need to be Castor and Pollux both to take on . . . to the crows with that little bastard. His father should have exposed him at birth or thrown him from the Tarpeian rocks, which is what I'd do if I ever got him home. . . . Damn, my head, my head . . ."

Rufus gagged, doubling over and retching. Quintus supported his shoulders.

"Come *on*!" whispered Manetho.

Up ahead, Manetho might fume that they were out of time, but *Rufus carried my stretcher. He forbade that I be abandoned on the desert or killed quickly when they thought I could not see. He taught me.* And Manetho wasn't a man to abandon a comrade, either.

"Who?" Quintus asked, his heart sinking to depths he would have judged impossible.

"He came up behind us . . . the lady and I . . . *Edepol*, sir, I'm glad you're here to take charge. . . ."

"Draupadi?" Quintus asked. "What happened?"

"Poor girl never had a chance. That useless traitor, that Lucilius . . . I'd like to have the purple stripe off their togas and them nailed up to a cross. . . ."

In the ruined hall, Lucilius had crouched at first with the Legionaries and the slaves, but then gone outside, pleading restlessness and the need to breathe untainted air.

And that was all that was clean about him! Quintus let his hands rest on Rufus's shoulders, trying to reassure the older man: but there was no reassurance for either of them.

Even as Lucilius had slipped outside, were the voices already eating away at his resolve? He had always been apt for treasons, as long as Quintus had known him. And this was not the first time he had tried to strike a bargain with an enemy.

It had been hard enough for Quintus with his old Roman grandsire and—as Lucilius thought—his ludicrous respect for loyalty to resist the voices that the Black Naacals sent out to tempt those who would stand against them.

What had they promised the patrician? Gold, it went without saying, and perhaps Draupadi, compliant or not.

"He hit me first, sir," Rufus said. "I went down. And then he grabbed for the Eagle—our Eagle! The lady snatched it away before he could lay his rotten hands on it, and I tried, so help me Minos and Rhadamanthus, I swear I tried to go to her aid. But he grabbed her by one arm and told her that he wouldn't kill me if she went along without using her magic on him. That was bad enough. And then he kicked me, and I went crashing into the wall, a real tyro's trick. . . . Gods, I've been a fool, bungled everything. Oh, Dis, to the cross with this *head* of mine. . . ."

"Steady there," Quintus muttered absently. "It's all right."

It would have been the cross or worse for all of them. The Black Naacals had Ganesha, with his great strength and power. And, while the old man had held out all these lifetimes and while he might well have endured until the final death that he had escaped in the whelming of his home, could he endure seeing a dear friend put to torment? Especially when the friend had been not just a student, but a daughter to him for all that time?

"She has the Eagle, sir," Rufus said. He stifled a groan—a sign he might recover if he concealed his pain. "I should be flogged, broken . . . one woman and I could not even protect her. . . ."

"Come *on!*" snapped Manetho. "They will betray us. Now we *must* hasten."

No! Do not think of Ganesha or Draupadi in torment. Do not think of the sacrifices of the Black Naacals. The priestess of the sun had power enough to use the Eagle; he only hoped that she would.

"The longer we stay here, the worse the chance. . . . Do you know what those priests *do* to their victims?"

Don't think of Draupadi's amber skin dappled with her blood or turned the color of chalk. Don't think of Ganesha's towering spirit quenched. And don't think of them. . . . They would put their *hands* on Draupadi. Maybe even Lucilius, who had wanted her and she had rebuffed him.

"First there will be a sacrifice. Then, they will begin," Manetho spoke, his voice hollow with dread.

Quintus had never expected to return to Rome, much less to return with the Eagle. He had, however dimly, begun to hope for some shreds of a life. Now, though, now, he must take the Eagle and wield it. A whole world hung in the balance.

"If they die, they die as soldiers." He heard his voice, so hoarse it was hard to recognize the words as his lips shaped them. "Rufus, you go back. Manetho, I'm with you. We will catch them in a circle. No one will get out alive."

Least of all ourselves.

But the idea of Romans, their eyes alight with anger and relieved tension, and the bloody drill of their short swords, advancing deliberately on the Black Naacals and cutting them asunder had its own attraction and even carried its own healing. Rufus struggled to his feet. What began as an unsteady walk finished up as a march.

Quintus turned to Manetho. "I know you would rather be with your own men," he said. "But with your help . . ."

"You must take care. It is you they want!" cried Manetho. "They know who brought in the strangers. You are young, strong. . . . They may wish to make you one of their number. . . . Sometimes it happens when one of our sons grows too strong and they have a vacancy in their ranks. . . .''

Now that was damnable—suborning sons as well as killing them. Let a strong man rise, and the slaves would never know if they could rely on him, or if, at the moment of sacrifice, they would look up at the Black Naacal holding the knife and see in his face the man who had once been son or brother or friend.

''They will have to content themselves with the terror they have already wrought,'' Quintus snapped. He would like to execute Lucilius himself: The patrician had betrayed not only his city and his caste, but all his world.

However, Quintus's first responsibility must be to rescue the Eagle. To wield it, if he could; and if not, to afford Draupadi and Ganesha a clean death before the Black Naacals unleashed their power. Perhaps he would even have time to fall on his own sword.

And the Eagle? If he could not wield it, he must destroy it. Most likely, that would eliminate the need to fall on his sword—or for any of the others to try it.

He had come, he realized, to the end of the skein of time allotted him by the Fates. With that realization came the death of hope—and the end of his fear. His sword gleamed in his hand, but did not quiver.

Abruptly he laughed. *"Morituri te salutamus!"* he cried, saluting the darkness.

Manetho glared at him. The poor bastard probably feared him almost as much as the Black Naacals. Yet he must lead his men and work with Quintus, whom he clearly found a strange creature if he could face death laughing.

But Manetho was brave. He led. And Quintus followed, his senses keyed up for this final battle.

Again, the banging of gongs and now, the braying of

horns and the sound that Quintus feared even more—the blowing of bone flutes, higher and more shrill than the priests' horns. Manetho shuddered. So long a slave, and now he was forcing himself to face worse than death. Quintus opened his mouth to utter the comforting words he himself had heard before his first battle. Again came the clamor of the priests' instruments. Energy thrilled in his blood. He felt stronger, fairly matched, and he no longer needed to place his feet with such care. The fear was gone, all of it. He wanted to share that comfort, for such it was, with Manetho, but the slave was a dark blot up ahead.

Even through the walls, Quintus heard the thunder. Lightning played across the gaps in the walls and danced in the waste, turning salt flats and stone slabs white. A wind blew. Remembering the storms he had endured with Ganesha and Draupadi—and the whirlwinds they had survived—he was not dismayed.

The lightning flashed once more. Now, the very walls themselves seemed to glow. Flames seemed to brush the hands of the figures in the battered friezes. Krishna had danced that way. But Quintus's talisman lay buried in the waste. Quintus decided that the sight was a good omen, if a fearsome one. *Fare forward,* Krishna had told him so very long ago. Told Arjuna, who faced armies, not a man with the blood of princes in his veins and the soul of a felon. Not Dark Priests. *Your battle is harder than mine,* came a voice in his head. Arjuna's this time, not the Dark Ones.

Quintus would fare forward, as he had been taught. It was relief. It was rebirth. And it was deadly danger.

31

MANETHO TURNED TO Quintus. "They have started," he said, tonelessly. They have taken the Naacals, and now they also have your weapon."

Now Quintus's reluctant guide would have only to shout. Surely, the Dark Ones had stationed guards in these honeycombed walls. Would the Romans face a second betrayal tonight?

The thought chilled Quintus for a moment, until he forced it out of mind. The Black Naacals might have the Eagle, but he somehow doubted that they could use its full powers. Still, since it was an Eagle of Rome, its loss was grievous.

More so was the loss of Draupadi, leaving an ever-growing ache in his heart. All his life, he had loved, only to have what he had loved snatched from him. Now, in losing her, he stood to lose even more than love: The whole world might pay for it.

Not if I can help it, he vowed.

Lightning illuminated Manetho's pale face, showing skin streaked with oily sweat, and eyes rolling from side to side like those of a horse frightened by a raging fire. With this evil ritual begun, Manetho reacted to slaves' fears: Run and hide, perhaps survive until next time— even if he also sensed that, if they did not fight now, there would be no next time.

What do you recommend? It would be cruelty to ask. But it was a question the Roman must have an answer for. Manetho knew this ruin; Quintus did not.

His own people were running out of choices. They might gather what water and supplies they could and retreat into the deep desert—if they could pass the barriers—and trust to Fate and skill to find more water before they went mad, and died. Or they might hide within this complex—assuming Lucilius did not betray them. Even if they hid successfully, there would come a day when their luck would run out.

The Black Naacals wanted him, Quintus, now—sacrifice or apprentice to their foul magic, who could say?

Neither was a choice for a Roman. What then were Roman choices? Quintus could rejoin his men, and they could fall on their swords. Or they could follow their own harsh code: Draw those swords, form a battle line, and attack as long as life was in them.

"Will you turn on us now?" Manetho demanded. Quintus's silence had made him, too, suspect betrayal.

"Put that thing away," Rufus grumbled, coming up to them as he gestured at the ancient blade the slave had drawn. "A man could die poisoned by its dirt before he bled out life from any cut you gave him."

Though terror had given Manetho keen ears, Quintus wagered that he had not heard the centurion pad up behind them. Accustomed to the darkness now, he saw that Rufus had slung his boots about his neck and carried his own blade.

The centurion gave the tribune a strange look. That look—Quintus had seen its like the night the man of the Legions had come to tell his family that his father had died. Hard news, it meant, to be borne as a man bears the dealings of fate.

"Sir," Rufus began, "I felt some better, and I went to scout out the Black Naacals' . . ." his mouth moved as if he wanted to spit, ". . . what they'd call a shrine. They're all there, along with those they took for their altar. I had thought if I could, I'd give them a decent death: no luck."

If Rufus had been able to reach Ganesha and Draupadi, would they have welcomed his "decent death"? Could they even die, after so long?

Manetho shifted from foot to foot, and Quintus guessed his wariness: The slave had only the sight and voice of the two Naacals—and terror thereafter. With their knowledge, their wealth of experience, and their study—which had once been the discipline of the Black Naacals before they turned to darkness—how easy it would be for them to adapt to a new form of power. For him, priests were like serpents: There were some whose venom killed after you took one step, and some whose venom killed after you took two steps—but you died just the same.

"You think they'd—" Ganesha's deep wisdom, Draupadi's supple grace, extinguished in a pool of drying blood, either in sacrifice or by Rufus's rough mercy.

"They wouldn't betray us. Not those two," Rufus said. "It's what I'd want for me. You would too, sir. And even if they're not Romans . . ."

"Never mind, soldier." In another minute, Rufus would have him wet-eyed—and this was no time for tears. "Anyhow, you did not succeed."

''No, sir,'' Rufus drew himself up. ''It's Carrhae all over again. We have failed.''

The boom of a great gong shuddered through the walls, its vibration shaking into them as they huddled against the worn masonry. Just so had they heard the gongs and bells and drums of The Surena's reinforcements and prepared to sell their lives in the bright sun so far away.

''Well,'' Quintus said, ''we have known we were living on borrowed time. So now we pay it back, eh?''

He had well expected that grim laugh from Rufus.

''It's worse than you know, sir. They have set a guard more dangerous than any we might have expected. The lady Draupadi herself.''

Quintus whirled to grab the centurion's shoulders, slamming him back against the rock. Chaos was come, if Draupadi could be turned against them. And he had been so sure that she would not.

''It's not like that!'' Rufus hissed at him. ''You know how worn out she has been. The way Lucilius turned, that seems to have been the last straw. When he brought her in, they talked to her, and she shook her head. That was when they grabbed her. I was going to go after her, but three of the boys held onto me. . . . I let 'em live. . . . They forced some drug into her. . . .''

Quintus heard himself moan.

''. . . and now she seems to have turned inside . . . not like a madwoman, but like a sibyl seeing visions. And what she sees, they can use. They can use *her*.''

''How do you know?''

''We saw her sitting there. Just sitting. I was surprised that she wasn't better guarded. So, one of the lads thought he could sneak up and rescue her. One less to worry about, eh? And he knew it would please . . .''

"Never mind that," Quintus said, holding onto a ragged calm. After hearing that his son was dead, his grandsire had thanked the messenger and called him "guest." Never mind that he was dying inside. "What happened?"

"They've got her staked out like a lamb for a lion! She *pointed* at him and chanted something. Sir, he wasn't expecting trouble. He trusted her! And when she chanted, he just marched up and saluted. 'Watch this,' says one of the Black Robes, and slits his throat in front of that runaway from the crows, that traitor. . . ."

"Lucilius just stood there?"

"Right before the altar. They've let him keep his sword and gear—haven't issued him a black robe yet. But they don't let him near the Eagle, and they don't treat him with the kind of respect he likes."

Maybe Lucilius had never been much of a tribune, but for him to stand there while priests slit the throat of a Legionary—crucifixion was too good for him.

Having given his report, Rufus stood waiting, as he always had, for orders.

Old war dog, Quintus wanted to say. *Tell me what to do.* Escape into the desert? Hide, and attack from within the ruins over and over again? Choose to die? But not even the centurion's years of experience had prepared him for this day. And it was not Rufus's duty to order, but to obey. Still, by his own example, Quintus had the advice he sought. *Do a Roman thing.*

Quintus drew his sword. "I shall not sheathe it again, save in enemy flesh," he said between clenched teeth. Manetho shuddered.

"Steady, man!" Rufus clapped him on the shoulder. "The tribune says we're going in there to fight, so we're going in there to fight. You *like* living this way? You'd rather die on the altar or like that poor fool who got his throat slit? At least now you can die like a soldier."

There were women, children in the ruins. They would die, too; but they would die in any case, whether the Black Naacals took them or by the half-understood powers they hoped to unleash overwhelmed this oasis. Families had died, too, Quintus knew, in the rising of Spartacus. And Ganesha and Draupadi would die, too. Poor Draupadi, trapped at the end in the illusions she spun so well. Perhaps the drug would wear off, and her mind would be clear at the last to remember he loved her—if that were not the last cruelty of all.

Manetho straightened. "You're going to fight. Even if you have no hope. We have *never* had any hope. So we will fight at your sides. Perhaps your gods will look more kindly upon us than our own have done."

"Good man," Rufus said, his voice oddly gentle. "Tribune . . . ?"

"Let's go," Quintus duly ordered.

He followed the centurion to a darkened room in which Legionaries crouched, armed and waiting. At the sight of their officer, the Romans lined up, ready to move.

Manetho gestured, and slaves seemed to pour from every crack, every corner of the ruined walls. Moonlight spun a frail light through a broken wall, then faded as clouds scudded across the disk. When the wind blew them past, the moon was darker, as if moving into eclipse. The slaves flinched from the bloody light. It would be good to see the sun again. Quintus did not expect to.

Manetho guided them deeper within the Temple complex, where the great walls rose about them like the broken teeth of a slain Titan, dead in battle. The slaves he led seemed young and thin to Quintus, too young for real battle.

"Pass the word," he told Rufus. "Each of the men is to take one of our friends in charge. Under his shield."

Don't let them die alone in the dark with no decent example to follow, he was going to say, but his throat tightened.

Empty-handed, a man who had served long ago as standard-bearer came to his side. A pity they did not have the Eagle. At the worst, they could have used it to blast this entire place. Now, the best they could hope for was to destroy it too.

There was no one here to see these last of Crassus's Legionaries victorious or once again disgraced—no one except the gods and, maybe, the *manes* of those who had cared for them. And near them stood their allies, the men of Ch'in, led by Ssu-ma Chao. He nodded at Quintus as the Roman approached. He too preferred to stand by his own forces.

They had Draupadi, poor, drugged girl, set up as a guard. He knew she would give the alarm, and he was equally certain he could not kill her.

As the gong rang out once more, the slaves crept closer. A cloud slid once again across the cracked face of the moon, then vanished, almost as if it had been eaten. Under the tainted moonlight, Manetho's men blended into the Roman ranks. The battle lines shifted to receive them; for a moment, Quintus's heart was gladdened to see how much stronger they looked.

Again and again, gong and drums sounded, until the vibrations could be felt through their sadly worn-out boots. The Dark Ones *must* know that they were coming. Lucilius would have warned them. If the gods were kind, perhaps Quintus could at least kill *him*.

The air thickened. For a moment, his consciousness

seemed to lurch sideways. By now, Quintus was used to that shock of displaced time. In just such a space apart, he had marched through a tunnel of wind and blowing sand to the oasis where they had found water and, seated by a fountain, Draupadi herself.

The way out from the arch would be closed now—even if they had Draupadi and Ganesha to break through the Black Naacals' magics. If they succeeded now, even if they won, their victory would be like that of Pyrrhus: another such, and they were lost.

The entrance to the shrine gaped wide before them. Once, great doors perhaps two or three spear lengths high must have swung to awe worshippers. Those doors were long gone: broken through and carried away, to be harvested by slaves for their metal over many years.

Despite the terror that seemed to settle from the air above, the battle lines moved steadily. Rome's pace. Rome's race. The standard-bearer stood as firmly as if he still held the Eagle. They would see it once more before they died. Quintus drew a bleak comfort from that.

The inner shrine was shielded by a vast dome. Through narrow lancets torn out of its massive walls, the moonlight poured in. Between each window rose a bronze stand, wrought in the semblance of a great serpent; smoking torches jutted from their fanged jaws. Patches of light and darkness appeared to float in the dome, so high that one sensed rather than saw them clearly. The gong rang out, and the entire space quivered. The darkness seeped out, encompassing the light.

A reddish glow pulsed from about the altar on which a body gleamed pallidly. With a shock of horror, Quintus recognized Ganesha, stripped of his robes.

Fury replaced horror as Quintus recognized Lucilius, standing by the Black Naacals, his harness gleaming as if he stood in attendance on a proconsul. Guarded as carefully as Lucilius himself and placed at some small distance from him gleamed the Eagle.

Again, the clamor of the gong, followed by the thunder of huge drums and the braying of horns carved out of bones the length of a man's thigh. Those patches of light and darkness floating overhead shifted, clouds of illusion to twist the senses. When they cleared away, Quintus saw Draupadi.

32

TIME AND PLACE shifted once more. Amber light, tiny flames flickering in brass bowls floating in a pool, the splash of falling waters turning their light into a dancing shimmer, and, gleaming in the light, Draupadi, reclining on cushions the way Quintus had first seen her.

They had given her a new gown of the clinging saffron cotton she favored. Her long hair had been combed out and gleamed on her shoulders, and her face appeared washed clean of the exhaustion and fear graven in it by month upon month of hardship. A ruby line marked the part of her hair and a bloody hand ornament dangled between dark eyebrows. Her eyes had been elongated by some cosmetic, and there was absolutely no recognition in them.

And no way to reach the enemy or the Eagle except to pass by her.

The fires' glow shifted, to create on the stone floor the illusion of a pool. It was all illusion, Quintus thought, cast by a woman lost within her own creation.

She had been wary, the first time they had met. And

Ganesha had challenged him to a deadly game. How had he ever dared to play? Well, this was the final round.

Quintus gestured, and some of the men fanned out. He himself must be the one to approach her, and they would have to guard him. He forced himself to stare beyond Draupadi: He saw no archers, but that did not mean that the Black Naacals did not have such posted. He would just have to risk it: There was no way to the inmost part of the shrine but to pass Draupadi.

"Guard me," he whispered and started forward.

Quintus's first impulse was to go around the water. *What water?* he reminded himself. They had drugged her, he knew. But drugs could wear off. He only hoped that, to protect Ganesha, she had not consented in some fastness of her being, to serve as guard: If so, she too had been lied to, for Ganesha lay bound as a sacrifice upon the altar.

Remember—illusion, he told himself. Gesturing to the force at his back to stay behind, he strode out, setting foot onto the shimmering area that looked so like water. A corner of his mind expected to sink, but his boots scraped on rock until he reached the carpets on which Draupadi reclined.

She held out a hand to him. Once before, she had held out a hand thus, seeking to delude him—but that had been not Draupadi, but a simulacrum. The real woman had intervened to protect him.

As he had before, Quintus grasped the outstretched hand. The skin pressed by his callused hand had been smoothed with oil, and it smelled faintly of sandalwood. The nails were shaped and gleaming, the fingers henna-tipped. And none of that was right. Draupadi's hand was shapely, true enough, but callused nearly as much as his own from helping with the pack animals, roughened by

grit-filled water, burnt from when she cooked over a dung
fire. And the ring that he had given her was gone.

But he took that decorative, deceitful hand and drew
Draupadi gently to her feet, holding her close against
him. "I've come to take you out of here," he said.

"There is only here," she said. She shook her head,
and her dark hair poured loose over those slender shoulders. He remembered the feel of that flow of hair in his
hands. "Look about you," she told him and smiled.

Lights. Water. As he watched, the light shifted, and
now he stood on a spit of land he remembered well. So
often in his childhood, he had used this place for a retreat. From it you could see the entire valley. Now
Draupadi had found it to share with him forever.

Her eyes fixed on his, and, he could find no other
word for it, drew him in. Her hands went to his chest, his
shoulders, seeking to pull him down to rest on the carpets. The smell of her hair and flesh made him giddy. Sit
and talk, he thought. What harm . . . talk? He doubted it.
Never had they lain together. This might be their last
chance. She would cast a veil of darkness over them, and
together they would dream their last dream: that they
were alone together.

But it would all be a lie. The Black Naacals would
stand witness and be ready to expose them to what remained of Quintus's legions: a last betrayal as their officer abandoned them to lie in the arms of the woman
who had bespelled them.

"It is time to go, Draupadi," he said gently. She shook
her head.

"We will get Ganesha and we will go." The dark eyes
flashed. Fear began to flicker in their depths, fear for her
teacher? Then part of her was awake, part of her was
fighting the influence of the drug.

"You have wandered far, Draupadi." He could make a song of her name to lure her back. "Too far. Now, come back!"

He put a snap in his voice, hoping to shock her awake.

"Why should we leave?" she asked, still drowsy. "Here is quiet. Here is peace. Here is all we shall ever need."

"Here is *death*," Quintus said. "Have you forgotten? You are in the keeping of the Black Naacals, and so is the Eagle. If they learn to use it, they will let the seas flow out to cover half the earth, then rule over the other half. Do you remember the time before, when that happened? *Do you remember?*"

She shook her head, fearful and reluctant.

"Draupadi, you remember. I know you do." He turned her face up forcibly to meet his eye to eye. *"Do you want it to happen again?"*

"No . . . oh no . . ." Tears spilled down her cheeks.

"Then you must come with me."

She was faltering, weakening. He began to pull her toward the "water" that lay beyond her carpets.

The gong and horns rang out. Just let him get her back, and the Dark Ones could raise all the alarms they cared to. Almost, they drowned out a death shriek. *Not Ganesha, please all the gods. Rufus, make them hold the line.*

As if the man's death fueled the illusions that the Black Naacals wanted Draupadi to cast, the images became stronger, fragmenting into a confusion of light, sound, and color. It was getting hard to breathe, let alone walk. Draupadi gasped and almost collapsed. If he had to carry her, how could he fight? He thought of the dagger he wore. Had she lived long enough among Romans to prefer their way out to surviving in any way that she might?

"*I* am not your enemy, Draupadi," he muttered. "They are. Fight *them*."

He pulled her along, expecting any moment a blow, screams of rage, perhaps, or some attack of the spirit that might leave him flat. Instead, she burst into tears. "I can't!" she wept. "I am old. I am hideous. If I leave this place, I will die and crumble into dust."

He had seen crying women before. Tears must mean she was weakening. He tugged this one past the bounds set by her illusions and her fears. She was clinging to him, her face close to his.

"Is that what you want, Quintus, *mea anima?*" Sarcastically, she brought out the Latin endearment. "This, for all time? *Kiss* me!" Her face, so close to his, shifted, the smooth tanned flesh shrinking from the bone, wrinkling almost into peeling strips. Her dark eyes glistened furiously in all-but-naked eyesockets, and her lips drew back from yellowed teeth. Her breath smelled not of cardamom, but carrion.

"This flesh you want—already, it rots and dies. Is my death what you want? Is *this?*" She tugged at her garments with one hand. Her breasts were no more than leathery flaps.

"Cover yourself," he ordered. He tightened his hand upon her wrist, hating how the fragile bones felt as his fingers pressed against them. She screamed, high, anguished, and hopeless like a victim of sacrifice. If she were mad or permanently twisted—better dead. And better that she meet her fate with a clear mind.

What would his men say if they saw him dragging a skeleton across the floor and calling it by her name? They'd think he had run mad, and they would kill him.

Mistress of illusion, he told himself. *And her illusions are twisted now.*

Gods only grant she wake. He pushed her through a patch of light that showed her ravaged face far too clearly. For an instant, his feet "splashed" in illusion. Then he was walking on "dry land" once more, well away from where she had been set to ensnare him.

She collapsed, weeping without tears, a dry, tearing sound that subsided gradually into mourning without madness.

If he turned her around, would he see the lady or the hag?

"Tribune . . ."

Perhaps only Rufus's voice could have forced him to that duty, the most merciless of any in his service. He bent, dagger in hand, over her. She lay, her eyes tightly shut in rejection, on her side now. Though she was less warm and beautiful than the illusion she had cast, she was still lovely.

"*Mea anima, mea vita,*" he whispered. "My soul, my life, awake. Look at me."

The eyes remained stubbornly shut.

Who knew what voices were speaking to her within the confusion of her mind? Quintus thought. He had suffered such barrages himself. He shook her roughly, but she turned her face away again. *Forgive me,* he thought, and slapped her face. Her eyes flew open in rage—and to the sight of her face, reflected in his eyes and the blade he showed her.

"*See* yourself," Quintus ordered. "You know the difference between truth and illusion. You are not a hag! And I will kill you myself before I let you be a traitor. You are Draupadi, and we need you. *Now do you understand?*"

"Alone," she stammered, ". . . the water rises, the earth shakes . . . all alone, and death all around . . ." Her face began to shimmer, to decompose again, and she looked longingly at the stage set for her illusions.

Quintus bent his head and kissed her, hard and fast. "Never alone. Do you understand?"

She clung to him for one blessed instant, then pushed free.

"Ganesha," she said, fear mounting. "And Lucilius tricked me."

"We are ready to fight," he told her. "Your part is over. Go back where you will be safe."

"My part?" She was keeping pace with him as they hastened back to the waiting soldiers. "And there is no safety here."

They reached the soldiers. She took up a position on one side of him, and the standard-bearer stood on the other.

Rufus barked the order to advance.

33

"**Wait!**" **Quintus flung** up a hand. For the first time, he countermanded one of the senior centurion's orders. Despite their peril, the expression on Rufus's face made him grin.

"Sir, they've killed one man already. They're stronger, don't you feel it?" For the first time, the senior centurion questioned an order. And it was a good question.

The lights under the huge dome were fading to the sullenness of a dying oil lamp, and with a smell even more foul. The darkness was gathering in the form of mists, a black dampness that raised hackles and a cold sweat. The eyes of the Legionaries showed white and shining against it. Some of the slaves had begun to tremble. One or two tried to drop to their knees, but the Romans at their sides held them up. They were used to discipline. Quintus hoped they would not try to bolt; it was too cruel to blame and kill men for a cowardice they had never been taught to withstand.

Now the clangor of the gong seemed to shed ripples of

darkness, too. They gathered and flooded upward, as if to touch the Eagle. The bronze, which had blazed so brightly before its captivity, appeared to tarnish before the Romans' very eyes: a bird in moult; a bird badly needing freedom from its confinement.

''I can pierce that.'' Draupadi moved her hands, even though they trembled, and her voice was hoarse from the spells she had already set that night.

She was exhausted, Quintus knew. But she would not rest until she had a chance to undo what she had done. In that regard, she was very like a warrior herself.

One of the Black Naacals strode toward Ganesha, passing by his previous victim with barely a glance at the pale, drained body. Then darkness covered it with a filthy pall. The Black Naacal's robe, where it touched the blood that had drained from the man, clung to his legs on one side.

The first time Quintus had seen Ganesha, they had fought, and Quintus had lopped off his head, or so it had seemed. The old sage had survived, for a wonder, and Quintus had always wondered thereafter if he had battled illusions. He had no such doubts about what they faced now and that there were some things that even demigods could not endure. Had not Bacchus been torn apart—or that strange Egyptian deity he had heard women whisper about? He owed Ganesha a life or a clean death. Rufus was right. Time, and past time, to advance.

''Wait!''

By all the gods of Hades, *Lucilius?* What did *he* want? The waning light flickered on the patrician's face as he placed himself between the Black Naacal and Ganesha.

''I did not know you were so fond,'' said the Black Naacal. His chuckle was like a blow. Lucilius reddened, then blanched, mastering himself with a control he had rarely shown.

"Why cast away what might be a weapon in your hand?"

"Cast away? Little traitor, I use what comes to hand. See, this senile wineskin of a man is filled with power. Tapping it, I drink; and I take that strength for myself. And then . . ."

The ground rocked underfoot. Perhaps the Black Naacal would grow so confident of his powers that the earth would open and swallow this place: victory of a sort for the rest of the world.

"They are coming."

"Spies, slaves, and outlaws." So much for the remnants of a great Legion and a Ch'in army.

"You need *her* if you are to use the old man. He cherishes her."

Ganesha did not move. His eyes were shut. What odd byways of memory and power did the old man now travel?

"There speaks a man besotted. Can you not wait for your dainty?" The Black Naacal began to turn away. "He did not break when we drugged her. What folly makes you think he will control her now—or even that we can get her back? These traitors break, but they do not bend. So, we may as well take his power and bend it to our will. You have your gold, and the promise of more when we stamp the face of the earth into an image of our devising. Do not seek for more."

"You swore I could have *her*."

"There will be other women for you. Now, traitor, stand back lest we avail ourselves of what little virtue you possess."

The Black Naacal slapped Lucilius's face, then back-handed it. The blow looked light enough, but a bloody welt formed on the man's cheek, and he staggered, fetching up against the basalt wall closest to the Eagle.

Light and darkness flickered about it, making the Eagle appear to be attempting to move. Lucilius was a traitor. But whatever else he was, he was a Roman, and he had followed the Eagle and served it after his fashion.

"Forward at a walk," Quintus gestured. Far behind him, Ssu-ma Chao repeated the order.

Under the gongs and chants of the Black Naacals, the scrape of the Legionaries' boots, the pad of the slaves' bare feet or the Ch'in footgear made little sound. They might have been ghosts, advancing stealthily, but always in plain sight.

Lucilius was watching them. His eyes widened. Let him shout, and they would be under attack before need be. But Lucilius did not shout. His eyes brightened, as with the tears of shame that he should have shed long ago. Even as his former Legion advanced toward their standard and their enemies, the patrician straightened himself and saluted.

Rufus caught his eye and spat.

The darkness thickened about the traitor, seeking to touch his eyes and lips and ears, as if trying to control him utterly.

Traitor he certainly was. And he had laid hands upon Draupadi. He deserved death, many times over.

Memory stabbed at Quintus—Crassus, surrounded by Parthians, fighting until he died. Quintus had fought for him until a blow to the head had toppled him. The old proconsul had been a venal failure and a fool, but he had died like a man.

"Lucilius!" Quintus shouted. The echo rang in the vast shrine. "Join us! Remember, you are a Roman!"

Lucilius's mouth worked. Color flamed on his cheeks, almost as vivid as the welt from the Black Naacal's blow.

"Come on, man!" *Mirabile dictu*, now Rufus was shouting encouragement. Now, all the soldiers were taking it up. One even yelled the gladiators' salute, as if he were, for all the world, a barbarian fresh from the forests across the Rhenus.

"Do a Roman thing," Quintus shouted. "Come back to the *patria*. Follow the Eagle!"

The Eagle loomed over Lucilius's head. It was brighter now, seemingly poised upon its standard as if awaiting some sign. Quintus looked up at it. Maybe it was a trick of the guttering light, but that bird watched him with eyes that were more than craftily wrought metal.

He called for the salute. After a moment, the slaves and the Ch'in copied it. The Black Naacals' chant rose to a frenzy.

"Lucilius!" Quintus shouted. "The Eagle! *Bring us the Eagle!*"

Rufus's war-trained voice repeated the command, louder than his.

The Black Naacal held the dagger poised above Ganesha's throat. And the hissing began, that squamous threat that had followed them from Syria, a sign that evil was manifesting and about to strike.

"Now, man! There isn't any more time!" *Why, you would think I love him like a brother!*

"For Rome!" Rufus shouted.

"*Roma!*" voices boomed behind him. Even the slaves had taken it up. "*Ro-ma! Ro-ma! Ro-ma!*"

Lucilius's eyes darted around the shrine and focussed on the Eagle. Weighing the odds again, was he?

He hesitated . . .

. . . And the remnants of his Legion advanced.

Quintus saw the indecision on his face. No more to be called traitor, by either side. To regain his pride, even in death.

Do the Roman thing, Quintus urged him silently. Even if none of them survived, Lucilius's spirit might stand before Minos and Rhadamanthus unashamed. There must be words that he could use to push the patrician into action—and then he found them.

"Come on, lad! One last throw of the dice!" he shouted.

To his astonishment, Lucilius laughed. Light crowned his pale hair. He lunged for the Eagle and grabbed its staff.

The great bird mantled its shining wings like a living creature, while the Temple's foundations trembled at the beat of those wings.

Lucilius held the Eagle aloft . . .

. . . And the Black Naacal brought his dagger slashing down in a gleaming arc toward Ganesha's throat, a death from which there would come no awakening.

"*Roma!*" shouted Lucilius, and smashed the standard down on the Black Naacal's skull.

He twisted around, heading for the men who had once been under his command. They were cheering hoarsely now, even the slaves.

Was it only another illusion, or did the shrine seem brighter? No, that was not illusion at all. The dark mists were burning away under the glow of the Eagle. Now the pale light before dawn began to pierce through the lancets in the great dome. The idea of actually seeing another dawn brought a surge of hope into Quintus's heart. The light intensified. One long beam of light slashed through the narrow window into the shrine, past the crumpled body of the Black Naacal, and past the Romans as they charged to touch Lucilius and the Eagle he upheld.

Once again, the bronze bird mantled. This time it screamed anger and defiance. And the staff that had supported it for so long erupted into flame, hotter than naphtha, that licked out to enfold Lucilius.

He had no time to scream or even grimace in agony. One moment, he appeared to glow in the light. In the next moment, he was incandescent. His harness fell away, and they could see exposed, as the flesh was consumed, the pattern of his bones: ribs and skull and the stubborn articulation of the arm that upheld the Eagle's flaming staff until the bones too were consumed, dropping into a little heap of calcined fragments.

Beams of light stabbed through the windows and transfixed the Eagle, and it screamed once again. As if the Flame used it as a lens, light darted from the Eagle's eyes toward the other Dark Ones and burnt them to ashes. Priests, servants, even the corpse of the first sacrifice . . . all consumed.

Still the Eagle glowed with unspent force. And Quintus remembered . . . *Pasupata had been unleashed. It devastated the field, yet he who had used it and his army had remained very still, lest it turn on them, too.*

Seizing Quintus's dagger, Draupadi ran forward toward Ganesha. Freed, the old man gazed up at the Eagle, then knelt as if he wished to touch earth before a superior being. Behind him, the slaves had gone prostrate in awe.

And the Romans drew themselves up and saluted their regained Eagle with a pride they were overjoyed to feel once more.

Some of that salute is for you, Lucilius, Quintus thought. *I hope you know it.*

With a last cry, the Eagle lifted from its perch, to circle

the inside of the Temple three times. Dawn was coming in now, a rising tide of light and life and purification. Out of the nearest window, a streak of bronze fire, the Eagle winged—and was gone.

Now Romans, Ch'in soldiers, the two White Naacals, and former slaves stood free beneath the great vault of the old shrine. Even the smoke stains had been scoured from its walls by the sudden splendor of the Eagle's flight. The white rock of its vault glowed, and the great dome seemed to quiver on massive piers. Above the altar, the great serpent coiled in majesty, and the eyes of its many heads shone gem-bright.

Tears poured down Rufus's leathery cheeks. "Our Eagle," he said. "Just when we won it back, it's gone."

"It was never ours," said Quintus, "but Rome's."

"And now it is flying back," said Ganesha. Draupadi had flung one of her veils, toga-fashion, about him, and even in that unfamiliar garb, he contrived to look dignified.

"It is your time now, Romans," Ganesha said. "And your world. What shall you do with it?"

Quintus wanted to shrug. They all had felt the barriers go up. If they could not be removed, what would they do, with no way now of returning home?

Ganesha laughed. "And has your kind been exiled before? I tell you, what one magus has done another one—carefully—can undo. And even if I cannot, let me tell you, young Quintus, your Rome will thrive. For this is Rome's time, as long ago it was our Motherland's. As for us, we too shall thrive. Who knows? Perhaps, one day even your Rome may be astonished when it sends out men and they find not strangers but more Romans ready to clasp arms with their brothers!"

Quintus spared a look at the little heap of lime and ash

that had been a Roman. Later, he would gather them up and give Lucilius an honorable grave so his tricky, volatile spirit might rest.

Draupadi knew his mind and handed him her headscarf to lay over them. Perhaps she and Ganesha could indeed free them from this place. But if not, there was food and the chance to grow more. There was water. There was stone to build with and, now that the Black Naacals were gone, allies to build with—possibly more powerful than any knew until they unlocked the secrets they had kept stubbornly hidden from the Dark for so long.

Ganesha and Draupadi bowed before the restored altar. Quintus no longer considered it an accident that the Serpent's eyes glittered in response.

Then, all of them left the Temple, hastening out into the open air. The wind, blowing through the Temple's vaults, pursued them down the corridors. It was like a fragrant breath. The sky shone more brightly than it had during all the days of their wandering.

Without, the Eagle still soared overhead, rivalling the sun. As it saw them, it shrieked acknowledgment. *"Ave atque vale!"* Quintus shouted at it. *Hail and farewell.*

Then it wheeled and flew westward, like a messenger returning home with news of a great victory.

They watched its path until it was only a gleaming speck in the dawn sky, and that speck, too, had vanished.

Then they stood staring at each other, all those survivors. Already, Valmiki, the closest thing that the former servants of the Black Naacals had for a priest, was in earnest conversation with Ganesha. And Rufus turned toward his officer.

"So this is where we get our land?"

"You'll have to wait for the mule, I'm afraid," Quintus told him, then laughed for the pure pleasure of it.

"From what I understand, I have the time to put in."

Quintus nodded and reached out for Draupadi's hand. Ganesha might be right in his predictions as he so often was. Perhaps he could indeed free them. And perhaps in another time, Romans might travel out into the desert and be astonished to meet their distant kin. But for now, Quintus had a farm to build and tend and a life to get on with, a life to share. How better to show this entire place's return to life but with a wedding? Draupadi turned to meet his eyes. She knew his mind now, as always, and smiled: no need for more now, before all these people, but later . . . ah, later . . . a life . . . a child, maybe strong sons and dark-eyed daughters . . . It was more than he had ever hoped. And more than Arjuna had been privileged to keep. *With all my strength—for all my lives,* he promised Draupadi in his deepest thoughts; and the seeress smiled.

He studied the ruined Temple. Those walls could be raised again, and some of the leftover stone would do well to build houses and, later on, aqueducts. There was no reason why this place could not flourish, and its people along with it.

Now he looked up to the sky. Desert sky though it was, he thought he saw a promise of rain.

Rome would prosper in the West, whether or not he ever saw its seven hills again. Here too in the East there was work to be done, and as Rufus might say, Romans to do it. By the honor of the Eagle, they would do it well.